JUNO H

KING
OF
FIRE
AND
FLAMES

King of Fire and Flames
Book 2: Courts of the Star Fae Realms
Copyright © Juno Heart 2024
All rights reserved.

Skull cover design by Artscandare
Sun and flames cover design and title page by
saintjupit3rgr4phic
Fae King and Queen Edition paperback design by Orina Kafe
Leaf and Arrow character art by Zolyna

Ebook ISBN: 978-0-6456242-9-8
Paperback ISBN: 978-0-6458956-2-9
Color Hardcover ISBN: 978-0-6458956-4-3
Special Fae King and Queen Edition Paperback ISBN:
978-0-6458956-3-6
Gold Foil Hardback ISBN: 978-0-6458956-6-7

v250214

No one loves harder than a reformed villain who has paid his penance in grovel and tears.

Leaf Z.O.R.

Chapter 1

LEAF

My head smacked something hard, and I jolted awake, blinking at a blurry shape opposite me. A person? No, a dust-damned fae. And a hateful one, too.

Esen's scowl materialized out of the gloom of what appeared to be the interior of a carriage. I stared at her pale face framed by blue hair as bright as a peacock's feather, sharp pain stabbing my temples.

I couldn't think straight.

What was I doing traveling in a carriage with Esen for dust's sake?

The last thing I remembered was crossing the Light Realm desert, giddy with excitement because I was getting closer to Coridon.

Closer to Arrow.

And then...

And then what had happened? I couldn't remember.

And where the fuck *was* I?

Heading to Coridon?

Or back to Mydorian?

As I shifted my numb legs, a bad case of pins and needles and an alarming thought struck. The pain in my temples reminded me of something I'd experienced before. It felt exactly like the aftereffects of fire magic.

The kind Quin had used to fight with in Mydorian.

I closed my eyes again, pretending to fall back asleep as unwanted memories slammed through my mind.

The sickening sound of my knife plunging into my twin brother's heart.

Feeling weak but happy as I recovered in my bed in Mydorian, Arrow by my side. Bidding him goodbye in the forest as he and Raiden left on urgent Light Realm business.

Then the boredom of waiting for him to return for my coronation.

The unbridled thrill of traveling to surprise him, and the glittering beauty of the desert near the Auryinnia Mountains as Luna and I rode through it.

Esen and Raiden appearing in a halo of golden dust. A fire mage with flame-filled eyes. Then his horrible, unbelievable words—*by order of the King of Storms and Feathers, you are under arrest.*

No. It couldn't be true.

Fiery agony seared my flesh, blistering my stuttering heart.

No, no, no.

It must have been a dream. A terrible nightmare.

But if so, why was Esen sitting in front of me, a cold smile on her beautiful face?

Not a nightmare, then. It was true.

On Arrow's orders, the Sun Realm had captured me, and I was trapped in their carriage on the way to dust knew where.

A fucking prisoner once again.

I wanted to scream. Bash my head against the metal walls of the carriage.

If I could tear out my heart to stop it from aching, I would do it without question. Right now.

Forcing tears to dry in my eye sockets, I ground my teeth, slowed my breathing, and unfurled my fingers from the cloak material around my chest.

I had to get a hold of myself and remain calm.

Never display weakness.

Ever.

Cool metal banded my wrists, but the rest of me, including my ankles, was left unrestrained. That was a mistake. I could kick Esen in the groin. Butt her stupid head.

And then what?

Raiden, the fire mage, and at least two other riders were outside the carriage somewhere. I was trapped with no way to escape. Nowhere to go.

Fucking brilliant.

Was this my fate in life, to always wear an oppressor's chains?

Opening my eyes, I smoothed my expression, clearing my throat with a pretend dry cough. "So, here we are again, Esen. You and me alone in a carriage, with another opportunity to bond. Get to know each other better."

Her thin smile grew, but she said nothing.

Blinds drawn, the carriage was dark and gloomy, and I had no idea if it was night or day out there. It was warm, though. Too warm. Much hotter than the Light Realm.

Raising my wrists, I shook the chain linked between them. "Black metal this time. I assume it's an improvement over the steel you used on my first journey to Coridon."

3

"You're finally awake, human." Blue eyes scanned my body, lingering on the black cloak draped around me. I picked at one of its embroidered golden feathers, longing to tear them all off. "What's the chain made of?" I asked.

"Xanthanian metal from the outer Star Realms."

I arched a brow. "The second strongest material in the realms? Well, I suppose the reaver elves won't be selling you Auryinnian silver anytime soon." My mouth twisted in a sneer. "At least you've finally stopped underestimating me."

She snorted. "I know exactly what you are. The *worst* kind of fae, mostly human with barely any reaver blood. And you know what? That doesn't make you special. It makes you a freak. If I were you, I wouldn't waste my time trying to escape. Nothing will get you out of those chains, and your reaver magic won't work here, either."

Never one to take a liar's word for the truth, I tried chanting the cloaking spell under my breath—a*uron khaban ana, auron khaban ana*—but nothing happened.

Concentrating with every part of my being, I tried to will the skin-tingling sensation of the cloak sliding over my skin into existence, the warm feeling of security. But again, nothing.

Damn. Damn. Damn.

I was totally fucked.

Again.

Storm magic erupted on Esen's palms, and she raised them toward me. I stifled a gasp. An unusual purple-brown color wove through the clear, blue light of her storm power. Fire magic.

How was that even possible?

I'd never seen magical elements from two realms combined like that, working together. Well, other than when Quin had fought me, fortified by the Sun Realm's fire magic. But that didn't count because, being human, he'd never had magic to start with.

Esen pushed her hands closer, and crackling flames danced in front of my face, so hot I feared for the safety of my eyebrows.

"Hey!" I shuffled deeper into the cushions. "Unless the asshole Storm King's instructions were to burn me to a crisp before we arrive at Coridon, you'd better take it easy. Otherwise, stop toying with me and just get it over with."

"I'm only playing," she said as her magic struck the right side of my ribcage.

With a sharp inhalation, I shoved the agony into the section of my mind where my lost memories had lain hidden before the sight of my younger brother Van's face triggered the spell's release.

Every time guilt struck about killing my twin brother, Quin, I forced it into that same recess in my brain where I kept everything I didn't want to think about or feel, such as the pain that thrummed through my blood right now.

And intrusive thoughts of Arrowyn fucking Ramiel. They were in there, too. Thousands upon thousands of them.

The King of Storms and Feathers had never loved me. He'd betrayed me. Cast me off like some used-up piece of garbage. Once, I'd considered him the love of my life, but now I knew him for what he truly was—the realms' greatest liar and deceiver.

My forever-enemy.

And the fae I vowed to despise long after I had destroyed him, sucked the last breath from his poisonous lips, and buried him under the desert sand of his precious Light Realm.

His body would rot slowly and disintegrate, transforming into the gold dust that ruled his life and had ruined mine. I could think of no other reason that he betrayed me other than in sick pursuit of greater sovereignty over the gold trade.

It was his only obsession.

Other than me.

Thinking of him, rage and sorrow shook through me, his stupid cloak of feathers around my shoulders scraping at the fresh wounds of heartbreak. I longed to rip it to shreds. And I would. At the first opportunity.

Oh, Arrow.

How could you break me like this? After everything you said. Everything you did. And all you promised.

For dust's sake, why?

A wave of nausea made me gag, but I dug my nails into the leather on the outside of my thigh, willing my limbs not to shake. Never would I let anyone see how badly he had hurt me. How grief and longing battled with the hate simmering through my blood.

The fae I had loved was now dead to me, and I would not let his ghost destroy me.

I had Van and the people of Mydorian to care for, a kingdom to put to rights. Against all odds, I'd returned to them once. And I would do it again.

Somehow.

Even if I went home in a body bag.

Esen's magic burned hotter, scorching my neck over the Aldara mark that I wished I could cut from my skin. *Burn it*, I thought. *Burn the wretched thing off.*

She snarled, and the fiery whorls of magic disappeared, reabsorbed into the wasteland of her bitter soul.

I smiled at her face, a mask of constipated violence. "So that's confirmed. You've been ordered not to hurt me. Good to know."

Esen's eyes narrowed. "As you are aware, I don't always follow instructions."

A memory of hot flames and ice-cold fear shuddered over me—the day she tried to push me into a vat of melted gold in Coridon's gold foundry.

Wracked with bitterness because I'd unwittingly stolen her king's attention, she had always despised the sight of me. Jealousy was indeed a curse, and unfortunately, mine to bear. Because at last, Arrow's feral guard dog had me exactly where she wanted me. Trapped, with no way to escape.

Hers to toy with.

But fuck her... I didn't plan to cower in fear, now or anytime soon. Not to her, and not to anyone if I could help it.

Squaring my shoulders, I straightened my spine. "Yes, I remember what a liability you were and still are to your king," I said, scanning her tight leathers and molded black-and-red body armor as she glanced away and tucked a strand of blue hair behind her pointed ear.

As far as I could tell, no swords were strapped to her body or knives hidden beneath her clothing. Perhaps she believed the borrowed fire magic was enough protection. And if so, I hoped for the chance to prove her wrong.

I inspected the interior of the carriage.

Black metal blinds covered the windows, and a wan orange light emanated from a lamp hanging above Esen's shoulder, saving us from traveling in complete darkness.

A bag rustled at Esen's feet as she rifled through it before tossing me a water pouch. Manners were wasted on her, and in captive situations such as this, definitely not required. So I drank deeply without thanking her.

I wiped my mouth and passed her the pouch.

Muttering, she shoved it back in her bag.

"Sorry, did you say something?"

"I *said*, we're going to the City of Taln, not fucking Coridon."

"What?" I lurched forward in shock, and she pushed me backward. "We're in the Sun Realm?" I tugged on the closest chain, and the blind whipped up, banging against the window frame. "How did we get here so quickly?"

"The portal between the realms. And you've been unconscious for a while."

"How did you get me in here? I don't remember a fight."

"There wasn't one. A fire mage knocked you out the moment you drew your blade."

I gaped at the black terrain, lit by columns of flames that shot from the ground at irregular intervals and sprayed sparks around a barren landscape. "What the dust are they?"

"Fire geysers," said Esen. "A volcanic lake flows beneath the entire Sun Realm, and if you don't watch where you walk, one will take you out before you even realize you've stepped on it."

"And to think I first thought the Light Realm was a hostile place. This is much worse." I studied Esen's expression, the delight she was trying to hide, flickering at the corners of her lips. "So, why be helpful and share that information?"

"I'm bored and find it entertaining to hear your silly thoughts spoken aloud as the dire reality of your predicament sinks in."

"Always so charming." Grunting, I shoved the window open a little, hot air with a smoky tang blasting inside and an instant film of sweat sticking my leathers to my skin. I fumbled with the buttons of Arrow's cloak and slid it off my shoulders, glad to be free of the rotten thing.

"Shut the window, you idiot," growled Esen. "The blinds were down for a reason."

Because it was probably the most useful command she'd ever given me, I did as she ordered. "Since you're in the mood to chat, why are we going to the Sun Realm?"

Her lips curled. "You'll be King Azarn's guest at the Fire Court while we wait for Arrow to arrive. Although, the term *guest* might be a bit of a stretch."

Arrow... *damn him.*

Of *course* I'd have to see the bastard again at some point. I should welcome the idea. How else could I stop his heart from beating if I didn't get close to him? Close enough to smell his fresh, stormy scent. Touch his golden skin. Feel the heat emanating from his body. And stare into traitorous silver eyes as I remembered how much I hated him.

Self-disgust curdled the water sitting in my belly as I recalled how excited, how blissfully *happy*, I'd been to arrive in the Light Realm after traveling three days with the sole purpose of surprising him. What a naive, lovesick fool I'd been.

But not anymore.

I would never be so foolish again.

Wait... my horse...

"Where's Luna?" I asked. "If she's hurt, I promise the fae responsible will suffer the same fate tenfold."

"Big words for a small captive."

Gods, she sounded like Arrow.

He had said similar things, constantly amused by how much venom a small human girl could spit. With a ragged sigh, I mentally opened the door to the room in my brain that contained all the bad shit I never wanted to think about again and kicked the Storm King's image inside it, turning the lock with a satisfying click.

"What? No smart-mouthed answer?" said Esen, her eyes dancing, clearly having the time of her life acting as my temporary master.

Breathing slowly, I stopped myself from smashing her nose with my chained fist, that prick's words flashing through my mind, chiding me.

What a violent little thing you are—he'd once said, his voice teasing, fake affection lighting his stormy traitor's eyes.

Shut the fuck up, Arrow, I told the unwanted memory. *I couldn't care less what you think anymore.*

Flashing Esen a serene smile, I said, "It sounds like you've forgotten I'm a queen."

"*Were* to be a queen. What you are now remains to be seen. But regarding your horse, she's currently tied to Raiden's. They're traveling behind the carriage."

Raiden.

Another two-faced prick.

It was so quiet outside that I'd forgotten the bastard was along for the ride. Other than the whoosh of the fire geysers, the rhythmic thud of hooves and jangling horse tack, all else was silent.

I hadn't heard a word from the other fae. Not the ones I couldn't see—Raiden and the flame-eyed mage with crimson hair who was somehow blocking my reaver magic. And not from the two visible through my window—the pair with long black hair escaping their helmets, trailing down their chests like ink spills.

One of them appeared to be a dark-haired version of the crimson-haired mage. Perhaps they were brothers. And possibly even twins. Sorrow squeezed my heart as my thoughts turned toward Quin. *Again.*

Another enemy I'd mistakenly chosen to love and trust. And now he was dead, his serum-soaked flesh rotting under a slab of marble beneath the Mydorian Palace in our family's ancient crypt.

I drew my mind away from the past and watched Esen shift her weight, something moving under her clothes on her right side. A small blade, if I wasn't mistaken.

"Esen, if the Storm Prick ordered my arrest, then why are we going to the Fire Court?"

A new smirk tilted her lips. "As you know, Arrow broke the peace accord because of you. To make amends, he promised to deliver you to Taln himself. But when I heard that the City of Mydorian still thrived and you were supposedly their lost princess, I knew Azarn would be extremely eager to meet you. As predicted, instead of waiting for Arrow to deliver you, he ordered me to take you directly to him. So... here we are. Together at last."

"What an interesting chain of events," I said dully, keeping my expression blank as my mind buzzed with the words Arrow had said to me in Mydorian. The hardest thing he'd supposedly ever done was stand by and watch me kill my brother, risking my life in front of him.

A lie.

He had also stated he felt physically unwell whenever he was away from me.

Another lie.

He apologized for every wrong he'd ever done to me.

All lies... along with every tender word he'd ever whispered in my gullible ears.

I seized hold of my spiraling thoughts, forcing calm to flow through my veins. Making myself *think* with my head instead of my heart for a change.

"Does Arrow know that Azarn's soldiers have me?"

"Not yet. But he'll soon be told and will no doubt hasten to the Fire Court to witness your extermination."

Yeah... I wasn't convinced. This whole setup felt wrong. The details of events relayed by Esen seemed murky at best. According to her, Arrow had agreed to hand me over as payment for his past misdemeanors. She didn't say he had *ordered* my arrest. And I knew better than to trust Esen. Was it possible this whole thing was a trick? A plot to make me believe Arrow had betrayed me?

I looked out the window again, flinching as a geyser showered sparks across the night sky, peering toward the back of the carriage where Raiden rode. I couldn't locate him, but I had no doubt he was there. I had seen him in the desert with my own eyes, and the presence of the Storm King's closest friend proved the circumstances of my arrest had most likely unfolded the way Esen had explained.

"I don't quite understand," I said. "All the kings of the realms are now aware I'm the heir to the Earth Realm crown, yet they still believe Arrow has the right to trade me to another king?"

"Of course. Why do you think the elves keep Mydorian cloaked? Humans are weak and hated by the fae. Your brother was too stupid to realize Azarn was using him to maneuver closer to the reavers and their precious gold mines. And Arrow? He has always believed he *owned* you and that you were his possession. But now you belong to the Fire King."

"You expect me to believe that Arrow would give anything he considered *his* to the fire fae. It's not in his nature to share."

"Oh, Leaf, did you never listen to the things Ari told you? *All* fae despise humans. But the fire fae hate Arrowyn even more than they hate *you*. In addition to the Bonerust incident, Azarn blames Arrow for the death of one of his sisters."

My jaw dropped, and Esen's face went blank as her brain caught up to her mouth, likely realizing she'd shared too much. "That's enough *bonding*, as you call it. I've been kind and, as usual, I've told you far too much. I don't know why your sad, green eyes elicit such pity inside me, but I'll work harder to resist them in the future. Rest now. The journey is nearly over."

Esen *kind*? And my sad eyes apparently made her feel sorry for me?

Impossible. She was never nice without an ulterior motive.

My mind raced like a rabid eponar across the desert—spinning this way and that with no clear sense of reason or direction—until one thought trumped the others. Had Esen perhaps slipped up and revealed something useful?

I already knew that Azarn hated Arrow with a fiery passion, but the information about his sister... about Arrow being responsible for her death... Well, that was new. And interesting.

Had Esen meant to share that with me? Or had she royally fucked up?

Leather creaked as she shoved the window open, poked her head out, and barked a single word. "*Melaya.*"

The red-haired mage appeared next to me on the other side of the glass. His brow was smooth, untroubled, but his dark eyes fixed narrowly on Esen with something akin to dislike.

She tipped her head in my direction and hissed three terrifying words. "*Make her sleep.*"

Twin flames ignited in Melaya's eyes. He snarled and flicked his fingers near my face.

Scorching pain burst inside my skull, then a black wave crested over me.

Chapter 2

LEAF

When I woke up, I found myself tied to a pole, a wall of flames surrounding me. Heart pounding, I struggled against the chains that linked my hands together behind my back, unable to even wipe sweat out of my eyes.

I released a volley of curses and bucked against the restraints.

Moaning, I squinted through the ring of fire magic, but couldn't see shit. Heat licked over my skin, scorching hot, but somehow the magical flames didn't burn me. Beyond them, only darkness loomed, and low voices murmured beneath the whoosh and crackle of fire.

Dust, where in the hells was I?

"Melaya," a male voice barked out.

The fire mage's smirk appeared between the flickering flames, and then the owner of the menacing voice sidled up beside him. A tall fae with a wiry build, chestnut hair falling in loose waves to the middle of his back, and an unpleasant aura hovering around his shoulders.

"Take care, Melaya," he said, the casual cruelty of his voice chilling, despite the suffocating heat. "I don't wish to roast the human just yet. She may turn out to be compliant."

I seized upon the word *yet* and let it tumble around the chaos of my mind. The fire fae planned to kill me. Perhaps not immediately, but eventually. That much was clear.

The mage shouted a command, and the ring of flames disappeared.

The fae issuing the orders strode toward me, and I finally got a good look at him. A crown of black flames writhed like windswept shadows around his brow, and flakes of charcoal sloughed off its wood, eddying around the male's shoulders.

The crown was a magical thing, as was the fae who wore it—Azarn, the Fire King. It had to be him.

Boot heels clicked over flagstones as he stalked a tight circle around me. My eyes adjusted, and shapes emerged from the shadows, the light from braziers dotted throughout the courtyard revealing figures huddled in a far corner, whispering secrets.

Probably Esen, Raiden, and perhaps a few counselors or torturers, all smacking their lips in anticipation of making me scream and confess to deeds I'd never committed.

Behind crumbling arched columns, the top section of a black tower thrust its turret through a star-studded sky, making me think that the courtyard might be located somewhere high, near an outer wall of Taln's palace.

At my feet lay Arrow's cloak, the embroidered feathers dulled by dust and grime. Given how much I hated it, the sight should thrill me, but it only made me sad.

The king seized my chin, turning my face for his inspection. "Are we certain this is the girl?" he asked, glancing over his shoulder.

"Of course," Esen replied, the staccato clack of her boots echoing as she strutted from the shadows. "I know the human well. Check her teeth. Not even the best glamour can hide bones. And she has the feather glyph on her neck, too."

A rough thumb prized my lips apart.

Azarn chuckled. "Yes, I see the gap. By all reports, it fascinated the Storm Idiot unduly."

Storm Idiot? I approved of this new nickname and planned to adopt it for my own use. That is, if I lived through the night.

The king's hand slid over the Aldara mark on my throat, but he pulled away with a hiss as the glyph activated, causing him pain.

"Curse Arrowyn Ramiel," he snarled, then turned to Melaya. "Can you remove the mate mark?"

The mage, a fae of few words, shook his head, unbothered by his king's growing fury.

"For your sake, Melaya, you had better find a way."

Not blinking once, the mage stared him down, and the king looked away first.

Helpless frustration rippled through me. I wanted to scream, spit, bite, and curse, but I gritted my teeth instead and focused on the Fire King's vivid gaze.

Those green eyes flashed bright against his dark jacket—padded shoulders tapering to a tight waist, embroidered with flames and tiny roosters of all things, all outlined in shiny red thread.

My first impression of Azarn was of a bitter sorcerer with low self-esteem, rather than the warrior king that Arrow had told me tales of. The fae who stood before me was a ghoulish crow. A gaunt raven king with the beginnings of a slight stoop weighing down his shoulders.

A smile spread over his face, the warm-toned skin stretching over sharp bones, creating cruel hollows below his cheeks. Two long streaks of gray framed his face, and a soft curve of flesh flopped over the silver belt at his hips, aging him beyond the youthful fae I'd pictured in my imagination.

Stroking the point of his short beard, he studied me intently. "You have no gift of tears for me, Zali Omala? No pleading and begging for your life?"

I spat on his boot, my teeth clacking as his swift backhand crashed my skull against the pole.

The king laughed and waved his hand at Esen. "The girl is exactly as Arrowyn described. Take her away before I lose my dinner. The stench of the human sickens me."

Raiden emerged from the shadows and unfastened my chain from the pole before locking my wrists in front of my body.

"Here we are again, *king's guard*," I said. "You mishandling me at a corrupt ruler's bidding. Demeaning duties for a fae warrior, don't you think?"

Avoiding my gaze, he said nothing.

Esen seized my arm and tugged me toward an overgrowth of ivy creeping its way over an arched wooden door. "And *you*," she grumbled, "still can't keep your foolish mouth shut to save your life."

I opened my foolish mouth to lash out a response, but the king's voice boomed behind me, thankfully interrupting my reply.

"Wait," he said. One more thing, Princess of Dirt and Bones—"

"Dust and Stones," I said, "if you wish to be correct. But you can call me whatever you like. Unkind words don't trouble me."

"May I suggest you consider how to use *your* words more wisely, human, because tomorrow, you will meet my son, Prince Bakhur. And if you wish to live, *he* had better like you."

Shit. That didn't sound good. And why in the realms should I care what his son thought of me?

As Esen creaked the door open and tugged me through it, laughter tittered behind me. Female laughter.

"Who were the ladies? Azarn's queen and her servant?" I asked.

"No, the king's sisters—Marcella and Ruhh," she replied.

Esen shoved me along a dim hallway lit by flames flickering in a bank of mirrors that lined the walls. Strange, but there were no sconces opposite them, and the flames seemed to burn from inside the mirrors themselves.

"Esen, I know Azarn had two sisters, and in the carriage, you told me one of them was dead."

"Yes, I did. Ruhh *is* deceased."

I stumbled on the first step of a wide staircase. "If she's dead, how can she be cackling in the shadows of a courtyard with her sister?"

"You'll see tomorrow," said Esen ominously.

I glanced over my shoulder at Raiden who had Arrow's cloak slung over his arm. "Did you carry me unconscious from the carriage and tie me to that pole?"

Silence was my only answer.

"What's wrong with you, Raiden? Left your tongue in Coridon?"

Esen paused on a small landing. "Stop pestering him," she said. "He hasn't been feeling himself of late."

I shrugged. As if I cared about the feelings of my captors. We stepped through a door leading to a narrow staircase that spiraled up the inside of a tower, and other than a few well-placed sconces, the stone walls were bare. We started up the stairs, Raiden behind me and Esen in front.

On the sixth step, with my hands spread as wide as the chain allowed, I lunged and ripped the knife from the sheath at her waist and kicked my boot up behind me, hitting Raiden's groin. Holding my breath, I drove the blade toward the blue-haired fiend's chest as a blast of magic threw me against the stone wall.

"Fucking dust." I dropped in a heap and stared up at Esen's grinning face. "How did you do that?"

"Same way your brother Quin did." Esen grabbed my throat. "Now stop wasting our time with old tricks and get up."

"What can I say? I'm a creature of habit," I said, wishing I could reach around and rub the bruises blooming on my back.

With a hand cupping his balls, Raiden groaned, then pulled me onto my feet.

"You all right?" Esen asked.

He nodded.

"Didn't I warn you to watch out for this one? She's worse than a feral orc."

While they dragged me up more stairs, eventually stopping on the seventh landing, I wondered why she'd needed to warn Raiden when he was already well-acquainted with my fondness for violent escapes.

Had he lost his memories as well as his entire personality?

Two winged trolls stood on either side of a carved oak door, and to my left, stars shone through a small, unglazed window. I stood on my toes and peered through it.

Raiden dragged me away, but not before I'd seen the jagged black rocks at the bottom of the tower. There would be no easy escape from my new lofty prison.

Esen unlocked the cuffs around my wrist and hung the chain from her belt. "Go inside," she said, opening the door.

Ignoring her, I smiled at the troll guards, but neither met my gaze, which was disappointing. During my time in Coridon, I'd learned much could be achieved by treating my captors with kindness—alliances forged and escape plots hatched once friendships were firmly established.

I should probably remember that whenever I spoke to Esen. If I could soften her up, she might prove useful. But was it worth befriending someone who sold their loyalty to the highest bidder?

She frowned as I stared at her, unmoving. "Zali, I won't ask again."

"Esen." I tried a smile, which she ignored. "Please tell me why I'm here in Taln."

Gripping my shoulders, she gently pushed me backward into the room. "You will stay here in your new chambers until the morning. You won't starve. Food will be served. At some point tomorrow, you'll be brought into the Great Hall. There, all will be made clear."

"But—"

Raiden swept past Esen and threw the cloak inside the room. As he started to close the door, I pressed my weight against it. "Wait, Raiden. Please. Can you get a message to your king?"

"Azarn?" he asked, his voice a little rougher than I remembered.

"No. The Storm Idiot."

Brown eyes stared at me, and Esen crossed her arms, tapping her boot against the floor.

I released a loud sigh. "If either of you can get word to Arrow, please inform him that he's a worthless piece of lizard shit, and that an unbroken fire dragon would be more loyal, more honorable than him. And tell him... tell him when he least expects it, I'll come for him, and it won't be a pleasant reunion."

Raiden snorted and slammed the door in my face, locking it briskly and leaving me to gape, slack-jawed, at my new temporary residence.

It looked comfortable, which surprised me. I wondered why the fire fae hadn't thrown me into a stinking dungeon far beneath their dreadful palace, like the Storm Idiot had done when I first arrived in Coridon.

I strolled around the room, taking inventory of all it contained.

Three metal oil lamps hung on hooks on the semi-circular walls, illuminating a canopy bed, a plump couch, a desk, a mirrored dresser, and a tall wooden closet. Behind a screen painted with flames, I found a door leading to a bathroom containing a tub, basin, and a toilet. Except for the white fur blankets and cushions, every item in the large room was black or a shade very close to it.

A bank of arched windows ranged on the stone wall facing the sea, unfortunately too high to access, but I sighed in relief at the window seat on the right side of the bed. Even obstructed by bars, the view of the crescent moon and dark ocean was beautiful. A pleasant place to sit, contemplate my fate, and plot my escape.

The palace was perched on formidable cliffs at the far point of a cape, so even if I somehow prized the bars off the window and jumped, I would wind up splattered on the rocks. Food for the crabs when the tide lapped hungrily in.

Although the room was attractive and comfortable, with air heated to the perfect temperature, and according to Esen, I would be well-fed, I hoped I wouldn't live here long. Even if that meant the fire fae killed me. Because if I couldn't escape, death was preferable to living out my life as a prisoner.

I shook the dirt from the Storm Idiot's cloak, contemplated throwing it through the bars of the window, and then folded it neatly on a shelf inside the large closet made of glossy red wood.

Then I stripped off my sweaty leathers and bathed in the tub before sliding into a black nightdress that had been laid out neatly on the bed.

Fighting tears, I slid under the covers and spent at least an hour or two worrying about Van and Ari, wondering if they'd heard the news of Arrow's betrayal. Praying they were safe.

Eventually, I fell into nightmares set in the pavilion in Coridon, with the Storm King touching me everywhere. And worse—whenever he stopped, I moaned and begged him to continue.

Chapter 3

LEAF

King Azarn's throne room had the claustrophobic atmosphere of a tomb. High windows granted entry to the late-morning sunshine, and flames glowed from inside long channels set into the marble floor, neither light sources strong enough to chase the shadows from the farthest corners of the hall.

As Esen shoved me though the enormous, open double doors, an ogre's voice boomed out, introducing me to the fire courtiers. "Fae of Taln, I present Zali Omala of the Earth Realm, the outlaw princess of Mydorian, and King Azarn's valued guest."

A hushed silence resonated, followed by hundreds of whispers.

Esen grinned at Raiden, both flanking me as they pushed me down a center aisle toward an oval, black-stone dais, where five fae perched on tall, narrow thrones, King Azarn on the largest, most ornate.

When we reached the bottom of the dais stairs, Esen pulled me to a halt. The king's spine straightened as he waved a ringed hand at me. "Zali Omala, you may approach."

With careful footsteps, I mounted twenty stairs, stopping in front of the king, my gaze not once leaving his. The scent of smoldering wood from his crown mixed with a heady perfume of frankincense assaulted my senses, the combination not entirely unpleasant.

"Welcome to the Sun Realm, Princess," he said, his body draped in black and the crown of dark flames licking his brow.

I cleared my throat. "I can't truthfully say it's a pleasure to be here, King Azarn."

Seated on his right, a striking female drew a sharp breath, as if shocked by my words. She wore a gown of soft folds of silver that shone like liquid starlight, her long black hair framing eyes of palest blue. In appearance, she was the Fire King's opposite, and if she turned out to be his queen, then I prayed the same could be said of her character.

I'd taken an instant dislike to Azarn, and I certainly didn't trust him. It would be some comfort if his lady partner was blessed with an entirely different nature.

"This is my wife," he said coldly, "Queen Estella, from the Crystal Realm of Night and Stars. Do you know of that kingdom?"

"Yes. I may be human, but I'm not a fool. And I happen to be in possession of all my memories again."

The queen inclined her head in greeting, and I returned the gesture, matching her somber expression. She pointed to the fae sitting on the other side of her husband. "Princess Zali, this is our son, Prince Bakhur."

The male rose in a flurry of silver-and-black material, bowed, and gave me a charming smile. He was predictably tall, his body well-shaped, and loose brown curls flopped over gold-flecked, hazel eyes that, unfortunately, reminded me of a gold addict's over-confident gaze.

With a subtle leer adorning his handsome face, he linked his hands behind his back, walked forward, and paced a tight circle around me. "You will do," he said.

My heart stuttered, then pumped double time. "What precisely will I *do* for, Prince Bakhur?"

Ignoring my question, he turned toward the female fae seated beside the queen. "These are my aunts, the king's sisters, Marcella and Ruhh. Ruhh is deceased, of course," he said, as if the sight of her browning bones, visible through a gown that had seen better days, and her mottled, transparent skin was nothing out of the ordinary.

"Oh, of course," I agreed, as though I too had a rotting specter as a valued member of my family. Then an icy shiver ran down my spine as I imagined Quin as my undead companion. I certainly wouldn't give him leave to sit beside me on the Mydorian dais, the way Azarn did with Ruhh.

Marcella leaned forward, rust-colored hair trailing over her emerald gown, and gave me a benign smile. Just as Sindar the sailor had said weeks ago, when he cursed the fire family on Captain Loligos's ship, her eyes were indeed a bright orange color.

And perhaps, once, the dead girl's had been, too, but with all shades other than white and brown leeched from her body, only malice remained simmering in her staring, translucent eyes.

By mortal standards, the prince and his living aunt, like most fae, appeared to dwell in the rosy bloom of youth, but I couldn't begin to guess how old the ghost-fae had been when she'd passed away. But if Arrow had something to do with it, as Esen had suggested, I planned to learn everything I could about her. Ignoring the prince, who hovered close by, I turned my attention to the king. "Please tell me why I've been arrested. What crime have I been accused of?"

"You murdered the Regent of the Earth Realm, your brother Quin Omala, who the Sun Realm recognized as the rightful Mydorian heir."

"For the time being, we'll have to disagree about who should wear the Mydorian crown, but when your mage captured me, he said I was under arrest by the order of Arrowyn Ramiel. Was he lying?"

Laughter rumbled through the courtiers that I hadn't yet had the courage to inspect. I knew what I'd see if I did. Cold glares, filled with hungry fascination for the strange, weak human. No friendly, reassuring smiles waited for me on the sea of faces below the dais.

The Fire King snarled. "When Arrowyn destroyed my blacksmith, Gorbinvar, in Bonerust, he broke a centuries-old treaty between our realms, then bartered with your life to avoid war. From that moment on, you were destined to live or die at the whim of my court."

Estella opened her mouth as if to interrupt, but Azarn gripped her clenched fist and pressed her knuckles against the armrest of her chair, indicating there was more to the tale than the Fire King was willing to share.

He released his wife's hand. "But when I learned the identity of Arrowyn's prized slave, I saw an opportunity. Your death would be a waste when your life could bring me many advantages. But even so, he must—" The king broke off as if he'd said too much, then steepled his hands in contemplation. "Still, you are a murderer of your own blood and must be punished for your vile crime. Fortunately for you, I am a man who enjoys gambling with fate, especially someone else's. So..."

He trailed off again, his focus shifting to his dead sister, Ruhh, who floated two feet off the ground behind the queen, her gaze still boring through me.

"And so?" I asked into the growing silence. "What were you about to tell me?"

"You have a choice to make, Zali of the Earth Realm. Complete a few tasks of my choosing for our amusement and the chance to marry my son. Or be put to death before the morning turns to noon."

A laugh burst out of me. "Marry your son? But that's ridiculous. Surely you're joking."

He blinked, his expression blank. "No. I'm as serious as the blade that will soon cleave your head from your neck if you choose the option to die instead of compete."

Compete? Who or what would I be competing with?

"Why do you want your son tied to a human? We have no magic. No great power. And you just accused me of a terrible crime. I can't believe you'd want me for a daughter."

He laughed, indicating Ruhh. "Why not? I lack one of my sisters. And you share a bloodline with the gold makers. Your kingdom, if I can call Mydorian that, is aligned with the reaver elves. If I am related by marriage to their precious Earth Realm queen, then I can help you control the gold."

"So this is about wealth and greed? How predictable. How dull."

"And don't forget power," he added. "*Everything* in the Five Realms is about power."

"Perhaps for the kings, who obsess over destroying what they cannot own. But I'm more concerned with maintaining peace and balance. Your plans disgust me."

"Are you refusing my offer, then?" he asked, dropping his head back against the throne and staring through hooded eyes. "My courtiers will be sorely disappointed. They adore competitions, and I *do* love to please them."

Cheers erupted below the dais, confirming the fire fae's enthusiasm.

Nausea churned my stomach, my mind racing. If there was any way to survive, then I had to at least try, which meant I'd have to complete tasks for the fire fae's entertainment. And if living meant I'd end up married to the prince—a wholly repulsive idea—then as his wife, I could at least wait for an opportunity to kill him, escape, find Arrow. And then end him, too.

I raised my chained hands, pushing unruly hair behind my ears, then lifted my chin. "And if I agree, what kind of tasks must I complete and how many?"

Azarn smiled, excitement sparking in his green eyes. "Three entertainments of my choosing. You will learn the details prior to their commencement."

"If I have no clue what I'll be facing, I won't have time to prepare."

"Precisely," answered Prince Bakhur. "That's the idea, you see."

"Do you want an Earth Realm bride or not?" I snapped. "If I die here, the reavers certainly won't work with you. So what's the point?"

"If there is no living Mydorian heir, we will simply find another method to ensure the elves' cooperation." Bakhur lurched forward, strong fingers pinching my chin as his gaze flicked over my face. "Either way, the Sun Realm wins."

I shoved his hand away and paced along the edge of the dais, ignoring the snickering courtiers below. Dying today simply wasn't an option, so my choice was made. I would compete to marry the Fire Prince.

I stopped before the throne, clasping my chained hands tightly in front of me, striving for calm. "If I agree to amuse you, King Azarn, are you willing to vow that you and any member of your court will not harm or assault me in any way until either I win or am defeated?"

Fire danced in his eyes. "Yes, I can promise you no harm will come to you until you're defeated. Now return to your chambers. I'm considering whether your first event might be our post-dinner entertainment tonight or perhaps the following night, so don't get too comfortable."

Willing my legs not to shake, I bowed my head, and then began to turn away. "One more thing," I said, whirling to face Azarn again. "Did the Storm King agree you could bring me here?"

He looked at his coat and flicked a speck of something off the fine material. "Yes. And I've already sent word to Coridon that you have arrived safely and invited Arrowyn to join us. I'm certain he'll wish to witness the festivities."

The *festivities*. How cruel fae were.

"Yes," I said calmly. "I'm sure he would."

I couldn't bear the thought of seeing Arrow, but even so, sickening heat infused my blood, excitement, I guessed—knowing I'd soon have a chance to slit his double-crossing throat.

I nodded at Raiden and Esen who stood behind me. "And these two, why keep traitors to their own kingdom by your side? Aren't you afraid they'll betray you, too?"

"I have mages to dampen the magic of other realms, allowing us to exert control over them. For example, I'm sure you've realized you cannot use your reaver cloak in Taln. And besides, I believe in keeping the distrusted close. Esen, in particular, is akin to a disfavored hound, eager to please whichever master tosses her the juiciest scraps of meat."

Esen flinched at his words, then straightened her spine.

What Azarn said rang true. Esen had always been ruthless, putting her own interests above all else. But no matter how I tried to frame it, I couldn't accept Raiden's presence in the Fire Court as easily as I did hers.

I caught Raiden's gaze. "How did you masquerade as Arrowyn's dearest friend for all those years? Do Stormur and Ildri know about your defection to the Fire Court? If so, they must be heartbroken and ashamed."

Brown eyes stared at the two Fire Princesses on the dais, not even flickering as he ignored my question.

"Enough prattle," said Azarn. "Return to your room and the comforts I've generously provided. You will need your energy if you hope to survive the first event."

My chains clanked as I shifted my weight but said nothing.

The king leaned forward, raising a brow. "Considering the circumstances, have I not shown you great kindness, Zali Omala? Can you not thank me for this service?"

I wouldn't thank him for one damn thing, comfortable room or not.

And *great* kindness was overstating the situation. Were all fae kings so delusional about themselves? Arrow certainly had been.

Damn. Not Arrow again. When it came to him, I refused to think of anything but his destruction. How pleasurable, how deeply *satisfying* it would feel, to punch his smug face many times over.

Esen tugged the chain between my wrists and hauled me down the dais steps. At the bottom, I looked over my shoulder. The queen and her son stared back. Marcella stuffed dates into her mouth, and the ghost girl—Ruhh—glared at me with evil intent.

Melaya and his twin stood off to the side behind the royal family, a fire pit burning between them. The unnamed twin's face was calm and blank, and no flames burned in his dark gaze.

As we exited the hall, I nudged Esen. "Is Melaya's twin as powerful as he is? He looks constipated, ineffective."

A quick glance passed between Raiden and Esen. "Nukala?" she said. "He is essential."

We climbed the tower steps that led to my room.

"Can the dead girl interact physically?" I asked.

"You want to know if she could pick up a fork and stab you in the neck?" asked Esen. "At certain times, yes. But her... condition waxes and wanes."

I snorted at the memory of my attack on the Fire Court's envoy back in Coridon as Esen unsheathed a small knife, digging it in my side. "No more questions."

On the threshold of my prison, I gripped Esen's arm. "Wait. I know you're in a bad mood." I gave a meaningful look to the blade in her hand. "But I have one more question. Why do you let him talk to you like that?"

"Who?" she said, pretending ignorance.

"The Fire King. For all you've done for him, spying in Coridon, capturing me, he doesn't treat you very well."

"Better than the Storm King did."

"How so? From what I saw, Arrow loved you and appreciated your strengths."

"My strengths!" She snorted. "And what are they?"

"You're a powerful female, smart and unmoved by emotions. An impressive warrior and an awe-inspiring lightning wielder."

Blinking fast, she stared at me, her mouth moving as if forming words of thanks, but then her expression shuttered, and she pushed me backward into the tower room. "Flattery will get you nowhere."

"It's not flattery. It's the truth."

The door began to close.

"Wait a moment." I pushed against a panel of wood. "When can I see Luna?"

A scowl creased her lovely face. "A prisoner is in no position to make demands."

"It was a request."

"Get in your room, human, and stop bothering me," she said. "I've had more than enough of you."

"How long until this so-called entertainment starts? Azarn said it might happen after dinner. What time does the court eat? And what am I meant to do while I wait?"

"I don't know." She pointed at the rolls of parchment and clay jars on the desk. "Write sad poetry about how mean the Storm King was to you. Play the board game by the fire."

A checkered board sat on a table, a cluster of silver and gold pyramids piled off to the side. "I don't know the rules. Will you teach me?" I asked as she unfastened my wrists and fixed the chain to her belt.

"I have duties."

"Perhaps when you've completed them you'll return."

"I don't think so." A wry smile teasing her lips, she shut the door in my face, and then locked it.

As the sun cast a ring of orange light around the tower room, I spun in a circle, my arms outstretched to release tension, stopping when I noticed a gown of dark leather and lace spread over the bedcovers.

Did the Fire King expect me to wear a dress for the first event? If so, he really did think me stupid.

A fire crackled in a small hearth, and I inspected the dress by its strange purple light, my fingers trailing delicate panels of black lace. It was lovely but would greatly restrict my movements. And unless the first event was a dance competition, I couldn't expect to perform well in it.

I smoothed my palms over the dirty leathers I wore, and then hurried to run the bath. After stripping, I sank into the tub and tried to relax.

My thoughts raced as I wondered what trials awaited me. Would Azarn test my courage with torture? Challenge my wit with riddles? Or was he only interested in what I could do with a sword?

Perhaps he hoped I would die fast, and then robbed of the Storm King's tribute, he'd have an excuse to attack Coridon or Auryinnia.

After bathing, I gazed at my reflection in the dresser's mirror and decided what I must do. Wasting no time, I tugged on a dark tunic with delicate crimson embroidery I'd found in the closet, wiped down my leathers with soapy water and set them out to dry. Then, I started training.

The semi-circular chamber was just big enough for me to move through fighting patterns, so after I stretched my limbs, I practiced in earnest, enjoying the familiar burn of muscles. Whatever happened tonight or tomorrow, I would embrace the challenge and face it head-on. I wasn't a quitter. Descended from a line of queens, I had people to protect, a land to care for. A brother who needed me. I would survive. There was no other choice.

I picked up the black gown and walked to the window, then flung it through the bars, watching the garment twirl down, down, down before it splayed over the rocks. Mesmerized, I imagined it was *my* broken body down there, as limp and lifeless as an unwanted dress.

Azarn might very well punish me for not wearing the gown during the first of his so-called *festivities*, but I didn't care.

No fae king would tell me what to wear and have me meekly obey.

Ever again, if I could help it.

Chapter 4

LEAF

The merciless sun scorched my skin as heat coiled in my stomach, and flames licked between my thighs, slowly teasing.

I released a moan of bliss, my body weightless and heels digging into rough tiles, seeking stability.

Was I back in Coridon?

With a gasp, I shifted my weight, leaning back on my elbows and opening my eyes. I squinted through soaring columns at a brilliant blue sky, then down at the golden head moving between my thighs. Naked, I reclined on the Coridon pavilion, hips over the edge and my legs draped over broad shoulders that seemed to hover in mid-air.

A warm mouth laved my flesh, strong fingers digging into my thighs, permitting no escape. I knew that wicked mouth. Remembered everything those cruel fingers had done to me.

Arrow.

No way.

This wasn't happening. It had to be a dream. Only a dream.

As I wriggled away from him, dark wings flapped, blocking out the sun and blowing hair across my face.

"Please," I said, another glide of his tongue sending shock waves through me.

Chaos reigned in my mind, my thoughts tumbling over each other. Was I begging for him to stop or continue forever?

"Keep still," he rumbled, his voice drawing a moan from my lips as he forced me to lie back, warm fingers curling around my breast and pinching my nipple, his other hand pressing my stomach, holding me in place.

"Leaf," he whispered against me, his voice a delicious vibration as he licked deeper.

I shuddered, pressing my heels into the hard muscles of his back and teetering on the edge of a powerful climax. A moment ago, I yearned to escape. Now, I'd murder him if he didn't finish.

"Don't stop," I said, and his head lifted, silver eyes burning through mine. Lips glistening, he smiled, and my heart shattered all over again as my brain caught up, and I remembered what he was.

A liar.

A betrayer.

"Why did you do it?" I asked. "*Why?*"

Wings beating the air, he took a deep breath to answer. But then a female voice interrupted my dream, the tone too cold to belong to the Sayeeda.

"Get up," she barked.

Fucking *Esen*.

Blinking sleep away, I scanned my surroundings.

The vision of Arrow and his golden pavilion dissolved with the dust motes swirling through the dull morning light of my current prison.

Oh, joy. I was a captive once again. Even in my dreams, how could I have forgotten?

Esen threw my bedcovers off. "If you want to visit your precious horse, then hurry up and get dressed. And I heard you moaning. What were you dreaming about?"

I would *never* admit the mortifying truth.

"About how thrilled I am to be alive," I said, pulling a black and red tunic over my head. I fastened my belt around it, and then stuffed my stockinged feet into boots.

Esen dangled the dreaded wrist cuffs between us. I held my hands out, and she fastened them quickly. "You're fortunate Azarn decided not to begin the entertainments last night. A good night's rest puts you at an advantage."

"Who said I had a good night's sleep?" I blushed, remembering this morning's dream.

Fucking Arrow. I hated him. So why would my self-sabotaging mind torment me with a dream about him doing such deliciously dreadful things to me?

"I'm surprised the Fire King is letting me visit the stables."

"I told him if you saw Luna, you'd likely fight harder and that if you had nothing to live for, you might give up and ruin Azarn's fun."

"Thank you, Esen. I appreciate that." Studying the blue-haired fae, I stretched my back, working out the kinks. "And even if you're planning to shove me off a cliff today and tell everyone I fell while trying to escape, it will certainly be nice to get some fresh air first."

She snorted. "The Taln air isn't very fresh."

I thought about the smoky, sulfur-tinged breeze that whipped through my window and silently agreed with her.

We left the tower room and began our descent. Halfway down the stairs, Esen cleared her throat. "You said some nice things to me yesterday, so I'm returning the kindness. But don't get any ideas about escaping. You're chained, your reaver cloak is blocked throughout the city, and I have fire magic. I'd burn you to ash before you took two steps away."

"At the moment, all I care about is Luna's welfare. Let's hurry before Azarn changes his mind." I gripped Esen's forearm and tugged her down the stairs, wondering if anyone had ever been nice to her before.

"Slow down a little," she said as I bounced off the last step into a small foyer lined with black and silver tiles.

"Sorry. I'm excited."

Taln Palace, or at least the areas I'd seen so far, was mostly dimly lit with few windows, and smoke from fire braziers and incense constantly watered my eyes.

Esen led me along confusing hallways that seemed to shift and change direction of their own accord, past fae wearing servants' uniforms of black tunics and white aprons, before finally stopping at a random corner and opening a narrow door tucked into a stone recess.

We stepped out into a still-dark morning, the scent of charred wood and the sulfurous tang of minerals teasing my nose. I sneezed, and Esen laughed.

"You'll soon adjust to the city's smells," she said.

"I hope not."

Restricted by the chain, I stretched my arms above my head as best as I could, releasing my tight shoulder muscles.

To the east, black cliffs dropped into a windswept sea, the distant rhythmic crash of the waves against the rocks matching the wild beat of my heart.

A warm wind blew wisps of smoke around us as we picked our way down the hillside on a winding, stony path toward a flat area of dark earth and scraggly trees.

Unlike the vibrant greens and rich browns of Mydorian and Coridon's golden streets and terracotta roof tiles, Taln's landscape was a dull palette of black and gray, broken only by showers of red sparks from the fire geysers.

Their radiant glow bathed the land in shades of orange and red. But when the geysers weren't active, even Taln's grass and trees looked depressing, leeched of nearly all color.

Jagged rocks, worn smooth by the harsh elements, jutted from the ground at intervals, their surfaces aglow as if burning from within. Several times, I tripped, and Esen tugged on my chain, stopping me from falling on my face.

As we trekked through a tunnel of dark trees with gnarled, overhanging branches, the heat grew unbearable, sweat slicking my skin.

I wiped the back of my arm across my forehead. "The fae in Taln must bathe a lot. It's so damn hot."

"Only in the areas not regulated by magic. As I said, you'll get used to it. Your body will acclimatize in a week or two, then you'll be wearing cloaks everywhere like the rest of us."

"I'd like to think I won't be here long enough for that."

Esen laughed. "Not looking forward to becoming the Princess of Fire?"

"I'd rather be crowned queen of my own realm. Anyway, Prince Bakhur isn't interested in me. And if the sham of a marriage did take place, I doubt he or his father would let me out of the tower afterward."

Bright blue eyes cut to mine. "Last night, Azarn clearly told you what he's interested in—the gold that you're connected to through the reavers." A small geyser exploded only five feet in front of us, and Esen tugged me out of the way just in time. "Watch where you're walking or your face will be burned off, and then your beloved horse won't recognize you."

"Face or no face, Luna will always know me. Arrow controls both the lightning weavers and the auron kanara. Mydorian can't supply Azarn with gold. He needs the Storm Idiot on side, and I can't imagine that asshole giving control of anything over to the fire fae. Can you?"

She snickered. "Other than you, no I can't."

The sun rose higher in the gray sky, burning most of the foul-smelling smoke away. Through the end of the tree tunnel, the silhouettes of distant buildings shimmered, blurring in the heat, like the body of Azarn's ghost sister—the pitiful, but terrifying, Ruhh.

Our footsteps echoed against flagstones as we entered a large courtyard surrounded by walls covered in tumbling roses so dark they appeared black. Hoping to test their perfume, I strayed toward them, but Esen plucked me back and marched us over to a large, rectangular building made of dark wood and gray stone.

Two guards flanked the open wooden doors, trolls with long curling tusks and orange eyes that reminded me of Gorbinvar. A cold shiver puckered my skin as memories of laying beneath the blacksmith shuddered through me.

It was all my fault. I shouldn't have escaped Coridon without a plan or an ally. *Shut up*, I told myself, squaring my shoulders and mentally slapping myself. I'd do exactly the same thing again if given the chance to flee Taln.

I regretted nothing.

Freedom was worth risking everything for.

Rows of stalls constructed from smooth, wooden beams and the same volcanic stone that the palace was hewn from lined the stables. Pulsating triangular symbols adorned its roughly rendered walls.

In a haze of dust, grooms worked at the far end of the building, sweeping hay and cleaning stalls, the sound of horses' whickers and stomps filling the air.

"Luna," I called out, and her white head appeared over the second stall on my right, her nostrils flaring and ears flicking forward.

I hurried over and pressed my cheek against the flat of her nose, breathing in her familiar scent as I whispered soothing words. I opened the half-length door and ran my hands over her coat before inspecting her feet, hugging her neck when I was satisfied that she was well and happy.

"She seems to like you," said Esen, leaning a shoulder against the stall's wooden frame.

"I raised her from a foal. Other than Ari, Luna is my dearest friend."

"The Sayeeda?" Esen snorted. "So everyone despises me, but that icy gold reaver elf has no trouble making devoted friends?"

Slowly, I turned to face her. "If you try being nice for a change, you'll make friends, too, Esen. And I also recommend that you don't attempt to murder any potential friends. Remember our near-fatal gold foundry visit?"

She laughed and pushed off the wall with her shoulder. "You haven't changed a bit. Still don't know when to keep your thoughts to yourself."

"I'd rather die than not have the last word," I teased.

"Suit yourself," she said, digging a piece of apple from a pouch and giving it to Luna. "I'd better take you back to the tower before you accidentally offend someone and get yourself stabbed."

"Can I take Luna for a quick ride first?"

"No. You'd be halfway across the realm before I even realized I'd been left behind."

"Come on." I made a pleading face. "Or... are you afraid I'm a better rider than you?"

A flash of fire magic rolled off Esen's palm, and I winced as it hit my shoulder.

"What was that? Did your power misfire? Or did you do it on purpose?"

"It's nothing. Don't worry about it." She looked away, flicking her fingers as if in pain. "Let's go."

Promising Luna I'd return soon, I dropped a kiss on her nose and exited the stables.

We took a different route back to the palace, meandering through gardens filled with plants and trees heavily laden with fiery-colored flowers that were planted in intricate arrangements—sweeping spirals mixed with more formal rectangular patterns.

A red sun hovered in the sky, casting pinkish light over black statues of winged fae, their limbs tangled together in the midst of fierce battles. A stone phoenix spread its wings in the center of a fountain spewing liquid fire into a pond, its light too dazzling to study for long.

While chatting with Esen, I paid close attention to my surroundings, mapping out the landmarks near the palace. If I could escape from my tower room, the forest that ranged to the north-west was likely the best place to head for. Trees meant plenty of hiding places, which was great. Unless beasts with long claws and sharp teeth already occupied them.

Swatting away red-winged dragonflies that buzzed around our heads, we crested the hill, and the black spires of the fire palace loomed before us. I touched Esen's arm to get her attention. "Thank you. You didn't need to organize my visit to Luna. I really do appreciate it."

"Don't thank me. Remember you're here because of me. If I hadn't alerted Azarn to your identity when I did, then Arrow would've found you first, and your circumstances would be quite different."

My gaze shot to hers, and I stumbled away from a shower of sparks that had erupted out of nowhere. Was I losing my mind or did Esen sound guilty?

And if Arrow had got to me first, would I be better off imprisoned in Coridon right now?

Better, I decided. Because I'd be closer to slicing the Storm King's head off with the first blade that I got my hands on.

In a courtyard that led to the palace's side entrance, a tall fae slid out from behind a stationary carriage, blocking our path. A flash of recognition jolted through me. The slight stoop, long auburn hair, and smug expression belonged to the Sun envoy I'd tried to kill with his own fork in the Coridon dining hall.

"Esen," he said with a bow of his head before turning a pair of dark, accusing eyes on me.

"Neeron," she replied, shifting to stand a little in front of me, an unmistakable gesture of protection.

"Ah, if it isn't the little human fiend herself. I'm happy to hear you're finally facing the consequences of your insults to both me and my realm."

An aura of barely repressed fury sizzled around his body.

I pasted on a smile. "You heard wrong, Envoy. I'm in Taln to marry your prince. One day soon, I'll be your queen. Queen of two realms, in fact." I patted his arm. "I feel certain we can put our differences behind us. Don't you agree?"

"No." Pure malice flashed in his eyes. "If Azarn's festivities don't kill you, be assured that I will."

"My magic is stronger than yours, Neeron." Esen shoved him backward. "Touch her, and I'll gladly turn the small, tightly wrapped package in your pants into finely mashed sausage and meatballs."

Without another word, Neeron scurried away, leaving us free to continue through the courtyard.

"Esen, I'm confused. By your own admission you got me into this mess, so why protect me now?" I asked as we entered the palace directly into a large storeroom, then strode through the black-walled kitchen.

"You're my responsibility," she replied. "I'll decide when someone is allowed to hurt you."

"Gods, you sound just like Arrow," I said. "Careful, or I might fall in love with you. I have a type, you know."

She barked out a laugh. "You do realize what you just admitted?"

"That love isn't bound by the shapes of body parts?" I teased.

She shook her head. "Your ability to joke when your circumstances are dire has always baffled me."

"Each to our own coping methods," I said. "And speaking of the prick, when's Arrow supposed to arrive?"

I hoped it wouldn't be too soon. I needed time to steel my heart before I could safely look upon the arrogant, deceitful face of my betrayer.

"I'm not sure. Soon." She gave me a cunning smile as we stomped up the stairs of my tower. "Aren't you looking forward to seeing him, Leaf? Even just a little?"

"No." At least, I hoped I wasn't. "And could you please try not to call me by the name he gave me?"

"Okay, *human* it is, then," she said with another sly grin.

As the door shut behind me and locks clicked into place, I ignored the lunch platter on the desk and the beautiful patterns of sunlight on the walls, my mind occupied with fantasies about Arrow's imminent arrival.

I pictured his silver eyes, wondering what color they'd turn at the moment of death. No storm magic enlivening the irises. No spark of life. Just staring blankly.

Perhaps dull gray or translucent white.

With my hand pressed against my chest, I collapsed on the bed, telling myself the only reason my heart pounded wildly was because I was excited that I'd soon see him die.

Nothing more.

Chapter 5

LEAF

That evening, just as I swallowed my last mouthful of dinner, the locks rattled outside my room and Esen entered alone, her expression pinched, not open as it had been during our visit to the stables.

"When you shoved me in here earlier, you forgot to remove this," I said, holding my chained wrists aloft.

"No. I didn't." She tilted her chin toward another gown that a servant had hung on a coat stand by the door. "Put it on."

"Why?" I rose from the chair, pushing it under a small, round dining table before smoothing my palms over my leather pants.

"The king wants you to wear it while you fight."

So tonight's event was a battle.

Of course Azarn wasn't interested in testing the strength of my mind. Well, fine, then. If he wanted blood and gore, I'd do my best to give it to him.

I cracked my back, thankful I'd spent the day training. Even with my wrists restrained, I'd moved through as many two-handed strike patterns I could think of, limbering my muscles.

"I'd like to see Azarn fight in a dress," I said. "Will my opponent be wearing one?"

Silent, Esen crossed her arms and stared at me through narrowed eyes.

"No? Then neither will I."

She rolled her eyes, then led me down the tower staircase and through the palace, while I quietly celebrated the fact I still wore my tunic and leathers. A sad victory considering I was possibly about to die, but a victory nonetheless.

In the Great Hall, servants collected the leftovers of a lavish feast from tables that lined both sides of the oval room. On a raised platform that loomed high above the court, a male flutist with silver hair so long it tumbled almost to the marble floor, played a dark atmospheric tune. He accompanied a singer who flew around him, the webbing of her bat-like wings translucent and her voice high and ethereal.

The musicians and courtiers fell silent as we approached the dais where the king sat surrounded by his family. I squared my shoulders, lifting my chin, refusing to show any signs of fear, my pulse racing, and my heart pumping erratically.

An oval, stained-glass window dominated the space behind the dais. Framed by magical flames, it spread the colors of a fiery sunset throughout the hall and illuminated carvings on the curved black walls. At night, the hall's true beauty was revealed.

The Sun Realm royals sat like statues carved in ice on tall, narrow thrones, their expressions frozen in unreadable masks. A thick silence enveloped the hall, each deliberate, slow thud of my boots the only sound cutting through it.

In a burst of swirling gray fabric, the king's ghost sister appeared out of thin air and shot along the center aisle, stopping in front of me, her slippers hovering two feet above the floor.

Cold fingers swiped over my throat. Correction, swiped *through* my throat, as if she wanted to strangle me with her ghostly hands but couldn't.

"Arrowyn Ramiel despises you, human," she hissed.

"So it seems. Did he hate you as well?"

Tears of blood leaked from her translucent eyes, and her body shook with fury.

"Ruhh dearest," the king called out. "Return to me at once. The best seat from which to enjoy the proceedings is the one beside me, and tonight it is yours."

Azarn stared down his nose at Queen Estella, and without a word, she rose obediently, then eased into the ghost girl's chair. In a cloud of dust and ragged material, Ruhh glided across the marble and joined her brother on the shining black dais.

One foot in front of the other, I told myself. And if that was all I could do, it was better than collapsing on the floor and giving up.

Never give in, and never show fear—that was the mantra I lived by. And I'd gladly die by it, too. Because Mydor blood would never fail.

Even after my death it would live on in Van and the reaver elves. Killing me wouldn't end my quest for balance throughout the Five Realms. In my stead, others would rise up and carry the eternal torch of peace. I was certain of it.

I stopped at the bottom of the stairs, staring up at the king, waiting for his instructions.

Leaning forward, he braced an elbow on his knee. "I've heard that you killed your brother, whose skills were enhanced by fire magic, with your human fighting ability alone. I find that difficult to believe. Tonight, I'd like a demonstration of your *supposed* prowess."

"You'll have me fight? That's the first *supposed* entertainment?" I asked, mirroring the word back to him.

He smiled. "Yes."

"But if I die tonight, there will be no Earth Realm bride for your son."

Azarn shrugged. "And as I've already advised you, there are other ways to control the gold trade."

Nausea churned in my gut. Arrow and the Zareen would never cede power over the gold to the Sun Realm. Coridon and Auryinnia had existed in a symbiotic relationship for thousands of years. They needed each other. And nothing King Azarn did to me would change that.

Torchlight flickered over the Fire King's obsidian throne, his hands gripping armrests of extravagantly molded gold, and his green eyes blazing as he studied me.

The same barely bridled excitement burned in the gazes of his family—except for Queen Estella of the Crystal Realm—a star fae whose detached manner was as mysterious as the galaxies surrounding the five realms.

My chains rattled as Esen stepped forward and unlocked them with deft movements, her eyes on the task and her breaths coming out short and ragged. What did *she* have to worry about tonight?

Esen wasn't poised to fight an unknown opponent and possibly get hacked to pieces or burned to ash in an enemy territory.

Dark flames writhed around Azarn's crown of ever-burning wood as he rose from the throne and addressed the court, his voice projecting arrogant authority. "Tonight, Zali Omala of the Earth Realm, a traitor to the Hidden City of Mydorian, will complete a challenge for the chance to see the light of another day."

My wrists ached and fear weighed heavy in my stomach, but I stood tall with my hands loose by my sides, breathing slowly.

Courtiers murmured, the air thrumming with excitement. I was sure every one of them hoped to see me fail, and I prayed I had the strength to disappoint them.

"Zali, tonight, you will walk the Dragon's Path," the Fire King said, sweeping his arm out in front of his velvet-covered chest as he strutted to the edge of the dais. "In recognition of your human weakness, other than the flames that enclose the pathway, I guarantee no other magic shall be used in this event. And no combatant will wear protective armor."

"Dragons?" My pulse raced. "I have to fight one?"

"There are no dragons present tonight. The flames are your adversaries."

"What flames?" I asked, whirling around and scanning the throne room.

It looked exactly as it had a moment ago. Fire fae sat at tables around the walls—ogres, trolls, jinns, and the more humanoid fae, all bristling with excitement, their wings, teeth, and other strange appendages grinding and flapping in anticipation.

Prince Bakhur, looking particularly thrilled, laughed as he joined Azarn. "Watch closely, Zali Omala," he said.

Father and son moved their hands in matching complex patterns, and wisps of fire formed a web in front of them. They flicked it outward, and a tunnel of flames swept along the length of the hall.

"Your task is to pass through the flames and emerge intact on the other side," said the king. "If you survive, you may have the honor of joining my son in a dance before you retire for the evening."

Oh, lucky me. What a prize!

"And when will the second event happen?"

"When it suits me, impertinent human."

I nodded and considered what I'd learned.

Azarn wanted a demonstration of my fighting skills. Did that mean I'd need to battle the flames themselves? Or was there more to the trial that he hadn't disclosed?

Raiden appeared and handed me a black-hilted sword. I closed my eyes, holding the weapon over my open palms. The blade felt well-balanced, and when I opened my eyes, firelight was reflected in the sword's sharp edge.

At least the fire fae had given me an excellent weapon.

Stepping backward, I slashed the sword through the air, wondering if I should slice Raiden's head from his shoulders while I had the opportunity. And since Esen stood beside him, I could remove two heads in one satisfying sweep.

But then the fire fae would kill me, and my plans to destroy Arrow and return to Van and the Mydorians would be dust. And I'd be nothing but ash, floating on the warm Taln breeze.

Two winged fae standing on either side of the fiery tunnel lifted large rams horns to their lips and blew simultaneous, ear-splitting calls to battle.

Silence fell over the hall as I stared at the writhing flames, summoning my courage.

"Well? What are you waiting for?" boomed the king. "Go forth and entertain us." He returned to his seat, then flicked his fingers at me. "Begin!"

I drew a breath deep into my lungs, raising my sword as I strode toward the tunnel, hoping I looked a lot more confident than I felt.

The moment I stepped onto the Dragon's Path, the magical space expanded, the wall of flames moving farther away from my body as the ground shook and heat scorched my skin. There was no smoke, but my eyes stung and my vision blurred regardless.

With dawning horror, I watched flames peel off the side of the tunnel, merge and form the shape of a tall fae. It raised its arm, holding a sword of fire, waiting for me to move.

Fuck.

How would I get myself out of this fiery shit show?

Violent determination was the only option.

Whispering the Mydorian battle chant, I started forward, my teeth gritted and hands gripping the sword for dear life.

With every few steps I took, more flames leaped toward me, and two more creatures appeared. Their fiery arms slashed across my vision, and I ducked and wove, slicing off limbs and piercing the creatures' hearts one by one.

Enormous, the fire beasts were terrifying, but thankfully slow, and before long, I'd slain three, then four, five, six, their bodies melting back into the tunnel walls the moment I stabbed their chests.

The most difficult thing about this challenge was the heat. It licked down my throat, and dried the moisture in my eyes, evaporating my sweat. My breath sawed in and out of me, and I tried to breathe through my nose to conserve energy, but couldn't get enough air in.

Both fury and determination boiled inside me, growing hotter with every slash of my sword. I had to make it through the tunnel. I couldn't let Azarn win. Nor would I allow the Storm

Idiot to triumph. I would marry the damn Fire Prince if it was the only way to survive and escape this unhappy realm of ash and smoke.

I just had to keep swinging.

As I reached the halfway point, the heat intensified, the flames roaring louder all around me. Feeling dizzy, I swayed, my strength wavering as glowing embers rained down and burned through my clothes, scorching my skin.

Outside the tunnel, noise from the courtiers, cackles, grunts, and roars, could be heard over the flames of the Dragon's Path. Most fae probably hoped I'd run from the tunnel with blackened skin, barely alive, so they could watch me die on the floor of the throne room.

Ignoring the taunting sounds, I kept two images fixed in my mind, the beloved faces of Van and Ari, and with every surge of heat, I reminded myself of the Mydorians who needed me and pushed forward with renewed vigor.

I refused to die tonight.

Another creature dropped from the ceiling of flames.

Time slowed as I spun and slashed, the end of the tunnel getting closer with each lung-scorching breath I took. Not much farther now. I could do this.

As I pulled my blade from another fire creature's heart, leaving a swirling hole of molten embers in its place, I glimpsed the *real* task Azarn had set for me. A tusked fire troll snorted and bellowed near the exit, his orange eyes painfully familiar.

Gorbinvar had been raised from the dead.

Chapter 6

LEAF

I mpossible.

In Bonerust, Arrow blew up the fire troll's smithy. I watched it happen. Not a scrap of flesh or single bone shard would have survived the destruction for Azarn's mages to reanimate with blood magic. But still, the resemblance to Gorbinvar was uncanny.

Perhaps I faced a relative.

"Zali Omala," the troll growled out. "Human slave of Arrowyn Ramiel, the time has come for you to pay the price for murdering my father, Gorbinvar of Bonerust."

Oh, shit. The smithy's *son*.

More than anyone, I knew what spite did to a person. It hardened organs and turned hearts into cold, brittle things. Bitterness was a slow but fatal poison. And there was no one more embittered than a son avenging his father.

"Who are you?" I asked, my voice a shaky whisper.

"I am Dorn, and mine is the last name you will ever hear, human."

With limbs as thick as tree trunks, the troll was nearly twice as tall as me—far from an even match—confirming the Fire King didn't care if I lived or died tonight.

Releasing a hard breath, I cracked my neck and rolled my shoulders, preparing to do a lot more ducking and weaving as I began whispering my people's war chant.

By branch and root, soil and stone, lend strength to muscle, heart, and bone. Crush all to live. Conquer and prevail. Mydor blood will never fail.

Mydor blood will never fail.

Saliva dripped from Dorn's tusks as he grinned, clearly relishing the idea of slicing me to pieces then sucking the marrow from my bones—if the tales of troll-battle traditions were true.

Brandishing my sword high, I spread my stance and waited for him to move. Hot embers fell around us, but we never spared them a glance. Who cared about a little burning flesh when your head might be hacked from your shoulders at any moment?

Dorn looked confident as he tossed his sword between his meaty hands and laughed. Straps of black leather crossed his bare chest, the rest of his body clad in tight pants and heavy boots. Azarn had kept his word, and no visible armor protected the troll.

He stalked forward, and I chanted the reaver cloaking spell one last time. But as expected, it didn't work. Fucking fire mages. If not for them, I could disappear, kill the troll, keep running until I reached a seaport, and never lay eyes on the Sun Realm again.

As Dorn's momentum increased, I lunged forward, running, then skidded past him, my blade slicing the backs of his knees.

With a roar he spun around, chasing me with lumbering steps to the other end of the tunnel.

The fire hissed and crackled, my heart pounded in my ears, and the troll's breathing was loud and labored. But no sounds could be heard outside the flaming walls.

The court was silent, waiting.

Dorn's grunts and wheezes gave me hope. He'd barely moved, yet seemed to struggle for each breath. Perhaps he'd been spending his days sitting on his ass, eating pies, and dreaming of gory revenge. Well, the time had come to live out his fantasy.

It was a shame he was no warrior—but a great bonus for me.

Blood splattered from his wounds as his sword swiped at me while I ducked and zigzagged up and down the tunnel, speed saving me from a brutal hand-to-hand combat with the massive fae. Each time his blade clanged against the floor, I checked to make sure my limbs were still attached to my torso, relief surging through me.

The arc of his blade kept circling, missing my head and my stomach by mere inches, and I thanked the gods his size made him slow and clumsy. He relied on brute strength, but I had different skills. I was fast, refused to give up, and I fought with the fury of a woman who'd had enough of being used and abused by power-hungry males.

This event might end with the troll slashing me into bloody ribbons, but so what? It was better to die fighting than surrender to assholes.

Running toward Dorn, I leaped at the last minute, issuing a short, sharp kick to his balls before I slid between his legs, slashing his thighs. He stumbled, then righted himself, blood trickling down his legs. Growling, he raised his palm, fire magic kindling blue and red between his fingers.

I shook my head. "You'd better not. You're likely to explode if I'm correct about the way Azarn plays his games."

"Fuck," he muttered, realizing the truth of my words. Then he roared as he hunched forward, coming at me again. Faster and harder this time.

Securing my footing with a wide stance, I rocked my weight, tossing the sword hilt between my palms. "That's it. Do your worst, Dorn. Do it for your poor, dead daddy."

With a scream of fury, he met me head-on, the force of his blade against mine hurtling me backward. I scrambled onto my feet, ran past him again, and slashed at his calves, then his back before he even had time to turn around.

A sense of power rushed through me. It felt good to swing a sword, to move fast, finally breathing in a controlled manner, despite the heat.

Crush all to live. Conquer and prevail. Mydor blood will never fail.

Never. Fucking. Fail.

As Dorn stumbled in confusion, I moved through a well-practiced sword pattern, slicing across his arms, then down the front of his thighs. With a feral roar and a lucky sweep of his big arms, he picked me up and hurled me into the air.

I flew along the tunnel, bouncing off the wall of flames before I dropped to the marble floor and rolled, scrambling onto my feet again at the same moment Dorn picked up his sword.

I watched his feet, the bend in his knees, waiting for his weight to shift as his bulky body prepared to spin toward me. The moment his eyes shifted off mine and his spine began to twist, I bolted forward, scrambling up his back before his blade had fully swung around.

Not wasting a second, I dragged my sword across his throat. A gruesome collar of blood sprayed from the fae's neck, soaking my arm and leathers. He released his weapon, and it clattered over the marble. I dropped to the ground as Dorn turned, one hand pressing the gaping slit in his neck and orange eyes wide with shock.

As his free hand reached for the floor, blindly grasping for his sword, I ran back several paces, spun around, then charged forward. Leaping up, I slashed at his neck two more times, and he fell to the floor, landing face-up with a thud. My muscles protested as I climbed his reclining body and plunged steel into his chest, making sure he would never get up again.

Groaning through gritted teeth, I raised the sword above my head again and again, thrusting through bone and flesh. My vision blurred. Everything around me—the flames, drifting embers, the hall beyond—dissolved into blackness, my hoarse, panted breaths the perfect music for murder.

Mydor blood will never fail.
Mydor blood will never fail.
Mydor blood.
Will... Never... Fail.
Never.

I saw my brother's face beneath me—Quin—laughing and taunting as blood flowed over his features. Then Arrow. His silver eyes staring and staring as his hand braced my hip, his iridescent wings spread out on the ground. Not moving. Just lying there, letting me kill him.

A firm hand pressed the middle of my back. "Leaf. That's enough."

With those words, the sounds of the Fire Court crashed over me. Deafening cheers, the roar of the fae. Laughter from Prince Bakhur. Ruhh's high-pitched screeches.

Panting, I let go of the sword, leaving it embedded in the troll's stomach, and looked over my shoulder.

Esen.

She held out a hand, and I took it, gaining my feet, then wobbling on shaking legs.

Surprising me, Esen braced an arm around my waist. "I think he's probably dead now. You can relax."

Nodding, I wiped blood and gore from my face. "Yes, I believe you're right."

I scanned my body. My leathers were singed and torn, and a grimy layer of soot and blood covered my skin. But I was alive. I had survived the first event.

The Fire King shouted something unintelligible, and the Dragon's Path of flames disappeared, the court falling silent once more.

Azarn beckoned me toward the dais, and Esen, her arm linked through mine, led me limping forward as I leaned nearly all my weight on her.

When I was close enough to see the king's face, both fury and triumph glittered in his emerald gaze.

"Zali Omala, you have survived the first entertainment and defeated an enemy," he said, his tone indicating he wasn't pleased with the outcome. "But the second task may prove more challenging."

I longed to correct him. Because tonight I'd faced two challenges—the fire creatures and the troll—but five sets of frosty eyes staring at me from gilded chairs kept me silent.

Not one member of Azarn's family smiled or directly acknowledged my success in any way. Cold assholes the lot of them.

"May I retire?" I asked, desperate to return to my room and tend to my cuts and bruises, the burns that grew more painful with each passing moment.

"No. But you may walk to the center of the hall, and my son will join you for a dance, after which you have my permission to leave us."

I bowed my head, masking my relief behind a tangled curtain of hair. "Are you certain your son will want to dance with me in this condition?"

Bakhur laughed, and Azarn heaved a long-suffering sigh and nodded.

With my head held high, I turned my back on the dais and walked to the middle of the hall, the sea of courtiers parting as if they feared me in my current blood-soaked state. Good. Hopefully, they'd think twice before crossing me.

A sudden hum of excitement rolled through the crowd. Ruhh screamed, and Prince Bakhur hissed out an audible breath. Weaponless, I drew my aching muscles tight, preparing for anything, but refusing to turn around and react to the courtiers' taunts.

Three beats of silence, and then a slow clap sounded from near the dais, the hairs on my arms standing on end. Goose flesh prickled my skin, and my Aldara mark flared to life, scorching my neck.

I spun on my heel.

A tall male braced his booted feet wide on the dais's bottom step. He pushed his hood back, revealing dark gold hair and a ferocious silver gaze that pierced through my skull before lowering to my ribcage and setting the pieces of my shattered heart aflame.

The ability to form words left me. My heart reassembled itself only to hammer and flail about my chest like a dying fish with a hook in its mouth.

I couldn't move as the fae's sensual lips parted. I dug my nails into my outer thigh, every muscle shaking.

"Well done, Princess Zali," he said in that familiar honeyed rumble. "Unfortunately, I arrived too late to see you fight, but courtiers have informed me that you remain as formidable an opponent as ever."

My fists clenched as I locked my jaw at the terrible sight of Arrowyn fucking Ramiel, flashing a lopsided smirk at me.

I thought I was prepared. Believed I was ready to face him.

But I wasn't. Far from it.

A rage-filled scream lashed against my lips, demanding release.

But I wouldn't yell, swear, moan, or show a single flinch of emotion.

I would *never* let that asshole see my pain.

Chapter 7

LEAF

The first stupid thing I did was wonder if the Storm King had ever called me *Princess Zali* before, and the second was allow a flash of longing to flow through my veins.

Why did the mere sight of Arrowyn Ramiel make my body betray my mind?

My nerve endings foolishly recalled every sigh of pleasure his touch had wrung from me. My bones, flesh, and skin didn't care that the male with his eyes locked on mine was the realms' greatest liar. A brazen deceiver, who'd turned out to be as despicable as I'd predicted when I first laid eyes on him from inside the slaver's cage at Farron Gilt Market.

In some cruel twist of fate, he appeared even more beautiful since I saw him in Mydorian a few weeks ago, and that made me furious. How dare a monster look so good.

A cold expression adorned his face, a pitiless smirk on his lips. An aura of supreme confidence surrounded him, like a trap, a forcefield of shimmering corruption, and my Aldara mark thrummed in blind, ridiculous appreciation.

Tonight, tight dark leathers hugged his long legs, shining metal caps strapped over his knees. As was his habit, he had left the ridged muscles of his stomach bare, his chest covered by the lethal plate of gold feathers. Other than his favorite feather ear cuffs, his head bore no crown or other kingly adornment.

I hated him, but adored every inch of his appearance. If a breathtaking, winged god rose from the hell realms to destroy Taln, it would no doubt look exactly like him.

He pushed the dark material of his cloak behind his broad shoulders, so it hung between the purple-black wings tucked close to his body, the thick hem falling against his calves.

The garment's glinting feathers seemed to mock me, reminding me it was an exact match for the one he'd covered me in after he stripped me naked and threw me in the river on the day we met. The one he gave me before leaving me alone in Mydorian. Before *betraying* me.

"*Promise you'll take care of yourself,*" he'd said, wrapping it around my shoulders in the forest. "*Keep this, then I'll always be able to keep you warm.*"

Fucking liar. As if he gave a shit about my comfort. His love was a cruel pretense. An elaborate ruse to make me compliant, so he could use me as leverage with the Sun Realm.

Memories tumbled over me of the many times I'd pleaded for his touch, his bite, his love. But no more. Never again would I sink so low as to beg for scraps of attention from my abuser.

"Arrow," the king's ghostly sister cried out, excitement thrumming in her airy voice. "You came."

The Storm King smiled at Ruhh, his skin paling slightly. "Of course. I wouldn't miss the festivities for all the gold in my realm."

The other sister, Marcella, guided Ruhh back to her seat, soothing her into silence as they went.

Two fae stepped out of the crowd and joined Arrow—Raiden and a younger male I'd never seen before. Wait... Raiden? How was that possible? Only a moment ago, he'd been standing on the left side of the royal family.

My gaze shot to the dais. There he was, standing straight-backed and dressed in Sun Realm armor, just like before. I blinked, and in his place, stood a fire fae with short black hair and a neatly clipped beard.

What in the dust was going on?

I whipped around to face Arrow and found Raiden and the young human male still standing beside him. Instead of the black and red Fire Court armor, Raiden wore dusty leathers and a dirt-flecked cloak. He braced a hand on his hip, lips twitching, fighting a smile.

What the fuck?

I glanced at Esen. *She* hadn't changed and still wore Sun Realm armor, her gaze focused on the floor and cheeks stained red as if she'd been caught doing something she shouldn't.

The truth hit me like an anvil to the back of my skull.

I'd been tricked.

A fire fae must've used transformational magic and stolen Raiden's image, impersonating him. But why?

The female fae who had guarded me over the last couple of days was authentic, often speaking of things that only the real Esen could possibly have known. But Raiden had barely said a word, and when he did, he'd sounded odd. Wrong. How had I been so stupid not to guess it wasn't him?

And what was the purpose of the Sun Realm pretending Raiden had defected to the Fire Court? Nothing in this scenario made sense.

Queen Estella rose and glided down the dais steps to greet Arrow. Linking her arm through his, she guided him up toward Azarn's throne, a ripple of midnight hair and an indigo gown studded with metallic stars flowing behind her.

"Is Estella a friend of Arrow's?" I whispered to Esen.

"She's a strange one. As cold and distant as the stars, except with him, for some reason."

I wanted to ask about the Raiden impostor, but bit my tongue and strained my ears to hear the conversation between Azarn and Arrow, hoping to glean useful information.

The young male who had arrived with the Storm Court party hadn't moved from the bottom step of the dais, his black curls framing a lean, handsome face, solemn eyes studying me. There was something familiar about him. The way he stood, loose-limbed, but alert. The strong line of his nose. The fact I couldn't place him bothered me greatly.

"You wasted no time in getting here, Arrowyn," Azarn said. "Meet any gold raiders on the journey?"

"We dispatched a small crew. And of course I hurried to Taln after hearing of your plans for the human girl."

Azarn chuckled. "I thought they would appeal to you. No regrets in giving her up? By all reports, the girl was your favorite bed slave."

Arrow shrugged a shoulder. "She had her uses. But after a while, all objects lose their shine."

An *object*, was I? And *the human girl*.

What an utter prick.

I pictured his deceitful head falling from his neck and splattering on the marble. I imagined stomping on it, turning his flesh to mush, just like I'd done to Dorn.

Prince Bakhur rose from his chair, swaggered over to the Storm King, and bowed.

"Bakhur." Arrow barely inclined his head. "Apparently, you're about to dance with my ex-servant. Brave of you."

"Oh, why is that?" asked the Fire Prince.

"As small and innocent as she looks, she's far from a sweet, little kitten," Arrow rumbled, his gaze fixed on me. "If you wish to keep your eyes, I suggest you watch out for her claws."

"Duly noted," said the prince as he started down the dais stairs.

"Wait," boomed his father, casting a sly look at Arrow. "I believe I would be better entertained if the King of Storms and Feathers danced with his murderous ex-slave. What do my courtiers think of the proposal?"

"Brother, please, no," whined Ruhh as the courtiers' shouts drowned out any further objections.

A dirge of music rose from musicians placed somewhere in the crowd—the drums slow but urgent, the strings a caterwaul of twisted paranoia. A perfect melody for a bitter reunion.

An atmosphere of violence surrounded Arrow's powerful frame as he strode down the stairs, stopping right in front of me. He ignored Esen beside me, who made a clumsy bow and backed away, leaving us to stare at each other with mirrored poses. Jaws clenched, fists balled, and hearts closed.

So... finally, here he was in front of me. My glorious, golden nemesis only four feet away. The fae who had ruined my life at least twice over. Oh, how I wished he had left me caged at the gilt market, saving me from endless heartache and pain.

But, no. Assholes have to asshole.

If only I still held the sword that mangled Dorn, I could end Arrow right here. Right now. I scanned his body for weapons, and other than the stupid feather breastplate, saw none.

With two large steps, he closed the distance between us and more, nearly knocking me off my feet. A dark-gold eyebrow quirked in either amusement or concern. Perhaps he was afraid of what I might do to him in front of the fire fae.

He was right to worry. Wrong to find it funny. Because, at last, I could touch him, spit on him, then scratch his pretty eyes out. I leaned forward, my fingers forming claws, but then the heat of King Azarn's glare burned between my shoulder blades. Revenge would have to wait for a more private occasion.

A brittle silence stretched between us, a chasm between each pounding heartbeat to the next as we stared, neither one prepared to look away first.

Arrow made a strained noise. A throat clearance or a grunt of discomfort. I kept my breathing steady. Forced my pulse to flow like treacle through my veins. Slow and calm.

Unbothered queen, I told myself—or *almost*-queen. That's what I was. Unruffled. Unaffected. Unmoved by rippling muscles and body heat like an inferno.

"Shall we dance?" he said, his low voice scraping my skin like evening stubble.

A big palm came to rest on my hip, the fingers of his other hand entwining with mine. I cupped his shoulder, each dip and curve of bone and muscle so familiar. So real. His skin was too warm and his pulse rapid beneath it.

I clicked my tongue in annoyance. When would he learn to dress for an occasion and stop swanning around half-naked, like an adolescent who'd suddenly realized he'd been blessed with a physique to make the gods drool?

With a gentle push of his palm into the base of my spine, our bodies slid together, my breath seizing in my lungs, heart fluttering, trapped against the cage of my ribs.

His stormy scent overwhelmed me—a bite of cold air before it rained, cloves, and a hint of the wine he'd had with his dinner. I did my best to forestall them, but unwanted memories rushed over me.

The way the Storm King had questioned me—a new servant—in the kitchen at Coridon, demanding to know about the home I had no memory of. The intensity burning in his gaze that night, possessive and commanding even then.

The guards who assaulted me, and then suffered gruesome deaths by the same hands that now heated my flesh.

The first time his lips touched mine.

The soaring gold columns of my pavilion.

His crescent-moon bedchamber.

All the lies he had told me.

We began to move, and coherent thoughts dissolved—even the murderous ones.

We danced a meandering, unsteady waltz, my body shaking to the rhythm of his ragged breaths.

Dark lashes glittered with gold paint as he stared down at my mouth. Then his gaze lifted, the heat in his silver irises shocking me into missing a step and stumbling, scorching my heart, causing terrible pain. And still, I couldn't look away.

Let him stare and attempt to fry my insides if he wished. He would never make me cower.

The murmurs of the fire courtiers grazed my skin as we danced past, their whispers describing the gruesome things they hoped Arrow would do to me. But other than stare in silence, the Storm King did nothing.

I almost asked him about Raiden and the fire fae's transformation, but then vowed to keep my mouth shut. It was best if my enemies thought me clueless to their tricks, no matter how obvious they were.

For a whole turn of the hall, I said nothing, then of its own accord, my mouth opened. "Well, did you do it?"

"Do what?" he asked.

"Betray me. Sell me to Azarn."

Fake outrage twisted his expression. "Your question suggests there's a chance you believe I might not have."

Lost for words at his flippancy, I stared. First at his traitor's eyes, then his liar's mouth.

He sighed. "Your faith in me was always a fragile thing."

"So what's your answer? This time, don't speak in riddles."

"In truth, I'm so fucking mad right now, I don't care what you believe."

"Oh, I promise you'll care one day," I said. "When I decide to make you pay."

Chapter 8

LEAF

His glittering lashes dropped, and he closed his eyes for three ragged beats of my heart, drawing a sharp breath as he opened them. "Take care what you say, Leaf," he whispered, barely moving his lips. "I'm sure the Fire Court has ways to discern our words."

Leaf.

Did he have no shame? How dared he address me by the pet name that was once all I possessed. The identity *he* gave me before he sold me to the Sun Realm.

"That's fine," I hissed. "I'll happily stop speaking. I have no desire to talk to a betrayer. Also, I forbid you from calling me by the ridiculous name you gave to a slave. I am not that lost girl anymore. I know who I am. Prisoner or not, one day, I'll wear the crown of my ancestors. So from this night onward, to you, my name shall be Vengeance. Or Heart Stopper. Take your pick. Both have a lovely ring to them."

"I think I'll stick with Zali. Or Princess, if I must."

"Still irks you, doesn't it? My royal status."

He sighed through gritted teeth, his breath rustling my hair. "It saddens me how little you know me."

"That's true. I don't know you at all. I never did, because while you were selling me to the highest bidder, like a love-sick fool, I was rushing to your bed when Esen captured me."

His steps faltered. "You were *what?*" His golden skin blanched, and he spun us around the dance floor at an alarming pace, my hair streaming behind me and his wings spread out like sails. "Esen *arrested* you?"

"Under *your* name, of course."

His lips formed a thin line, a storm flashing in his eyes. "There's your fucking betrayer, then. It's Esen, not me."

A combination of fury and doubt washed over me. I shrugged a shoulder, feigning indifference. "No matter how Esen altered your plans by interrupting my travels, the result is the same. Here I am in the Sun Realm, property of King Azarn, just as you wanted."

A muscle ticked in his jaw. "Oh, yes. That's exactly what I wanted. Of course I longed to see you enslaved again. How could you possibly think that I—"

"Still, I would bet my life you can't bear to see another man take what was once yours, even if *you* don't want it anymore."

Rage sparked in his gaze, followed by an unhinged emotion that made me flinch away from him.

"That's right, *human.* Even after everything you've said tonight, I'd love nothing more than to bend you over that banquet table and fuck the insolence out of you, and I wouldn't give a damn who witnessed it."

My entire body flashed hot. Then ice cold.

"Wish for it all you like, King of Slaves, but I will never *ever* lie beneath you again."

His lips quirked at my insult. "Never is a long time, *Princess of Little Faith*. A lot can happen between now and the end of time."

I shrugged. "Well, at least you still have one devotee here in Taln. The dead girl, Ruhh. Killed her, did you? Tell me how and why."

"Wouldn't you love to know. What will you give me for the tale of it?"

"I don't need to hear it *that* badly. I already know enough disgusting things about you to curdle my stomach until I die."

He leaned close and whispered against my lips. "Do you now?"

"*Yes*. And as I said, you sicken me."

"I predict you'll live to regret those words, *Princess*," he said, hissing the title like a curse, a promise. A husky threat that slid along my spine and dampened the skin between my thighs.

Self-disgust rose, hot bile scalding my throat. How could I find anything that faithless wolf said remotely exciting? Habit, I guessed. My body was used to responding to him. Used to reacting to his voice, his touch, remembering them as sources of pleasure and joy.

But no more.

I'd rather die than let him touch me like *that* again.

And he could threaten all he liked, but it wouldn't change a thing. My face would still be the last thing he saw as he drew a final breath, and I tore his entrails from his gut.

"Enough dancing." Azarn rose, clapping his hands together once. "It bores me." He nodded at Esen. "Take the human away. I have much to discuss with King Arrowyn before I allow him to rest from his travels."

Arrow bristled at the king's words, his hands falling away from my body. He cut me a bow, facing away from the dais as he whispered, "Have they hurt you? Tell me now, Leaf." His gaze tracked over the gore on my tunic.

Ignoring his question, I dropped my gaze to the dark marble. "*Arrowyn*," barked the Fire King.

Arrow spun on his heel and stalked away, the weight of his fury enveloping me, as if he'd wrapped his brand-new cloak around my shoulders. A prickly burden I neither wanted to feel nor would let affect me.

As he mounted the dais, the hand by his side flexed twice. Two spasms of either disgust or anger. Disgust that he'd had to touch me? Or fury that Azarn wielded some kind of power over him?

As Esen led me past the flame-lit faces of the tittering crowd, I felt Arrow's gaze on my back, my Aldara mark pulsing in response. An answer to a question neither one of us wanted asked.

Thanks for marking me, fuck face, I thought, *and for ruining both our lives.*

My limbs weak with exhaustion and shock, I leaned on Esen as I walked through the corridors of the palace, feeling Arrow's presence all the way back to the tower room.

"Get some sleep," Esen said as she locked the door, leaving me to scrub the blood from my skin in a hot bath before climbing into bed, every bone in my body aching.

I'd been asleep for a while when the sound of clicking locks woke me. As the door creaked open, I bolted out of bed, then crouched beside it, ready to leap onto my assailant's back and claw their eyes out.

Silence followed. No steps. No movement.

Who could it be?

Arrow stalking toward me through the shadows? My inactive Aldara mark told me it wasn't. Perhaps Esen had decided to finish what she'd started back in Coridon. But that didn't make sense. Her sharp personality had lost so much of its edge since I'd been in Taln, I was beginning to suspect she *liked* me.

"Where are you hiding, little murderess?" said a tall slender shadow with a silky-smooth voice. "I'm not here to kill you. I promise. Hurry and show yourself."

With a sigh, I got to my feet. "Prince Bakhur, what could be so urgent that you must disturb my sleep?" I asked, even though I was certain I knew the answer.

At the flick of his wrist, a wall sconce burst to life, and he prowled toward me. Refusing to cower, I kept my bare feet planted wide and raised my chin as if I were dressed in Mydorian armor, rather than a too-thin nightgown.

"I found your fight with Dorn rather... stimulating, Princess of Dust."

I laughed. "You couldn't have seen much through the flames."

"In Taln, we are fae of the sun. Flames illuminate all things to our vision. I saw you clearly. I witnessed your fierceness, your determination, and I longed to congratulate you on your win. So here I am."

"Congratulations could have waited until morning."

His amber eyes glittered as he gripped my chin, tilting my face up. "Congratulations could wait, yes. But *this* required immediate attention," he said, seizing my wrist and guiding my palm to the hard bulge in the front of his trousers.

Something sizzled, the scent of burning flesh watering my eyes as Bakhur spat out a curse, stepping backward and away from me. "Fuck the Storm King and his mark."

"Does it hurt to touch me?" I asked, unable to hide the joy in my voice.

Bakhur grimaced and glanced at his groin. "Depends what I'm thinking about at the time."

How interesting. How perfect.

Gratitude for the Aldara mark flowed through me. Whatever magic made it impossible for Bakhur to assault me, right now, I was extremely glad of its existence.

"The mark makes our marriage impossible," I said, my thoughts racing.

A dark brow rose. "Oh? Why so?"

"It would allow no intimacy. You couldn't get heirs or even pleasure from the union."

His low laugh prickled over my skin. "There are other pleasures than full consummation and many ways to get a babe inside a womb, Zali."

Revulsion turned my stomach, his smile growing as I shivered.

Bakhur was an odd one—charming at times—but beneath his smooth veneer lay a cruel, calculating nature. Fairly typical of his species, I supposed. And I knew from experience fae couldn't be trusted to treat humans well. Not even the one I'd given my heart to understood the true value of possessing a human's love, given in faith to a much more powerful being.

"Let's try an experiment, shall we?" Bakhur asked.

I said nothing as he turned me away and pressed my hands against the cool glass of the bay window, terror weakening my limbs.

He muttered a spell, and my nightgown fell to my elbows, exposing my back. His fingertip slowly traced the skin over my spine.

Hissing in a breath, I tried to swing around and elbow him, but found I couldn't move. My muscles had seized—frozen by dark magic. His nail traced patterns over my back, red-hot pain searing. The Fire Prince was burning my flesh.

Sweat dripped between my breasts, and my blood boiled with useless fury. Trapped and rendered immobile by his spell, I stared through the tower window at the moon, its bright light mocking me.

"*Let me go*," I thought, unable to push any sound through my lips. "*Let me go. Let me go.*"

Out of nowhere a growl sounded, and Ruhh appeared, her tattered slippers hovering above the floor. "Nephew, the girl wants you to stop. So stop. *Now.*"

"Oh, Ruhh dear, you always were a wet blanket. The only time you had any real life in you, was when Father announced that he would ask Arrowyn to marry you."

Ruhh snarled, lank hair hanging around a gaunt face, her pale eyes large above prominent cheekbones. Water dripped from her gown onto the wooden floor. She had the look of a drowned rat, her clothes damp, the remaining skin wrinkled and puffy. Perhaps she had died in water.

A chill skittered down my spine as I pictured Arrow drowning her with ease. He was callous enough to do it.

"Go now, Bakhur, or I shall tell your father you've burned runes into his valuable guest."

Runes? My suspicions were confirmed. Bakhur was an evil prick. And the last person I wished to be wed to.

Mentally, I added him to my list of targets.

One day, he would pay, too.

The prince watched as I reached my hand as far as I could and ran my fingers over my back, feeling the raised patterns on my skin. He snickered in delight, and then left my room without a word.

"You should stay away from my nephew," said Ruhh, perching in the air above the edge of the bed. "He was working magic into your skin, attempting to get the Aldara mark off and also testing how much he could hurt you while it remained." She flew a circle around my chamber. "Take care. Inflicting pain is Bakhur's greatest passion."

I collapsed on the window seat, hugging my knees to my chest as I contemplated the dead girl hovering in front of me. "How did you die, Ruhh?"

She pointed out the window. "See that tower in the distance?"

I nodded.

"It is Taln's tallest. Arrowyn rejected my father's marriage proposal, so poor Ruhh was tumbled from it and fell a very long way down."

An odd way to phrase it. Not to mention how weird it was to refer to herself in the third person. A massive red flag, in fact.

Preparing to tease her, I kept a straight face and arched a brow. "Really? I had no idea Azarn felt that way about the Storm King."

She gave me a gray-toothed smile. "The offer was for *my* hand, obviously."

"Oh, I see. And so your life was ruined, *ended*, because that asshole didn't want you."

"Something like that." Ruhh's smile twisted. "Which makes me the perfect person to help you end *him*."

"Who said I wanted to kill Arrow?" I asked.

"What woman betrayed by a male doesn't at least wish to rip his eyes from his sockets or slice his cock from his pants?"

"Likely none," I replied.

Ruhh clapped her hands. "Then it's settled. We will talk more soon. I'm certain you'll find my plan appealing."

"Plan?" I asked, leaving the window seat and heading toward the bathroom to pour water over my stinging back. "What plan?"

Without answering my question, Ruhh's gray gown burst into flames, and she disappeared, leaving me to wonder if her hatred for Arrow was good news or bad news.

Knowing my luck, likely the latter.

Chapter 9

LEAF

On my seventh day as the Fire Court's *guest*, Esen burst through my chamber door at lunchtime. "Get up, Zali. The king requires you for the second event."

"*Now?*" I asked, choking on a mouthful of flatbread as I sat in the window seat, still wearing my nightgown. "During the day?"

"Yes, *now*," said Esen, crossing her arms. "It's in the Fen Forest, where it always feels like nighttime. So you could wear your sleeping attire if you really wanted, but I recommend you hurry up and put your leathers on instead."

Since the previous event, I'd spent the last four days recovering in my room. And hiding from Arrow—let's not forget that.

And, yes, I knew I had work to do... Taln City's layout to study, the mystery of my arrest to unravel, an ex-lover to murder. But while my body was weakened and vulnerable, I couldn't bear what the sight of Arrow might do to my heart.

So I'd taken the cowardly option and hidden in my chamber.

I pushed a tray of food along the sill, and a pile of books tumbled to the floor. "Are you going to stand there and watch me get dressed?"

"I've seen it all before when Arrow paraded you around Coridon dressed in glittering strips of cloth."

Rolling my eyes, I rose from the window seat, pulled my nightgown off, then tugged on leather pants and a snug, molded leather corset, compliments of the Fire Court, before flinging a new cloak around my shoulders. Flames and tiny dragon wings decorated the thick material, a vast improvement on Arrow's cloak adorned with golden feathers.

"What can you tell me about today's event, Esen?"

"Nothing."

"Please, I know you've never liked me, but think about this: we're just two girls being used by males and doing our best to survive. We're the same, don't you think? Help me, Esen. Give me a chance to beat them."

She chewed her lip, avoiding my gaze, but I could tell her resistance was softening.

"Aren't you tired of being used by them, too?" I asked.

She kept her eyes on my boots as I laced them up, her face blank. Then she threw her hands in the air. "Fine. I want to hate you, Zali. I really fucking do. But Azarn is an arrogant prick, and I wouldn't mind wiping the smug smile off his face. So perhaps I will give you some tips, after all."

"Azarn hopes I'll die in one of the events, doesn't he?"

"I don't think he cares either way. What he really wants is chaos. Lives for that shit. If you did die, he'd have an excuse to attempt to gain control of the gold trade by fucking with Arrow and the Zareen."

"Sounds like the Fire King should be eliminated, not me," I said. "As long as it serves their disgusting schemes for power, tyrants don't care how many people die horrible deaths in their name."

"Perhaps. But it won't be me who kills him. Not today, and not while Melaya is by his side."

Interesting, I thought, as we left my room and hurried out of the palace toward the stables. Azarn seemed over-reliant on his mage, which meant I had to find out more about his power. How it worked. And if there was a way to destabilize it.

"No chains today?" I asked Esen, waving my hands as we dashed through the statue garden. Lit by bright sunshine, they looked particularly grotesque, every splotch of mold and peeling paint visible.

The sun warmed my skin, and not one cloud floated in the azure sky. If I had to die, today was a fine day to do it.

Esen gave me a withering side glance. "I think you're smart enough to realize you'd be dead before you got three feet away."

"But I feel like you're warming up to me, so there's a slight chance you might just let me keep running. Might be worth the risk."

"Oh, Leaf, you're relentless." Shaking her head, blue hair tumbled around her face as she laughed. "Today, your task is to find a specific plant in the forest. If you succeed, then similar to the last trial, you will fight an opponent. And if you survive that, you'll only have one trial left. The worst, so I've been told."

"Great," I said, with zero enthusiasm. "What's the deal with the Fen Forest?"

"Treacherous place. Holes filled with burning lava lurk beneath the pine-needle floor. Fall into one and you'll never come out again. By all accounts, it's not a pleasant way to go."

"No kidding. How do I avoid them?"

"If you concentrate and block out other sounds, you'll hear their hiss and crackle when you walk nearby. Be sure to step elsewhere."

"Thank you. That's helpful."

In the stables, a single groom stood near the entrance, holding the reins of a large gray horse. "Where is everyone?" I asked.

Esen smirked. "In the forest. Waiting for you." She took the reins from the stable hand, then thumped my back, pushing me toward the horse. "Hurry up and mount. Sable won't hurt you. She has a mild and steady temperament. Unlike you."

As soon as my butt hit the saddle, Esen mounted behind me.

"If you wanted to get close to me, there are more comfortable ways than sharing the same saddle," I joked to distract myself from the nausea churning in my stomach.

Esen nudged the horse into a trot. "Very funny. No one at Taln, apart from Arrow, is stupid enough to give you a ride of your own. We'd spend the next week hunting you down."

"I'm flattered you think so," I replied. "Why would Arrow give me a horse?"

"Because where you're concerned, he's a fool."

"*Was* a fool," I corrected, ducking as we skirted an overhanging elm branch. I scanned the rolling hills and the pine forest in the east that grew closer with Sable's every hoof beat.

Very few geysers shot from the ground in this lusher, treed area behind the palace, where the air almost smelled fresh and clean. As I drew a deep breath into my lungs, the sky over the woods suddenly darkened, looking gloomy and dramatic.

Perhaps not such a nice day to die, after all.

"Can you tell me about the plant I have to find?" I asked as we reached the edge of the forest.

Esen slowed Sable to a walk and spoke in a low voice against my ear. "A hidden plant called the blood orchid. It's carnivorous, and the petals are rumored to possess great power, but I'm not actually sure what they do. A courtier told me they'd heard it suppressed Azarn's magic."

"But from what I've seen," I said, "the king let's his mage do most of his dirty work. I didn't realize he had much power."

"Azarn is lazy and allows Melaya too much freedom. You remember the price fae pay to wield magic? Before you arrived, Arrowyn would often sleep for days to recover from large expenditures of storm magic. Sun Realm fae suffer likewise."

"So how do I find this blood lily?"

"Blood *orchid*," Esen corrected, pushing pine branches aside as Sable trotted into the eerie darkness of the Fen Forest.

The smell of burning wood and smoldering embers hung heavy in the air. I looked around for signs of smoke or flames, but found none. Charred bark covered many of the tree trunks—the remnants of fire damage—and the leaves of nearby branches glowed blood-red, as if imbued with magic.

"Esen," I prompted. "Did you hear my question?"

"Yes. And did *you* hear me say it's called the *hidden* blood orchid? I have no idea how to find the damn thing because it's not meant to be found."

"Has anyone in Taln seen it before?"

She sighed. "If I tell you everything that I know about it, will you promise to stop nagging me?"

"Yes, of course."

"There's an old story about a herb gatherer who stumbled on the creature who protects the orchid, a fire demon who takes the form of a snake. Apparently, the kitchen hand smelled decaying flesh just before it appeared."

"What did the plant look like?"

"The fae didn't hang around long enough to find out. He ran back to the palace like ten hell hounds were biting at his heels. But he *did* say the encounter happened in the darkest part of the forest, near wet, boggy ground, so perhaps the plant prefers those conditions. This morning, the kitchen was abuzz with tales of past quests to locate the orchid. The head cook, Lorana, swore her grandfather died on one such ill-fated mission."

"How did he die?"

"The serpent fae appeared and tricked him into a bargain with fatal consequences. If you can outsmart the creature, Leaf, you stand a chance of returning with the plant."

"Okay, but how do you know this happened if the cook's grandfather died?"

"Good point. His brother went along for the adventure but ran off as soon as the bargain with the serpent fae was lost, leaving him to face a gruesome death alone."

"What a coward," I said, then heaved a sigh. "So in the forest, I should head away from the sun and listen out for water?"

Behind me, Esen adjusted her hold on the reins. "Sounds like a plan."

"And a shit plan is better than none," I said.

A deep layer of pine needles muffled our progress through the undergrowth, which was hindered by thick ferns and branches that scratched our limbs as we passed.

"Leaf, watch how Sable chooses her steps carefully. The terrain is dangerous, and she knows it."

Smart horse.

I drew a breath to admonish her for calling me the annoying, prick-given name for possibly the third time this morning, but Esen shushed me with a hiss. "Listen! Can you hear that?"

Tuning in to my surroundings, the relative stillness told me there were no birds in this forest, only creatures of mud and earth, every one of them quiet. Underneath the thud of Sable's steps and the whisper of warm air through leaves, I finally caught it—a soft crackle and pop in front of us and a little to the left.

"There it is," I said, pointing toward the sound. "A fire hole."

"That's right. Whatever happens, don't forget to listen out for that sound. I'm starting to hate Azarn more than I dislike you and Arrow. And maybe... maybe I'm beginning to wonder if I chose the wrong side."

"You did. But, please, don't include me in the Storm King's camp, the lying asshole. I'm on my own side. The side of the oppressed and downtrodden. The girls' team. And thank you for preferring me over Azarn."

She laughed. "Try not to be *too* thankful. If you hadn't notice, we fae tend to take advantage of gratitude."

That was true. They always did.

A twisted tunnel of gnarled ironwood trees widened into a large clearing, and in its center, scrolled gates leading to a stone-walled amphitheater loomed. Through the gates, the entire Fire Court was gathered on the crumbling stone steps that formed tiered seating around the arena's edges. Magical flames from large braziers and eerie light from luminescent mushrooms cast a green hue over the fae's sharp features.

It was roughly an hour past midday, and as Esen had warned, it looked like twilight.

Sable's steps echoed on stone as we rode into the arena, and the courtiers fell silent for a moment before resuming their raucous chatter.

Fireflies flitted through the crowd, tangling in the fae's hair and clothing, but they were too busy drinking and gossiping to notice. The king and his family sat in the rear center of the arena dressed in black clothes with silver embellishments that flashed like tiny diamonds.

I scanned the crowd once, then twice more, but Arrowyn Ramiel was nowhere to be seen, which proved he was a coward. What was the point of handing me over to the Sun Realm if he didn't watch them destroy me?

Unless his aim wasn't to hurt me, after all.

A wave of doubt engulfed me as I searched for his face in the crowd. What if he hadn't betrayed me? What if he was in Taln to *help* me?

But then I recalled how he'd rushed away from Mydorian soon after Raiden arrived, as if he couldn't escape from me fast enough. And the two miserable letters he'd written. Dry, passionless wastes of parchment.

The other night, when he arrived at Taln and Azarn made us dance, Arrow hadn't specifically denied his role in my arrest. But perhaps I'd goaded him into an argument too soon and not given him the chance to speak up. Old habits died hard, I guessed.

Getting under the Storm King's skin had once been my favorite entertainment.

King Azarn rose and lifted his palm toward his subjects. "Silence, fae of the Supreme Sun. Today, the Princess of Dirt and Stones—"

"Dust and Stones," I muttered.

Azarn cleared his throat. "The Earth Princess has entered the Arena of Ashen Souls, and if you prick your ears, you'll hear her ragged breathing as she walks forward for my instructions. The human speaks boldly, but her body betrays the truth. Enjoy the elixir of her fear."

The courtiers laughed, a few with long snouts howling. In every direction, dappled, green light twisted the limbs and features of orcs, trolls, jinn, and other fire fae into hideous shapes. The dark wings of the more human-shaped fae stirred the air in excitement.

Many fire fae were as beautiful as the night sky, but the bitterness in their unfriendly gazes rendered their handsome faces ugly. And going by the scowls directed my way, no one here wished for my survival, least of all their king.

"Dismount and walk to Azarn," said Esen. "Don't do anything stupid. Melaya will kill you before you can draw breath to run."

I did as she said and marched forward, my chin raised and shoulders squared, wishing I could wipe my clammy palms on my clothes, but refusing to give in to the urge.

"Azarn," I said, inclining my head as I stared up at emerald eyes floating in his gaunt face.

"Welcome. Today, you must venture into the forest and return with a petal from the blood orchid. If you succeed and make it back to this arena, you will face your second opponent in battle. Once again, use of magic will be banned."

"May I have a clue or two to help me find the plant?"

"No, you may not."

I ground my teeth. "Then can you at least tell me what it looks like?"

With a long-suffering sigh, he flicked his cloak off one shoulder and leaned over his knees. "The orchid is quite small and therefore difficult to locate amongst the foliage. But once you see it, it's easy to recognize by the long petals of a crimson so dark they appear black. Fire feeds it, not water. How you locate it is your business. If you're not back within the hour, we'll assume you're dead and find my son a different bride."

"But what if I'm not dead, only having trouble returning?"

"Well, you soon will be. So there's nothing for us to worry about."

Easy for him to say. He wasn't the one who'd get eaten by the serpent fae who guarded the orchid. The same creature that Azarn had failed to mention, which only confirmed my suspicions: he definitely didn't want me as a daughter-in-law.

I wished I understood more about how the Fire King's power worked. Did it play a part in blocking the magic from other realms in Taln? Or did Melaya alone achieve the incredible feat?

The king and his mage must be vulnerable in some way. Every being in the realms had a weakness. I simply needed to discover theirs.

"Esen," boomed the king, interrupting my musings. "Guide the human to the forest gate, and the courtiers will entertain themselves while we wait to see if she returns." His merciless eyes bored into mine. "And if you don't make it back, then farewell, Zali Omala. I can't say it's been a pleasure to know you."

"Likewise," I whispered through stiff lips. Esen's palm pressed into the small of my back. "Wait," I said, not moving. "King Azarn, please, can I take a weapon?"

"You cannot."

Queen Estella's pale gaze flicked to her husband, her knuckles white against the burnished gold of the chair's armrest. Marcella snickered, and Prince Bakhur only stared at me while the runes on my back itched painfully.

Surely death would be preferable to a husband who reveled in cruelty.

"Since I'm essentially your fiancée, Bakhur, do you have any tips or advice?" I asked.

He tapped the point of his chin. "None I can think of. Oh, wait, yes. Here's a tip. Don't eat the petals of the orchid. Instant death if you do."

"Good to know," I said with a smile, silently cursing him into the hell realms.

Refusing to bow or beg for my life, I turned away from the royal family and let Esen lead me to a narrow metal gate set between moss-covered walls at the south end of the arena, its swirls and patterns stained with rust and age.

"Never thought I'd say such a thing to you, but good luck, human. Don't fall down a fire hole and get your stubborn ass incinerated."

"And I never thought I'd say this either, but I hope I see you again, Esen. These past days, your sour company has really grown on me."

As she laughed, I put on a brave face and winked, then stepped through the gate into the shadowy forest.

A sudden wind sprang up, whipping my braid across my face.

But nothing moved. No bird, no shrub rat, no serpent creature.

Bracing my boots wide, I stood as still as a fire-garden statue, listening to my surrounds as if my life depended on it.

Because in all truth, it *did*.

Chapter 10

LEAF

Taking great care to watch where I stepped, I tried to quiet my ragged breathing, then walked toward the darkest part of the forest.

The air was humid and stifling, and every few minutes, I stopped and wiped sweat from my face with the sleeve of my tunic, wondering how in the dust I would find one tiny plant that didn't want to be found in this chaos of greenery.

All around me, towering trees and twining vines climbed toward threads of sunlight, and a low mist wove through the undergrowth, wrapping mossy rocks in its damp tendrils. The lack of birdsong was eerie, depressing, and it took great effort to shield my mind from spiraling thoughts of doom.

I had to find the orchid. I needed to survive the next battle. Dying wasn't an option. Whatever it took to make it out of Fen Forest and take down my opponent, I would do it.

I stopped walking and tuned into the soft rustling sound of leaves, noticing a subtle, irregular chime beneath it that sounded like distant music. Wait... no... was it running water? According to Esen, the orchid grew in damp locations.

Trekking downhill, I pushed aside low-hanging branches, crawling at times over the prickly undergrowth, guided by intermittent sounds of what I hoped was a creek tinkling in the distance.

I stopped a few times to catch my breath, finding the heat unbearable as I listened for the hiss of fire holes and made sure I was still on course to find the water.

Not long after, I arrived at the bottom of the hill where a willow's graceful limbs swept the marshy banks of a creek. The air was cooler here, the soil beneath the swaying grasses soft and damp, ideal growing conditions for the blood orchid.

Swatting away insects, I crawled through reeds, around rocks, wet blades of grass and ferns tickling and scratching my skin. The pungent scent of rotting leaves and damp earth teased my nose as I carefully parted thorny vines and inspected purple-petaled flowers, a mix of anticipation, hope, and panic pounding through my blood.

After roughly ten minutes of searching, I hadn't caught a single glimpse of any flowers with black or dark-red petals. The entire forest was a vivid palette of green and brown splotches and slashes, reminding me of Mydorian. A wave of homesickness rolled over me. I stood up to stretch my back, whacking my forehead on a branch.

How much time had passed since I'd entered the forest? Maybe half an hour, and hopefully not a minute more. If I found the plant, I still had to get back to the arena in time to fight an unknown opponent. Whatever species of fire fae Azarn matched me with, perhaps an orc or a jinn, I hoped they were as slow and lumbering as Dorn.

I longed to take off and run through the forest as fast as Quin and I had done when we were children, slashing and tearing at the forest until I found the magical plant. Or fell down a stupid fire hole.

So far, I hadn't seen or heard a single one, and I was beginning to think Esen had made them up just to slow me down. I never should have trusted her. I was a gullible fool, fabricating a friendship with my prison guard because I was lonely. And pathetic.

After more careful probing along the water's edge, I walked back up the hillside a little, and then down to the creek again, carefully scanning the lush landscape.

Where in the hells was this dust-damned plant?

A dark shadow passed over me, and I searched the tree canopy above, hoping I wouldn't see the bone-chilling sight of Taln's famous dragons bearing down on me with their jaws open. Nope nothing there. Whatever it was, probably a sleep-deprived owl or bat, had probably found a nice tree branch to roost on.

Standing still and panicking wouldn't get me any closer to finding the orchid. I had to get moving before time ran out and the fire fae left me in the Fen Forest for dead.

Narrowing my gaze, I stared at what looked like a lizard moving through a water-logged clump of rushes a few feet ahead. I focused on the sounds around me, hearing no sizzling hisses. No roars from dragons. As I lifted my foot, ready to take a step, the stench of rotting flesh filled my nostrils.

Branches snapped nearby, and the air temperature rose several degrees.

"I wouldn't step right there, if I were you," rasped a voice over badly ravaged vocal cords.

I looked down. Directly below my foot, the ground undulated as if something bubbled beneath the soil. Finally. I'd found a fire hole. A *silent* one.

I whipped around.

The serpent fae leaned on a tree trunk a little way up the hill, slick dark hair framing the sharp angles of a handsome face with black lips so thin they were barely visible.

He was as tall as three fae standing head to toe with black and red scales covering his muscular torso. But instead of legs, a thick tail spanned out from his hips, the tip waving through the red mist that curled around his lower body.

"Shit," I breathed, unsure where to put my foot down.

"Jump to the left," the serpent fae advised. "You'll probably make it."

Was he trying to trick me?

My instincts told me he wasn't lying, so I took a breath and followed his instruction, landing on solid ground with a huff of relief.

"You've been listening for the sound of fire bogs, which is correct. Unfortunately, some of them are silent."

"Been watching me, have you?"

"Since the moment you stepped through the Ashen Souls' gate into my forest."

My eyebrows shot up. I thought I was good at catching spies, my senses well-honed and alert to the signs of someone following me, but apparently, I was out of practice.

Nearly choking on a too-deep breath, I smoothed my expression, trying to hide my disgust. Born of the fae realms, the serpent fae was fascinating to look at, beautiful even, but his putrid scent was appalling, and I tried hard not to gag and offend him.

"Like those who came before you, I suppose you're seeking the ember blood orchid?"

"I am," I admitted.

"For what purpose?"

How much of my tale should I tell him?

I debated for a moment before deciding to stick with my habit of being honest whenever possible. Lies only trap us in suffocating webs of our own making, impossible to untangle.

The truth was always best.

Afraid to take a wrong step, I breathed slowly, quietly, so as not to trigger the serpent fae's prey instincts. Raising my chin, I met a set of orange eyes glowing with malicious intelligence.

"I am Zali Omala, heir to the Earth Realm throne. King Azarn has taken me prisoner. But if I complete a series of what he likes to call *events* or *entertainments* successfully, I'll be allowed to marry his son, who I have no interest in, instead of being murdered."

The creature's tail whipped the air behind him. "Azarn," he spat. "I have no love for the Fire King. And one of these trials involves my orchid, does it?"

"Yes. I must return within an hour from when I entered the forest with a petal, or he'll leave me here to die at... well... at *your* hands, I suppose."

A chuckle shook his broad chest. "If not mine, then there are many other hungry beasts hiding in these woods. I see you have no weapons."

"No. Nothing at all to defend myself with."

"Except your wit—if you happen to possess one. I am called Vyprin."

"Nice to meet you. At this point, anyway."

Serrated teeth flashed as he grinned. "Fortunately for you, human girl, you told the truth. Most fae who dare come near my precious plant lie through their hungry mouths. I killed every one of them."

"Does that mean you'll give me a petal?"

"No, but I *will* give you a chance to earn one. Answer two riddles correctly, and you shall have your petal and a fast route back to the Arena of Ashen Souls."

"And if I answer incorrectly?"

A thin, black tongue slithered between his lips, licking moisture from his chin. "Then you will be my dinner."

"Not a very attractive bargain, if I'm honest. You might give me unanswerable riddles."

"I won't. And if you do lose, I will let you eat a petal, which will grant you an instant, painless death. Then I can take my time and enjoy a delicious meal without all the irritating screaming."

Considering the bargain, I stared up at a slice of gray sky visible through the treetops behind the fae's shoulders, and a huge, dark shadow passed over it. Vyprin glanced up, too.

"Is that one of Taln's famous dragons?" I asked.

"No, it's the nosy Storm King, trespassing on my territory."

Arrow? What in the hells was he doing here?

"Ignore him. Are you willing to play a game with me?"

"I'm still not convinced."

Vyprin sighed and folded his arms. "My honor is all I have left of my former life. So believe me when I vow the questions are quite solvable. At least if you have half a brain to think with."

What choice did I have? I probably couldn't find my way back to the arena in time without Vyprin's help. And Arrow, flying above like a giant bat, was less-than-zero use to me.

"Fine. Give me the first riddle, then."

"You're a little bossy for a human, aren't you?"

"And you're not the first fae to tell me that."

The serpent slid a little closer, his putrid smell overwhelming. "I live in flames but am never consumed by them. What could I be?"

"Do I have a time limit to answer in?"

He rolled his slitted eyes. "Simply *think*. Then speak."

Hm... What lived in flames but was never consumed by them?

Wood? No, of course not. Wood was fuel and completely consumed by flames. Ash? It was created by fire, a byproduct of it, so perhaps not. Tree sap? No, sap added the crackle and pop, but was most definitely devoured by it.

What were other components of a fire?

Light? Warmth...

"*Heat*," I blurted out before I could change my mind, always a risk taker.

He waved his clawed hand at me. "That particular riddle was too easy."

"It was a lucky guess. Give me the second, and we'll see if you get to make a meal of me."

Vyprin bowed, an overly polite gesture for someone who hoped to devour me slowly.

"Listen carefully. An old troll wished to leave his gold to one of his three children, but since they were all obedient, he couldn't decide which one deserved the honor."

"Why not share it equally among them? That would be fairest."

"The last thing troll fathers can be accused of being is fair. If you live to an old age, do you plan to share your wealth among your grasping offspring?"

I hadn't thought about having children, but I understood the point of his question.

"Of course. It would prevent them from killing each other to become my heir." The vision of three golden-haired babes crashed through my mind, and I mentally swatted the picture away.

If I ever did decide to have children, Arrow would be the last male in the realms to father them.

Vyprin sighed. "How boring you are, Zali Omala. So, the troll father gave his grown children gold feathers and instructed each of them to buy something that would fill his granary to the ceiling. Because it was cheap, the eldest son bought straw, but once it had been laid out, it compacted and didn't fill the storehouse. The second son bought wood, but not quite enough. The youngest child, a raven-haired daughter, purchased two things and managed to obtain her father's fortune. What items did she buy?"

"*Two?* Their father failed to mention they could buy two things."

"Nor did he say they couldn't."

Ah, the daughter was clever. I wracked my brain, trying to imagine what two things could accomplish the task. Wood and straw together? Still difficult to calculate the exact amount required. Plants and soil that would grow over time? No, they would need sunlight to thrive.

Think, think, I told myself, sweat trickling between my breasts and my legs shaking. This was the Sun Realm, so the answer might relate to the fire element, like the previous riddle had.

I drew in a sharp breath, my heart beating hard against my ribs. "Could she have brought a candle and a fire lighter into the room? Light from a fire source would fill the entire space."

Disappointment curved the corners of his mouth down, his shoulders sagging. "Yes, you are correct, and now I must let you leave." He slithered to the side, flicked his palm, and the mist around his lower torso dispersed, revealing a three-foot high plant, its tendrils crawling up the base of an old oak tree.

The black blooms resembled a spider about to pounce, and they dripped dark-red sap over the forest floor. The scent of death intensified, and I realized I'd been smelling the magical plant all along, not the serpent fae.

Stepping forward, I reached for a petal. Vyprin hissed, and I yanked my hand back immediately.

"The orchid eats flesh and is quite vicious toward those who seek to destroy it. Allow me." His torso bent in a sinuous movement, and he plucked a whole bloom. The plant growled, and the petals still attached to it reached for the serpent male's fingers, a line of blood appearing on his skin.

Vyprin made soothing noises, and the orchid's leaves stopped vibrating. He placed the velvety flower on my palm. "Only give the king the single petal he asked for. Hide the rest. You'll find them very useful."

"What do they do?"

"You consider yourself clever, therefore, you can work it out. Now you must leave." Without warning, he lunged down, tugged my hand to his mouth, and then bit it.

I let out a cry of pain and closed my eyes as the ground rushed toward me, thinking Vyprin had gone back on his word. But when I came to, I found myself slumped in front of the Ashen Souls' gates, the sounds of clanging swords and a cheering crowd audible beyond them.

Stumbling up, I brushed off my tunic, then pushed on a rusty handle, my breath whooshing out of me at the sight inside the arena.

Azarn's queen battled a fire jinn, wielding a sword as long and dark as her midnight hair. Lifting the blade overhead, she let out a wail and brought it down onto her opponent's head, cleaving him in two with one strike. She threw the sword into the crowd, then spun around the arena in a celebratory dance, the stars on her dress glinting in the muted, green-tinged light.

Shock and excitement vibrated through me.

The transformation from quietly spoken queen into a fearsome warrior was extreme. Estella looked terrifying, but wonderful. And my mouth hung open as I watched her whirl and shake her arms at the sky like a goddess.

Finally, she stopped in front of Azarn, her chest heaving and eyes glittering. He rose from his throne and raised an arm to silence his courtiers.

Then the Fire King's head turned slowly, his gaze searching the arena until he looked directly at me. "Zali Omala," he boomed. "Meet your next opponent, Queen Estella of the Crystal Realm."

Chapter 11

LEAF

A zarn couldn't be serious. He wanted me to fight his wife? His *queen*?

Dust, what a royally twisted family. I'd rather die than marry into their fucked-up bloodline.

Estella stalked around the perimeter of the arena, her gown flowing behind her like a triumphant banner, arms raised, rousing the crowd into new heights of ecstasy each time she stabbed the sky with her sword.

Including her in the event meant Azarn didn't hold much value in her life. Unless he knew for certain she was unbeatable.

And if she was an exceptional fighter, why hadn't she already sliced her nasty husband's throat while he slept? If I were her, I would have gotten rid of him ages ago.

The arena smelled of dank misery, as if thousands had battled for their lives on this very ground and lost. Perhaps I would soon be one of them.

The Aldara mark on my throat sizzled, and I whipped around to face the dais. The Storm Prick himself sat beside Marcella, and Ruhh hovered behind him like a wickedly grinning bad smell. Arrow's eyes speared through mine, piercing my heart.

With his knees spread wide, he reclined against a scrolled headrest of gold, his feather ear cuffs glinting in the gloomy light, and large palms resting on his thighs. He appeared to be at his kingly leisure, as if he didn't have a care in the realms and was looking forward to witnessing my demise.

His purple-black wings were on display, erect as if ready for flight, contradicting the relaxed state of his limbs. I frowned, wondering if it really had been him flying over the Fen Forest while I was with the serpent fae.

Arrow's lips parted, his chest rising and falling with an obvious sigh, and my heart stuttered in pathetic response.

Stupid heart. It needed to get a life.

"Did you bring me the blood orchid, Zali?" asked Azarn, beckoning me forward.

I pulled a single petal from my pocket and marched forward, placing it on my palm when I reached the bottom of the stone dais.

A servant ran down the stairs, snatched it from me, then delivered it to the king.

"What power does the petal hold?" I asked.

"That is none of your business." Azarn strode back and forth in front of his family, who sat statue-still on their thrones as if unmoved by the unfolding events. Perhaps they knew better than to voice their opinions.

Only Arrow sat slightly forward, his fingers digging into his knees and knuckles white, far from relaxed now.

"Please remember," said the king, "in today's tournament, magic is banned and no killing allowed. Permanent maiming is acceptable, of course."

Oh, *of course*. I would expect nothing less.

I swiveled on my heel and faced the queen.

A strange intensity shone in Estella's eyes as she dipped her head, acknowledging me, not violence or determination, but something more mysterious.

She took slow, deliberate steps toward me, her movements graceful, as if we were about to dance around a ballroom. A hint of sadness touched her smile, and it felt as though she peered into my soul, uncovering my insecurities and failings, my every hope and dream.

"Do not worry, Zali. No matter what happens, I won't use magic against *you*," she whispered, her heavily accented vowels long, but her words clipped short.

"Wits and swords," I said, bowing my head in respect. She was a queen after all, and quite a formidable one.

According to rumors, Estella was ancient, a masterful wielder of the Crystal Realm's particular brand of star magic. With my own eyes, I'd witnessed her incredible skills with a sword, but I thanked the dust she couldn't use her cosmic power during our battle today.

It couldn't have been much past the early afternoon, and yet the last of the daylight sank behind the trees, the arena now lit solely by flames from braziers, torches, and the eerie mushrooms that scaled the stone surfaces.

Esen appeared and threw me a sword; the same one I'd killed Dorn with. I slashed it in front of me in a lemniscate pattern, controlling my breathing, centering my weight over my hips, and locking all thoughts of Arrow behind the door in my mind that I labeled: *Danger. Do not open.*

As Estella closed the distance between us, the forest beyond the ancient stone walls came alive, creaking and whispering, distant creatures snarling and howling. But the fire courtiers remained still and silent, not scratching with a claw or rustling a wing. A tense backdrop to the impending clash.

She whipped her arm out to the side. Her sword appeared above the crowd and whizzed through the air, landing neatly in her outstretched hand.

Moving fast, the queen struck first, her blade slicing through the air with precision. I blocked the attack with all the strength I could muster, my arms vibrating with the impact. She pushed me back, her eyes searching mine, that flicker of sadness moving from her lips to her icy gaze.

Estella moved with otherworldly grace, redirecting my strikes without losing breath. Each thrust was swift and exact, her blade stopping a mere inch from my body, over and over. Determined to survive, I took more risks, countering with lightning-fast strikes, my feet grounded, maintaining balance and strength.

After a few minutes, I was certain the queen held back her true strength. She could have taken my arm off three times over if she'd wanted to. Sparks of light trailed Estella's blade. Not magic, but likely produced by the metal itself, which must have originated from the Crystal Realm, the land of her birth.

Under my breath, I chanted the Mydorian war song, repeating the last phrase again and again—*Mydor blood will never fail.*

We danced around each other, our swords ringing through the arena in a symphony of violence. Sweat dripped down my face, and my muscles ached, but as long as I could hold my weapon, I wouldn't yield.

Our swords clashed repeatedly as we spun and twisted, grunting with each impact. Without magic, we were equally matched in height and strength, but she was faster. Her ferocity felt fake, an act to please Azarn, and I wanted to win more than she did, that much was apparent.

The grueling dance continued for ten minutes or so, my muscles burning, my lungs aching, but then the Mydorian forest of my childhood enveloped me, and my brain shifted into a different state, like it used to when I trained with my brother Quin. Before he'd attempted to destroy me.

I always beat him because I practiced the hardest and for the longest. And in Taln, over the last week, I'd kept my muscles strong, exercising in my tower, performing endless sit-ups, push-ups, and resistance training until I fell into bed exhausted each night.

I had no idea of Estella's capacity for endurance, but if I had to, I could spar all night long.

The next time she advanced, I feinted left, then spun out of her attack, running to the other side of the arena. The courtiers roared, probably because I looked like a coward fleeing their queen's wrath. To gain momentum, I ran up a wall, flipped back onto my feet, then bolted toward the queen, screaming like a sea kelpie bursting from a wave to leap upon their prey.

Estella dipped into a crouch, then attacked, crossing the arena at speed in a series of startling, one-armed cartwheels. I blinked and her sword slashed from my shoulder across my chest, blood staining my tunic.

Clutching the front of my body, I gasped for air, nausea battling panic inside me. The Fire Court erupted in cheers and howls of triumph. Their queen was winning.

With two hands, Estella held her sword vertically in front of her body, the hilt level with her stomach, the blade a long shadow over her face. "Sartoriahn galaxiaros," she breathed.

Bright light flashed, silver searing the backs of my eyes, blinding me. A shimmering mantle of magic settled on my shoulders, wrapping so tight I could hardly breathe.

"Don't panic," Estella said. "Look around you."

I did as she said, my jaw dropping in astonishment. Beyond the translucent field of magic that encircled us, every fae in the arena, including the royal family, appeared to be frozen solid, their skin waxy and gray, their eyes vacant.

Cosmic magic. I'd heard awe-inspiring tales of the Crystal Realm's star power, but this was the most incredible thing I'd ever seen.

"Azarn prohibited magic," I warned, my voice trembling slightly. "And you said yourself you wouldn't use any."

"His courtiers are fine. Do not worry. And I won't harm you, Zali. I promise."

How many broken vows had I heard from the fae? Their words were meaningless.

"Why wouldn't you? Your husband wants me dead. Your son hopes to torture me for all eternity. I'm nothing but a pawn in their schemes to control the gold trade."

Her pale-blue eyes flashed white. "You and I are the same. Imprisoned by men with limited vision who are greedy for power. I'm not a willing participant in their game, and I don't believe you are, either. We want the same things—balance in the Star Realms, peace. I can help you achieve that, Zali."

"All right." I nodded, lowering my sword as relief washed over me. "Tell me how to get out of Taln." I wasn't sure if Estella could be trusted, but it couldn't hurt to hear her out. Anything was better than having no plan. No allies.

"The first thing you should know is Melaya's magic-blocking power is not infallible. He is strong because he controls his feelings and emotions. His weakness is his twin brother, Nukala."

"That's useful information. Tell me more about Melaya's brother."

"Unfortunately, in this space, my words are bound and limited by old magic, and I cannot reveal more. But you are a twin yourself. I implore you to reflect upon that."

"I will. But, please, I need to get out of Taln."

"We cannot discuss that here," she hissed, grabbing my wrist and squeezing hard. "Listen carefully, Zali. When the star shield dissolves, I will be lying on the ground and your sword *mus*t be at my throat. Tell no one you have more blood orchid petals. Hide them..." Tremors shook her shoulders, and her eyes rolled back in her head. "I can't sustain the time lock much longer. I'll speak to King Arrowyn. We need a plan. Now get your blade ready. Quickly."

"Arrow? I'm stuck here because of him."

With a groan, Estella collapsed on the ground. I raised my sword and touched its tip to her white throat as the forest shuddered, flames flickered, and the fae began to stir around us.

At the sight of their queen under my blade, chaos broke out, rows of trolls, orcs, and jinn tumbling over each other, snarling and growling. Azarn called for quiet, and silence settled over the arena.

I threw my sword to the side, then reached down and helped Estella to her feet. She played the part of an overpowered opponent, gliding back to her seat with her head bowed against her husband's fury as he snarled out a reprimand. After Estella took her place beside him, she stared vacantly into the flame-lit arena, as if her mind was in another time and place.

Only then did I allow my gaze to shift toward the winged male whose breastplate of gold feathers and silver eyes gleamed in the firelight. He looked smug and calm, but probably would've worn the same expression if I were lying on the stones with my limbs hacked from my torso.

Hovering behind Arrow, Ruhh mouthed indecipherable words at me, likely a spell or a curse, wishing me speedy travels to the hell realms.

Esen arrived at my side. "Well done again, human," she said. "You have a talent for survival."

I took a breath to reply, but Azarn rose from his chair and pointed a flame-tipped scepter at my chest. "Tomorrow, you will face your final opponent, and the rules will be a little different. Your adversary can try to kill you, but you may only attempt the same if their killing blow fails."

"That's hardly fair," I said.

Bakhur wore an unpleasant smile, and I wondered what he'd prefer to see tomorrow. My gruesome demise. Or my triumph, so he'd have a human bride to torture.

"If you don't like the rules, you can always decide not to participate," said Azarn.

"Will you allow me to select my own opponent?"

The king smiled, twirling the point of his beard between bejeweled fingers. "That depends. Who would you choose?"

I grinned back at him. "You."

Looking ready to chop my head off, Melaya stepped forward, a flaming sword in his hand.

Arrow's laugh boomed out, sending shivers down my spine. With his head casually resting against the back of his chair, the Storm King gazed at Azarn through hooded eyes.

"The human wishes to ruffle your feathers, Azarn," he drawled. "And you're obliging her."

The Fire King paled. "Melaya, sit down. *Now.*"

The mage obeyed, his flame-filled eyes never leaving me. There was no doubt in my mind Melaya wanted me dead, perhaps even more than Azarn did.

Esen took me by the arm. "Let's go before you irritate someone into lopping your head off."

As we turned to leave the arena, at the corner of my vision, I saw Arrow stand, but quickly sit back down, as if he wanted to chase after me, but remembered himself just in time.

Silver moonlight illuminated Sable eating grass outside the arena walls, exactly where we'd left her hours ago. I gave Esen a questioning look.

"She's glamored to stay where I leave her. And before you ask, no, it's not cruel. Taln's horses are treated very well, and Sable is perfectly happy."

"If you insist," I said, mounting after greeting the horse with a quick nose rub.

As Esen settled in the saddle behind me, Ruhh appeared, her ankles crossed as she sat on a gnarled tree branch like a spooky ghoul.

"Fuck," breathed Esen in my ear. "Stop doing that, Ruhh. What in the flames do you want?"

The ghost girl's eyes widened. "Don't speak to me like that, soldier girl. My brother wouldn't like it."

"Oh, I don't think he'd mind too much." Esen nudged Sable into a walk. "You're here for a reason, so hurry up and tell me what it is."

Floating beside the horse, her cheek resting on her palm as if she was reclining on a towel at the palace's bathhouse, Ruhh said, "I want to take the human back to her tower myself."

"Why?" Esen asked.

"So I can talk privately with her."

Esen laughed. "No. Absolutely not. Now get back to your crypt before I summon an exorcist."

Fear flickered over the dead girl's face. "Must you always spoil my fun, King's Guard?"

"Yes," Esen replied. "I know the type of games you like to play, little ghostling."

Cruelty ran in the veins of the Taln royal family, I thought, as the runes on my back prickled.

Ruhh snarled and disappeared, her gray gown dissolving into the darkening sky, and Esen urged Sable into a gallop, ensuring I couldn't question her about Ruhh's schemes.

As we passed the castle wall near the fire gardens, my Aldara mark sizzled. Arrow again. It had to be. I whipped my head around, searching the shadows, but found no sign of the Storm King.

A breeze from above blew my hair over my eyes as Esen pulled the horse to a stop, then Arrow landed in front of us, folding his enormous purple-black wings behind his back.

For a moment or two, possibly three, I gazed at the dark iridescent colors, the wing tips glowing in the moonlight. I'd forgotten how beautiful they were, how mesmerizing.

"King Arrowyn," said Esen in a flat greeting.

Staring at me, he said, "Get off the horse."

Esen dug her fingers into my ribs. "Don't move," she told me, then to Arrow, "Why would I trust a traitor with her?"

"If I'm a traitor, then that makes three of us. Let her dismount, or get down and fight me, Esen. Choose now. I'm not feeling very patient."

"Do as he says," Esen whispered against my ear.

"I'm not interested in anything he has to say."

"Don't argue with me, Leaf. Just do it," Arrow replied, his voice low and menacing.

My Aldara mark throbbed, and his gaze fixed on it, his nostrils flaring as if he could smell my fear and perhaps other... disappointing feelings.

The moment my boots hit the ground, he charged at me, grabbing my throat and pushing me against an external wall of the palace. "Stay out of this if you know what's good for you," he barked over his shoulder at Esen who'd leaped from the horse and followed close behind us.

"I can't stop you, Arrow, but I can stand here and listen to every word you say, bearing witness."

Arrow growled, his eyes boring into mine. He stroked the Aldara mark on my throat. "Good. It's still active. Bakhur wants to hurt you, but he can't because of my mark."

"That's your job alone, is it? To hurt me?"

He rolled his eyes. "We've had this conversation before. My answer hasn't changed."

"Actions speak louder than words," I snarled back. "And yours, thus far, have been abhorrent."

Grunting, he pushed me harder against the rough stones, his fingers flexing on my throat, tight but not causing pain yet. "And what about your actions?" he asked.

"*Mine?* What have I done that comes near to equaling your betrayal?"

"Oh, Leaf," he said, his voice husky and breath caressing my cheek. "How your words wound me."

Fire sizzled through my veins, setting every part of me alight. His touch infuriated and excited me. Made me want to scream and slap his perfect face until every speck of shame and self-disgust had left me.

How dare my body burn like it wanted him. Like it needed him. My flesh was weak, and my thoughts were no better. Chaos reigned in my mind as I stared at his lips, wondering how they'd feel against mine, a sick part of me willing to do anything to find out.

I shook my head and pushed against him, but he was as unyielding as a fucking mountain.

"If you have anything of importance to say," Esen told him, "then for gold's sake, hurry up."

Arrow breathed out a curse, and Esen hissed, "Melaya's coming. I can feel him through the mergelyn bracelet Azarn makes his soldiers wear."

"Be careful," Arrow whispered, then flicked out his wings, a dark shadow engulfing me before he rose up and disappeared in a gust of wind.

We scrambled and mounted Sable, and she bounced into a trot just as the twin fire mages rounded the corner, Melaya's eyes blazing with their usual cheery aggression.

"Good evening, Melaya. Nukala," I said in a pleasant tone to mess with them. "I hope you both enjoyed today's entertainment."

Sweeping past us in the direction of the fire gardens, Melaya said nothing, while his brother stared over his shoulder at me with curious black eyes.

"Can't your brother speak?" I called out. Esen shushed me, but I ignored her and continued teasing the mages. "If he could, I'm sure he'd tell me it was quite an achievement to beat the Fire Queen."

"Oh, Zali," Esen admonished. "Will you ever learn to keep your mouth shut?"

Rubbing my chin, I pretended to consider her question. "No, I don't think so. My parents raised me to stand up for myself, and it would be disrespectful to their memories to do otherwise."

Esen chuckled, urging Sable into a canter.

All the way back to my tower, I gave thanks for the way she had softened toward me. In the last few days, this fae who had once tried to kill me seemed gentler, kinder, almost protective of me.

Perhaps in time, she would be a true friend and ally, and I could take her back to Mydorian, two victorious females, riding high after destroying our enemies.

The Storm King and the Fire King.

Chapter 12

LEAF

The next day after lunch, Melaya, instead of Esen, collected me from the tower for the final event, his eyes burning holes through the back of my skull as I finished braiding my hair, one question spinning through my mind.

If I survived today, would Azarn let me live? Because it was clear he didn't want me to actually *marry* his son. I had no doubt he'd stop at nothing to ensure my demise in the final fight. His entertainments were a ruse, an excuse to kill the one female in the realms who had influence over what he wanted most. Gold.

My stomach churned as I smoothed my tunic over my leathers and turned to face Melaya. At least I'd finished most of my plate of baked fish and fresh bread. A good meal made everything infinitely more bearable. I just prayed it wasn't my last.

With my hands cuffed in front of me, the fire mage pulled me down the stairs, through the palace's back corridors, then to the stables—all parts of the palace I was familiar with. Unfortunately. Other than my visit to Luna, I'd mostly been confined to my room, and that troubled me.

If I managed to escape, I had no idea in which direction to flee. I couldn't even find my way to the palace's storehouse and certainly had no clue where the nearest ports were located. At every opportunity, I'd driven Esen mad with endless questions, which got me nowhere, since she remained tight-lipped until she lost her temper and swore at me.

"Where's Esen today?" I asked Melaya as he threw me on a large white horse and fastened my chain to the saddle pommel. The beast's impressive black wings flared out from muscular shoulders, blowing my hair over my face. "And Nukala? I rarely see you two apart."

"My brother and Esen are occupied," the mage said, mounting behind me. "It hasn't gone unnoticed that she was warming toward you."

Damn. I hoped Azarn wasn't punishing her for being *nice* to me.

The breath whooshed from my lungs as the winged horse leaped over an erupting fire geyser, and then soared through the air, arriving at the Fen Forest in no time.

As Melaya marched me into the arena, the Fire King silenced his courtiers with an abrupt wave of his hand before turning to greet me. "Welcome, Zali Omala, Princess of Dirt and Stone."

I sighed and swallowed a retort. Azarn got my title wrong on purpose, and I refused to give him the satisfaction of appearing affected. Today, I'd silently tell him to go fuck himself.

"If you survive the final entertainment," he continued, "you will marry Prince Bakhur and become a member of my family."

"Then I'll be your daughter," I announced loudly, causing laughter to ripple through the courtiers. I quickly scanned the dais and the crowd, searching for Arrow, unable to find him.

That was strange. If he wanted to see me fail supremely, now was likely the best time to do so.

Azarn grimaced but didn't contradict me. If I won today and he didn't kill me, I would soon be his relative by marriage. And as long as Bakhur found a way to impregnate me while I bore the Aldara mark, I would be the mother of the heirs to his kingdom.

Esen strode across the arena, her mouth grim as she unchained me, then handed me a long knife, and not just any knife. It was *his* knife—Arrow's. The one made of Auryinnian metal that he'd thrown to me after Quin tumbled us from the Mydorian palace's balcony. The very knife I'd used to kill my brother.

Nausea rolled through my stomach. "I'd prefer a sword, if possible," I said, my firm voice masking a turmoil of emotions. Fear. Anger. Sadness.

Azarn laughed. "Fight with *that* knife or with your bare hands. I don't care which. The choice is yours."

I bowed my head and gripped the hilt tighter.

"Now it's time to meet your final opponent," said Azarn, his words rough with barely contained excitement.

The arena gates creaked open, and the entire Fire Court drew a collective, ragged breath. I spun on my heel, my neck hot and my Aldara mark prickling.

My heart stopped beating.

Arrow stood on the other side of the arena, moving closer.

I took three steps backward, bewildered. My jaw snapped shut as my gaze bounced between the Fire King's cruel green eyes and Arrow's lopsided smirk.

A high-pitched laugh came from the dais, and I finally noticed Nukala seated at Azarn's feet, his chest bare, his head resting on the Fire King's lap, and black hair spilling over his legs.

There was something very odd about Melaya's twin. A riddle that needed solving. But not now. I had bigger problems to solve than the puzzle of a powerless fire mage.

I spun back to Arrow. "Is this a joke?" I asked, stupidly revealing my shock. It never helped to show an enemy my true feelings. Whether it be fear, surprise, or heartbreak—I locked my emotions inside me.

But *this*—this was too fucking much to repress.

"King Azarn has never *been* more serious," said the Storm Prick, tossing and catching a bone-hilted blade with infuriating calm.

While my pulse thundered in my ears, he stalked toward me like a Mydorian forest cat, his limbs loose but strong, ready to pounce and destroy his prey in an instant. In that moment, I saw beneath the facade of the golden king. The sensual lightning god. Beautiful. Fearless. In control.

It was all a game.

He wasn't civilized. He was a savage, reveling in violence and cruelty. Fae scum, just like I thought the day he'd thrown me in the river, and then left me to my fate in Coridon's dungeon. Drunk on his beauty, over the weeks of my captivity, I'd let the pleasure of his lying mouth and murderer's fingers blind and bind me to him, like those poor, feckless auron kanaras.

What a fool I'd been.

Running my thumbnail over the carvings on my knife hilt, realization struck. Azarn had just handed me an opportunity. A gift. I could try to kill Arrowyn Ramiel today. Something I'd dreamed about since the day of my arrest.

I could do it now.

End the Storm King.

Stab the smug smirk from his lips.

JUNO HEART

I faced Azarn, and let my gaze skim the silent members of his family, motionless in the seats around him, as if they'd been painted into the scene. A glamorous but depressing family portrait, only their lips twitching like hungry ghouls, impatient to feast on my soul.

"Remind me of the rules again," I said.

"Arrowyn Ramiel may do anything he likes to you, even kill you. In return, you can wound him, but not fatally. If you murder the King of Storms and Feathers, your life is forfeit."

Ah, what a neat little plan to finish us off. No matter who won, the two greatest pains in Azarn's ass would be neatly dealt with.

Instead of protesting, I nodded as if the rules were fair, but everyone present knew they weren't. Even Arrow, who stared at me with such raw intensity that for a single foolish moment, I remembered how it had felt when he looked at me that way while buried deep inside me.

I spun the knife in my hand, clicked the bones on each side of my neck, then started toward him.

"Wait," said Azarn, stroking Nukala's hair. "I have more instructions. If you make it out of the gate into the Fen Forest, good luck to you. But know this: two greivon dragons will fly above you at all times, eager to sink their talons into your flesh if you attempt to escape."

What in the realms was a greivon dragon? Regardless, if they decided to burn me to a crisp, all I could do was wave my knife around and shout a lot. I'd be dead before I even tried to run.

"Well then, shall we begin, Princess?" said the Storm bastard, circling me slowly.

I held my nerve, spinning on my heel as the words he'd spoken the day he left the Mydorian forest weeks ago whispered through my mind.

"*Remember who you are—my winged gift, forever my Aldara*," he had said. He'd also sworn to always come for me when I needed him. To raze realms to save me. Pay any cost to keep me safe. No matter what. And, now, here he was—about to try to *kill* me.

What a rotten liar.

"No armor?" I asked, raising a brow as my gaze slid down his body. Bare-chested, he was dressed only in black leather pants with metal kneecaps and heavy, calf-hugging black boots, his wings hidden. "Not even your famed breastplate."

"Surprised? You should be used to seeing me half-naked or just... naked." He licked his lips and scanned my body. "You've grown thinner since we last met. Aren't they feeding you properly?"

Something dark flickered in his gaze. It looked like anger, perhaps sparked by a memory of our shared past. Or a desire to rip my heart out through my ribs.

I clutched my dagger tighter, its hilt cold in my palm. A warm wind howled, blowing my braid over my eyes, obscuring Arrow momentarily. When I flicked my hair away, he'd moved closer, his weapon raised into a strike position.

Once, he said he loved no one and nothing and never would, and those were the words I would cling to during the fight. For it was Arrowyn Ramiel's truth. Back in Coridon, he'd stated it clearly. I just hadn't been listening properly at the time.

As we circled each other, I inched in the direction of the Ashen Souls' gates. If I made it into the forest and found the serpent fae, Vyprin, perhaps he would help me for a price.

"Are we going to dance like this all day?" Arrow asked, keeping pace with my slow-weaving movements.

"If you like. You always professed to despise the activity, so I'm more than happy to oblige."

He barked out a laugh. "Oh, I never despised doing anything with you, Leaf."

"Shut up and fight me," I hissed, furious at his repeated use of the stupid slave name he'd given me.

Without warning, Arrow moved swiftly, deliberately, his blade glinting in the sunlight. I skipped back and to the side, slipping behind him. My heart pounded as he whirled around, a wild storm raging in his eyes.

He was stronger, but I was nimbler.

Arrow lunged forward, his strikes powerful. I moved out of their force with speed, destabilizing his balance, our grunts and curses causing roars of delight from the Fire Court.

We moved close again, then broke away. It was a game, and he loved toying with me, prolonging his fun.

The smell of the desert still clung to his clothes, and his own scent—warm skin and sandalwood—made me dizzy. I shook my head and gritted my teeth. No swooning allowed today. This was a battle, not a lovers' reunion.

I whispered the Mydorian battle chant under my breath. *By branch and root, soil and stone, lend strength to muscle, heart, and bone. Crush all to live. Conquer and prevail—*

"Mydor blood will never fail," finished Arrow.

"What?"

Our blades slid and entwined in a furious clash of steel until he twisted his wrist and locked the hilts together, his warm breath ghosting over my lips. My own breath snagged in my throat as Arrow clenched his teeth and tugged me closer. "I never wanted this."

I parted my lips and pretended to fall into him, as if I were about to kiss him. The risky tactic worked, and in confusion, he frowned, loosening his grip on the blade. I whipped my long knife in a figure-eight pattern and stepped slightly back, releasing the bind.

"Didn't you?" I asked. "Then perhaps you shouldn't have sold me to the Sun Realm, then."

He advanced again. "You're a fool. You've never been able to see what's right in front of your face. Never seen *me* clearly."

"You're right. I'll always regret that I didn't see beyond your fake smiles and sweet lies to the conniving demon beneath them."

Arrow's eyes darkened, and he relaxed his forearm, pointing his blade toward the ground.

The crowd roared out taunts and gave the Storm King bloodthirsty instructions.

Kill her. Kill the human. Remove her guts and throw us the tender entrails. Show us who you really are.

Chapter 13

LEAF

My shoulder blades hit the Ashen Souls' gates, and without turning, I reached behind me and fumbled for the latch.

In a fake, courtly gesture, Arrow turned a palm up, directing it toward the forest beyond the arena walls. "Please go ahead. I'm sure you recall how much I enjoy chasing you."

Thunder clapped directly above us, heavy rain beginning to fall as I slipped through the gate and ran for my life.

I stumbled and fell, sliding along the ground on my butt. I heard Arrow behind me, not running, but just calmly stalking me like the predator he was. I knew I couldn't beat him in hand-to-hand combat. He was nearly twice my size and three times as mean. Even so, I'd make him work for his victory.

I leaped up and darted forward, feigning a thrust toward Arrow's heart. He parried the blow, his blade scraping the air in front of my cheek.

As he fought, his eyes turned the color of thunderclouds, a dark and violent gray. We shuffled forward and back, circled giant tree trunks, while frustration boiled inside me. He was too damn strong, and all I could do was duck and weave fast, once even skidding between his legs.

Still toying with me, he laughed when I popped up behind him, then laughed harder when I stabbed his arm. His boot grazed my thigh, sending me stumbling backward.

Rain and blood streaked his skin, and Arrow continued to laugh as if he was having the time of his life. Or losing his mind. Mad prick. He hadn't changed a bit.

But neither had I.

And I wouldn't stop fighting until he killed me.

I ran up a tree stump and leaped, flying toward him, my dagger aimed at his chest. He pivoted, narrowly evading my blade, and countered with a fierce spin and a strike that sent me reeling. He could've killed me then, but he hadn't.

Why was he holding back?

The answer struck me like a bolt of the Storm King's lightning. He was a bored desert cat, and I was the scurrying mouse. A bit of fun. He could play this game forever.

I barely blocked his next attack, my dagger quivering under the force of his strength. This close, he could snap me in two without breaking a sweat. With a brief flex of muscle, his body could crush mine. Part of me wished he'd hurry up and do it and put us both out of our misery.

But instead of ending it, he stared and stared as his breath panted out and the depths of his deceit hit me. Arrow had no intention of killing me.

So who was he trying to fool with his act of violence—me or Azarn?

Ferocious screeches echoed in the distance, the sound growing closer. The dragons. Fuck.

I craned my neck and looked up. Two black creatures flew above, their breath scorching the treetops with each pass.

Arrow's wings appeared, flaring wide above his shoulders like protective armor.

"Is that allowed?" I asked. "Azarn prohibited the use of magic."

A smirk tilted his lips. "I'm not using magic to fight you. I'm protecting us from the greivon beasts. They don't obey rules and are likely to swoop you off and decorate their den with your bones."

"And we can't have them taking your fun away, can we?"

His eyes darkened further. "That's one way to put it, Princess."

"Come on. Ignore them and fight me," I said, dropping into a crouch and circling around him through the ferns. "Let's finish this."

He shook wet hair from his eyes and adopted a defensive stance, studying my every move, but not making any of his own.

Branches and twigs cracked beneath my boots, and growls rumbled from the sky.

"Stop moving," he commanded, and I obeyed. "There's a fire hole to your left. Move into the clearing with me. There's no danger here."

"Other than from you."

He breathed a laugh through his nose. "Do you really believe that?"

"Let's find out, shall we? Stop holding back you winged ass and *fight* me. Otherwise, Azarn will kill us both."

"As you wish," he said, spinning then lunging forward. In four quick movements, he had me pressed against the rough bark of a giant tree trunk, his breath stirring strands of my hair and his blade's edge kissing my throat.

Despite his labored breathing, I knew he wasn't tired; far from it.

I fought like a demon against his hold as he maneuvered my free arm behind me, using his weight to keep it trapped. Then he seized my other wrist in an iron grip, preventing me from striking him.

Unhinged fury burned through my blood as I scraped his lower leg with my boot. He held tight, forcing my surrender, but I bucked against him until he trapped my boot tips under his, immobilizing me.

No, he definitely wasn't tired. The hardness that dug into my body told me exactly how much he enjoyed this. Power and control made him hot, just like it always had.

"I hate you," I said, watching rain slide down his cheeks like tears.

"I know."

Wind from the dragons' wing beats tangled our hair together. Strands of dark gold and dirt brown, the sight making me sick to my stomach.

The Storm King had won again, holding me captive, trapped, just the way he liked me. It was a pity I'd spent a delusional period of time in Coridon believing he actually *cared* about me.

Well, I was done worshiping the Light Realm's false god. Sick of being at this male's mercy. All I wanted was for it to be over. Forever.

"Kill me." Squeezing my eyes shut, I jerked against him. "*Do it, Arrow*. I never want to see your smug face again, and if that's the only way to achieve it, then so be it. I'd rather be dead than at your mercy for one second longer."

"Open your eyes."

I shook my head.

"I never took you for a coward, my Aldara. Look. At. Me."

Drawing in a painful breath, I cracked my lids and found myself drowning in swirling pools of molten silver.

"You of all people should know things are never how they first seem, Leaf."

"Usually, it's much worse. Hurry up and kill me, then I won't have to watch you and Azarn turn the Five Realms to shit. Give Ari my love."

My mind raced with desperate schemes. If he believed I'd given up, and if I could distract him somehow, maybe I could get enough space between us to break away and plunge my blade into his neck.

I clenched the knife hilt, and his fist tightened around my wrist. Why hadn't he disarmed me? Struggling against his grip, I bucked again, and he hissed out a curse.

"Stop it. I'm not going to kill you."

"And I'm not a fool. You heard Azarn. You have no choice."

"You *are* a fool," he replied, his voice low and urgent. "You're the fool who once cared for the fae who enslaved you, believed in his redemption, then with little proof, had the gall to think he *betrayed* you. Do you deny it?"

"Of course not. It's the truth. You never tortured me physically, never cut me or bruised my flesh on purpose, only attacked my dignity and pride. This made me believe you weren't a monster. But I was wrong. I hated you once, and I despise you even more now."

"Liar." He sheathed his knife at his hip and wrapped his fingers around my throat. "You *loved* me."

"Can a prisoner truly love their jailer?" I asked, my pathetic tears blurring his features. "Can an absence of cruelty be mistaken for care? Yes, I was once stupid enough to believe that.

But the day Esen and Melaya arrested me in the desert, all those foolish assumptions shattered my heart. How I wish you'd left me in the gilt market cage to rot."

"Believe me, if I'd had the slightest inkling of the pain that you'd cause me, I fucking well would have."

Silence hummed through the trees, broken only by the sound of our ragged breaths and the dragons' soft rumbles to the east.

I sighed. "Arrow, this is ridiculous. We can't stand here all day. *Do* something. *Please*."

He nodded, brows drawing together in an agonized frown. "Damn it, Leaf. I'm sorry, but I need to make it stronger. Don't know how long it'll last, but—"

"What? Make what stronger?"

Realization dawned as his gaze slid over my throat, but before I could react, his warm lips pressed against my skin, and he bit me without warning.

No, no, no, I thought as my head fell back against the tree, my eyes rolling with intense, mind-numbing pleasure.

As his fangs slid deeper into my flesh, heat and desire flooded my veins, and I asked myself, was it *my* longing or *his* that I felt flowing through me? An intoxicating poison. Destroying me.

"The Aldara bond," he murmured, his words slurring against my neck. "Must be strong to speak to you."

What in the hell realms was he talking about?

It made no sense, but as a deep groan rumbled in his chest, a spark ignited inside me. Clarity. This was it. My one and only chance to gain the upper hand. To kill Arrowyn Ramiel, my torturer. My beloved.

I allowed a moan to escape my lips and writhed, pressing my hips against his, teasing, as if begging for more.

"Leaf," he whispered, taking my lips with horrifying tenderness.

The shock of his kiss nearly undid me, and I fought with every fiber of my being to stay in control. To not succumb to the wretched part of me that wanted nothing more than to dissolve in his arms. Wanted to believe he was still mine. My sanctuary. And that we belonged together forever.

The soft, wet warmth of his mouth was a fatal drug, melting my bones and any remaining strength I possessed. His sighs, the graze of his teeth—pure torture and unbearable. Memories of every time he'd touched me flooded over me. The thrill, the fear, the complete and utter bliss of being his.

Of surrendering.

Oh, merciless gods, I never thought I would feel this again, his heat, his muscles coiling tighter beneath my fingers. I wanted more. I wanted *everything.*

Mydor blood will never fail. Don't give in to him. Don't... give... in.

The dragons called to each other in bubbly chirps and low growls, growing closer. One roared and shot a line of fire nearby, setting three trees alight.

Arrow's wings lifted, enfolding me in a warm blanket of iridescent feathers.

Another roar sounded as heat from the dragon's breath blasted above our heads. Arrow swore and glanced up, stepping backward, distracted.

Perfect.

Snarling, I gritted my teeth and sliced my blade across his neck, not deep enough to do real damage. Then with all my might, I stabbed his chest, just a little to the right of his heart, missing my mark. I twisted the blade as his eyes widened in shock.

Stumbling backward, he hit a tree, and then slid down its trunk to the ground.

I crouched beside him, my palm pressing the golden skin around the knife, prepared to leap away should he try to strangle me with the last of his strength.

"Is it really that easy to kill you, Storm King?" I asked, unwanted tears pooling in my eyes, threatening to spill over.

"Kill me? No." He cast a brief look at the blade sticking out of his chest and laughed. "You've wanted to see me like this for some time, Leaf. Tell me, does it feel good?"

Yes, I thought. *Yes, it fucking did.*

As the dragons emitted piercing screeches, turned, and flew toward the arena, relief surged through me, grateful I wouldn't be their dinner. I was alive and hoped to stay that way, at least for the foreseeable future. Dust knew how Azarn would react to my victory.

"My vicious, most-intoxicating murderess, please... Please don't leave me." He coughed and reached a shaking hand toward my cheek, stroking damp hair away. "You must realize I never stopped loving you."

I laughed. "Never stopped? According to your own words, you never started. You told me you cared, insisted many times I was yours and that I belonged to you. But you never once said you loved me."

"Did I not? Well, I thought it more times than was good for me. A constant refrain, my thoughts of love for you drove me to the edge of insanity."

"Interesting how you say such things only as I'm about to twist my blade deeper into your heart."

"Technically, it's my blade. And you missed my heart, little Leaf. Your lack of faith in me is the fatal strike. If anything kills me, it will be that and that alone."

I reached for the knife hilt, and his bloodied fingers wrapped around my wrist. "Listen. They're coming."

Arrow tipped his head back against the wet earth and watched the approach of five fire mages, Melaya leading them, his twin prancing behind as if he was on his way to a midsummer picnic.

"Remember what I vowed to you back in Mydorian," Arrow said, his voice barely audible. "What I promised you... I will always protect you. Always come for you. Trust that... if nothing else. While you've been trying to kill me, I've had no choice but to play the part of your enemy to *save* you. In the palace... what I say is monitored. Find Zaret. He can explain."

Grendal's son was here? That must have been the young human who arrived in Taln with Arrow and Raiden.

The mages appeared a few feet in front of me, and with a tiny flick of his fingers, Melaya released a burst of magic that sent me flying across the forest floor. Chanting, they enfolded Arrow in chains of fire, and then dragged him away, his silver eyes fixed on me until he disappeared through the gate.

Silver eyes that lied.

Arrow only pretended to be my savior to save his life, but I knew better than to believe his stories. I'd learned my lesson. He was a betrayer. A total asshole.

And I'd come very close to killing him, which meant that I'd won the final event.

A cold shiver rolled down my spine.

I had survived.

But what would the Fire King do with me now?

Chapter 14

LEAF

The rain had finally stopped, and Arrow was gone. A long breath shuddered through my lips, my legs weak and shaking. I grabbed a low branch, swaying on my feet as my head spun. It was only exhaustion. Nothing more.

I didn't care if the Storm King died, and if he did, then, great, I'd accomplished my goal, and only joy should make me swoon. But unfortunately, it was more than that.

Shame, regret, even sorrow coursed through my veins. Part of me couldn't imagine living in any realm where Arrow didn't exist. I had to face it—my mind was a conflicted mess.

Footsteps crunched over bracken and fallen leaves as more fae poured into the forest—Azarn and Estella first, Bakhur following close behind.

The queen's eyes flashed at me, relaying a message I couldn't interpret. Not in my current state of exhaustion. I could barely stand upright, let alone think straight. Perhaps she meant to reassure me that her husband would let me live. But surely there were better ways to achieve that... like with a secret visit to my tower, where we could hatch a plan to destroy him.

Azarn sidled up to me. "It appears you almost killed King Arrowyn, Princess," he said, a touch of awe in his voice. A similar excitement glimmered in his son's eyes. "Fortunately for you, he still lives. For now. But if he does dies from the injuries you caused, then your life is also forfeit."

Estella shot an icy look at Azarn. "Husband, Arrowyn is much weakened and will die without attention from our healers."

My chest constricted with a confusing mix of pain and triumph. "Will you allow him to die, King Azarn?" I asked.

He laughed. "Arrowyn Ramiel's continued good health is still required. Come. We must announce your victory to my courtiers."

"To kill a fae swiftly," Estella whispered as we fell back a few paces and entered the arena together. "You must strike the heart dead center, deep enough to stop it from beating before their natural healing power repairs the damage. But I implore you not to try to use this tactic on Arrowyn. There is much to tell you when circumstances permit."

I eyed the two enormous dragons crouched in the center of the arena. At least ten times the size of a tall fae, they huddled together, stretching their long necks and red-tipped wings, yellow eyes searching the crowd, perhaps for a tasty appetizer. Rancid-smelling smoke puffed from their nostrils, eddying through the air.

They were formidable beasts, and I hoped I never had cause to get too close to them.

"Is it wise to describe how best to kill your kind, Estella? Given the chance, I could use the tactic on you."

"The last fae you should attempt to murder is your only friend in Taln."

Meaning: Estella thought of herself as my ally.

Wasn't she worried I might share the news with Azarn or her son to gain an advantage? And advising me not to harm Arrow; now that was stretching our burgeoning friendship. No one had the right to ask that of me.

The things he'd said in the forest spun through my mind, taunting me as my palms dampened and sweat broke out on my brow.

You must realize I never stopped loving you.

Did *he* realize I had trust issues? Major ones.

To believe his words, I'd have to accept that he told the truth while I held his life in my hands. That he'd never been my enemy. Had always tried to protect me. And that he cared for me above all else.

But it wasn't possible. Evidence suggested the opposite was true.

The letters he'd written while we were separated after Quin's death—two passionless missives over a three-week period. If he had truly cared and wanted to hide it from the Sun Realm, he could have visited me in secret. The man had wings, after all.

So many had hurt me. Davy in Coridon's Underfloor cell. Grendal. Esen. The sailors on Captain Loligos's ship. My own twin turned against me. *Everyone* betrayed me. I couldn't let myself trust anyone again—perhaps except for Ari, Van, and Raiden's mother, Ildri. *Ever.*

Estella drew me onto the dais where her stiff-backed family waited, and then Esen arrived carrying a velvet-wrapped parcel. She nodded at the queen and placed it on her open palm.

"Zali," Estella said, projecting her voice for the entire court to hear. "Since you've triumphed in all three of King Azarn's entertainments, soon you will become the daughter I have long wished for. From now on, your movements within our city will not be restricted."

My pulse hammered, and I struggled to keep my expression blank. This was incredible news. Moving freely about the palace and grounds, it wouldn't take long to discover the best escape route and—

"Zali?" said the queen. "Can you hear me?"

I blinked, focusing on the item Estella held out, an ankle bracelet fashioned from black metal and carved with flames. "This connects you to Melaya and prevents you from leaving the boundaries of Taln."

My heart sank as Estella knelt and slipped my shoe off, then fastened the anklet to my leg before re-tying my bootlaces. For all intents and purposes, I had won every event, pretended to be docile and compliant, never making a fuss, and yet here I was—still a captive.

Azarn and Bakhur joined us, the king ranting about the strength and wonder of his son and heir, his claims highly doubtful. Then he waxed lyrical on the beauty and invincibility of his kingdom, but I hadn't seen enough of the Sun Realm to comment. Finally, bored with my lack of response, he left the arena, his family trailing behind him with all the joy of a somber funeral procession.

Slowly, the courtiers followed, filing past me with curious stares. When I was alone, I settled on the king's throne and tugged my boot off. I pushed, prodded, and dug my nails into every line of the anklet, searching for a crack or weakness.

"Don't waste your energy," said Ruhh, appearing out of thin air as she was so fond of doing. "The mergelyn anklet can't be removed unless Melaya releases the spell."

Groaning in frustration, I tightened my laces and stood up, brushing leaves and dirt from my leathers and swaying on my feet again. My stomach rumbled. Dust, I was starving. I could inhale a whole loaf of bread right now. Maybe even two of them.

I descended the dais stairs with care, and then strode out of the Arena of Ashen Souls, my gait a little unsteady. Hopefully, I'd never see the dust-damned place again. Not even in my nightmares.

"Where to next?" Ruhh asked as she floated beside me, her ghoulish smile lined up with the left side of my face.

"Oh, you're still here," I said, grimacing as I realized I had a long walk back to the palace.

"They left a horse for you." Ruhh pointed toward the sunset at the largest spindle tree I'd ever seen, its branches alight with magical flames and Sable munching grass nearby.

Fiery sparks shot from the earth, and the horse reared up, snorting in fear. "What genius left her next to a geyser? Maybe they hoped she'd get burned to a crisp before I found her."

Ruhh laughed. "Of course not. Sable just wandered over to the juiciest grass. Hurry up and mount. I have something to show you."

"What is it? I'm tired and not in the mood for games."

"Wouldn't you like to use your newfound freedom to explore?"

"Most definitely. But I need water, food, and a bath first."

"Then I shall meet you near the fire moat in two hours. Follow the palace wall south from the exit Esen leaves your tower by.

I'll show you how to stop Arrowyn for good and not take the blame for his demise."

"Oh?" A mix of shame and excitement churned inside me. That was what I wanted, wasn't it? The Storm King's death?

"Please come, Zali," said Ruhh. "Make sure you bring the blood orchid petal with you."

"How did you know—"

"I'm a spirit. I can travel anywhere. See everything. Trust me."

Trust her? That was the last thing I should do. But I'd be lying if I said I wasn't intrigued by her offer.

I mounted Sable and returned to my tower room to eat and bathe, not wasting time exploring the palace along the way, even though I longed to satisfy my curiosity. I was also keen to investigate how far through Taln's boundaries I could travel before Melaya would arrive to punish me. But both those things could wait until tomorrow.

After a blissful bath and a brief nap, I dressed in a clean tunic from my closet, and then hurried down the tower stairs to meet the ghost princess, my mind still sluggish with sleep.

What remained of Ruhh's gray-white skin shimmered under the moonlight as she floated out of the shadows near the palace wall. Above her, the night sky loomed, an indigo blanket threaded with glittering stars. Fireflies danced through the humid air, and in the distance, a geyser erupted, illuminating the trees near the edge of Fen Forest.

"Right on time, Princess," she said as I picked my way around rocks on the dark, uneven terrain. "Did you bring the petal?"

Raising a brow, I patted my pocket and let Ruhh guide me through the darkness to the fire moat that ran behind the palace. Lava flowed over the moat's edge, tumbling off the nearby sea cliffs, down into the glowing mouth of a cave set into the rocks.

I grabbed hold of a boulder and leaned forward, squinting into the dark as I tried to make sense of what I saw.

"Don't ask," Ruhh said. "The less you know about what happens in that cave the better."

Of course her comment only increased my curiosity, but the cave would have to wait, too. "What did you want to show me?" I asked.

Ruhh floated closer, damp air enveloping me as she stroked her fingers through my hair. "When rubbed on your skin, the orchid petal will make you invisible, just like your reaver's cloak."

"I thought they were poisonous." I really shouldn't trust her. She could be lying, but if what she said was true, invisibility was a useful weapon.

"Vyprin wants everyone to believe the petals are dangerous. If their true value was common knowledge, there would be thousands more fae bones piled up in his den."

"I imagine he'd enjoy that."

"No, he is lazy and prefers to spend his time sleeping. Tell me, Zali, do you love Arrowyn Ramiel still?"

My fingers curled into my palms until my knuckles cracked. "No," I replied, raising my chin.

Sparks exploded in the moat, blinding me as three creatures formed from the lava, flames flickering over their long limbs as they rose up. Their jaws snapped near my face, and they emitted strange crackling purrs before their bodies sank back into the river of fire, disappearing.

Ruhh cackled and flew over the moat, spinning somersaults before hovering in front of me, her bare toes inches above the rocks I stood upon.

"What in the fae realms were they?" I asked, my jaw hanging open.

"The khareek—lie seekers. They're quite greedy for them and enjoyed yours very much."

Oh. Embarrassment scalded my cheeks. Had my answer to Ruhh's question summoned them to the surface of the moat? Because somewhere deep down, a foolish part of me still loved Arrow—almost as much as I hated him.

"How long does a petal's magic last for?" I asked.

"One petal... hm, not very long. Approximately half an hour, but it depends on how you apply it and on your individual body's reaction. Is one petal all you have?"

No way would I answer that question. Instead, I'd ask my own as a distraction. "Why should I trust you, Ruhh?"

"Because I know what you hope to achieve here in Taln. They've told you Arrow ordered your arrest, and ever since then, the thought of killing him consumes you."

I swallowed hard, but said nothing.

She leaned close and whispered against my ear. "My thoughts are similarly occupied. You could finish Arrowyn Ramiel off before he recovers from his battle wounds. We wouldn't be the only ones rejoicing in his death."

"Why bring me here? You could have told me that on the ride back from the arena."

"Because the khareek reveal lies, and I need to know if you still want to kill Arrowyn. *Do* you, human?"

Gritting my teeth, I focused on the memory of my arrest. On Melaya's words when he greeted me in the Light Realm desert: *Zali Omala of the Hidden City of Mydorian, by order of Arrowyn Ramiel, the King of Storms and Feathers, you are under arrest.*

"Yes, I still wish to kill the Storm King," I replied as we spun and faced the river of fire. It flowed calmly, only tiny sparks floating on its surface.

"You speak the truth," said Ruhh.

"And if I'd lied?"

"I would've pushed you in the moat."

"Ruthless," I said, begrudgingly impressed. "If I rub the petal on my skin, will it harm me in any way?"

"Not unless you swallow it."

I checked the moat, finding its surface still calm. "Good. Thank you for being honest," I said.

"Don't waste your breath thanking me. Instead, make yourself invisible and pay Arrowyn a visit."

"Why don't you kill him yourself?" I asked.

"Would if I could, but I can't wield a knife very well in my current state."

"Fair enough. Where might I find him?"

"Where do royal guests usually stay in a palace?" she said sweetly.

I sighed. "That's not very helpful."

"A spell has been cast against me disclosing his whereabouts. Melaya thinks of everything, except for those pretty orchid petals. Now hurry up, Zali. Tonight, the Storm King is weak. You won't get a better opportunity."

I hated taking orders from anyone, let alone a creepy ghost girl. But she was right. Time was of the essence. I carefully unfolded the cloth I'd tucked a few petals inside, the rest of the flower hidden in my room in case Ruhh tried to take it from me.

"Can I apply it anywhere?" I asked, staring at the velvety petal on my palm.

"Yes, but the best place is over your heart, and be sure to rub it in well."

I smeared the petal underneath my tunic, and my palm came away sticky with dark fluid. Breathing slowly, I waited, my heart racing. Nothing happened for several moments. Then a rush of nausea hit me, and I felt it—the satisfying sensation of magic rushing through my blood.

Ruhh laughed as I whispered the ancient elven chant, disappearing from the ghost girl's view.

"Zali?" she called out. "You don't need the reaver chant. The petals hold their own power."

I knew that, but old habits were hard to break.

Ignoring her, I bolted past the palace's curved outer walls until I came to the main entrance. I raced up the external stairs toward a pair of massive black doors etched with tiny bones and flames, shivering as the two guards flanking them sniffed the air with their wolf-like snouts.

Reflected flames from candelabras and wall sconces shone in the grand foyer's polished obsidian floor, and a heady blend of spices and roasted meat flavored the air. Without thinking, I followed the trail of the mouthwatering scent.

Moving silently, I hurried along twisting corridors that led me deeper into the palace as they morphed from grand and light-filled to narrow and dark without logic or reason. The palace had a will of its own, and it wanted to deter my progress.

Thankfully, I didn't spook easily.

A dark corridor suddenly opened into an ornate foyer. Music and laughter filtered through the cracks of large, molded black doors, the smell of food intensifying. I'd found the entrance to a feasting hall packed with raucous courtiers. My stomach growled, and I asked it to kindly pipe down until I had time to attend to its demands.

A grand, black-marble staircase stood on the other side of the foyer, two smaller bone-white staircases sweeping upward in graceful arcs on either side of it, leading to smaller towers. I hurried up the middle staircase, guessing that a visiting king would sleep in the largest tower, unless Azarn had insulted Arrow and given him a chamber in a less prestigious location. Which was more than possible.

Halfway up the stairs, two female jinn wearing white aprons over black tunics and carrying medical supplies—folded bandages and glass vials of bright-colored liquid—appeared on a landing, then marched down a hallway to my left. I watched them disappear through double doors etched with a golden phoenix at the end of the passage.

I tiptoed toward the door and pressed my ear against it. Male voices mumbled, too low to identify. Checking the mirror that hung on the opposite wall, making sure I was still invisible, I waited. Blood rushed through my ears, the sound louder than the conversation inside what-I-hoped-would-be Arrow's bedchamber.

After about ten minutes, the jinn healers exited the room. I ducked sideways, and they strolled straight past me. I crept forward again and listened at the door, straining to make out the words being muttered on the other side.

The voices rose, and my heart stuttered and slammed against my ribs. They belonged to Arrow and King Azarn.

I'd found the right room, but if only I could decipher their conversation. My fingers flexed toward the doorknob, but I quickly drew my hand back.

The petal's effect could wear off at any moment, which would be disastrous in front of Azarn. I had to be patient and wait until he left.

And if I made it inside the room, only to reappear in front of Arrow, I hoped I'd have time to lodge my knife deep in his heart before he could react. Then, finally, he'd be dead.

Pain strummed my insides, but I breathed through it, steeling my resolve. No matter what Arrow had said in the forest today, nothing could change who he'd been when I first met him.

A slaver. My jailer. The male who had tried to control me.

A fae who had kept me against my will.

And for that, he had to pay.

Chapter 15

ARROW

"**W**hat would destroy the human?" Azarn asked, stopping his pacing, and leaning a shoulder on a carved bedpost in my room. "Since you kept her caged for some time, Arrowyn, you must know the key to breaking her spirit."

Shifting my weight on the mattress, I sighed softly, but kept my face as blank as I could manage with my own fucking knife sticking out of my chest.

The king's mages had sealed the wound, preventing my life force from seeping out, but the blade couldn't be removed safely without assistance from Taln's healers. I hoped they'd arrive sometime this fucking century. I was beginning to think Azarn wanted me to die while I waited for them.

Weak from blood loss, I struggled to focus on the Fire King while rehearsing a careless tone in my mind before I spoke. Leaf's life depended upon Azarn believing I was indifferent to her fate. That I didn't care about her. But nothing could be further from the truth.

"Why the need to destroy her?" I asked. "Mere hours ago, I thought I heard you declare her as your son's intended bride." An event that would only occur over my dead body, I added in my head. "I destroyed your most loyal of courtiers, Gorbinvar the blacksmith, not the human. I don't understand your obsession with her."

Unfortunately, I did understand, for I shared his passion quite thoroughly. But instead of wanting to ruin her, I needed Zali Omala to be mine, safe for all time, and recognized as such in all realms, by all beings, fae or human.

I was the ruler of the Light Realm, High Lord of the Gold Accords, and Azarn was nothing but a petty thief. Without question, I would prevail, and soon, my Aldara would be free.

Azarn pushed off the bedpost and resumed trekking back and forth across the floor rug, his black-silk robe whipping the air behind him. "The girl is a future queen," he said. "I use the term *queen* quite loosely, of course, since she belongs to the most despicable race ever to inhabit the realms. Due to her reaver blood, she holds power over the gold trade. The disgusting creature attempted to kill my own envoy at your court! The sooner Zali Omala and her *people* are exterminated, the better for all fae kingdoms. Coridon included."

I very much doubted that.

In truth, what Azarn really meant was that he couldn't bear to let a human girl have the upper hand, to possess greater control over the gold trade than he would ever have. Fortunately, for all the kingdoms of the realms, Leaf was no power-grabbing oppressor. Her heart and intentions were good. Benevolent even.

But regardless, I needed her back in Mydorian, safely cloaked by the reavers, where neither Azarn nor I could get my hands on her.

That was my goal. To save her from all fae—myself included. More than anything, Leaf wanted to be free, and I would stop at nothing to give her that gift. But deep down, I knew when the time came to leave her in Mydorian, I would never have the strength to let her go. She was my one vice, my fatal addiction. I would never give her up.

So if that made me a hypocrite or an asshole or both, so be it. I'd gladly wear the title.

"It seems the Earth Princess, a tiny scrap of a girl, has gotten under your skin," I said, shivering and pulling the bed sheet to just below the knife jutting from my chest.

"She's aligned with the reavers, related to them by the blood in her veins. I would rather see that blood soak the ground and the gold trade control returned to the fae kingdoms alone." A laugh shook the Fire King's shoulders as his cheeks flushed red. "Of course I mean returned to *you*, Arrowyn. And I will be beside you, always supporting your efforts."

Losing count of the lies pouring from Azarn's lips, I struggled to suppress a sneer of disgust.

Azarn's dreams were simple, obvious, yet impossible to achieve. One day, he hoped to control Coridon. Or at the very least, my auron kanara. But without their feathers, the reavers' blood couldn't convert to gold. And even if the Sun Realm annexed my land, to keep the birds alive, he'd need lightning magic and lots of it. And for *that*, he needed my cooperation.

Azarn was in a bind, but too blinded by greed to notice.

Over the years, the Sun Realm had stolen both kanaras and lightning weavers from my kingdom to conduct illegal experiments on. But even the traitor Esen, a strong lightning wielder herself, couldn't keep many birds alive for long without my presence.

I alone tethered the lightning weavers' magic to the source. And more importantly, through my bond with the Zareen of Auryinnia, I *was* the source.

Coridon's pact with the reaver elves held the key to not only retaining power, but to maintaining balance in the realms. Reavers were unable to create lightning themselves, but when the Zareen gifted each new Storm King with wings on his crowning day, bestowing him the power of magical transference, he then boosted all Light Realm fae's power. None more important than the lightning weavers.

If the true measurement of dominion in the Star Realms was the amount of gold a fae controlled, then the Zareen was the most powerful being of all. Azarn was either oblivious to this eternal truth or had chosen to dismiss it as mere rumor.

More fool him.

Carefully gripping the hilt of the knife—the last place Leaf had graced me with her near-fatal touch—I breathed through the pain of her lack of faith in me and addressed Azarn again. "If you hate humans so much, why deal with her brother? He was the very worst of the species, vain and weak, an untrustworthy fool who deserved the poetic justice of his end. Killed by his own twin sister."

At the word *twins*, Azarn blanched. I thought of Melaya and Nukala, wondering if recalling them had disturbed the Fire King for some reason.

He waved his hand in a dismissive gesture. "Quin Omala was a gold-addicted moron who was easy to manipulate."

My stubble rasped as I scratched my jaw and pretended to contemplate options for weakening my Aldara. Whatever I told the Fire King needed to sound plausible, convincing.

"In answer to your question, Azarn, most of all, the human despises being humiliated. Feeling powerless. If I were to feed off her, I could drain her slowly, weaken her will and make her malleable to your needs."

Azarn's brow rose in interest. "What would justify such an occurrence? I'd prefer my wife not to be alerted to our schemes."

"You tell Estella that to fully recover from my injuries, I must feed daily from my Aldara. If necessary, sometimes twice a day. Although, I'll do my best to feed as infrequently as possible. The process is... distasteful."

"Why did you mark her in the first place, then?"

"For the same reason you have her here in Taln. To maintain control of the gold through her blood connection to the Zareen."

"Since she tried to kill you, Arrowyn, I don't imagine she'll comply without a fight."

Remembering what dissolved my little human's formidable resolve—*lust*—I would make damn sure she did.

I gave Azarn an indifferent shrug and gritted my teeth against the pain of my next words. "You're her current master, so order her to submit."

The Fire King's crown of flames wavered, almost sputtering out as he slumped into a chair and thumped the back of his head against the headrest. "Fine. I'll have my scribes write up the decree. Go ahead and do what you will to her. Or at the very least, do what you must. Break her if you wish. My mages should be able to put her back together. And if not, you and I will enslave every reaver alive, and then share the gold trade profits for as long as it suits us both."

Share? What bullshit. Azarn didn't plan to share a single gold feather with me. Leaf was only alive because he hoped to use her to control me. As much as I wished for the opposite, the Fire King wasn't a complete fool. I had to play this carefully and convince him she meant nothing to me.

"Of course, your... *visits* must be supervised by my guards, and they will hear everything you say. Proceed carefully, won't you?"

Stupid of him not to realize I had a very good way around that.

I laughed. "So distrusting."

"Can you blame me, Storm King?"

He had a point. "No. If I were you, I'd do the same. And I don't mind your guards attending. They'll cause her greater humiliation, which will only enhance the process for me. I don't mind performing in front of others."

A knock sounded at the door, then on Azarn's barked invitation, two healers entered my room. Without speaking, the tall female jinn, with coiled braids of fire writhing like snakes around their shoulders, proceeded to remove the knife from my chest and stitch the wound with magical threads.

It took all of ten minutes, and Azarn watched their every move, likely praying I'd drop dead during the procedure.

The healers' work instantly recharged and restored me, but I feigned otherwise for benefit of the fire fae. The more they underestimated me, the better.

Azarn left soon after, bidding me goodnight and leaving me to relive every moment of today's battle with Leaf. Being close to her again had filled me with euphoria, but at the same time, it was frustrating as fuck to realize she didn't trust me and claimed not to love me anymore.

But one thing was certain; she still wanted me. And badly. The perfume of her desire had wafted from her skin in heady, drugging doses.

While in the Fen Forest, if she'd asked me to do anything, anything at all, I would have dropped to my knees and proclaimed myself her servant.

Thrashing my head against the pillow, I groaned, my blood burning in my veins the way it did whenever Leaf was nearby. Images of her dilated pupils, the black swallowing emerald-green irises, and the erratic pound of her heartbeat as I'd trapped her against the tree drove me insane.

I needed her safe. Wouldn't rest until she was out of harm's way. The trick was to achieve it without looking like I gave a shit.

My thoughts spiraled into darkness, fear for Leaf trembling through my limbs. Where was she now? Was she safe? What horrors would the Fire Court inflict upon her now that she'd won Azarn's events? And fucking Bakhur had better stay away from her, or I'd rip his curl-blessed head off his neck.

Like a sudden flash of sheet lightning, my glyphs activated and burned the way they did when Leaf was near. Could it be...?

No, not possible, but still I froze and breathed softly, quietly, watching shadows and waiting. Feeling the air snap and sizzle and buzz over my skin.

Ever so slowly, the door cracked open, just wide enough for a small person to slip through the space. A Leaf-sized gap.

A fire geyser exploded outside the window, the light bathing the room in crimson. My blood hummed exactly the way it did whenever my Aldara was close enough to touch.

Shock drummed my heart against my ribs. "Leaf?" I croaked out as I pushed my weight onto my elbows, then climbed out of the bed. I spun slowly on my heel, my eyes wide and my skin prickling with awareness.

Leaf was in here.

I could fucking feel her.

But how? How the fuck did she activate her reaver's cloak with Melaya's block in place?

Scanning the room, I saw nothing unusual, then suddenly my blade vanished from the nightstand. She'd picked it up, her cloak absorbing its visible form.

I cracked my knuckles and willed calm through my veins. Then breathing slowly, I strolled toward the room's arched window and leaned on the stone frame, looking out across the fire fae's kingdom. Ancient stars glittered in a black sky, the darkness below broken by the city's flickering torches and the odd fire geyser erupting.

Counting heartbeats, I waited for her to make a move.

One. Two. Three. Then four, five, and six.

Still nothing happened.

At the count of ten, I felt it, a disturbance in the air, my human's scent peaking—a little different now. The notes of sweet apples and midnight-flowering auron roses were tinged with something darker. A little bitter. Fear. Anger. Desperation.

Whipping around, I reached out blindly and latched onto her wrist, *hard*, so it would fucking hurt and stop her in her devious little tracks.

She hissed, and I wrapped an arm around her, crushing her body to mine as I searched for the knife hilt, seized it, throwing it across the floor while she bucked against me, like a trapped, unbroken filly.

I backed her against the wall, sliding my hands up the familiar paradise of her curves until my palms braced her face. "If I could only see you, little Leaf, this moment would be perfect," I whispered. "Instead, sadness fills my heart."

A bolt of pain struck, and I spat a curse, my body jerking against the agony.

"Poor Arrow. Are you sad that you couldn't see my knee strike your groin?" she growled.

"I'd very much like to see any part of you touch me."

Capturing petal-soft lips, I pressed into their moist heat and kissed her. My body shuddered as if the power of a thousand storms rolled through me. She opened to me, sighing, and then, gold save me, moaned like she'd missed my touch. Missed *me*.

With each desperate kiss, her invisibility cloak flickered, and parts of her body became visible. Tonight, she wore a black tunic embroidered with flames and a Fire Court cloak. Not *my* cloak. Not the one I'd given her before I left Mydorian.

I caught a glimpse of her lashes fluttering like moth wings on the dusky hills of her cheeks, the shine of her skin, glowing with health. She'd been paler on that terrible day I left her in the Mydorian forest.

I'd wanted her so badly. Longed to take her with me. To never let her go. But instead of following my heart's desires, I'd listened to the voices of caution—Raiden and my Sayeeda.

A moan wrenched from my chest, so loud I almost missed her command to stop. Although it nearly killed me, I stepped back, still gripping her shoulders as her cloak flickered on and off, like a malfunctioning glamour.

"What's wrong?" I asked.

"The invisibility is wearing off. I must go before someone finds me here."

Wearing off? That was an odd way to phrase it.

I nodded as my thumbs twitched on her collarbone, my fingers curling tighter. "It's probably for the best."

"Arrow, stop squeezing me like a Mydorian forest python. Let me go. I'll come back another night and have a third attempt to murder you."

"Third? I'm certain your count is higher." I gave her a wry smile and forced myself to take another step backward. "You must be disappointed to find me still alive, then."

"Yes. And sad to learn a knife to the chest couldn't kill you."

"Mm. Must strike the heart, I'm afraid. Right in the center. And very *deep*. You'll need to use all your strength for the task."

She walked to the door and opened it, then glanced over her shoulder as I called her name in a plea, a prayer for mercy. "Leaf, wait a moment. Please. Are you all right? Have they hurt you?"

Green eyes widened in surprise or annoyance. "I'm fine."

"Then expect me in your room tomorrow night," I said, hoping I'd see a flash of something other than hostility in her features.

"Why?" she asked, frowning harder.

Pain worse than when she'd plunged my knife into my chest tore through me.

"Why? Because I'm trying to *help* you. Please, listen to me. I must—"

"I'll never believe another word you say, Arrow," she said, the door clicking shut with such fuck-you finality she might as well have slammed the damn thing in my face.

I slumped on the bed, resting my elbows on my knees and clenched fists tugging my blood-streaked hair.

Why? Why did she have to be so stubborn?

Cracking my neck, I rose from the bed and downed three glasses of water. Then wasting no time, I got dressed and hurried to the smaller of Taln's three taverns, where Raiden and Zaret preferred to drink.

I had to prepare them, warn them that my human was still hostile, disbelieving.

And about to run headfirst into disaster.

Chapter 16

LEAF

T he next day, I sprang out of bed early and enjoyed my newfound freedom by exploring Taln's rambling market district that wound down a grassy hillside beneath a slate-gray sky, the air thick with cooking smoke and spices.

I spent the morning inspecting wares laid out on market-stall tables, pestering hooded traders from the Ice Realm, blacksmiths, glassblowers, and bakers with questions, feigning interest in their magical trinkets and edible delights—enchanted blades, fire runes, amulets, potions, and health elixirs.

My aim was to learn everything I could about my newly acquired jewelry item, the repulsive mergelyn anklet, and get rid of the dust-damned thing as soon as possible.

Grizzled, long-haired warriors dressed in leathers and not much else wandered through the crowd, some buying weapons and others drinking ale from large tankards on roughly hewn tables set around the town mill.

I perched on a stool nearby, eavesdropping, before finally concluding their conversations about hunting tactics and best bedroom practices to make their partners scream were of little help to me. As soon as I finished my drink, I kept my hood low over my face and slipped past them.

At the very bottom of the market, I found twenty or so cages nestled in the walls of a shallow cave set into the hillside. They were filled with dragon-like creatures about the size of the cats that wandered the palace like royalty wearing bejeweled collars.

The caged dragons' pathetic mewling tugged at my heartstrings, and despite how badly I longed to set them free, I couldn't. I knew doing so would only get me confined to my tower again.

Or worse.

When my belly growled, I trekked back up the hill to the food stalls and used the gold feather Esen had given me this morning to buy a bowl of spiced soup and a sticky pastry for lunch. Blending in with the fae, I took a seat on a crowded table in front of a tavern and ate while watching Taln's famous dragon riders take their second whirl through the sky since the sun had risen.

As I licked the last of the pastry's honey from my fingers, I spied Raiden bartering with a trader. I slinked through rows of clothing hanging on long rails and watched him purchase a gold pendant with a single tear-shaped ruby, framed by shining black pearls. It was beautiful, the type of jewelry one gave to their beloved. And I smiled to myself, knowing exactly who Raiden had bought it for—Arrow's golden Sayeeda.

A wave of sadness engulfed me. I missed Ari so much.

I'd give almost anything to have her here with me in this twisted court of lies, and I was certain Raiden felt the same way.

I followed Arrow's dark-haired guard up and down black-walled streets and alleys until he came across the very person I had hoped to find—the human youth who'd arrived six days ago with the Storm Court retinue.

In the forest, Arrow had mentioned Zaret was here and advised me to seek him out. But could it really be Grendal's son? It made no sense that a human who'd lived in a gold raiders' camp would travel with the fae king who had proclaimed so often and so loudly to hate our species.

The males chatted amiably, Raiden laughing as he stroked his jacket pocket, where Ari's pendant lay safely tucked, before he clapped the boy's shoulder, and then continued alone up the hill toward the palace.

I wasted no time, ducking around groups of fae and stepping in front of the young man. "Hello," I said, offering my hand in greeting. "It's nice to finally meet another human in Taln."

A gray hue washed over his dark skin. "Princess," he stuttered, cutting me a deep bow, and ignoring my outstretched hand. In obvious discomfort, he flicked his gaze toward the market stalls, down to the ground, then finally back to my face. "How can I... uh... help you?"

"You could start by shaking my hand and telling me your name."

Laughter rumbled in his chest as he recovered from his bout of shyness and took my hand. "Arrow warned me you were blunt," he said drawing me through the crowd and toward one of the smaller fire gardens near the sea.

Fucking Arrow. Why was he the only thing anyone seemed to speak about and, worse, all I could think of? Self-disgust slid through my veins as I remembered the kiss we'd shared last night, the way I'd melted at his touch. In the space of three shakily drawn breaths, the walls around my broken heart had collapsed, and all I'd wanted was for him to call me his Aldara again. His only one.

And tell me that I was *his* and no other's.

The loud cawing of gulls woke me from my daydream of soft, seeking lips and molten silver eyes as the birds circled directly above, mocking me with their cruel cries.

The boy cleared his throat. "I'm glad what they say about you is true. Perhaps you'll forgive me if I speak in the same manner."

I smiled. "I appreciate straightforwardness," I admitted as I studied clear gray eyes framed by thick brows and dark hair that curled around the strong bones of his face. "I'm tired of the way fae forever talk around their secrets, rarely getting to the point. Speak boldly. It will be a refreshing change."

"I am Grendal's son, Zaret. I've heard a lot about you."

"Zaret? It really is you, isn't it? You have your mother's gray eyes." My fingers grazed his cheekbone. "Arrow said you were here, and I hoped it was true. But given all that's happened, it's hard to trust a word the Storm King says anymore."

A grin stretched his face, so similar to Grendal's mischievous smile that I knew without a doubt she was his mother.

"Will you sit with me?" he asked, perching on a flat boulder overlooking a field of fire geysers.

I settled beside him, and then took his hand and squeezed it. "Do you despise me for what happened to your mother, Zaret?"

He frowned. "Not at all. The Sayeeda, Ildri, and Arrow, they all explained what happened the day she died in the tea garden. My mother did a foolish thing in the hopes of saving me from a life of addiction. But in doing so, she betrayed you, her one true friend. The gold trade was the real cause of her death."

"Yes, and that's Arrow's fault. His court treats their servants with such savagery, allowing them to become addicted to serum as a means to control them."

"Much has changed in Coridon since you left. Servants no longer wear serum bracelets. And as long as they vow not to join the raiders, they are free to leave the city if they don't wish to work in the palace or the mines, where the pay is best. But most stay, glad to be employed and live comfortably."

For a moment, I said nothing as I watched a geyser erupt, spraying sparks across a field of grass. A fae appeared with a bucket and ran around putting out spot fires.

"You're telling me Arrow found you, *befriended* you, and abolished the Light Realm's slave trade in a matter of weeks? You can't expect me to believe that."

"Yes, Zali, he did. And I must tell you it was all for—"

I elbowed his ribs, cutting him off as the light breeze carried a raspy voice up the hill. "What have we here?" the voice mocked. "A human uprising in the Court of Fire and Flames?"

I looked over my shoulder and found Prince Bakhur and his pompous, shit-eating grin stalking toward us.

Releasing Zaret's hand, I wiped mine on my thigh and forced a smile. "Join us, Bakhur. We were just discussing what an asshole King Arrowyn is."

"My favorite topic." Bakhur turned to Zaret and snarled. "Leave, human. Do it fast if you know what's good for you."

Zaret rose without haste, strolling away as if he hadn't a care in the world. His casual arrogance reminded me of the Storm King, an obvious role model Zaret had been paying close attention to.

Flicking his cloak up, Bakhur sat beside me. "Father wouldn't like to hear of you fraternizing with the human."

"Why not? I'm human, too. I find it comforting to speak with my own kind."

"King Azarn doesn't care much for your comfort."

Nor did his son, I guessed.

Bakhur nodded at my mergelyn anklet. "I've heard many rumors about that device. A persistent one being that it allows Melaya to hear snippets of your conversations. Apparently, it's sporadic and unreliable, but if you gather with the human boy or members of the Storm Court again, your words may very well get back to us."

"You surprise me, Bakhur, admitting the Fire Court is afraid of a harmless conversation between friends."

"Nothing you do is harmless, Zali."

Unease surged through me. Could Melaya really spy on me through the mergelyn anklet? From now on, I needed to take the utmost care of what I said and to whom.

Planting my boots on the rock and hugging my knees to my chest, I released a heavy sigh. "Anyway, I'm tired of hearing *Melaya this* and *Melaya that*. No one speaks about his brother, Nukala, and yet your father seems very fond of him. What's his story?"

At the mention of Nukala, the Fire Prince's skin blanched white. "Nukala isn't spoken of because he's a bore. A useless, powerless fire mage."

"But, fortunately, a pretty one," I said, forcing a smile and wondering if Bakhur was telling the truth. Why would the king fawn over a weak, impotent mage? Unless the king was infatuated and besotted with Nukala, it didn't make sense.

As I got to my feet, Bakhur gripped my wrist, holding me in place. "Skip dinner in the hall tonight and attend my private bacchanal instead. You won't regret it, Zali. I can tell you tales about the Storm King that will take your breath away. You will consider me a mouse compared to the fae who caused the death of countless females over decades."

Arrow had only worn his crown for the past two years, so I was reasonably sure Bakhur had confused stories of King Darian for tales about his son.

"I'll think about it," I replied, then bid Bakhur goodbye and hurried off to find Zaret.

He knew things about Arrow that I didn't. Perhaps even how I came to be at the Fire Court. I needed to coax every detail from Grendal's son before I went mad wondering if the Storm King was a villain or, shock-horror, actually *my savior.*

Despite a thorough search of the town's three taverns, trading shops, and the common areas of the palace, I had no luck. The Storm Court party was nowhere to be found. However, the afternoon wasn't an entire waste, because I took the opportunity to test the limits of the mergelyn anklet.

It didn't take long to work out that if I tried to walk or run past Melaya's magical boundaries, I passed out cold. Even when I ventured waist deep in the churning sea below the cliffs, my mind went blank and I regained consciousness on the black-sand beach, as if an invisible forcefield had ejected me.

The same thing happened at the bottom of the fire geyser field, at the edge of the forest, and again when I scaled a section of the city wall, climbing the thick, overgrown vines like a ladder. I woke up on a table of chicken fillets, a winged butcher scowling down at me with his sharp talons flexed.

In need of a bath, I retreated to my room and tried to set aside feelings of despair. I'd discovered that escape from the Fire Court was nigh on impossible, so I attempted to distract myself from my hopeless situation by rifling through memories of home. I remembered precious times spent with my parents, my brother Van, but not Quin—the twin who had broken my heart and increased my trust issues tenfold.

And *never* Arrow. I did my best to pretend he hadn't been to Mydorian and helped me win back the crown from the usurper who'd held my birthright hostage.

I chased all images of the Storm King from my mind, replacing them with scenes of playing boardgames with Father or hunting with Mother, because if I let them in, I would need to ask myself a very difficult question.

Why would Arrowyn Ramiel do so much to help me only to later hand me over to another realm?

I quashed the thought before it took root in my mind, reminding myself that all fae were liars. They hated my species. And the Storm King was likely playing a long game to destroy me.

Why?

Because through me, he could control Mydorian and make a fortune from a legitimate gold trade in the Earth Realm, increasing his wealth and ultimate power in the other realms.

In my experience, greed trumped love nearly every single time.

And to believe it, all I had to do was convince myself Zaret had fabricated the changes made in Coridon since I was last there.

That would be easy.

If nothing else, I was skilled at sticking to my delusions if I thought they might protect me from future heartbreak.

Chapter 17

LEAF

While I dressed for dinner, I contemplated Bakhur's offer to attend his little party.

Although an evening of criticizing Arrow sounded tempting, scowling at my golden nemesis across a dining table would be an infinitely more satisfying experience than listening to Bakhur whine about him for hours on end.

So, certain I'd made the correct choice, at the bottom of the stairs that connected my tower to the rest of the palace, I turned left, making my way to the Great Hall instead of seeking out the Fire Prince and his spiteful friends.

During dinner, as usual, chaos reigned in the hall. The atmosphere was smoky and dark, the food spicy, and the music and laughter loud. The heat blasting from countless braziers and an enormous fireplace on a side wall raised constant beads of sweat on my brow. The fire courtiers liked things hot.

With Bakhur and his aunt, Marcella, absent, I sat at the high table between Estella and Azarn, Arrow on the Fire King's right, and Ruhh hovering by his side.

If the ghost princess hated Arrow as much as she claimed to, why did she address him in that sickly sweet voice and run her cold fingers through his hair so frequently? Grinding my teeth, I vowed not to look at them so I could enjoy my dinner without losing it.

As I ate my clay-pot stew of spiced root vegetables and apricots, I sipped wine and peppered the queen with questions about the Crystal Realm, her birthplace, doing my best to block out Ruhh and Arrow's conversation.

Estella answered my questions in a guarded manner, relaying very little useful information about her land, powers, or how she might help me escape. As she spoke, her expression was wary, as if she suspected I might suddenly announce what she had done in the Arena of Ashen Souls. And tell her husband who she really was—a queen who possessed more power than he could ever dream of having.

A queen who I hoped was still my ally.

After dinner, the king rose and strutted across the front of the dais to address his courtiers. "Tonight, a particularly pleasing event will take place," he told them. "For your entertainment, a traitorous orc will dance over a fire for as long as he is able to stay conscious."

I choked on a mouthful of wine.

Orion—it had to be.

My heart pounded erratically as my dinner curdled in my stomach and three guards entered the hall. Chains jangled as they dragged a hooded prisoner to the middle of the floor, where a small pyre was being erected. Melaya glided forward and worked fire magic into a rope that he used to tie Orion to a large pole above the fire.

"Don't worry, Zali," said Azarn. "This won't be the death of your friend. We have more... *interesting* plans for the orc."

I nodded at the Fire King as if I didn't give a shit about a one-eyed sailor who had recently risked his life to help me escape from the Light Realm. But nothing could have been further from the truth. I would spare no effort to find out where they held Orion captive. After tonight, I would do anything to see him released from his bonds.

Clearing my throat, I gently placed my wine cup on the table, knowing I couldn't witness Orion's torture without losing my stomach contents. I had to get out of the hall fast.

"May I be excused, Estella?" I asked. "I'm so tired and still haven't recovered from yesterday's fight with Arrowyn. Don't think I'm quite ready to view another *entertainment* yet." I put finger quotes around the word entertainment, and the queen smiled, pity simmering in her blue eyes.

"Of course, Zali. We must speak soon. I will call for you at an appropriate time."

As musicians played cheerful music, reminiscent of a jig, I kept my head down and left the hall, unable to bear the sight of Orion's suffering. All because of *me*.

Under the full moon's glow, I took the route that wound past the fire moat, desperate to calm the turmoil of emotions tumbling through me. Near the sea cliffs, a fresh breeze blew off the ocean, chasing Taln's sulfurous-sweet air toward the forest.

Crossing my arms, I took a deep breath. I'd often wondered what became of Orion after Captain Loligos and his men sold me to the Earth Realm soldiers. Now I knew. And I really wished I didn't.

When I'd met Orion briefly in the Port of Tears, back then, I'd been vulnerable, with no memories, no idea who I was, and he had treated me with such kindness and risked his life to help me.

And now, he would pay a terrible price for his bravery, simply because Ari had asked a favor of him.

I had to find a way to get Orion out of Taln, even if it meant I might never be free myself. I couldn't expect others to help me while I sat back basking in comfort. That would be unjust. Unfair. And I strove always to set an example for my people.

Friendship and loyalty were worth risking our lives over.

First, it was crucial I discovered where the fire fae kept their prisoners. Then I'd need help to form a plan from someone that knew Taln well. Ruhh would assist if I offered her something worthy in return, but since I'd failed to kill Arrow, I doubted she'd trust me again, which left Estella as my only option.

I was beginning to think the ghost girl wanted *me* dead instead of the Storm King so that nothing stood in the way of getting her bony hands on his impressive, but traitorous muscles. Hadn't she realized I was mostly over him?

As I climbed the stairs to the tower room, I checked my inner pocket, feeling the soft cloth that contained the orchid petals. I had seven left, and for me, their effect seemed to last about an hour, not nearly long enough to break an orc free from prison and get him safely out of the Fire Kingdom. I wondered if using two petals would increase the duration of invisibility.

Fueled by fury about Orion's plight, I performed my nightly exercises until my muscles shook and sweat coated my skin, then I took a bath, contemplating what Bakhur had told me about the mergelyn anklet.

Was it true Melaya could hear my conversations at times? Or was Bakhur trying to dissuade me from hatching plans with

Zaret? And if Melaya could eavesdrop, was there a way to tell when he was listening?

Even subtle magic was detectable if you paid attention to the right cues. So from now on, I'd be on high alert for the signs, such as the sudden tingling of extremities, ringing in my ears, crackling of my hair, or unexplained nausea.

I desperately needed to speak to Zaret again. He could explain everything that had happened in Coridon since I'd left. Fill me in on the details of how Arrow had supposedly reformed the city's slave trade, while betraying every fond memory I had of him and allowing the Sun Realm to capture me.

How had I ever let myself fall in love with a two-faced monster? A callous fae who thought nothing of tearing my heart to shreds?

I cleaned my teeth and brushed the long side of my hair, finger-combing the clipped side that grew longer every day, the whole time praying Melaya hadn't let Orion suffer too long in the hall.

Yawning as I peeled back the bedcovers, three loud raps sounded on the other side of the door, followed by a male's voice. *Arrow's* deep voice. "Princess, open up."

Dust. He *had* warned me he would visit tonight, but naively, I'd taken his words as a threat, an attempt to frighten me, nothing more.

"Wait a moment," I said, slipping on a robe, the silk cool against my bare arms and legs. As I opened the door, my jaw dropped.

Flanked by two burly Fire Court guards, Arrow held an unraveled parchment between two fingers, jostling it in front of me. I flicked a sneer at the scroll, and then an eyebrow up at him.

He flapped it under my nose. "It's a signed order from Azarn. You must read it."

"I'm not in the mood." I feigned another yawn and pushed against the door, but Arrow's boot shot out, keeping it open.

"Oh, should I come back at a more convenient time?" he asked in a sarcastic tone.

"Yes, please. And let me think when that might be..." I stroked my chin, as though considering my non-existent schedule. "How about *never*?"

One of the guards took charge of the parchment as the small party hustled inside my chamber, and Arrow stared at me as the bearded fae began to read out loud.

"By the order of King Azarn Thrusheel, Arrowyn Ramiel, ruler of the Light Realm, has been given leave to take life-sustaining blood from the veins of his marked Aldara, twice daily if he so wishes, until the king withdraws his permission."

With a broken shout, I leaped at Arrow, my fists swinging.

"Don't touch her," Arrow barked as the guards' weapons clattered behind us.

He caught me in his arms, tossed me on the bed, then used his bodyweight to hold me down.

I struggled like a wolf in a trap, but it was no use. He was too strong. Too ruthless.

"This isn't fair," I said, the closest I'd ever been to giving up as I thumped his chest armor with my fist. Swallowing a sob, I caught my breath. "I'm sick of being a pawn in the stupid games males play."

"Agreed," he said, his lips barely moving as confusion shuddered through me.

What did he mean by *agreed*?

He frowned down at me as our ragged breaths combined, our faces too close for comfort. The feather glyphs on his skin turned from dark crimson to gold. My pulse skyrocketed, the Aldara mark burning my flesh, and my bones melted like summer honey. Damn. I hated how his nearness affected me.

I turned my head, hoping he wouldn't notice my blown pupils, the tell-tale signs of desire blushing over my skin.

"Look at me," he rasped.

I shifted my head, but kept my gaze fixed on the erratic pulse at his throat.

"Leaf."

"That's not my name."

"*Zali*, then. Stop fighting. Why make this harder than it needs to be?"

"An easy question for an oppressor to ask. For the one subdued, the answer is clear—there is no other option than *making things harder*."

Silence hummed through the air, our rasped breathing the only sound in the room. What in the hells were the guards doing right now? Standing by, watching, and grinning? The humiliation was unbearable.

Arrow's thumb stroked down my neck, while his hardness pressed into my stomach. I heard him swallow, practically drooling while he prepared to bite me.

"Don't do this," I whispered. "Please."

"I've no choice," he growled softly as his fangs sank into my flesh, lips suckling the long muscle in my neck.

As he drew slowly on my vein, a cry of pain and ecstasy tore from my throat. "*Relax, little Leaf. I won't hurt you. Never hurt you. Promise.*"

What the fuck? I thought, as my body jerked in shock. Had he somehow spoken in my mind?

"I can hear you, reckless one. Guard your thoughts if you have any secrets you wish to keep from me. Concentrate on the blood flowing between us and focus only on what you wish me to hear."

"Which would be nothing. Why didn't you tell me we could do this?"

He groaned against my neck and gripped my chin roughly. *"It mostly only works during feeding. But I knew you'd hate it—the invasion. And because I care about you... I suppressed it."*

"That's rich, claiming to care about me now."

"I've never stopped. You, Zali, are my precious gem, my light, my fire, my earth, and ice."

He drew deeper on my vein, and I gasped, my hips bucking against his hard length.

"Hold still, human," he said out loud, "or your throat will be shredded."

The guards laughed, sounding thoroughly entertained.

My fingers twisted in Arrow's hair at the base of his neck, as though I would tug him away. But I didn't. I held him in place as if my life depended on it.

Closer.

Tighter.

Forever.

"You sold me to Taln," I thought carefully, focusing on each word so he would understand. *"You said you'd always come for me. You told me that more than once, Arrow. But you didn't come."*

"*Shh, I'm here now,*" he soothed. "*No more words. The ruse must be acted out. I have so much I wish to say to you and no time. No time at all.*"

"*Tell me one thing,*" I thought as he took a last sip, then licked my wound. "*Does your power work in Taln?*"

He gripped my neck tighter, as if he would strangle me, his fingers digging into my muscles. "*No, I'm afraid not. Your blood gives me strength. The small amount I took from you in the forest allowed me to use a very light glamour on Azarn to ensure he would agree to let me visit you. But no amount of blood will help me access storm magic through Melaya's block. But don't worry. I have a few ideas about how to get you out of Taln.*"

"*And they are?*"

"*A conversation for another day. Now get up and act like you hate me.*"

"*That shouldn't be difficult,*" I said as he pushed off the bed, leaving me shivering in his absence.

For the guards' benefit, I said aloud, "I'll always hate you for this, Arrowyn Ramiel."

Ignoring his grimace and the wave of dizziness that rushed over me, I slid off the bed, staggered to the closet, and pulled out my cloak. No, not *my* cloak. It was *his* cloak.

It had never truly been mine.

I dangled it from my finger as if it was a filthy rag. A broken promise. A withered heart.

"Take it," I said. "I never want to feel it on my skin again."

He blanched. "But it's yours." He stepped closer and dropped his voice to an urgent whisper. "Please."

"Take it, Storm King, or I'll throw it in the fire." He stared at the cloak, and I released my grip and let it drop on the floor.

The guards hissed in audible breaths. Purple flames crackled in the hearth. Outside, the rhythmic chirping of nearby crickets could be heard over the gentle crash of waves against the cliffs.

With a soft sigh, Arrow picked up the cloak and hung it on a hook by the door. Then his gaze flicked to the guards, indicating that what he was about to do was for them alone. By the time he looked back at me, his expression had turned to stone.

Storming forward, he backed me against the wall next to the window, the same way he'd done last night in his room. But this time, our rapt audience shifted their weight, weapons clinking in anticipation of violence.

Everyone in the realms had heard tales of the Storm King's ruthless nature, but I was finally beginning to grasp that the stories were wildly exaggerated.

"Talk to me like that again, human, and I'll show you exactly who's in control. Want me to fuck you in front of them?"

"You wouldn't dare," I spat out.

"Azarn gave me leave to do whatever I wanted with you. It would be no crime," he snarled back.

Was this still an act? It felt so real. The cruel prod of his body against mine. The furious steel flashing in his eyes. Only moments ago, he had declared his devotion, and now, he threatened violence and humiliation. Confusion spun through my mind. Could I trust him?

Without warning, warm lips crashed against mine, swallowing my muffled cry as he kissed me more cruelly than he'd ever done before. Instead of fear, hot flames engulfed me, licking at my core.

His teeth scraped, tongue stroked, and his fingers dug so firmly into my flesh I thought I'd pass out or spread my legs and beg him to plow into me and end the torment. Take me on that long, blissful ride to oblivion.

The kind of oblivion only *he* could give me.

Right now, the entire Fire Court could've been watching, and I would've willingly let him have me.

"Learn to behave," he growled, breaking the kiss and thudding my head against the wall, his fingers braced behind my skull to take the impact. "*I love you*," he mouthed, then pushed off the window frame and strode out of my room without a word.

Another shock of cold air rushed over me, and I swayed, dizzy and disoriented. What the fuck had just happened?

The guards smirked at me before following Arrow, slamming the door so hard the windowpanes shook from the force.

I slid down the wall until I hit the floor, covering my Aldara mark with my palm. The place where Arrow had bitten me pulsed with each beat of my heart—a slow, soothing rhythm, a stark contrast to the chaos whirling inside my mind.

I tried to sort through my racing thoughts, desperate to make sense of what had occurred.

Arrow had said... he said he *loved* me.

Or had I imagined that part?

I wracked my brain, wondering if he'd ever said those words to me before, part of me longing to believe it was true. Wanting to trust that he had always cared for me, had never stopped, just as he claimed.

I shook my head, dipping my face into the cradle of my hands. It would be a death sentence to believe him. To nurture hope, like a fledgling in a nest, waiting for its family to return before a wild storm set in.

Arrowyn Ramiel was a compulsive liar.

And life had taught me that, eventually, everyone betrayed me.

Arrow's attempt to regain my trust was nothing more than a part of his plan to maintain power over the gold, destroying me in the process—a future queen of the race he so despised.

Or was it?

When the guards' vision had been obscured, he'd touched me so tenderly, looked at me with such sweet longing that I'd believed him.

But now, I hardly knew what to think.

One thing I did know was that I'd wasted the opportunity to ask him where the Fire Court was likely to be holding Orion.

Tomorrow, I would find out for myself.

And in the meantime, I would try to make sense of every wonderful word that Arrow had said tonight—both aloud and through our bond.

Chapter 18

LEAF

"Zali, wait," Esen called out in the distance as I picked my way down a steep path in the rain, heading toward the sea.

Taln Palace loomed above like a giant black crow hunkered on a cluster of treacherous rocks, and behind me, Esen swiftly approached. Unlike me, who slipped and slid every few steps, her fae speed and grace allowed her to cover the difficult terrain with ease.

Plowing onward, I waved my hand over my shoulder in greeting, but didn't stop, determined to find the fire cave I'd seen from the cliffs when I was with Ruhh at the moat two nights ago.

"Where are you going in such a hurry?" Esen asked as she leaped off a rock wall to walk beside me.

This morning, the weather was wicked. Steady rain pelted the cliffs and churned the sea into wild, frothy waves that mirrored my agitated mood.

"Exploring. And I absolutely love starting the day getting drenched and whipped by a brutal sea breeze," I said, grimacing as I swept wet hair off my face. "It's very refreshing, don't you think?"

"No, not really." Esen laughed at the soaked state of me, then threw a ball of fire magic at my chest. It whooshed over me from head to toe, drying my hair and clothes in an instant and lashing them around my body.

"Nice," I said, straightening my tunic. "But tell me, do I have any hair left on my head to braid tonight?"

"Don't worry. Perfumed oil, a circlet, and a few ribbons do wonders for partly bald heads."

I patted my skull, finding my unruly brown mane mostly intact. "Not much point wasting your power to dry me off, Esen. The rain's not letting up any time soon."

"Sorry. I got carried away in the moment. Glad to see you're still alive," she said. "The whole Fire Court has heard about the Storm King's feedings. There are wagers you won't last the week before he drains you dry or fucks your weak body into a pile of broken bones."

"Charming," I said, guessing Arrow hoped the entire Sun Realm believed that and would, therefore, leave me alone for one of two possible reasons.

Option one: he had told the truth and was in Taln to help me.

Or two: he wanted the Fire Court to know he was the only fae allowed to toy with me.

The lost girl I had buried deep inside me preferred the first option. *She* hoped there was a sane explanation for why he'd sold me to Azarn and Bakhur. But the girl I'd become since—the one who killed her own brother after foolishly giving her heart to her fae owner, well... I just couldn't let myself trust him.

Not yet, anyway.

If it turned out that Azarn was the reason I was trapped in the Fire Kingdom, then Arrow would still need to do a whole lot of groveling to be forgiven for leaving me alone in Mydorian for so long. And, also, for being such a shitty letter writer.

I rubbed the Aldara mark on my neck. It seemed suspiciously convenient for Arrow that the bond that allowed us to converse in our minds only renewed while he drank my blood. He knew the act made me lose my mind and burn for him, which made me all the easier to manipulate.

Self-disgust filled me. How could I fall so effortlessly under his spell again?

I stumbled over a rock and grabbed Esen's arm to regain balance.

"It strikes me as odd that you claim to be glad I'm alive when you've tried to murder me at least once... that I know about. I thought you hated me and only cared about how fast you could gain the approval of whichever king you happened to be colluding with at the time."

"Perhaps I've seen the error of my ways." She jumped off a slab of rock onto the path below that zigzagged down the side of the cliff, then held her hand out and helped me leap down to join her.

Stopping for a moment, I checked if I could feel tendrils of Melaya's magic slithering over my skin. Finding nothing that indicated he might be listening in, I continued. "I'm searching for the fire cave hidden in these cliffs," I said, pondering if it was stupid to trust her with my mission. But if she ratted me out to Azarn, I'd just blame my curious nature. "Ruhh showed me the dust-damned thing the other night, but now it's disappeared. I can hear its fire sizzling in the rain, so it must be close by, but the paths I've tried so far just lead me in circles. Can you help me find it?"

She shot me a narrowed glance, then helped me navigate around a salt bush blocking the path, showing me how to cling to its trunk and swing out over the tumultuous sea far below. I followed her method while trying to erase the image of my body smashed to gory pieces on the rocks.

When we were safely on the path again, she asked, "Why do you wish to visit the cave so badly? There's a reason why it's off limits to the likes of you."

"I'm curious. I only want a quick look inside."

She laughed. "You might regret your curiosity. It's dangerous in there, and once you've seen something horrible, it can't be unseen and will haunt you every time you close your eyes."

I shook my head. Fae were so dramatic. "Sounds like you're speaking from experience, Esen."

A salty wind whipped my hair over my eyes for the hundredth time today, the rain still pouring and slowing our progress as we wound down the side of the cliff.

About a third of the way down, Esen put her palm out to stop me. "Okay. We're here."

Heart hammering, I scanned the black cliffs and a clutch of emerald-green birds roosting in a craggy nook. "I don't see anything."

Esen smirked. "Watch closely." She muttered a spell, and a golden phoenix-shaped sigil appeared in midair. When it dissipated and the smoky haze cleared, the mouth of a large cave was revealed, its interior shielded by a wall of fire.

"Why was I able to see it glowing from the cliff top the other night?"

"Because you were with Ruhh, and she *wanted* you to see it, which tells me that she's up to something. Don't be drawn into the ghost girl's plots. She's trouble."

"I'm always careful around her." I hiked an eyebrow toward the cave. "Lead the way."

"You don't look too worried," Esen said.

"Perhaps if you told me what's in there, then I might be."

She laughed, tucking wet hair behind her pointed ear. "After you," she said as she swept her hand out in a graceful arc, as if guiding me into a lavish ball.

Taking a long breath, I walked through the wall of fire. Although the sound of the flames crackled ferociously at my ears, they felt like a silken veil brushing my limbs as I entered the cave.

For a moment, I stood blinking in total darkness. Then Esen waved a hand, her magic igniting torches that cast orange light throughout a small cave, its walls charred from fires that looked like they'd burned for centuries so thick was the scarring.

As Esen strode toward the rear wall, a passage became visible. "Come on. We don't want to be here any longer than necessary. If we're found... it wouldn't go well for either of us, and we don't want that. Understand?"

"Yes," I said, my heart rate accelerating and a wave of dizziness engulfing me. This could be a trap. Esen might lock me in here forever or slit my throat or even...

Relax, I told myself. *Death is but another journey. Be brave. Mydorian blood will never fail.*

And if mine did, then surely the Zareen would agree to work with a male of my line in my stead. My brother Van was strong-willed, good-hearted, and I knew he'd make a wonderful ruler if needed.

I followed Esen through a rocky tunnel that opened into a vast cavern somewhere in the heart of the cliff. It was lit by a pyre of green flames burning inside a small pit in the middle of the limestone floor.

Veins of magic pulsed along intricate fire symbols etched into the walls. Dark Unseelie magic. The kind my parents had taught me to stay away from.

My gaze tracked upward, my breath rushing out of me when I saw what—or rather *who*—dangled above the fire pit.

Orion.

His limbs were tied to poles of Xanthanian metal, black and glittering like stars in a clear sky and shaped into a large inverted triangle. A lattice of enchanted flames made a circle of bars around him, forming a prison of dancing fire. Shadows flickered over his body, distorting his slackened face into a mask of horror. His white tusks and bushy beard had been cut off, his gray skin yellowing like sun-bleached paper.

The suffering the orc endured was sickeningly apparent. I swallowed bile, my entire body shaking. I wanted to run from the cave and scrub its memory from my brain. At the same time, I wanted to stand here forever, so Orion's sacrifice would be carved into my heart for all time.

With every fiber of my being, I prayed he wouldn't become a martyr for those who sought peace in the Five Realms. Orion deserved to live. To thrive. I just had to figure out how to get him down from there.

Hot embers floated through the shimmering, sour-smelling air, and no matter how many deep breaths I took, I couldn't seem to draw enough oxygen in.

"They're burning him alive," I finally rasped.

"Not quite. Orc, wake up," commanded Esen, her expression full of pity, despite her harsh words.

A moan rumbled from Orion's chest, then he slowly raised his head, his single, red-rimmed amber eye fixing on me. Another moan split his lips—the sight of me adding to his anguish.

"Leaf," he croaked. "Go... Please. I beg you."

Bathed in the glow of shifting green and black patterns, he looked like an ancient fire god sentenced to burn forever in the hell realms, his agony a lesson for any fae who longed to revolt against Azarn.

Wiping tears from my cheeks, I stepped closer. Orion didn't scream or sob, but the sweat dripping from his skin told the tale of his pain.

"Get him down," I said, lunging at Esen and wrapping my hands around her throat. "Right now. Or I'll kill you."

"Impossible," she said mildly, allowing me to back her against the wall. "You're human and no match for my fire magic. One snap of my fingers and you'd be dead, unable to help the orc. I suggest you calm yourself, Zali. Your temper has only ever increased your troubles."

"You sound like Arrow again," I said, the words rushing out before my brain caught up to my mouth. I released Esen and turned back to the orc. "Can you speak, Orion? Give me your knife Esen. Please, let's cut him down."

As I began to step over the first line of flames, Orion groaned. Esen grabbed my arm and dragged me backward. "Idiot. Those flames will kill anyone who breaches them."

Frustration surged inside me. "Then how in the dust will we get him down?"

"We can't. You need a member of Azarn's family or Melaya to break the spell and dissolve the prison of flames. There's nothing you can do for him. The Sentura Pyre is a torture meant to endure forever. The flames themselves sustain the barest semblance of life, no water or food required, so that the victim will experience pain for as long as possible."

"That's vile." I raised my palms in a plea of guilt. "Orion, I'm so sorry. This is *my* fault. Tell me how to help. I'll find a way to free you, no matter the cost. I promise."

He shook his head, emitting a dry moan through cracked lips.

"Your family... can I help them? You once mentioned your mother who lived under a mountain. Please, Orion, tell me how to find her."

Drops of sweat sizzled in the flames as his chin slumped onto his chest.

Esen walked toward the exit. "Come, Zali. You've got what you wanted. Now you know what's inside the fire cave."

"I'll be back," I told Orion, swallowing sobs, my head aching with impotent fury. "Don't doubt it."

As we neared the passage that would lead us out of this dust-forsaken place, Orion coughed, then cleared his throat. "Leaf... Only fire fae can... open this..." His words trailed off, his eyes rolling back in his head.

"Only fire fae can open what?" I asked.

"*This cave*," he hissed.

Esen grabbed my arm, dragging me into the passage, Orion's eerie whisper echoing behind us.

What did he mean by only fire fae could open the cave?

Only fire fae could open the—

"*Esen*," I barked out as the truth sank in. "What in the fire-fucked dust have you done? You're one of *them* now?"

Chapter 19

LEAF

Outside the cave, rain slashed at our faces, our hair tangling together as I pulled her close.

"How?" I yelled over the roar of the wind. "What did you do, Esen?"

Her cheeks flushed red, and she gave a faint laugh. "I've always been one of them. I was *born* a fire fae."

"What?" In shock, I spun on my heel and started walking up the path. I stumbled on a slab of slippery rock and gripped Esen's arm for support. "That's not possible. I've seen you wield storm magic."

"King Azarn planted me at the Storm Court as a spy. I only recently found out. Apparently, it took his mages centuries to find a child whose power was strong enough to be subdued then transformed into storm magic. But they did it. They found me. Killed my family and dumped me at the gates of Coridon."

Pity and horror churned through my stomach. At such a young age, Esen had been used, abused, and twisted into a servant of the Fire King's greed. On some level, she must have felt warped, wrong, her true essence incompatible with the lightning magic running through her veins.

A lot of things about her made sense now, especially her bitter personality. As was the way with most hate-filled beings, she'd been damaged at a formative time and had suffered greatly.

"But why didn't the fae of Coridon notice something was amiss? I mean Arrow's father must have been—"

"Melaya's ability to block and repress power is formidable." Watching me warily, she heaved a sigh, then grinned. "Come on. Let's keep walking before we drown. I'll answer all your annoying questions when we arrive at the beach."

"In this rain?" My boots crunched and slipped over stones as we started down the hill. "Can't I interrogate you in comfort by the fire in my chamber?" As soon as I said the word fire, my heart clenched, and the image of Orion hanging over the Sentura Pyre assaulted me. His hollow, twisted features. The sweat coating his leathery skin. So much agony. And all because of me.

"I'd prefer to do it out here," said Esen. "Where the sound of the waves will ensure no one can eavesdrop."

I tuned into my body, searching for any strange sensations. "Melaya's not listening in, Esen. I feel no signs of another being's magical interference. In fact, since I was given the anklet, I'm fairly certain that I never have."

"Good. But I still prefer to be outside, where the wind and rain will hide my tears."

Shocked, I shot her a glance. With her tough exterior, it was easy to assume Esen didn't have any feelings. But clearly, I'd been wrong.

Nearly at the beach, I pointed up the hill. "It would be better if we headed back to the palace. I need to find Estella and—"

She cut me off with a snarl. "Do *not* tell the queen I took you into that cave. Please, Zali. It will be the death of me."

"Who should I speak to, then? Who can help me free Orion?"

"No one," she said, jumping off a flat boulder onto black sand and gesturing for me to follow. "No one can help you do that."

Wrong answer. Someone had to be willing to help. If there was no other choice, I'd even ask Arrow, which would test his much-professed loyalty and clarify if he was indeed a liar. A matter on which I remained uncertain.

Not a single gull or sea eagle swooped through the slate-gray sky looming over us. Esen's sobs were audible above the crash of waves and the sizzle of raindrops hitting nearby rocks. My heart broke for her, and I longed to gather her in a tight hug and offer comfort.

With my face upturned and arms spread wide, I spun on the sand, sucking cool air deep into my lungs to clear the horror of the cave from my mind. I stopped turning, my heart filled with compassion, as I took Esen's hand.

"Did you suspect you were different to the Light Realm fae?" I asked.

The leather armor covering her chest creaked as she heaved a sigh, her black and red cloak whipping around her body. "No. They wiped my memories when they dumped me at Coridon, a bit like what happened to you, Zali. Our stories are quite similar."

I nodded and pressed my palm to her cheek, wet with rain and tears. "We *are* alike, Esen. We're not enemies. Not if we choose to be friends."

She smiled through her tears. "You're right in a way. As a child, I *did* feel wrong inside. Somehow, I knew that I was different, unworthy of the storm fae's love. Anger flowed through my veins, sustaining me, and I made myself hate everyone except Ildri and Stormur, my foster parents. I loved my brother, Raiden, too. And I foolishly adored Arrow in the exact way one shouldn't love a male like him. I hated you because from the moment he first saw you, something about you called to his damaged heart. I longed for him to look at *me* that way. I thought if I got rid of you, one day, he would."

I squeezed her shoulder. "Esen..."

"Don't pity me. Please... anything but that."

I forced sorrow from my features, then stepped away, no longer offering comfort, since it was the last thing she wanted.

"While Arrow was in Mydorian helping you kill your brother, Azarn sent a messenger to Coridon who revealed my true identity. The Fire King asked for a meeting, and filled with hate for Arrow, the fae that had put you—a human—above me, I did as Azarn asked. And then I learned the horrible truth about what they'd put me through to transform my fire magic into lightning. Instead of feeling used, I felt wanted, needed, as though I'd finally found my place. My purpose."

"But something changed," I guessed. "What was it?"

"I saw how the fire fae used you, Zali, as if you were nothing. Chattel to be bartered. Manipulated. Imprisoned and controlled. Jealousy stopped me from pitying you when you experienced the same treatment in Coridon. But your ancestor married the great Zareen. Her blood flows in your veins, and yet Azarn has no respect for that. No respect for *you*, even though your magical bloodline demands it. And I finally realized he only cared about what I could do to help him build power and wealth. I meant nothing to him. I never had."

"I understand. Men like Azarn will always underestimate us, but if we unite and stand together, we can wrest the power back from them. Will you help me, Esen? If you do, I'll give you a position you deserve. A high counselor to the Queen of Mydorian perhaps. And if that role doesn't suit you, then I'll find another that does."

For the longest time, she said nothing, but at least her crying had ceased. The rain continued to pelt down, our clothes hanging like wet sacks, stuck to our bodies.

Finally, Esen smiled. "I want to be your ally. I really do. But more than anything, Zali, I want to be your friend."

With a gust of delighted laughter, I lurched forward and wrapped my arms around her stiff frame, hugging her tightly. She bore the affection for the span of a few heartbeats, then wriggled out of my arms.

"We must go," Esen said. "I need to find Arrow and beg his forgiveness. Enlist his help as best I can while Melaya's magic ties my tongue in knots."

As we trekked up the mountainside, I pondered her words, a new-found hope brimming in my heart. If Esen planned to seek Arrow's help, then she must believe that his cozying up to the Fire King since he'd arrived in Taln was just an act. Nothing more.

"Tell me the truth," I said as we neared the fire moat. "Did Arrow betray me? Or did Azarn trick me into believing so?"

Blue hair curtained her face as she shook her head. "I can't speak about that. Melaya has cursed my speech so that I can't disclose Sun Realm plans that directly concern Arrow. Even if there was a way to break the spell and tell you, it would be the end of me. A long and *painful* end. But I advise you to think carefully about what I *did* tell you and everything you've seen since your capture."

"I will," I said, my heart turning somersaults against my ribs, because her words *almost* seemed to confirm that Arrow was on my side.

Giddy with hope, I grinned at Esen as we rounded the south wall, then climbed the steps into the main foyer of the palace. "Your magic, storm and fire combined, must be incredible when unleashed."

"One day, I'll show you." She flashed a smile. "I'm no match for Melaya... but I will be quite the asset in Mydorian. Azarn's soldiers have a training session I must attend. Go now and spend time with the royal family. Appear meek and mild—if you have it in you—and watch *everything* like a sea hawk."

Hurrying through the palace, I wondered who else knew about Esen's astonishing revelation. Did Arrow or Raiden realize that she'd been born a fire fae—*here*—at Taln?

Esen and I were so similar. Our memories and pasts had been wiped, stolen from us by Azarn and Quin, who had used us for their own twisted means, and when we'd served our purposes, discarded us like foul-smelling shit they had trodden in.

United, we would make men like them pay. Together, we could fuck them up and make them sorry they had ever underestimated us.

For the first time since arriving in Taln, I felt a weight lift off my shoulders.

Now, I had Esen as a friend and ally.

And possibly Arrow, too.

The part of me still hopelessly, foolishly in love with him was busy swooning and performing a victory dance inside my head as I headed toward the Great Hall, hoping to find Azarn and his family on the dais, eating lunch.

As I marched along the shape-shifting passages, I kept my gaze fixed ahead, away from the endless mirrors lining the walls. Today, their dark surfaces reflected images of horned fire fae that spat a tar-like substance at anyone who made the mistake of glancing at them.

Disorientated and doubting my ability to locate the hall, I rounded a corner and came across Ruhh hovering like a ghoul at my eye level.

"Shit," I said wittily, leaping backward to stop myself passing through her translucent body, which I'd learned from experience was a terrible feeling for both of us. "Could you please stop being such a... a ghost and scaring the life out of me at inconvenient times?"

"Wish I could," she replied, her raspy laugh raising hairs along my spine. "How have you been occupying yourself this morning, human who was unable to achieve the simple mission of killing her ex-lover?"

"Simple? Ruhh, I tried to kill Arrow. *Twice*. The other night, I made it into his bedchamber, but he knew I was there the second I entered. And why didn't you tell me that fae can only be killed by a knife to the *heart*, not the chest, or throat, or the dust-damned stomach."

"That isn't true of all fae—only the kings and queens."

"Okay. That's confusing but useful information. Where's your family?" I asked. "Since I'm soon to marry your nephew, I should probably get to know them better."

"Eating lunch in the fire conservatory. I will kindly show you the way."

I dipped a mock bow. "Oh, yes, you're a translucent beacon of benevolence."

"*Indeed* I am kind today. Not that you deserve such courtesy. Fortunately for you, your motivations interest me. I'll take you to the conservatory via the route that passes by the stables so you may see Luna briefly. Since the mergelyn anklet has given you freedom to move about the city, I've watched you visit your horse, and I like it best when you ride her through the fire gardens. I keep hoping she might stumble onto a geyser."

I rolled my eyes. "Charming."

"I do my best," she said with a grin, before zooming along the corridor, forcing me to sprint after her like we were children playing a game of tag.

Chapter 20

LEAF

R uhh led me to a secluded corner of town, where the tower-like structure of the fire conservatory rose high above the surrounding pine forest. Crafted entirely from vibrant stained glass, its gleaming spire speared the sky and seemed to go on forever.

As I followed Ruhh through the entrance, my mouth fell open in awe at the building's dark beauty.

While the weather had improved and sunlight peeked through the clouds, not a single ray shone inside the conservatory. Instead, magical flames danced along a channel beneath the windows, casting an eerie glow over the entire space. Shadows slinked across the silver-tiled floor, while vibrant red and orange hues from the stained glass adorned the lush foliage sprawling over most surfaces.

"How do the plants grow without sunlight?" I asked Ruhh.

"Magic, silly." She cackled and sailed off to hover behind the royal family, perched on scrolled silver chairs arranged behind a long black table so polished that it reflected their figures upon its surface.

Carefully navigating around streams of magical substances that flowed along the floor, some channels coursing with water, others with fire, I moved toward the high table until I stood in front of the Fire Prince.

"Hello, *Zali*. Why don't you join us?" said Bakhur, patting his lap. "I've saved you a seat."

Azarn ignored me, focusing on his meal. Estella shook her head slightly, and Marcella dropped her fork with a loud clang as if shocked by my arrival.

"There is a spare place beside me, human," the king's sister said. "Come and tell me all about your time in Coridon."

Coridon.

I stifled a groan of longing.

The Storm Court was a golden, light-filled paradise compared to the smelly hellhole that was Taln. In truth, I preferred Arrow's city a million times over the Sun Realm capitol, an opinion best not shared with Marcella.

"Call me by my name instead of human and I'll gladly sit with you," I said, pasting on a perky smile.

"Zali, please join me," she replied with a gracious nod and an equally fake smile.

As I took a seat at the end of the table, Ruhh zipped over and floated above my right shoulder, ghostly wisps of her dress caressing my skin.

"Sister," Marcella said, curling strands of long, red hair around her finger. "Let Zali and I speak in private. Go talk to Estella. She and her maidens will soon begin planning Bakhur's wedding to the mortal. Perhaps you can share your dreams for the ceremony you would have had if the Storm King had been gracious enough to accept father's offer for your hand."

Ruhh let loose a shriek of fury, then disappeared, a trail of green dust floating through the conservatory's arched doorway in her wake.

Marcella shrugged, her lips twisting cruelly. "It is quite difficult to get Ruhh to *stop* speaking about her fabled wedding to King Arrowyn. Strange she had no desire to lecture Estella about it *now*."

"Quite strange," I lied.

Marcella had made it clear she enjoyed torturing her poor deceased sister, and sympathy for Ruhh surged through me.

She poured wine into an obsidian goblet, then passed it to me.

"What happened to the orc that was dragged before the court last night?" I asked, even though I already knew the sickening answer.

"The one who helped you escape Coridon?" She waved her hand dismissively. "He is in prison, of course."

"Will he be killed? Or released after serving his sentence?"

"Neither." She reclined slightly as a servant dressed in a regal crimson coat, which concealed the top of his goat-like legs, deposited two crystal bowls of spun sugar and cream on the table in front of her.

"I see you have a good appetite," I teased.

A russet eyebrow rose. "One of them is for you, wise mouth."

"Wise mouth? I assume that's a high compliment in the Sun Realm," I said, scooping the dessert into my mouth while trying not to moan. The flavors were to die for. Not literally, I hoped, wondering if they'd dare to poison me.

"Why must your king punish a mere sailor so severely?"

"A mere sailor?" Marcella repeated, spitting flecks of cream on my tunic. "Helping *you* escape from Coridon without Azarn's permission was treason, and those who commit such acts don't fare well in the Sun Realm. How do the people of Dirt and Stone treat their betrayers?"

"Dust and Stone," I corrected as I leaned close to her ear. "Surely you remember my brother Quin's fate."

"But Quin Omala wasn't a traitor. He worked in partnership with *my* brother, the King of Fire and Flames."

"Which still made him a traitor to *his* queen, and to refresh your memory, that's *me*."

"Perhaps. But as yet, you wear no crown." She nodded toward my feet. "And instead, an impossible-to-remove mergelyn anklet."

I bristled at the mention of the stupid device chaffing my skin. I had to find a way to get the dust-damned thing off. Even the thought of it monitoring my every move drove me mad.

"And before long, I'll be married to your nephew, Bakhur. Then I'll be a princess *and* a queen."

"But *still* wearing Melaya's marvelous device," she whispered across my cheek.

"True." I smiled sweetly. "Any chance you'd like to share some tips on how to remove it?"

Marcella laughed. "I find you rather tolerable, Zali. For a powerless mortal, you have surprising courage."

I almost shot my mouth off and reminded her I had reaver blood. Thankfully, I didn't. It was best if Marcella thought of me as weak and helpless. It served my purpose, which was to get Orion out of that terrible cave and as far away from Taln as soon as possible.

I had no idea how I would achieve it, but I was certain Estella and Esen could help. And Arrow. I was beginning to think he might be handy to have around, too.

"Where's the Storm King hiding?" I said, licking my spoon.

"Ask Ruhh. She's always following him around. But Nukala tells me the Storm Court party can often be found at the Roundwood Tavern. It's flooded with sunlight and is close to the portal between our realms, so you can understand their attraction."

"Oh? Do you think they're planning on leaving soon?"

She shook her head. "Not by that route. They gained entrance to the town via the portal, but Melaya has since warded it against their exit. They'll have to ride out of Taln. Or fly, in Arrowyn's case."

"And they must already know this, or you wouldn't have told me, am I right?"

"Precisely," she agreed.

"Why doesn't Melaya overthrow your brother? He appears to hold all the power."

"Not everything is as it seems, Zali," she replied, her gaze traveling along the table until it landed on the king.

"And Nukala? He doesn't do much except fawn over Azarn. Is his sole function to entertain the king and spy on Arrow's party?"

She crunched a piece of twisted candy between her teeth. "As I said, not everyone is as they first seem."

"Every*thing*," I corrected. "You said not every*thing* was as it seems, not everyone."

"No wonder you drove Arrowyn insane," she said with a huff. "You're a stickler for details."

I scanned the table. Bakhur and his father were deep in conversation, their dark heads bowed together. Ruhh had returned and performed a ghastly dance for Estella, her mottled bones highlighted red by the stained glass and flickering flames as she spun, her mouth set in a distorted grimace that may very well have signaled pleasure.

"Bakhur doesn't seem very interested in me," I said to Marcella, feigning disappointment.

"He's a prince. His ego requires stroking. He invited you to eat with him, and you rejected his offer. You should seek him out more often. Enjoy his company."

Marcella was right. Despite the impossibility of relishing time spent with Bakhur, I needed to appear as though I might make a biddable wife. Earn his trust, so I could one day exploit it.

Smoothing my braid over my shoulder, I stood up, smiling at Marcella before strolling behind the row of seats and stopping at Bakhur's side.

"The dessert was delicious," I said for want of a better opener.

His head jolted up, gold eyes fixing on me with malicious interest. "Ah, my future bride has returned. Tell me, if I asked nicely, would you sit on my lap now that the sugar has sweetened your temperament?"

It took all my strength not to roll my eyes so hard they'd fall out of my head. "Thank you, but I've been sitting too long and prefer to stand. Bakhur, no one has spoken to me about our marriage arrangements. I presume it's still going ahead. We... really are betrothed?"

"Yes, of course." Bakhur sighed. "Now you're boring me, human." He waved his hand, and the low flames that licked along the conservatory walls burst into motion, leaping high and forming seven fiery bodies, three times larger than a tall fae.

I watched in horror as they spun toward the table in an explosion of sparks and embers.

"How do you like my fire tanourans?" asked Bakhur.

The creatures writhed and twirled to the rhythmic whoosh and crackle of their own movements, black eyes staring blankly ahead. Ruhh laughed, clapping her hands in delight. But I couldn't stop myself from flinching every time the tanourans' arms reached toward me.

I cleared my throat. "They're very... *warming.*"

He scoffed, then flicked his fingers at me, a dismissive gesture if ever I'd seen one. "Go speak to Mother about the wedding. The arrangements have nothing to do with me."

"I will. When is your next private party? I'd love to attend, since I missed the last one." Lowering my voice, I whispered in his ear, "I look forward to getting to know you in a more relaxed environment."

Beside us, King Azarn snorted. "I'm sure my son will enjoy *your* presence, Princess. But Bakhur's company is something you must surely learn to *endure.*"

"I will do my best." I bowed my head and started toward the queen, who sat still and composed, as if deep in meditation.

"Queen Estella," I said, placing a hand on her shoulder. "Can we speak about the wedding?"

She stared ahead, her iridescent, indigo-and-black gown sparkling with stars that moved like they floated on water, the material alive with magic.

"Don't disturb her," Marcella called out. "The queen is communing with her family from the Star Court. She reacts with aggression when startled."

Withdrawing my hand slowly, I said, "Thank you for the warning, Marcella. Please tell the queen I would like to meet with her to discuss the wedding as soon as it is convenient."

I dipped a flustered curtsy and did my best not to run as I marched toward the exit while the fire dancers whirled around me, embers falling on my clothes and the smell of burned cloth assaulting my nose.

Esen had joined the two soldiers guarding the door outside the conservatory, and she pushed off the wall as soon as she saw me. "Come, Zali," she said, "I'll make sure you find your way back to the tower."

"I don't need hel—"

She silenced me with a glare, and I muttered something nonsensical about the conservatory disorientating me, which wasn't entirely a lie.

"Arrow will come to your room as soon as he can, probably during dinnertime," she hissed. "I implore you to *listen* to him for once."

My heart exploded in my chest. "Did you tell him what the fire fae did to—"

"Sh..." She cut me off for the second time with a glance at my mergelyn anklet. "As per King Azarn's order, you must make ready to help the Storm King heal. In the meantime, speak no more to me, Princess of Dust. Your grating voice exhausts me."

"Likewise," I murmured, smothering a laugh with my fingers.

The walk back to the tower was solemn, the silence broken only by the sound of our footfalls and breathing as we climbed the stairs to my chamber.

At the door, I turned and touched her arm. "Would you like to come in? If you enjoy books, perhaps I can read to you. Or we could just... train together. Might be fun."

Pressing her finger to her lip, she shook her head. "Just in case," she mouthed, dropping her gaze to my ankle again, a look of genuine disappointment on her face.

That damn stupid anklet. It was more than possible that Melaya couldn't eavesdrop through it and Bakhur had only said so just to stop me from scheming with my friends. But Esen was right. It wouldn't be wise to say too much just in case.

After an hour of exercise, I bathed, dressed in a simple silk gown, and then took a book of rather gruesome murder poetry over to the window seat. As the sun set, gulls and fire hawks swooped through a gold-tinged sky, hunting for their dinner in the last of the daylight.

Instead of reading, I stared over the cliffs toward the sea, thinking about Arrow.

It was getting harder to believe that he had betrayed me. When I put it all together, the sequence of events, everything he had said and done, his innocence was the only thing that made sense.

So, perhaps he did care about me, and all was right in the realms, after all.

When my eyes grew heavy and I entertained the idea of taking a quick nap before dinner, a fist pounded on the door three times. Then I heard a deep, rumbling voice.

The Storm King had come to visit his Aldara.

"As promised," he said as the latch turned, "I'm here to feed from you, *Princess* Zali."

Arrow and the same two guards from last night entered my chamber, their windswept hair and cloaks carrying the scent of woodsmoke and brine.

"Oh, you came," I said, meeting the intense gaze of the fae who had once enslaved me. I forced my lips into a sneer. "I was beginning to think you'd lost your nerve."

Chapter 29

ARROW

L ost my nerve?

Truly my Aldara was the realm's biggest shit stirrer. The fury in her green eyes hit me with the power of a thousand lightning bolts, causing shock waves to radiate through my body.

She fucking hated that I could just stroll into her room without consent and do anything I liked to her. Which was understandable.

But she probably hated *me* with a fiery passion because she believed I held her captive against her will. *Again*. But nothing could be further from the truth. Convincing Azarn to allow the feedings was the only way I could get close to her and strengthen the Aldara bond. To protect her.

And fuck her misplaced scorn. I was Leaf's hero, not the villain in her story, and I wouldn't stop trying to prove it until my dying breath.

Sitting in the window seat, she gazed dreamily at the sunset as if I wasn't there, chin on her knees, hugging them tightly against her chest. The guards took their places on either side of the door, their armor creaking and clanking, but Leaf didn't turn around.

"*Look at me*," I said in her mind.

"Go away, Arrow. I'm not in the mood," she said, staring out of the window.

Pain lanced my shoulder blades as my wings manifested, black and purple feathers flaring at the sides of my vision. I stalked forward, grabbed the book she clutched, and threw it across the room.

Anger blazed in her eyes.

"Get up," I growled for the guards' benefit.

"Now you're abusing books?" she said. "What did Poems for a Perfect Murder ever do to you?"

"*Stole your attention from me*," I replied in her mind.

Her eyes flared in shock. "*How can we speak through the bond when you haven't taken my blood yet?*"

"*It's still strong after last night's feeding.*"

Firelight danced over her face, and her gaze softened as it trailed over my wings, my feathers shivering in delicious response. She bit the corner of her smile, hiding it from the guards by rubbing her face.

Interesting. Perhaps her anger was an act, too.

"I told you to get up." I held my hand out, which she ignored before jolting to her feet, her cheeks glowing red.

"*My anger is for the guards,*" I said in her mind. "*Never you. Ignore everything I say out loud. The truth will be whispered through our bond. Listen closely to every word. To my every plea. I beg of you, Leaf. Let my heart speak to yours.*"

The feather glyph on her throat pulsed as she edged backward toward the wall beside the bed, her breath ragged and uneven.

"I'm frightened," she whispered, covering her neck with a shaking hand.

"An appropriate response," I said aloud, prowling forward before speaking in her mind again. "*My Aldara fears nothing.*"

Bracing my palms against the wall on either side of her head, I dropped my face close to hers. "Show your throat, human, or I'll rip it open without care for scarring."

I dared to meet her gaze and found a tempest of green staring back at me. My eyes dropped to her laboring chest, then to the peaked, rosy buds visible through the silky material of her gown. With one hand, I pushed her head to the side as my other palm drifted over her stomach, then up to cup her breast. A groan rumbled in my chest as my thumb skated over her nipple.

"*Arrow,*" her bond voice whispered, the needy sound making my cock twitch in response.

Lust racing through my blood, I kissed her neck in the exact way I wanted to worship her lips, but dared not in front of Azarn's men.

"*Nothing tastes as good as your skin,*" I said, shoving against her roughly, making her wince. "*Sorry. Sorry, my love. My queen. Most precious Aldara. They must believe I despise you.*"

At my words, her body melted against mine, her limbs softening as her fingers twisted into the loose shirt I wore unbuttoned around my chest plate of gold feathers.

I nipped her earlobe, and she moaned aloud.

"*For gold's sake, Leaf. Control your reactions in front of Azarn's mutts.*"

The bond cord connecting our hearts vibrated harder. "*I can't,*" she replied.

"*Fuck, I want to be inside you so badly.*"

"Do it," she whispered out loud.

"Such a risk taker. You'll be the death of me." I turned back to the guards. "Get out," I growled.

The stupidest one straightened his spine. "By order of King Azarn we must remain with you at all times during the Aldara feedings."

"Fine. Stay and watch me fuck the human if you don't mind being scorched by lightning. Your mage's blocking magic cannot dampen the bond's ancient power. Be warned, you won't enjoy what it does to your breeding organs. If you've a collective brain in your heads, get out, and don't come back until I call you."

The fire soldiers scurried from the room, all color leeched from their skin, reminding me of youths pissing themselves on the field before their first battle.

Leaf's arms wound around my neck, and then she tugged my head down, breathing a sigh into my mouth. "First, make me forget. Then help me remember everything, Arrow. Each sweet word you ever said to me."

Brushing my nose against hers, I laughed. "Which do you want most? To forget or remember?" I teased.

"Both. I want everything you can give me, as long as the fire guards won't hear us."

I stared into Leaf's lust-glazed eyes, drowning in forest green, the color of her home, and thumbed her lips apart, revealing the beloved gap in her front teeth. Then I trailed my finger over her Aldara mark, sparkling like molten gold on her throat.

"I'd wager five bags of gold feathers that in the hopes of keeping their cocks in working order, they're standing guard halfway down the tower steps."

"I believe you're right." Her laugh ghosted over my lips. "Hurry up and kiss me, you idiot. We don't have much time."

"You've changed your mind? Now you just want to be kissed?"

She slapped my shoulder. "You're enjoying having me at your mercy."

I grinned shamelessly. "I can't deny it."

"Control still makes you hot."

"Yes, always," I whispered against her skin as I turned her away and pressed her forearms against the wall. With feverish movements, I began unfastening the buttons that notched her spine.

She wriggled, trying to turn around. "Please, Arrow. Not my back."

I froze. "Why not? What's wrong?"

"Nothing. Please... just..."

I loosened my grip, allowing her to turn around. She smiled, her hand snaking down my stomach before pressing lightly against where I ached the most.

Clicking my tongue, I gripped her wrist. "Distractions won't work. *Show* me what you're trying to hide, or I swear I'll lose control and betray my cover. I'll take those two fucking guards out there, and I will—"

"All right. Calm down. It's nothing," she insisted, facing the wall again and leaning her cheek on the cool stone with a sigh.

The light in her chamber was dim, the sky outside dark, and only purple-and-red flames flickered from the hearth, illuminating the room and my Aldara's skin.

Confused, but undeterred, I kissed the top of her spine, freezing instantly as my lips brushed raised bumps on her skin. My hands wrapping her shoulders, I moved her toward the light of the fire and peeled the crimson fabric away from her body. My blood boiled at the sight of flesh-colored runes burned into her back.

Fire magic, worked into my love's skin by that fuckface Bakhur.

No one else would be moronic enough to touch, let alone mark, my Aldara. But the Fire Prince would pay for hurting her, many, *many* times over. All the ways I could end him spun through my mind. Slowly cooking his organs, first his cock, then his golden eyes, was by far my favorite idea.

A tremor rolled over Leaf's shoulders, but she kept her back turned, unwilling now to look me in the eye. "Arrow, please stay calm or the guards will hear. Then whatever game you're playing in the Sun Realm will end."

The only game I played was the one that would set her free. But maybe now I had another objective—the death and destruction of Azarn's son and heir.

"Tell me who did this," I growled, even though I already knew the answer.

"I haven't forgotten your vengeful nature." She looked over her shoulder and whispered, "If I tell you, you'll only put us in danger."

"So be it. The Fire Prince is a dead man anyway."

She shook her head, then turned to face me. "Why are you so obstinate? So set on revenge?"

"Me? I cannot believe you accuse me of something that you excel in. *You* are the stubborn one. Disobedient and willful, recklessly risking your life over and over." My heart melted at her expression of outrage, and I smiled. I couldn't help it. "But have I told you what else you are? Unique. Beautiful. Precious. Mine. Only mine."

"A perfect answer," she said, stroking my cheek. "Let's agree to worry about Bakhur later. Right now, I want to feel you inside me, around me... everywhere. Quickly. Don't waste a moment of our time together."

"As you command."

Like an explosion of auron kanara feathers, hope burst inside my chest as I walked her backward to the bed, then laid her down gently.

Did my stubborn human finally believe me?

"Leaf?" I began, my voice shaking. "Do you understand at last that I never betrayed you?"

"Sh, not now," she said, trying to draw me down onto the bed. "Let me pretend we're back in Coridon. Just love me, Arrow. Please."

"*Always*," I said. "I will always and forever adore you."

With trembling hands, I slid the gown up her thighs, exposing her body to my devoted appraisal. Through a hooded gaze, she tracked my every move, her skin pebbling at my touch, her breath labored. Tantalizing moisture glistened at her center.

I'd barely touched her, and she was wet for me, needing me badly. And yet I knew I desired her more. Certain I would die if I couldn't bury myself in the sanctuary of her body.

"Nothing else matters," she murmured, as if reading my thoughts.

In case someone entered, I shrugged off my cloak, but kept my shirt on and unlaced my pants. Even though I longed for every part of our skin to be in contact, at this time and in this place, it was impossible.

"*Soon*," I told myself, the thought connecting through our bond.

Leaf shook her head. "Not soon, *now*. Kiss me," she demanded, shuffling her weight onto her elbows, bringing our faces closer. "Come inside me. Hurry."

"You're as demanding as ever," I said, pushing her backward, then climbing over her.

She writhed beneath me, one hand pulling my head down, the other fumbling at the laces on my pants.

With a laugh, I framed her face with my hands, then kissed her slowly. Each time she tried to rush me, I nipped her lip and soothed her with a soft whisper.

I'd been waiting for Leaf to look at me this way again since the moment I learned that the Sun Realm had captured her, tricked her, and placed the blame on me. I had to know if she trusted me. Her faith in me was more essential than oxygen. More vital than food or water.

Before we went further, I had to be certain she understood. That she knew I would always be her hero, and only her villain if she asked me very, *very* nicely.

Chapter 22

ARROW

"Leaf... I'm so sorry," I said between bitter-sweet kisses. "Sorry for everything. I should have been gentle, revered you from the moment I laid eyes on you at the gilt market. Never frightened you. Not once. To atone for my sins, you can lash my body a thousand times a day. Starve me. Beat me. Anything as long as you never stop needing me. To me, you are more precious than gold. More vital than air and lightning. More necessary to life than blood. Let me show you."

"Yes," she murmured. "Show me. Please, hurry."

My wings enfolded her, creating a cocoon that insulated us from the bleakness of Taln. "You are safe with me, little Leaf," I said, sick with the need to carry my Aldara away from this terrible place. "You'll always be safe with me. Each tear I shed is a vow to you, a prayer, and a wish that you will return my love forever."

With a gasp, she wiped moisture from my cheek. Fuck. Since when did I cry?

Even when my family died, I screamed and raged, but shed no tears for their loss.

This was yet another lesson my human had taught me.

To be vulnerable.

To risk rejection, if I must.

Because living without her wasn't an option.

"Oh, Arrow," she breathed my name on a soft sigh. "Please don't worry. Everything will be all right."

We smiled at each other, tears shimmering in our gazes. Then I kissed her, the taste of salt on her lips the sweetest potion.

I couldn't decide which part of her to worship next. I wanted all of her. Now. Now and forever.

She cried out as I drew a nipple into my mouth, biting one softly, then the other. A low moan vibrated in her throat as my fangs pierced her flesh, and I drew blood from the side of her breast. Only two small sips. Enough to make her arch off the bed and drag my hips forward with greedy, clutching hands.

Shaking with anticipation, I slid my hand down her body and teased my fingers through her wetness. "Fuck, Leaf. You're so ready for me."

She made a broken noise, halfway between a laugh and a groan. "Yes, no more waiting. Please, Arrow."

"As you wish," I said, sliding into her heat with one fluid movement.

Finally.

A sense of blissful belonging washed over me. This was home. Wherever she was. As close to her as possible. My love. My Aldara.

She gasped, stroking my back before running her hands over my chest plate, then along my twitching stomach muscles.

"So good," I said through gritted teeth. "This is all I've wanted since I left you in Mydorian... to be with you. To be as close to you as I can get."

"And now you are. So for the love of dust, get moving before those guards come back."

With great care, I drew back, then inched forward, the delicious friction testing my control. She writhed gloriously beneath me, urging me to go faster and harder, but I didn't.

I couldn't.

First, I had to make sure she understood.

When I found the perfect, slow rhythm that made us sweat, on the verge of losing control, I stroked her body, her cheek, cuffed her neck with all the tenderness my ruthless heart could muster.

"I will protect you always. Never doubt it. From the night I saw you lift that fork to the Sun envoy's neck in my dining hall, an unbreakable spell was cast. *Your* spell, my Aldara. At that moment..."

Words failed me, the sight and feel of her warm, wet body, threatening to shatter my resolve.

Raising her hips, I changed the angle slightly. "I... I didn't know it then, Leaf, but that night I had fallen from the highest mountain peak in the realms, fallen irrevocably in love with you. And since that moment, I swear on the souls of my dead family, all I've wanted is to keep you safe. Keep you close. See you smile... preferably at me."

"Oh, gods," she moaned as I raised her hips again and thrust higher, sliding against her favorite spot.

"There are no gods, only one goddess and her servant king. We are King Arrowyn and Queen Zali. Arrow and Leaf, bound in bliss for all eternity. Do you believe me, my Aldara? Do you believe that I never failed you? That I never..." I moaned, shuddering helplessly. "Never betrayed you?"

Dark hair fanned over the bedcovers as she shook her head.

"No?" I froze with my hips pressed against her, my cock pulsing deep inside her exquisite velvet warmth. "You don't believe me? Then I had better stop." My fingers digging into her flesh, I prayed to the gold that I had the strength to remain still for as long as it took her to surrender.

"Please," she said, bucking and tugging my shoulders. "Don't stop."

"Then tell me your name."

"Zali."

"No. The name of your heart."

"Zali," my stubborn lioness repeated.

"Say the name I gave you... *Leaf.* Say it, and I'll fuck you any way you want."

She cradled my cheek and smiled into my eyes. "I'm called Leaf. And although I've spent a long time hating it, in truth, it's the name I like best. Given to me by the only male who makes me cry, and burn, and long for him like no other. The only one who knows that I like it hard and *very* fast."

I required no further encouragement.

Bracing my hand above her head, I leaned into the work and gave her exactly what she'd asked for—long, hard, punishing strokes that made sweat slick our skin as we groaned and raged and panted together.

"You're never... leaving... my sight again," I demanded, perhaps unreasonably.

"But Mydorian. My people."

"Damn it... Leaf. I—"

"Arrow, please... Don't think about what's beyond our control. Not now. *Believe* that all will be well."

Then she said my name again and again, an incantation, a spell, and as her muscles coiled tighter and clenched around me, I sank my fangs into her neck over the Aldara mark. She came apart at once, crying out, gripping me tighter. I shuddered hard, pressing my fingers over her mouth to silence her cries.

Sweet, dark blood coated my tongue as her life force slid down my throat. Euphoric, primal hunger rocked me to my core.

Need.

And solace.

Leaf's essence bound our hearts and souls together, and the bond demanded I keep her in my sight at all times. How would I find the strength to walk out of this room and leave her at the fire fae's mercy?

Determined to extend her pleasure, I cursed against her skin to stop myself from breaking, roaring, and bringing the whole fire kingdom down upon us. My feather glyphs blazed hotter than ever, blood flowing through my veins like a wildfire.

So close to pain, the pleasure was unbearable.

Too fucking good.

I never wanted it to end.

Not yet.

Then beyond my control, a force stronger than lightning quaked from my stomach and spread outward, ricocheting through flesh and bones until I exploded. I squeezed my eyes shut and shook like an avalanche.

Collapsing on top of Leaf, I kissed her neck softly, her lips too hard, and then feather-soft.

"Ouch, your chest plate," she reminded me, and I lifted my upper body off her.

"Still hate me?" I asked with a grin.

"Yes," she said, her cheeks blushing the sweet color of desert rose petals.

"Liar."

She laughed. "Get up, quickly. The guards could come in any moment." She wriggled out from under me, stood in front of a long mirror, and began repairing her ruined braid."

"Leave it like that. It will suit the scene we're playing."

She nodded and helped me put my clothes to rights as we laughed like mischievous children.

"I take no pleasure in any realm, in any *thing* without you," I said, bracing my hands on her hips and peppering kisses on her cheeks. "Food has no flavor. Nightmares besiege me. I haven't had a moment's peace since we parted. Does it please you to know you've destroyed me, my Leaf?"

"Of course it does." She grinned and fastened my cloak. "Now, where should I stand? Here? Or should I lie on the bed and cry for the guards' entertainment?"

"No, I couldn't bear it." Without thinking, I took my old cloak from the coat stand and wrapped it around her shoulders, breathing in the precious scent of her—warm, musky human with a hint of jasmine, combined with my own scent. The best smell in the five realms.

She shrugged it off, and it fell on the bed.

"Please, Leaf. I beg you to keep it and think about everything I've told you. We'll speak more tomorrow. Give the cloak back to me then if you must. And tell me that you know I didn't betray you. Could *never* betray you."

"The guards," she whispered. "Can you do me one favor? Get Ari here. I miss her so much."

A bolt of jealousy pierced my heart. I brushed a strand of hair from her lips and nodded. "I will do my best."

Pinching her cheeks hard, she said, "We need to make this look real."

"Yes, and I'm sorry for this," I said, tearing her dress so it hung from one shoulder. When she bit her lip, drawing blood, I caught her face in my hands, pressing my forehead to hers. "No, Leaf. You take things too far."

"They must believe you assaulted me. The ruthless Storm King wouldn't treat me gently."

"Those rumors are based on my father's reputation, not mine. I have never hurt a lover. Never hurt a slave, or a princess, or even a queen. When will you stop thinking the worst of me?"

"I admit I can be a slow learner. You should know that by now, Arrow." She stood on the tips of her toes and grasped my shoulders. "But I'm finally paying attention. I promise. Call the guards."

I kissed her one last time, walking her backward toward the bed, then laying her down. "If any of those Fire Court fucks touch you, tell me straight away. They'll be added to my list of dead men."

She bounced up off the mattress. "*Dead men*," she scoffed, as if I'd never killed anyone on her behalf before. She slapped my ass, then ducked behind me so I couldn't retaliate.

I spun on my heel. "Hey, get back here."

"Did you forget that you're powerless in the Sun Realm? You won't be killing anyone, whether they touch me or not."

"Won't I? We'll see about that."

"Orion, the orc who helped me board Loligos's ship. He's a prisoner, trapped in—"

"I know. We'll deal with it. Tomorrow morning I have a meeting with Azarn's counselors and some traders from the Ice realm. After that, I'll find you."

"All right," she said, smiling at me in a sweet, open way. A smile I thought I would never see again. "We desperately need a plan."

Damn right we did. With my power blocked, getting out of Taln safely wouldn't be easy. But the Sun Realm's queen held the key to our escape. The secret conversations I'd had with Estella had revealed she hated Azarn with a fiery passion, which would work to our advantage.

"The night of the last trial, how did you appear invisible in my room?" I asked.

"The serpent fae gave me petals from the blood orchid. I rubbed one on my skin and became temporarily invisible. That's its power."

"Good. Keep the rest well-hidden."

"I will."

"Will you be at dinner in the hall?" she asked.

"Yes. And it will fucking kill me to ignore you. I love you," I whispered. "More than you'll ever understand."

As I stared at her gap-toothed grin, the City of Taln seemed to turn upside down, the horror shaking out of it, and everything in the realms felt right again. I would gladly spend eternity in the hell realms if it were the price of seeing her smile every day and night for the rest of my life.

I opened the door and shouted for Azarn's men to return, struggling to suppress my own grin as the word *tomorrow* spun through my mind, a sweet, unbearable torture.

How would I wait a whole night to touch her again without losing my mind?

A wave of dread surged through me. Fuck. We'd forgotten to talk through our bond.

What if Melaya heard us?

I guessed if he had, I'd know about it soon enough, because Azarn's mage and his soldiers would be crashing down my door before dawn.

If so, bring it on. I'd never had a fight I didn't enjoy.

And in all truth, I was dying for a reason to break Melaya's nose.

Chapter 23

LEAF

The earthy tang of old parchment coated my tongue as I licked my finger and turned another page in a book about the history of Sun Realm magic.

Thankfully, the guardians, as the Taln librarians preferred to be called, were busy cataloging new titles from the Ice Realm and had left me alone to flick through a dusty tome called *Masters of Mythology: A Case Study of Magnificent Magicians and Mages Throughout the Ages.*

Earlier, I had grabbed a pile of books from the Historical Magic section and retreated to a snug corner nestled behind rows of shelves beneath the domed-glass ceiling, in a section of the library perched high above the town.

In one direction, the cozy nook overlooked the library's entrance far below, and in the other, the mountains beyond the forest, making it the perfect position to study any fae coming and going from the building and waste time daydreaming as I stared out at the view.

No one had entered for at least an hour, so I skimmed through chapters undisturbed, searching for information about the magic behind the Sentura Pyre and my mergelyn anklet, concluding that the fae of Taln weren't avid readers.

Twenty minutes later, a jinn who, for some reason had taken the shape of a centauress, arrived to water the library's trailing vines and potted plants with a long spout that connected to her bulging saddlebags. She completed her duties quickly, leaving me to concentrate on reading instead of flicking her curious glances every time the clip-clop of her hooves sounded on the parquet floor nearby.

The soft-blue sky suddenly darkened to burnt peach as sparks rained down in a glorious shower of fire. What caused the spectacle, I couldn't say. But the sight stole my breath, and I stared at it until my eyes glazed over, indulging in memories of Arrow and how delicious his big, warm body had felt, shuddering inside and around me.

I had sworn I'd never fall for his pretty lies again. But it was clear now that he'd been telling the truth all along. He *did* love me and had come to Taln for one reason only—to get me out of it. I could no longer deny how I felt about him. The Storm King hadn't betrayed me, which meant I was free to love him until the day I died.

Pretending to read, I flipped another page, the crisp sound evoking memories of my bookshelf-lined bedroom in Mydorian. I recalled the bliss of lying beneath heavy blankets, letting my imagination soar beyond the palace walls into the thrilling realms of distant lands and other lives.

I had also been a frequent visitor to Mydorian's light-filled library. With its whitewashed floors and silver branches of an enormous sapoula tree holding up the domed, open ceiling, it was quite a contrast to Taln's three-storied, dark-wood building full of secrets and shadowy corners.

I studied the long, crimson tassels of candelabras that hung from the ceiling like upside down love-lies-bleeding plants and the candles burning on reading tables. The flames cast a purplish light over the flowering creepers that climbed the shelves, providing relief from the somber, closeted atmosphere.

Facing the mountains, I closed my eyes for several moments, promising myself I'd only think about last night one more time before returning my attention to the book.

"Hard at work, I see," said a voice from above, startling me out of my reverie.

Damn. Guilty heat flushed over my cheeks. I glanced up, finding Arrow looming over me dressed in leathers and a cloak, the golden feathers on his chest plate tinkling as he shifted his weight and crossed his arms.

"Hello," I said, the image of him unfastening those exact pants all-too fresh in my mind.

"What are you pretending to do in the library?" he asked, frowning.

I snapped the book shut. "I'm not pretending. I'm hunting for useful information. What are *you* doing here?"

"I've been hunting *you*. I told you I'd come looking for you after this morning's meeting. Didn't expect to find you here, though."

"Why not? I *can* read you know."

"Yes. You can read very well. Everything except me, apparently." A smirk replaced his frown. "Found anything interesting?"

Prompted by the Storm King's arrival, a guardian emerged from a high level of an internal tower, cleared his throat, and hurried halfway down a spiral staircase that ran the full height of the black-crystal-clad structure to stop just above us. Oval windows in the tower overlooked each level of the library, likely for monitoring visitors while the guardians worked inside it, busy with administrative tasks.

"Is all well?" the silver-haired male asked, the movement of his crimson wings fluttering the long whiskers of his mustache and wafting his robes around his stooped frame.

"Perfectly fine. Thank you," I answered with a cheery wave while concocting a lie. "King Arrowyn has come in search of books on ice sculpting. He considers himself exceptionally skilled in the art. Did you know that he runs competitions in the Light Realm inside a purpose-built ice conservatory to protect the sculptures from the desert sun? He's quite determined to win this year's event and is seeking new inspiration for his designs."

The old librarian looked thoughtful. "It's doubtful we keep anything on the subject. As you can imagine, with our kingdom's heat, it's not a popular pastime, especially not one *kings* are known to engage in," he said with a judgmental sniff.

A map of the library appeared in the air in front of him, tiny flames morphing into what looked like a catalog of books that the guardian flicked through with a crooked finger. "No, I can't see anything specifically on ice sculpting. Has the competition being going for long? I've never heard of it."

"It's not a well-known event. Arrowyn proudly started it in his twentieth year. But please don't go to any trouble. I'll help him look through Taln's art collection. I'm sure something there will ignite his creative passions."

The guardian dropped a bow and retreated up the steps, leaving me alone with Arrow's hostile stare.

"Ice sculpting?" he growled. "Really? That's ludicrous. As if I would—"

I swallowed laughter and grinned. "I'm sure it's a fine activity for a Storm King. And to be honest, I think you'd look very attractive chiseling away at sculptures, half-naked as you worked."

"Huh. Might have to try it one day," he said with a smirk. "I can think of many uses for the ice that you might enjoy."

Patting the cushion next to me, I brought out the book I'd hidden behind my back when the guardian appeared on the staircase. I checked for any physical signs that Melaya might have been eavesdropping—skin tingling, nausea etcetera—and found none. "I *have* discovered something interesting in this book. It says..."

He held a finger to his lips, silencing me as he mouthed the word, "Wait."

Thunder clapped, and the city streets below sizzled, steam rising off the paving stones. Arrow looked over his shoulder and out the window, staring as if mesmerized by the fire rain.

"What causes the phenomenon?" I asked. "It's beautiful."

"Come with me, and I'll show you."

He held his hand out, and I grabbed it, allowing myself to be tugged to a shadowy corner of the library. Arrow backed me into the stacks, the smell of old books and dust teasing my senses. Soft lips kissed me tenderly, first my mouth, and then the side of my neck over the pulsing Aldara glyph.

"What are you doing?" I asked, so breathless I could barely speak. "I thought you were going to show me something about the fire showers."

"No, I decided to ignite my creative passions, just like you told the guardian I would."

"See? I always end up being right, don't I?" I teased.

"If you kiss me again," he breathed in my ear, "then you'll definitely be as right as the gold-flecked desert. As perfect as the sun that blazes above it. And as—"

"Oh, do shut up." I laughed, smashing our mouths together and silencing his ramble. "Why waste time arguing when we could do this instead?" I said between kisses.

My head spun, my limbs loose and languid, and for a few minutes, I forgot that we stood inside a library, located in a hostile realm.

But reality soon intruded, and I remembered that if we wanted to escape Taln, we had a lot of work to do, and locking lips leisurely would have to wait.

I pushed Arrow's chest, reluctantly breaking our kiss. "How is this showing me what causes the fire rain to fall?"

"It isn't," he said, his dark-gold hair a ruffled mess and his breathing rough and heavy. "Obviously." He let his face fall into the crook of my neck and rumbled the words against my skin. "But I can't stop thinking about last night."

"You can't stop thinking about my blood?"

His low laugh sent a shiver down my spine. "No, your *everything*, Leaf. Eyes. Smile. Voice. Smell. Taste. Laugh. And in case you've forgotten, you're mine. Mine. *Mine*," he rasped. "Forever mine as I am yours in life and death."

"I'd prefer not to contemplate our deaths right now."

"No? Then think about this," he said, his fangs sliding into my neck and drawing blood. Only a sip, but enough to make my head fall back in response, something heavy tumbling from the shelf onto the floor.

"Arrow, the book..."

"*Ignore it,*" he replied through our bond, his silver gaze hot as he raised his head.

"*More.*" I wound my fingers into his hair and tugged him back to where I needed him.

"Absolutely not." His forehead pressed against mine. "*You need your strength, and I only took enough blood to speak through our bond. I have a plan. We'll return to your cozy reading corner, converse about things of no consequence, bicker, and then I'll leave in an apparent rage. You'll wait five minutes, and then meet me by the fire moat.*"

"*Why there?*"

He rolled his eyes. "*For once, instead of arguing, please just follow my instructions.*"

"*Now you're worried about being discreet? Anyone could've walked around the stacks and seen us. Bakhur, even Azarn, who I've heard loves to lurk around his city, hoping to find someone plotting his demise.*"

"Are you ready?" he asked, leading me back to the couch where my books waited on a low table.

"As I'll ever be."

"You're quite wrong, Princess," he said in a fake pompous tone. "My ice sculptures shouldn't emulate forms from other realms." Frowning, he sat beside me and angled his head toward the window. "*Look carefully at the pair near the library entrance playing a board game,*" he said through the bond.

Two cloaked men that looked a lot like Raiden and Zaret moved clay figures over a board, joking and laughing as if they hadn't a care in the world.

"*You've set watchdogs near the entrance?*" I asked.

He smirked. "*Yes.*"

223

I crossed my arms, forcing a frown. "I disagree. I think featuring fae from other realms in your art is actually a radical act of peace. You should try it."

As I spoke, Esen approached Arrow's guards across a courtyard dotted with statues of winged orcs and trolls. Rising, Raiden smiled and slapped Esen on the back, then she squatted down and joined the game.

"I have no desire to sculpt fire fae," Arrow rumbled, sounding cross.

In shock, my gaze cut to his. *"You've forgiven her?"*

"It's a long story. Now please continue our tiresome, petty argument out loud."

Stacking the books on the table, I huffed out a sigh. "But, King Arrowyn, I've seen your ice work. You have a talent for sculpting bodies, buttocks in particular. I think you'd do a magnificent rendering of Prince Bakhur."

Arrow laughed, turning it into a growl as he shot to his feet. "Are you suggesting I have a... a fascination for the Fire Prince?" he shouted.

I tried hard, but failed to stop my shoulders from shaking with laughter. "And what if I am?"

He shook his head slightly, warning me I'd gone too far. "This is the last time I come to you for artistic advice, Princess Zali. You've been no help at all today."

I shrugged. "Fae kings often react poorly to constructive feedback."

With a whispered curse, Arrow turned on his heel, his cloak whipping out behind him as he marched away. The words *"Fire moat,"* echoed in my mind as he swept through the library doors. *"Five minutes. Don't be late."*

The old librarian appeared at the top of the stairs again. "Is King Arrowyn all right?"

"Oh, yes," I replied, picking up the mythology book. "Don't mind him. He's very sensitive about his creative process."

The fae harrumphed, and then disappeared in a whirl of black robes.

I contemplated the book on my lap, running my finger over the gold-embossed runes and dragons on its red cover. It mostly contained long-winded tales of the deeds of ancient fire wielders.

One particularly harrowing story detailed the scene after a battle, where the fire mages set a lake alight and burned the Ice Realm families who were taking refuge in it. Another recounted how the fire fae had conquered the lost tribes of sand dragon shifters in the Light Realm thousands of years ago, a story I thought best not to share with Arrow.

At least not until we were safely back in Coridon.

I used my final minutes in the library to run through what I'd found in the books—mostly things that I already knew.

The Sun Realm's strength stemmed from the fire fae's ability to transform their appearance and in their mastery of the dragons that flew over the city with their trainers each dawn, perfecting complex battle formations.

Flipping through the book one last time, it fell open on a page toward the back. I ran my finger over a passage about twin mages, the words partly concealed within the embossed illustration of a palace consumed by flames.

It said: *With each pair coming to ascendancy during the reign of a Sun Realm king, mergelyn twins are the key to a ruler's success. Lose one, the other fails. One dies, the kingdom falls. Protect the powerless, for he is the holder of the other's glory.*

A short, but extremely interesting piece of information.

Heart pounding, I wondered if I'd stumbled across the secret to bringing the Fire King down. If we could somehow gain control of Nukala, perhaps it would be easy to disable his brother, Melaya, and remove the block on our magic.

I snapped the book closed and returned it to the shelf, sliding it between tomes of bardic poetry and quickly scanning the rows around them. Each book in the section contained the word *poems* or *songs* in its title, while the surrounding shelves were designated for volumes of art history.

A Case Study of Magnificent Magicians and Mages had been misplaced, possibly not intended for the eyes of the average reader. Or a captive princess from the Earth Realm.

I brushed dust off my hands and headed toward the exit, eager to share my newfound information with Arrow and feel the delicious burn of his silver gaze trailing over me.

Chapter 24

LEAF

In daylight, the moat looked different—much less sinister than the other night. Its fiery surface swirled gently, like water in a breeze. Sparks floated lazily above it, and I wondered if the lie-eaters would make an appearance today.

"So what are we doing here?" I asked Arrow, sneaking up beside him.

He turned and scanned my body, his hot gaze curling my toes. "We're going to summon the khareek and sell them some lies, and in return, they'll help us speak privately just in case..." his words trailed off as he grimaced at the anklet around my leg.

"How do you know the moat-dwellers can do that?"

"As it turns out, you're not the only one who can read. I went to the library *last* night and did some research of my own."

That explained why he wasn't in the hall at dinnertime. Not that I'd been looking for him *too* often.

"Arrow, in the book I found today, it said—"

"Sh." Warm fingers pressed my lips. "Don't speak yet."

I exhaled sharply. "I'm sure I'd feel something if you-know-who was listening in."

"Better to be safe than sorry," he said.

Then, without a word of warning, the Storm King started singing. Feather glyphs flowed bright gold over his skin, as they often did in my presence, and his voice hummed from deep in his chest. Chill bumps broke over my arms, a shiver skittering down my spine.

Who knew that Arrowyn Ramiel could carry a tune?

"Hidden talent?" I whispered, and he shot me a withering glare, not skipping a beat of the hypnotic melody.

The song reminded me of the music sung by the northern traders that often passed through Coridon, slow and eerie, with an abundance of harsh consonants, but no clear words to decipher.

The surface of the moat churned, and three creatures burst out from the lava-like water, the sight ten times more disturbing than the night I first saw them with Ruhh.

In unfortunate, gruesome detail, the sunlight highlighted their charred bones and melting flesh, and as soon as one fiery limb dissolved, another formed in its place. The khareek writhed in a state of flux, burning and remaking themselves in a constant cycle, horrible to witness. But if the creatures were in pain, they showed no outward signs.

Silent now, Arrow inclined his head in greeting.

"Prettily done, Storm King," said the tallest khareek, swaying knee-deep in the moat as his rasped words slurred and his tongue and mouth dissolved in a blur of dripping flames.

"Can we... do anything to help you?" I asked. "You must be in pain. Are you trapped in the moat?"

"Nooooo," the word crackled out of the fire creature's regenerating mouth. "To be khareek is to be blessed, human. To us, pain is pleasure. Pleasure is pain. But if you wish to help us, you may tell us delicious lies. We are always hungry for those."

Feeling Arrow's gaze boring into me, I gave him a cool look. "What's wrong?"

"I'm just wondering if your relentless compassion will eventually rub off on me."

"According to rumors, it's already happened."

The Storm King opened his mouth, but said nothing, his eyes still fixed on mine.

"Don't make us wait," said the mouthpiece of the trio, interrupting my staring competition with Arrow. "Feed us, and we shall decide if your lies are worthy of our magic."

Arrow took a deep breath, but I stepped forward before he could speak. "Taln is a wonderful city," I declared loudly.

The khareek laughed, and the smallest one slithered closer. "The Storm King should speak. His lies will be more potent than *hers*."

Arrow waved a hand toward me. "See this girl here?" The khareek nodded eagerly. "I do not love her or even care about her fate."

"Good," hissed the creature, flames surging over its body as it writhed drunkenly. "Quite delicious. Tell us more untruths, Storm King."

"Of course." Arrow grinned at me. "I betrayed this girl who stands before you, and because of me, she is trapped in Taln."

The khareek shrieked in delight as my heart rejoiced. Arrow had betrayed me, and I was in Taln because of him—both statements nothing but sweet, sweet lies.

"More, more," the creatures chanted.

"Zali Omala, the Princess of Dust and Stones, is never my first thought when I wake, nor my last before I fall asleep. I don't worry about her safety, and I swear I've never longed for her touch so badly I'd rather die than endure a life without it."

Howling, the creatures' bodies bent and coiled in a dance of ecstasy, their black eyes fixed on the sky as if the gods themselves descended from the clouds to gift them with untold blessings.

Arrow's eyes blazed as he whispered directly to me, "I would never lay my life aside for Zali. Or do almost anything to keep and to treasure her."

"Lies. All lies," sang the khareek. "Beautiful, tasty lies."

It felt strange to hear Arrow call me by my childhood name when the one he'd given me finally felt so right. Only hours ago, I'd railed against it. But never again. Not now that I knew for certain how he felt about me.

"I think I may have overindulged," said a khareek, releasing a loud burp as it began to sink down into the moat.

"Wait," their leader commanded, holding its companion up by an armpit. "We must ask what the king and queen wish from us in return for feeding us so well."

"Oh, I'm not a qu—" I began to correct, Arrow's glare silencing me.

His wings manifested, flaring high above his shoulders, the right one lowering and embracing my body, drawing me closer. "With respect, ancient Khareek," Arrow said, "all we wish for is the gift of privacy."

"A lovers' concealment?"

"Yes," he replied. "We've been apart long weeks and wish to speak to each other without risk of others overhearing us. And I promise we mean no harm to the realms and seek only to restore balance."

The creature's black eyes burned through my skull. "Does the Storm King speak for you?" it asked, its left shoulder collapsing and melting into the moat.

"In this case, yes. Most definitely."

The khareek yawned. "What you have said is true. Your wish is granted."

The fire creatures opened their mouths and jets of lava spewed out, spraying our bodies. I flinched, expecting pain, but felt none.

As the khareek sank under the moat, one said, "Whenever you come here together, no being will be able to see or hear you, not even through magical means."

A semi-translucent globe of flames cast by the khareek burst around us, waves of heat billowing off its walls, a little too warm for comfort.

Arrow took my hands, pulled me close, and kissed me tenderly. Too quickly, he drew back, his palms framing my face. "Being unseen by others was a nice addition. We'll meet here whenever we need to discuss... delicate matters."

I laughed. "Hm. I suppose that doesn't include *partaking* in *frivolous* matters, such as kissing."

"I wouldn't rush to that conclusion."

I flapped the neck of my tunic away from my chest. "It's quite hot in here."

"Feel free to disrobe," he said with a cheeky grin. "Your comfort is always my greatest concern. Tell me what you learned in the library."

"I found a book about Sun Realm magicians that contained a brief paragraph on twin mages."

A gold eyebrow rose. "Despite years of work, my scryers haven't discovered any information about the fire mages. What did the book say?"

"If one mage is lost, the other fails. And better still, if one dies, the kingdom falls. And something about the powerless holding the other's glory. Whatever that means."

"So it's Nukala we must target."

"I think so." I nodded, my heart hammering with barely bridled excitement.

I could hardly believe the dramatic turnaround in my circumstances over the last twenty-four hours. Arrow stood beside me, smiling like I was a beam of sunshine on a rainy day. He was on *my* side and making plans to help me right King Azarn's many wrongs.

Tears stung my eyes, and I blinked rapidly to remove them. "What do you know about Nukala? He's an odd one. Keeps to himself. Doesn't say much."

"Agreed," Arrow said. "He's a particular favorite of Azarn's. That's all I know."

"We need to talk to Estella. Did you realize that she let me win our battle in the Arena of Ashen Souls? Arrow, she used cosmic magic to stop time. It was the most incredible thing I've ever seen."

"Yes. She told me she would do so before the event. Otherwise, I would've done everything and anything to stop it from going ahead. I know she wants to help us, but her mind is... fractured from the trauma of her forced marriage to the Fire King. She hides away. Often speaks in circles. I fear she may not be reliable."

"But perhaps our only chance?" I asked.

"Yes," he said.

"And Ari? Any news?"

"Azarn has agreed to let her visit Taln."

Hope bloomed in my chest. "That's so exciting and... surprising. How did you manage that?"

Arrow's mouth twisted. "I told Azarn it would be an insult to expect you to marry his son without my Sayeeda's help to prepare you for the occasion. Raiden has already left and will return with her shortly."

"Raiden? That'll be an interesting journey."

Arrow grinned. "And likely too short a duration for what your dirty mind is imagining, Princess mine."

"Princess? I thought I was your queen," I teased.

"*You* are my everything. The Empress of my Soul, who rules my every thought, wish, and desire. The mistress of my body, especially of my aching c—"

"Much better," I said, laughing. Then a wave of fear washed over me, and I dropped my gaze to the ground.

With a finger, Arrow raised my chin. "Leaf, what is it?"

"You don't think I'll have to actually marry Bakhur, do you?"

"Over my rotting corpse will you join yourself in any shape or form with that sniveling, indolent abuser. He doesn't deserve to have you spit on him."

"But you deserve me?"

"Of course. We were made for each other. Do you still deny it?"

"Do you admit you've been a prick? A villain?"

"In the past? *Maybe* that was the case." He drawled the word maybe out to a ridiculous length, as if it would make my accusation less true. "It's possible I didn't always proceed wisely, especially where you were concerned."

I pinched his cheek. "You've been a brute."

"And you love me for it," he said, chuckling as his arms came around my waist, squeezing me tightly. Then his expression darkened. "How can I make you understand the depths of my remorse for the way I treated you when you first came to Coridon? I've been drowning in regret, guilt, and shame. If I could chop off parts of my body and still bring you the same pleasure, still protect my people and kingdom, then I'd gladly hack them off at once and present them as tributes. Which would you like first, my right hand or entire left arm?"

"Your cock should do nicely," I said. "Give me that now, hard and fast, and consider yourself forgiven. All debts paid and more."

Giddy with happiness, we laughed between sweet kisses. Then he whispered over my lips, "Dearest Leaf, surely you must realize I never betrayed you. I rushed from Mydorian because when Raiden arrived, he told me he'd uncovered rumors concerning a fire fae planted at my court, and he suspected that fae was Esen."

"Of *course* it was Esen," I said. "Azarn has been busy playing a devious, long game."

"And still is," Arrow continued. "The fire fae, using Esen, tricked you into thinking I'd ordered your arrest. Deep down, you know I would never do such a thing. I think part of you enjoys the idea of me as a villain, but it's simply not true. It never was and never will be. I'll always be on your side, Leaf. From the moment I learned you we're stolen, I've had no choice but to pretend I didn't care and go along with their sick charade."

"Why?" I asked, a single tear rolling down my cheek. "Surely there was another way."

Arrow's thumb stroked my wet face. "*Why?* It was the only way to protect you, my love. The stars could fall from the sky and I wouldn't flinch as long I knew you were safe. Please say you believe me or end my misery now."

He drew a knife from a sheath on his thigh, wrapped my fingers around the hilt, and pointed the tip at his heart.

The rusty bars that caged my heart melted away, causing an avalanche of tears to tumble down my cheeks. It was time to admit my mistakes. Of course he had told the truth. I don't know how I ever doubted him.

"Fine," I said through sobs. "You can call me Leaf whenever you like as long as you call no other yours. *Ever,* understand? Only me. Or I'll rip your balls off with my teeth."

His brow rose. "Interesting idea. Perhaps we could act the scenario out when we return to Coridon. For the purpose of research."

"By the way, you won't be getting your cloak back, either."

He grinned. "Good. It's been yours since the day I met you."

I smiled back, my heart overflowing with happiness. "Now, what the hells do we do next?"

"Nothing until Ari arrives in a couple of days. Then we'll make plans to release Orion and get us all out of this gold-forsaken excuse for a fucking kingdom. The reavers have access to knowledge about the old magic of the realms, and the Sayeeda has been in Auryinnia with her sister, trying to find ways to break Melaya's power block."

"And in the meantime, all I have to do, is pretend I want to marry the Fire Prince."

He looked skyward as if seeking calm. "And I must stop myself from killing him."

A nearby shout startled me—someone calling my name. I squinted through the veil of flames and saw Esen and Prince Bakhur marching down the path toward the cliffs. They'd passed quite close to the khareek's sphere of magic and hadn't noticed us. And we'd been too focused on each other to see anything else.

I strained to make out their conversation.

"Leaf told me she'd be in the library, searching for books on Taln wedding traditions," lied Esen smoothly.

"I wish to know where she is at all times," said the prince, his light-brown curls ruffling in the sea breeze. At the cliffs, they turned left toward the Fen Forest.

Smiling sadly at Arrow, I said, "They're looking for me. I'd better go. We have much to discuss, and it's too difficult to speak sensibly through the bond when you take my blood during feedings. I can't concentrate. If I can get away from Bakhur, I'll meet you here at dusk tomorrow. Just before dinner, when the court is busiest."

Dragging me close, he kissed me without mercy, then held me at arm's length. "Be careful."

"I will. The sooner Ari gets here, the better. She always knows what to do," I said, taking a step away from him.

"Before you go, will you..." he glanced at his boots, shifting his weight, before staring at me with an anguished frown. "Tell me your name again. Please."

I knew exactly what he wanted.

With my hands pressed against my heart to stop it from exploding out of my ribcage, I began to turn away, as if I would leave. Then, slowly, I looked over my shoulder, revealing a smile.

"My name is Leaf," I said. "Always and forever I'll be your Leaf."

As I pushed through the dome of flames, Arrow's voice rumbled behind me. "Fucking finally," he said.

I laughed, skipping toward the Fen Forest like a giddy child, not a prisoner in a land I despised.

The human condition amazed me. As long as we found love, we could experience happiness in even the worst of circumstances. And I guessed that was true of all species.

Even the fae.

Chapter 25

LEAF

As it turned out, I couldn't meet Arrow for the next two nights because Prince Bakhur barely let me out of his sight. He insisted I accompany him to one dull event after another—fencing lessons, meetings with his tailor, drinking sessions with his creepy friends, even watching him nap as if we had nothing better to do.

Which *he* clearly didn't.

Standing by while he mocked and belittled courtiers and servants was a terrible challenge. Wearing a fake smile, I did my best to move the bully prince along, silently thanking Esen for never leaving my side. Her presence protected me somewhat from Bakhur's cruelty. If he'd tried to burn more runes into my skin, I would have broken his nose.

And probably gotten myself killed.

Now, dusk had turned to night, and I was perched in Taln's Great Hall, nodding and smiling at an unusually talkative Bakhur during dinner. When I finished my dessert, I noticed that Arrow, who often sat beside Estella, still hadn't appeared in the hall, and I began worrying something terrible had happened to him.

I scanned the room again, checking he wasn't seated at the table reserved for the Light Realm fae, when a firm grip tugged my elbow. Dust, not Bakhur again.

"When we have children, Zali," he said between loud slurps of wine, "do you realize they'll be heirs to not one, but two, possibly even three kingdoms?" He rolled a big mouthful of half-chewed crepes on his tongue, flecks of cream dotting his chin.

"Mouth closed while you eat," I said, tapping his nose in a revolting show of fake affection. "It's an Earth Realm custom. Indulge me?"

"I'll try," he said, gazing at me with regret, as if disappointed that I had no desire to study his mashed-up food.

Mirroring his pitying smile, I squeezed his velvet-covered forearm. "Why don't you have any brothers or sisters, Bakhur?"

"I do. Stepsiblings. After my birth, Mother claimed to be unable to conceive further children, so the king fathered three more sons off his concubines."

"Really?" I studied the faces of the fae below the dais, searching for Azarn's sharp nose and bright green eyes, set in youthful faces. "And they're at court?"

Bakhur scoffed. "Of course not. They're illegitimate and work in the kitchen."

My mouth hung open for so long the prince grew impatient and barked out, "We can't have them trying to usurp the rightful heir, can we?"

"I suppose not," I replied, thinking I'd very much like to help his stepsiblings start an uprising.

"Oh, look," said Bakhur, interrupting my careful inspection of the servants that were collecting dishes from the nearest tables.

It was difficult to make out features in the dimly lit hall, but from what I could tell, Azarn's children weren't among them.

"Zali," said the prince, elbowing my ribs, "look who has arrived."

My head shot up, and I scanned the hall again. Near the entrance to the kitchen, a bright form shone in the shadows, slowly moving closer, like a golden beacon. Then under the light of a large candelabra, the solemn, dear face of the Sayeeda emerged. I leaped to my feet before quickly sitting back down, confused how to react in front of the Fire Court.

"Ari," I breathed, unable to contain a grin.

Azarn laughed as he rose from his chair and strutted along the front of the dais, his calculating green gaze fixed on me. "Well, Zali, are you happy to see the Sayeeda?"

Not looking away from her, I said, "Yes. It's quite lovely to see a familiar face."

"Then you should greet her accordingly," said the king, sweeping his hand toward the three fae who had stopped below the dais on the black marble floor—Ari flanked by Arrow and Raiden.

I bolted down the stairs and sprang into her arms, sending her stumbling backward. Arrow reached out to steady us as Ari's low laugh tickled my ear.

"Little Leaf," she whispered. "It warms my heart to see you looking so well."

I thought of the rune marks burned into my back but knew it wasn't the time or place to mention them. She would discover them soon enough.

"I'm so happy to see you," I whispered back. "Are you all right? How are Ildri and Stormur?"

"I'm excellent now that I've seen you, and your friends in Coridon are all fine and looking forward to reuniting with you. Now, please, get us out of this dreadful hall as quickly as possible."

Linking my arm through Ari's, I turned toward the dais. "King Azarn, do I have permission to return to my chambers with the Sayeeda?"

"Yes, you may," he said, resuming his seat next to Estella. The queen stared blankly into the middle distance as though unaware an esteemed reaver elf, the Zareen's sister, had arrived in her hall.

Arrow and Raiden sat on the dais stairs, stretching their long legs in front of them as they watched servants use fire magic to remove tables from the hall, clearing space for the after-dinner dancing. They appeared uninterested in what Ari and I were doing, but I knew the opposite was true. Both males valued our safety beyond measure.

Before I turned away, my gaze met Arrow's. He winked at me, then resumed chatting with Raiden, settling in to watch the fire courtiers caper about below them.

"I can't believe Azarn allowed you to come to Taln," I told Ari as we left the hall by a side exit. "Why did you arrive through the kitchen?"

"I take pride in my role as Mistress of Spices, and in each new city, the kitchen is the first place I visit. The way a kingdom stores and prepares food, treats their staff, reveals much, and Taln has shown itself to be a city in decline."

I didn't doubt it for a moment.

We hurried along the palace's shifting hallways until we found a familiar small landing, and then mounted the stairs to my chamber.

"Azarn is a fool," Ari said as she stood in my bay window looking out over black cliffs and the silver sea. "Because we reavers maintain the Gold Accord with the Light Realm, the fire fae believe we are a passive, harmless species. They do not fear us. Not even the Zareen. But they should."

"Tyrants don't have enough sense to be afraid of anything," I said, joining her at the window. "Where are your sleeping quarters?"

"One floor below yours. Our rooms are an exact match." She leaned on the sill and studied the whitecaps crashing against jagged rocks. "Azarn is aware of your reputation as an escape artist."

I laughed, squeezing her in a tight hug before sitting on the bed. "Unfortunately, yes."

"Arrow tells me that you thought he orchestrated your abduction, and he's worried part of you still believes it."

"Oh, Ari, I'm an idiot. I should never have doubted his loyalty, but when Esen and the fire fae who'd transformed his face into Raiden's arrested me, doubting Arrow was the only thing that made sense. Is that why he hasn't visited me and renewed the Aldara bond the last two nights?"

"No. It's because he doesn't want to weaken you. But he *has* told Azarn he's still subjecting you to the feedings."

Subjecting me? Whenever Arrow sank his fangs into my flesh, it was hardly an ordeal. I had begged him to drink from me on more than one occasion, possibly hundreds of times.

"Moving on to more important topics," I said, waggling my brows. "How was your trip? It must have been very nice to finally have Raiden all to yourself."

Ari pushed shining curls behind the long blade of her ear, golden cheeks darkening to russet. "It was... wonderful. Lying with him was everything that you warned me it would be. Astonishing. Blissful. Life changing."

I pressed my fingers against my mouth. "So why did you two wait so long? Every fae in Coridon knows you're mad for each other. Nice pendant, by the way," I added, nodding at the tear-shaped ruby framed by black pearls I'd watched Raiden purchase at Taln market four days ago.

"It's the loveliest necklace in the realms." Ari rubbed her fingers over the central jewel. The bed barely dipped as she sat next to me, a glittering smile on her lips. "Reavers only share our bodies with our sworn mates. The Zareen flew to Coridon and made our union official before we left for Taln."

"Oh, Ari, that's brilliant." Gripping her hands, I kissed her cheek. "I'm so happy for you. Raiden must be bursting with joy. I can't count the times I watched him skulk around Arrow's chambers, hoping for a glance of you. It was very entertaining. And the Zareen doesn't mind that he's not of royal birth?"

"Not at all. Reavers bond for love. Position and power means nothing to us."

"Who made the leap first? Who finally decided to be brave?"

She blushed again. "It wasn't me. After you left Mydorian, I received a raven courier from Arrow asking me to return to the Light Realm as quickly as possible. By the time I arrived, he and Raiden had left, leaving word that they'd gone to the Fire Court on urgent business."

"They didn't tell you I'd been taken?"

"No. It wouldn't have been safe. They had to play their parts in Azarn's game and couldn't risk giving themselves away."

"No, I suppose they couldn't."

Ari cupped my cheek with her palm. "Dear one, I knew something was terribly wrong. I felt it in my blood. But I also knew Arrowyn would do everything, stop at nothing to fix the problem, and my role was to bide my time, pretend all was well in his kingdom and await further instructions."

"And so Raiden spoke up when he came to collect you?"

"Yes. It had frightened him to learn that even the king's Aldara could be stolen from him. Raiden didn't want to waste a moment more without me knowing how he felt. He got down on his knees in Coridon's kitchen in front of the staff and declared his undying devotion."

Clapping my hands, I screeched, and Ari covered her ears, laughing. "Raiden's a true romantic, then. You're very fortunate."

She gave me an odd look. "As are you, Leaf. You've been blind to Arrowyn's love, that is all."

With a meaningful glance toward my anklet, I held my finger to my lips, remembering we should be careful in case Melaya happened to be listening. Then I focused internally, checking for the tell-tale signs of activate magic and finding none.

Silk rustled as Ari shrugged her cloak off and walked to the window again, stopping with her body half-turned toward me.

"Taln is a horrible city. Fire geysers spew sparks and sulfurous gases day and night, a merciless sun scorches the arid ground, and yet everyone wears cloaks and burns fires in their rooms as if they were in the Ice Realm."

"The weather is strange," I agreed. "It's sweltering one moment, then cool the next."

"The Fire Court's magic is mysterious and unstable. But the Zareen knows about the ancient mergelyn anklets and assures me they cannot be used to spy on you. It's impossible. Queen Estella's people are capable of such magic, but the fire fae's skills lie in transformation and dragon control. They're fast, efficient fighters, but like most power-hungry species, over-confident in their capabilities."

Relief washing over me, I said, "A passage in an old Taln book hinted that the city's mages are the key to bringing Azarn down, but Melaya... he seems almost indestructible."

"No one is unbeatable, Leaf," she said, fanning herself with the hem of her gold tunic. "I know from experience you pay attention to your enemies. Surely you've already learned Melaya's weaknesses."

"Yes, his twin, Nukala. Remember how Quin believed if I died, then he would too? That misconception was the only reason he kept me alive instead of having me murdered. I'd bet every auron kanara in Coridon that he heard about the foolish twin-soul idea from his dealings with the Fire Court."

"Without a doubt," she agreed.

Pointing at the knives strapped to the Sayeeda's hips, I stood up. "Azarn really does think you're harmless, doesn't he? We need to kill Nukala. The verse in the old Talnian text made me certain of it."

"That may be so, but for now, we must be patient. Watch me carefully." Ari disappeared, reappearing a heartbeat later as her laughter soothed my anxious heart.

"Melaya's block doesn't work on you!"

"I am the Storm Court's bonded reaver elf, the sister of the Zareen. I'm made of stronger stuff than a mere fire mage."

"Then we can use your invisibility cloak to get Orion out of the fire cave. Did Arrow tell you what Azarn has done to your friend?"

Fury twisted her features. "Yes. But if I have my way, Orion won't be there much longer."

"I'd give nearly anything to escape Taln," I said. "But I'd rather stay here forever if it meant I could get Orion out instead. I can't bear that he's suffering because he helped me."

Ari patted my arm, comforting me. "My cloak can cover up to five others if they stay close to me, but we need a fire fae to help us break the spell of the pyre."

"Not just any fire fae, either. It must be a member of the royal family," I said. "Will you ask Estella to help?"

"Leave it to me. The less you know for the moment, the better."

Three soft raps sounded at the door.

"That will be Arrowyn," said Ari.

"Just a moment," I called out. "I'm not dressed."

"Fine with me," Arrow murmured, laughter in his voice. "Azarn's guards are cowering some distance down the stairwell."

"I'm still with Ari, gossiping about Raiden. Give us a minute?"

Arrow grunted, likely worried we were talking about him—which we soon would be.

I reached for Ari's arm, tugging her close and hitching my chin toward the door. "Why did he bring Zaret to Taln? We both know he's not fond of humans, especially gold addicts."

"Thanks to Arrow, Zaret is now an *ex*-addict, and he refused to stay at Coridon with Ildri and Stormur, who are his foster parents. Many times, he has heard the tale of how you made Arrow promise to take care of him. Leaf, Zaret would die to protect you."

With my heart melting, I got up and opened the door, flinging myself into Arrow's arms. "Thank you," I said, peppering his face with grateful kisses. "Thank you for keeping your word."

Laughing, he walked me backward into the room and kicked the door shut. Strong arms banded my waist as he lifted me off my feet, dangling me in the air for a moment. "Tell me straight away what I've done to deserve this spontaneous affection so I can repeat the action several-hundred times a day."

"Ari just told me what you've done for Zaret. I'm so grateful, Arrow. Thank you."

"Zaret is a good man. He reminds me of you, Leaf. Uncompromising in his opinions. Never afraid to criticize me when he disagrees. In your absence, he has acted as my conscience."

"Because you don't possess one?" I teased.

"I've always had one," he said, strolling over to embrace his Sayeeda and kiss her cheeks. "But after the death of my family, it took a tiny human spitfire to remind me how to use it."

He stalked forward and guided me to the window. Dropping into the seat, he tugged me onto his lap and wrapped his arms around my waist. "So what did I miss?"

"We were speaking of Orion," said Ari. "About getting him out of the cave."

Arrow gripped my chin and turned my face toward his. "Leaf, it is an extremely dangerous task. One I'd prefer you not to be involved in."

"No. Promise you'll include me. It's my fault Orion is suffering. I need to see him released."

Arrow's sigh ruffled my hair. "Fine. We may need to use the orchid petals that made you invisible the other night."

My entire body flushed hot as I remembered how he'd kissed me in his room while I flickered in and out of visibility, and for a selfish moment, I wished we were alone. I quickly told Ari about the serpent fae and the orchid petals he'd given me.

"If there are only a few of us, we should save the petals for our escape and use my reaver cloak instead," she said.

"Did the Zareen tell you anything about how Melaya's blocking power works?" I asked her.

"It's veiled in mystery. But it *is* true that the twin mages, not the king, possess the most power in the realm. Melaya has set blocking wards throughout the kingdom. Beyond the Fen Forest, your own reaver cloak would likely work, as would Arrowyn's storm power."

"If the brothers are so powerful, why don't they get rid of the king and take control of the city?" I asked.

"Estella," Arrow replied, his thumb stroking the sensitive skin of my forearm and his chest plate of feathers rough against my back. "She is the key to Azarn retaining power."

I sat up straighter, twisting to face him. "The queen is?"

"Why do you think he took her from the Star Court?" Arrow plucked me off his lap, placed me on the window-seat cushions, then got up and paced across the room. "As you've probably realized, theirs was far from a love match."

I frowned. "I thought it was an arranged marriage that benefited both kingdoms."

On my bed, Ari folded her legs beneath her. "They may frame it that way now, but no, it was far from amicably arranged. With Melaya's help, Azarn tricked her, subdued her formidable cosmic power and just... took her. The queen has no lust for gold or desire to control kingdoms. She keeps the mages in line for the sake of Bakhur."

KING OF FIRE AND FLAMES

"Exactly," said Arrow. "Estella hates Azarn and will no doubt move against him eventually. Her realm only wishes to be left in peace. The star fae can stop time, suck matter into black holes, uncreate life, and do unspeakable things with their power. Thank the gold they are mostly a peace-loving species."

"But what prevents Estella from taking action or from leaving?" I asked.

Ari sighed. "The bonds between Azarn and Estella cannot be broken without bringing harm to her son."

"She'd have to kill Bakhur to be rid of her husband?"

"That's right," said Arrow.

Hugging my knees to my chest, I thought through what I'd learned, not entirely sure it all made sense. "But why would Melaya help Azarn bring a queen, whose power was considerably stronger than his, to Taln in the first place?" I asked.

"There's more to it than just Estella keeping Melaya in check, Leaf," replied Ari. "For him to keep his position and full powers, he must always obey Azarn's directives."

I rubbed my temples. "Why?"

"Because at the twin mages' birth, unbreakable blood bonds were woven through their bodies, making it impossible for them to disobey whoever had been *officially crowned* the current King of Fire."

"How do you know?" I asked.

"The Zareen shared ancient knowledge with Ari, and since our arrival in Taln, Zaret has been spending a large sum of my gold bribing select fae. His sources hint at a similar story."

Excitement bubbling over, I clapped my hands together, grinning. "So given her hatred for Azarn, surely Estella will help us get Orion out of that fucking cave."

249

"No, Ruhh will," said both Ari and Arrow at the same time.

"*Ruhh*? The girl who killed herself because you wouldn't marry her? The same one who asked me to kill you while you were in bed recovering from a battle wound?"

"Ruhh has forgiven me, and Ari relayed a special message to her from the Zareen. One that means more to her than anything."

"So you *did* kill Ruhh," I said, shooting onto my feet and pacing in front of the bed.

Arrow sat next to his Sayeeda and watched me with a wary expression.

"Leaf, I admit it was a... a terrible situation. When I came to visit Azarn to make amends for your attack on the Sun envoy, Neeron, she threatened to have you killed in Coridon. And I knew she had the means to do it. We argued at the Lake of Fire, and she slipped and fell in. I simply... well, I didn't help her get out. I couldn't let her hurt you in any way. *Ever.*"

"Then why did Ruhh tell me she jumped from the palace?"

"I threw her body from the tallest tower to make it look like she had. Azarn has no proof that I was responsible for her death, but blames me anyway." Arrow laughed. "In truth, he isn't wrong."

"It's really not a laughing matter, Arrow. You're quite deranged. Do you know that?"

He gripped my shoulders, stopping my restless pacing. "I don't think you understand how far I'll go to protect you. No atrocity would be too vile and no being safe should they make the mistake to stand between us. Don't you think I would've already razed Taln three times over if it would ensure your safety, love?"

"No more," I said, pressing my face against his chest plate. "Promise me that from now on, only good deeds will be committed in the name of our love. And by the way, are these gold feathers still poisonous in Taln?"

"Unfortunately, no." His deep voice rumbled against my cheek. "My first good deed in honor of our love will be to free the orc from the fire cave."

I stared up at him. "How? And when?"

"Tomorrow at dawn we'll meet at the moat. Ari will bring you under her reaver's cloak, and we shall save the petals for defeating Melaya and his brother."

"Wouldn't it be safer to do it at night?"

"No," Ari said, guiding me to settle on the chair in front of the mirror. "They won't expect us to make a move in plain sight. Arrow must leave now and finalize the plan, and you and I will prepare for tomorrow by conserving our energy and getting a good night's rest."

Arrow moved Ari out of his way and stole a kiss from me. "Good night, my Aldara. Sleep well."

As the Storm King exited, Ari began unpinning my braids. As she brushed my hair, the slow strokes soothed me into a frowning silence as I thought over everything that had been said tonight.

Ari put the brush on the dresser, then squeezed my shoulders. "Leaf, I can hear you worrying. Please try to relax. Arrow and I have a plan in motion. A good one. Trust us."

What choice did I have? I couldn't rescue Orion on my own.

Chapter 26

LEAF

When I woke up the next day, the sun had already risen, and a soft mauve light slanted through the cracks in the curtains. With a gasp, I leaped out of bed, then stumbled around my chamber as I tried to get my bearings.

Where was Ari? Had she slept in, too?

I threw on clothes—a dark red tunic over my Mydorian leathers, Arrow's feather cloak wrapped around my shoulders—then opened the door.

"Morning," I said, surprised to find Raiden and Zaret standing outside my room. "I'm going for a walk."

"We'll join you," said Raiden.

"Uh, probably not a good idea. I didn't get much sleep last night so won't be very good company."

"We don't mind getting our heads snapped off. And Arrow asked us to keep you safe, Zali," said Zaret. "You should remain in your room until he returns. I'm sorry."

Right. So those dust-damned traitors had left without me. Or at least they *thought* they had. Arrow must have forgotten how I reacted to orders. I ignored them.

"Oh? And where is Arrow?" I asked, holding the edge of the door and swinging it back and forth in a distracted manner. "And have you seen Ari this morning?"

Raiden smiled, subtle creases bracketing his warm, brown eyes. "I think you know very well where they are. And in case it all goes to shit, he wanted you as far away from the scene as possible."

"Okay, that's reasonable. I'll take a bath, then. And since you're so concerned about my safety, I'll even leave the door open a little so you can hear if I drown."

Making sure the gap was wide enough for me to fit through, I smiled sweetly, then hurried to the bathing room. I ran the water, clunked some soap about in the tub, and dropped a couple of towels on the floor to mimic the sound of my clothes hitting the floor. Then I pulled an orchid petal from my pocket and rubbed it over my chest.

Magic shivered through me, and I swiveled to face the mirror. Good. It was blank. I turned the faucet off, splashed my hand through the water for a minute, then quietly slipped through the door and past my well-meaning guards into the crisp morning air.

Soon, the chill would disperse, and the sky would be ablaze with dragon fire, but for now, even the dragons and their trainers slumbered soundly in their beds.

When I arrived at the fire moat, no khareek, sneaky Storm King, or two-faced reaver elf were waiting for me. I hurried to the cliffs and peered over the edge. Still no sign of Arrow or Ari, but at least the fire cave was visible, tiny sparks swirling from its mouth, eddying in lazy patterns toward puffy white clouds in the lightening sky.

My heart pounded as I climbed down the slope onto the path cut into the cliff side, and then proceeded toward the cave, terrified of what I might find when I arrived.

At the cave's entrance, I took a deep breath then marched straight through the wall of fire and the first torch-lit chamber. I moved quickly into the concealed passage toward the back, then followed the rocky tunnel, gasping as I came out into the larger cavern where my friends stood around the pyre of green flames.

Tied to the unbreakable triangle of Xanthanian-metal poles, Orion was unconscious. Green light from the flames flickered over him, the magical bars of the prison sadly still intact.

Arrow held a sleeping Bakhur in his arms, and Ruhh of course, hovered directly above his shoulder. Esen and Ari whispered intently together in the middle of the limestone floor, and fire symbols pulsed along the walls as if in response to the intruders.

Distracted by the strange scene, I collided with a protruding slab of rock and stumbled, my boots scuffling loudly as I regained my balance.

"What was that?" asked Arrow, his glyphs igniting as he looked around the cave.

"It's only Zali," said Ruhh.

Three heads swiveled in my direction, their brows raised and eyes wide.

"The fuck," growled Arrow. "Where?"

"She's used the petals again," continued Ruhh, "and is invisible to your eyes, but not mine. Because of my... deceased state, most forms of magic don't work on me."

"And I can see you all clearly," I said. "Why aren't you under Ari's cloak?"

"I'm conserving my energy while we're in the cave," she replied, squinting in my general direction. "Where are you, Leaf?"

I stepped forward and gently grasped Ari's hand. "I'm here. I'll stay on your left side."

Arrow came up beside us, and like a blind man, used his free hand to pat my face, my shoulders, then squeeze me roughly. "You should be asleep. Why won't you let me keep you safe?"

I tucked a chunk of gold hair behind his ear. "I'm invisible. If anyone turns up, I can run fast. I'll be fine. But thank you for caring. Now, what's the plan?"

Orion moaned and lifted his head, his single orange eye staring at my friends through a haze of floating embers. My gut churned at the sight of him. He looked terrible, his body soaked with sweat, mangled tusks faded to chalky white, and his dark hair and beard stringy and bleached of color. It was hard to believe he was still alive.

I moved closer to the pyre, the stench of suffering and magic strong. "Get him down. Please, someone... Ruhh?"

Arrow propped Bakhur on his feet, holding him against his side. "Ruhh, what should we do next?"

"To break the Sentura spell, Bakhur's saliva must be added to the flames," she said.

Arrow held the prince face-first over the pit, and Ari gripped his chin, keeping his jaw open.

"Try massaging his cheeks," I suggested.

Ari squeezed and rubbed, Bakhur's lips forming comical shapes, but no spit dripped out.

"Fuck this." Arrow crouched down and shoved Bakhur's face even closer to the flames, shaking him until his tongue lolled out. Finally, half-choking, Bakhur spluttered, and a long string of drool sizzled down onto the pyre.

Lifting Bakhur into his arms, Arrow leaped backward. We stood with our hearts in our mouths, waiting for something to happen.

"It didn't work," said Esen after a few minutes.

Then Orion moaned, and the belly of the mountain seemed to rumble and groan, the ground shaking beneath our feet. Outside, thunder cracked across the sky, and I glanced at Arrow. His hands flexed with the need to connect to its power, and he threw his arms up, fingers spread wide. But the storm refused to answer his call.

Rocks and crystals cracked off the cave's roof, debris shattering around us. The runes on the walls flashed bright green, then turned a dull shade of ocher, like the branches of a dead swamp tree.

With a loud whoosh, the pyre's flames twirled upward, transforming into billowing gray smoke that hit the top of the cave then disappeared with an ear-popping sucking sound.

Emitting a broken whimper, Orion slumped forward, his body straining against his bonds.

"It's all right," I said, stepping into the empty pit and hugging his knees carefully. "We'll get you out of here."

Esen used fire magic to sever the dragon-hide ropes binding his wrists and ankles to the poles, and then lifted him from the frame. "He weighs nothing," she said, laying him on the ground with great care.

"Leave me... please. Not safe," Orion muttered, his broken words barely audible. "Dead anyway."

"Orion, please don't say that." I bent and brushed sweat-soaked hair from his face, untangling it from the remains of his tusks. "We won't let you die."

"Leaf? I can't see you. Are you..."

"I'm here, but I'm invisible, as you soon will be, too. Safe under the Sayeeda's cloak."

Ari held a water pouch to Orion's cracked lips, and he drank deeply, somehow managing to keep the liquid down. She broke up pieces of dried meat and tucked them into the sides of his cheeks. "If you haven't the strength to chew and swallow, just suck on them. I'm putting more in your pockets."

"It's all arranged, Orion," said Arrow as he nodded for Esen to pick the orc up again. "As we speak, in the second bay around the coastline, a fishing boat waits, cloaked by the reaver elves on board. They are healers and have ample food, water, and comfort to offer. On the Light Realm coast, eponars are waiting to carry your party to the sanctuary of Auryinnia, where the Zareen herself and your wife will oversee your recovery."

"My wife?" Orion croaked.

Arrow nodded. "Yes. You must hold on. You have much to live for."

"How?" I asked, as Ari whispered the reaver chant—*auron khaban ana*—calling the magic forward, but not fully activating her cloak. "How did you organize all of this in so little time?"

"Speaking of time, yours is running out. You must speak later," urged Ruhh as she flew through the cavern like an angry wasp. "It's no longer safe here."

Arrow led us through the dark passage, his deep voice echoing in the confined space. "On the night that Azarn tortured Orion in the hall, Esen began working on a plan to get him out of the

Sun Realm. She's trusted here and could communicate with our contacts in other realms."

So, it seemed he had fully reconciled with his ex-guard and held no grudge against her for aligning with the fire fae or conspiring to arrest me. Arrowyn Ramiel continued to surprise me.

Outside, a raging storm attacked the cliffs above and the sea below, Arrow shuddering with each flash of lightning as if it had struck him between the shoulder blades.

If enduring a foul storm was the sole consequence of breaking the Sentura-Pyre spell, then we'd gotten off very lightly.

Ari activated her reaver cloak, and to stay in its range, we traveled close together, slipping and sliding down the rocky trail toward the beach, with Esen balancing Orion on her shoulder and Arrow carrying the unconscious prince rather carelessly, his night robes trailing the sand.

When Bakhur woke up, he would have a brutal crick in his neck.

Chapter 27

LEAF

I t didn't take long to work out that if I stayed close to Ari, in the range of her reaver's cloak, I could see everyone in our small party. But I still wasn't visible to them.

The blood orchid's magic was fire based, incompatible with the deep-earth power of the elves of Auryinnia, and therefore reacted unpredictably.

"How long will it take to arrive at the meeting place?" I asked, swiping wet hair from my eyes.

"About fifteen minutes if we move fast," said Arrow. "Keep talking, Leaf. I need to know where you are at all times."

"I can do that," I replied as I tugged on Ari's tunic. "What did you do to Bakhur?"

"Estella created a sleeping potion for him. He's had a large dose," said Ari, not looking back as she spoke, the wind flapping her soaked, golden tunic around her calves.

"Bakhur's *mother* gave you a sleeping potion?" I tripped over my feet in surprise. "Your powers of persuasion are truly astounding."

Ari laughed. "*Estella* suggested we use Bakhur to break the pyre's spell."

"Gods, that was... nice of her, I guess."

Granting Arrow's request, I blathered on about the rumbling storm clouds and the tiny creatures living in the rock pools I leaped over, and he grunted or laughed, responding to each trivial comment.

We followed the shoreline around a sharp bend, staying close to the cliffs, the rain finally abating when we arrived at a small bay about ten minutes later.

Sand squeaked beneath our boots, jewel-toned sea glass glinting in the sunlight amongst the coarse grains. White caps raced like spirited silver ponies into the shore, and a group of gulls circled above the sea as they fished for breakfast, their urgent cries evoking memories of picnics on the beach with my family when I was a child.

Ruhh flew ahead and skimmed over the waves, the ragged edges of her gown trailing in the foam.

"Fuck. The boat isn't here," said Esen.

Ari released the reaver cloak, then whistled, wading into the sea. The slick backs of three dolphins crested in the distance. They swam into waist-high water and circled the Sayeeda with friendly splashes and cheerful chirping noises.

"Come quickly." Ari waved at Esen, urging her to bring Orion forward.

The dolphins formed a row, pressing the sides of their bodies together in a tight line, while Esen stomped into the gentle surf. She draped Orion over their backs and clamped his fingers around two dorsal fins. "No matter what happens, orc, do not let go."

"Be safe, Orion," I called out. "I'll be seeing you soon in Auryinnia."

The dolphins traveled in graceful arcs until they reached the middle of the bay, Ruhh flying above as the reaver elves' hands appeared on the edge of the invisible boat and pulled Orion's limp body aboard. First, his forearms vanished, then his head and shoulders, followed by his torso and upper legs, then finally, he was gone.

Ari walked out of the surf and stopped in front of me. "Don't worry, Leaf. The boat is well-equipped with two skilled sailors and three elves. The orc will be fine," she assured me.

"Thank you. Until we hear that he's reached Auryinnia safely, I'll be praying to every god in the realms," I said.

With his free hand, Arrow felt for me, hitching Bakhur higher over his back before pulling me into his other side. "Orion knew the risks when he helped you board Loligos's ship, and he chose to do it anyway. You would've done the same for him if your positions had been reversed."

Two sharp screeches reverberated across the sky, and Ruhh flew like a tornado above us, agitated.

"The grymarians are awake," she hissed. "We need to run."

"What? What are grymarians?" I asked, my gaze scanning the cliffs and finding only gray rocks and scraggly, shrub-like trees. "I don't see anything."

"Over there," said Esen, pointing a little to the right of where Ruhh was facing.

"Ari, activate your cloak again," ordered Arrow, squinting into the diffused sunlight. "Shit," he breathed, squeezing me harder as two gray figures morphed out of the cliff face.

The grymarians leaped into the air, and before we could move a muscle to flee, they landed without a sound on the sand only a few yards away.

The winged creatures were at least a head taller than Arrow, their wiry, muscular builds covered in opalescent black scales. From the neck down, the male and female pair looked like any other fire fae, their powerful, naked bodies gracefully shaped, but their faces were something else.

Dark green scales slithered over large brows concealing luminous silver eyes, adorned with slitted black irises, all framed by stringy brown hair resembling seaweed that had long ago washed ashore.

Their cold eyes tracked over us, assessing before attacking. Twisted black horns curled above their long ears, the tips covered in gore.

"Whatever those things are," I said, "I think they can see us. *All* of us."

Wringing her hands together, Ruhh circled wildly above us. "They're guardians. My brother never mentioned that he had set them to watch the pyre, but I should have guessed. I should have *known*. I'm just a stupid dead girl."

She slapped her forehead, and I tried to grab hold of her as she buzzed past, but my hands slipped through her spectral body. "It's not your fault, Ruhh," I whispered.

The grymarians raised dark-red wings, crosshatched with scars, and then leaped into the air, screeching toward us.

"Run," yelled Arrow, dropping Bakhur on the sand before scooping me up and throwing me over his shoulder as his legs swung into motion. "Everyone stay close to Ari so she can cover us with her cloak."

"Arrow, don't leave Bakhur behind," I said, my hips bucking in protest. "And I don't think the reaver cloak works on them."

"There's no other choice. Your safety is all that matters."

"I'll get him," yelled Esen, tracking back to collect the prince.

We ran in the direction of the palace, not once looking behind us, but just as we neared the path that led toward the fire moat, the dragon-like fae alighted on the sand in front of us. I slid off Arrow's back, clasping his hand as my boots hit the ground.

Clouds of black smoke wound from the creatures' clawed hands, filling the air between us. Mesmerized, I reached out to touch it.

Ruhh hissed. "Don't even look at their magic, Zali. Its purpose is to draw prey close, keeping them placid and the meat nice and tender."

"Gods, I sure hope we're dead when they start feasting on us," I said as Ruhh shot into the air, disappearing, and leaving us to our fates. But I held no hard feelings. She'd done all she could, and I just hoped she made it back to the palace safely.

At the sound of my voice, the creatures' heads canted, their slitted irises widening. I'd assumed they could see me, but as they sniffed the air, tracing my scent, I realized that they couldn't. I didn't know which god in which realm I had to thank, but the magic of the orchid petals seemed to work on the grymarians.

Keeping her gaze averted from me, Ari raised a finger to her lips, pretending to brush something away, perhaps an insect, a clear sign for me to stay silent.

"My energy is depleted, and my cloak has failed," she whispered between gritted teeth. "They can see us, but not you, Leaf. Go now. Hurry."

Arrow released my hand. "Go," he said gruffly. "For once, do as I ask."

"Not leaving without you," I whispered.

"Yes, you are. Look carefully at the beasts' magic. Someone's coming. If you won't leave for your own sake, then go for ours. We'll need someone to get us out of this mess."

"What do you mean?" I asked, squinting at the guardians. "Who's coming?"

The beasts prowled closer, the black smoke thickening until the outlines of three bodies became visible. Then Azarn, Melaya, and Neeron stepped out of the dark haze.

"I told you, My King," said the sneering Sun envoy. "I knew they were up to something when I saw the human leave the fire cave with Esen a few days ago. As soon as I noticed the guardians take to the air this morning, I guessed what terrible deed the storm fae had accomplished."

Melaya flicked his fingers, and Ari's reaver cloak retracted.

Azarn's crown of black flames swayed in the breeze as he stepped closer to us. Growls rumbled from the grymarians' chests, their animal stares fixed on my friends, who were now completely visible.

"Sayeeda, what interest have you in the orc's survival?" asked Azarn.

"He is a particular friend of my family's," said Ari. "His father helped our Zareen during the War of Attrition. Elves never forget a kindness and aim to repay it tenfold."

"Did you bring gold serum into my land? Is that what you used to poison my son?" He nodded at Bakhur's limp form, still snoring gently in Esen's arms.

Ari met the Fire King's gaze, not flinching. "Yes," she lied. "It acts as a sleeping tonic on sensitive fae. I took a chance it might work on him. And it paid off."

Azarn's jaw ticked as he strutted back and forth in front of our line, his hands behind his back as if making a decision. Finally, he stopped in front of Arrow, so close I could smell the scent of sleep on his royal bed robes.

"Even though you deserve it, Arrowyn, I don't believe I shall kill you just yet," said Azarn, turning slightly toward Esen. "And although you chose to protect my son from the guardians, you were part of this foolish plot and perhaps instrumental in its design. You betrayed me and must join your former master in the dungeon."

Silent, Esen bowed her head.

"Retrieve the prince," barked Azarn, and Neeron took Bakhur from Esen, stumbling a little at his dead weight.

Waves of fury rolled off Arrow's body, prickling my skin. Without a doubt, he longed to blow the City of Taln to dust, his actions hindered only by Melaya's power block.

The fire mage bristled, flames leaping in his eyes, as if he'd love nothing more than to snap the Storm King's neck. It would be quite a sight to witness—the two of them engaged in battle, their powers unrestricted. But alas, that wouldn't happen today.

Azarn wrapped his dark robe tighter around his chest and leaned close to Arrow. "From now on, your gold reaver will serve *me*."

"That's impossible," Arrow ground out. "There are ceremonies, rituals that must be completed. The Sun Realm has no Accord with Auryinnia."

"That is true. But perhaps the Sayeeda's terms of service will be a little... *different* to the bond you shared with her, Arrowyn. Regardless, I believe we will get along quite well."

"If you hurt her—"

"What will you do?" Azarn asked, grinning as he circled him. "Having repaid my friendship by releasing an enemy of my court, you're in no position to make any demands."

Arrow released a frustrated sigh. "Orion's sentence was too harsh. Savage, in fact. Killing him would've been kinder. You've already made him pay for his betrayal a thousand times over."

Azarn laughed, his fingers combing through his beard. "How ironic that the ruler known for stringing slaves from a pavilion high above his city, carving them up, and letting their blood paint the sides of his palace while they died slow deaths, even thinks to call *me* harsh. *You*, Arrowyn Ramiel, are the savage."

"King Darian did those horrible things, not me. I have never taken pleasure in another being's suffering. I will never be like you or my father."

"All that matters is that you pay for today's crimes. Put him in chains, Melaya," Azarn ordered. "And while I decide what to do with you, Storm King, you will reside in a cell, and your Aldara will be punished for your deeds. Zali will be my son's pet, and through her, we shall control *you*. You will write the Zareen pretty letters and maintain the Gold Accords with Auryinnia. From now on, my court will manage the trade or the human you profess not to care about will suffer. Fight us now, and she will be tortured immediately. As we speak, my soldiers are on their way to find her."

Beside me, Arrow ground his teeth together.

Shit, shit, shit.

"If you know where Zali is, you had better tell me now," said Azarn.

"Zali prefers to sleep late. I assume she is in her room," said Ari at the same time as Arrow said, "This has nothing to do with the human."

Melaya conjured a red beam of magic, blasting it directly into Arrow's chest. He collapsed on the sand with a thud.

Fuck, fuck, fuck.

He had better not be dead.

I waited three seconds before I saw his chest rise and fall. Then I turned and bolted up the hillside. At the top of the cliffs, I stopped briefly and watched Melaya produce another mergelyn anklet from a ball of flames that spun on his palm before he fastened the damned thing around Ari's leg.

With loud screeches, the guardians took to the air, and I sprinted toward the palace, praying I would make it to my room before Azarn's guards arrived.

Chapter 28

LEAF

P raying the orchid's magic would keep me invisible, I raced up the tower stairs, then dashed past Raiden and Zaret, who were arguing with two of Azarn's guards outside the door to my chamber, which, thank the dust, was still ajar.

"And *I'll* say it again—you *still* don't have permission to enter," Raiden told them as I darted into the bathroom and ripped my clothes off faster than a bandage stuck to a wound.

I leaped into the now-cold bath water and scrubbed my skin mercilessly, attempting to wash the petal juice from my skin while the argument continued outside.

Boots pounded on the stairs, then I heard the Fire King's voice, rasping so low I couldn't make out his words.

"As I said, Zali is in the bath." Raiden's voice again.

"Move aside," said Azarn.

Oh, gods. If he entered the bathroom and saw... *nothing*, I'd be royally fucked.

"Princess Zali, are you in there?" asked Azarn from my bedroom.

"Yes. But I'm not dressed."

"And she hasn't left her room at all this morning?" Azarn asked, voice muffled as if he'd turned away.

"Of course not," Raiden replied. "We've been positioned here since before dawn. What's going on?"

"Did Arrowyn order you to guard her?"

"Yes," replied Raiden.

"King Azarn, if you tell us what has happened, perhaps—"

"Never mind," said the king, cutting off Zaret. "Guards, arrest them."

The sounds of a scuffle reverberated through the walls—muffled thuds, grunts, weapons clashing, then boots scraping as though Azarn's soldiers dragged Raiden and Zaret down the tower stairs.

"Guard her door until I tell you otherwise," said the king to his men. "And leave the door ajar so you'll hear if she gets up to mischief. The Earth Princess is not to leave her room. Understood?"

"Yes, Your Majesty," gruff voices rumbled.

Silently, I climbed out of the bath and dried off. By the time I'd gotten back into my clothes, a quick check in the mirror confirmed that I was still invisible. At least I'd learned something new. Water had no effect on the orchid petals' magic.

The Storm Court fae were likely imprisoned in the palace cells or held under guard in their rooms. So currently, my options to help them were limited. But before the petal's effect wore off, I needed to find Estella and beg her assistance. While she had no desire to endanger her despicable son by getting involved herself, the fae of the Star Court wielded significant power. Perhaps she could convince them to intervene.

But first, I had to track her down.

Fortunately, during the last two weeks, I had paid special attention to the royal family's habits and learned that most days, the queen ate lunch alone in her private garden behind the fire conservatory. According to Ruhh, she never let anyone join her. Not even her precious son, Bakhur.

It was easy to slip past Azarn's guards, who were busy bouncing fire balls down the stairs to see whose would be the first to ricochet off the walls and back onto the landing in front of my chamber.

I jumped over their beams of magic, essentially hopping down the stairs, and when I reached the bottom, I breathed a sigh of relief to find all my limbs still attached and in reasonable working order.

Passing court servants and a few soldiers, I hurried through the city, thankful no one could see me as I ducked out of the path of merchants' carts and darted away from the spray of erupting fire geysers dotted throughout the gardens.

Before long, the conservatory's stained glass came into view, glinting under the midday sun. I stopped a moment to catch my breath and admire its captivating beauty. Then I zipped past the guards and pushed through the entrance, blinking in the darkness for a moment until the flames around the bottom of the windows ignited.

Behind me, the clueless guards grumbled about the gust of wind that had blown open the door and seemingly ruined their day.

My footsteps echoed as I ran past tropical plants glowing red and blue in the diffused light, and then skirted around the empty black table that Azarn and his family had occupied four days ago.

A loud whooshing noise crackled behind me, and a quick glance over my shoulder confirmed the seven tanourans had peeled their fiery bodies off the walls and now danced with gusto toward me.

I ran faster until I slammed into the back wall made of opaque glass, sparks from the advancing fire creatures scorching my clothes. The glass shuddered beneath my thumping fists.

"Estella, it's Zali. Please let me in. I need to speak to you urgently."

Silence.

The tanourans came so close I could see the gape of their eye sockets and mouths filled with razor-sharp teeth and fire. So much terrifying fire.

"Estella! Please, Azarn is holding Arrow prisoner, and the tanourans are about to burn me alive."

An opening materialized in the wall. I stepped through it, spinning on my heel in time to see the glass melt closed behind me.

Surrounded by darkness again, I squinted and blinked, hoping my eyes would soon adjust. Slowly, the glow of colorful mushrooms and flowers became visible, growing in clusters below the glittering branches of an enormous weeping willow. On the ceiling high above, stars ranged in an inky sky, as if the sun had no dominion here and it was always nighttime inside these enchanted walls.

Ruhh had called it the queen's garden, but it was more of a room, glamoured to appear like the outdoors at night. A strange in-between place that thrummed with old magic and I had no desire to dwell in for long.

The remains of a luncheon were laid out on a small table—a crystal goblet on its side, silver plates scattered with bread and cheese crumbs. Behind the table, the queen herself sat facing a pond, her long hair streaming around her like a cape of darkest midnight.

I cleared my throat. "Queen Estella, I'm so sorry. I hope I didn't interrupt you," I said, meeting her far-away gaze as her head swiveled in my direction, the movement more birdlike than fae or human.

She smiled and beckoned me over. "The petal's effect is wearing off, Zali. Parts of your body are flickering in and out of visibility. And you're not interrupting me. I was merely spying on the Star Court and missing home. I welcome a diversion from my sadness. Please, come sit and tell me what has happened."

I settled on the queen's left, laughing when I saw my reflection in the silvery water—my face and limbs wavering like a mirage in the Light Realm desert.

Estella waved her hand, and magic vibrated against my clothes, tickling my skin. "That's better," she said, scanning me from head to toe. "Now, I can see you. I'll give you a piece of jewelry when you leave that will keep you invisible until you remove it in your chamber. It's more reliable than those wretched orchid petals."

"Thank you," I said before taking a long breath to slow my racing heart. "I think Azarn has locked Arrow and Esen in a cell somewhere, possibly Raiden and Zaret, too. And he's taken control of Ari."

"The Storm King's Sayeeda? That was bold of him, but my husband is ever a fool in the pursuit of power. Did they get the orc to safety?"

"Yes, and Bakhur is safe, too. Although, it was a close call. Azarn arrived just as the grymarians were about to make a meal of us."

"A mother always feels when her children have suffered great harm. I knew Bakhur was well. You were fortunate Azarn showed up when he did. If he hadn't, you would all be dead."

"I never thought I'd be grateful for your husband's interference, but I guess I am. Sort of."

"Zali, you must get the storm fae out of the dungeon below the moat and help Arrowyn restore balance to the realms. Azarn must die, perhaps even Bakhur, too. I wish things were different, but he has chosen to follow in his father's footsteps, not mine. As Taln's heir, he will only seek to destabilize the realms for his own ends."

A branch snapped overhead, then a snow-white owl swooped onto Estella's right shoulder, its crystalline wings shining like faceted rainbow moonstone.

"Hello, Feydar," the queen said, stroking the creature's head while it inspected me through wide, golden eyes. "I know you dislike traveling in the daylight, but I need you to find Azarn and tell me what he is up to. Also, please find out how the Storm Court fae are faring. Take care, and hurry back with your report."

With a deep hoot, the owl launched off Estella's shoulder and disappeared into thin air, the sound of its wings flapping the only sign it flew through the doorway she had opened.

"Don't worry, Zali. Your friends should be safe. We have time to make a plan," Estella said, stroking my cheek with cool fingers. "My husband won't kill Arrowyn and the Sayeeda. He needs them alive to keep Auryinnia in line. Without the Storm King, the auron kanara cannot be fed, the reavers will die without their feathers, and the entire gold trade will grind to a halt."

"I know," I said. "Without Arrow, *all* the realms are destabilized."

Estella smiled, displaying a row of pointed teeth. "And yet, not long ago, you were scheming to kill him yourself."

Heat flushed over my cheeks. "I'm far too vengeful. It's a terrible character flaw. I know it. But I promise I'm working on it."

Estella laughed. "You and the Storm King are well-matched."

"Tell me about Melaya's brother. How do we get to him? He's the key to defeating Azarn, isn't he?"

She nodded. "My husband keeps Nukala locked in his apartments, only letting him roam free every now and then to appease Melaya and show his pet off to the court."

"Can you enter these apartments?"

"Of course, but I rarely do. I cannot bear the sight of him caged. As you have seen, Melaya's block limits my power, but it is *still* usable. Nukala has a fetish, a fantasy if you like, about intimacy with humans. He is fascinated by your species."

"Why?" I asked.

"In this court, he is weak. Most fae don't realize that without him, Melaya's power is significantly reduced. Nukala despises being seen as powerless and yearns to control someone weaker than himself. I will tell him that as punishment for the Storm Court's release of Orion, Azarn has agreed to let him play with you for a short period."

"He wants *me*?"

She laughed. "In truth, any female human would do, and at present, you're the only one available. I will visit Nukala on the evening of your wedding and inform him you'll be brought to his chamber just before you say the vows that will make you Bakhur's wife. He will take great pleasure in the idea of having you before his prince does."

"Okay," I said through a grimace, hoping I wouldn't actually be left alone with Nukala. "Then what?"

"I'll tell him I've discovered that water neutralizes your Aldara mark. I'll run a bath under the pretense of allowing him to do whatever he wants with you for one hour and convince him to get into the tub to wait for you. When he does, I'll overpower him and hold him under water for approximately twenty minutes. This will block Melaya's power but won't be long enough to kill Nukala. His magic will allow him to breathe underwater for at least that duration of time. Your court will have a small window of time in which your powers will function normally. I suggest you make the most of it."

"Why not kill Nukala? Wouldn't that solve all our problems?"

"As soon as Nukala died, Melaya would know it. He'd kill Arrowyn and alert the entire court to your attack. Even with his power reduced, none of you would survive his wrath."

"But with his twin dead, Melaya couldn't reinstate the block on our magic. It would be a fair fight between him and Arrow, right?"

"Wrong. Even death cannot sever the mergelyn twin's connection. Residual magic will flow between them for some time, and the block will likely return for an hour or so before petering away."

"Shit. So how does holding Nukala under water work?"

"It's simple. Water extinguishes fire."

"Oh, I see. And after you let Nukala out of the bath, what will he do to *you*?"

"He is always drunk. He will fight badly, but I'll only kill him if I must. Only in self-defense and after you've disposed of Azarn."

"What you did the day we fought in the arena was truly breathtaking. You could use your cosmic magic to kill them all. Destroy the mages and Azarn. Why haven't you?"

"At the time of my marriage to Azarn, magical blood bonds were created to ensure that if he was ever murdered, our son's life force would leech from his body in a slow, excruciating death. I've worked tirelessly to rehabilitate Bakhur, hoping I could guide him toward the light of kindness and empathy, never wanting harm to come to him. But now I see there is no other choice."

"So you've put up with Azarn's tyranny to save Bakhur?"

"Yes, and also, if I killed Azarn and Melaya, the Star Court would view me as a criminal and a traitor to my adopted home. I couldn't bear returning to them in disgrace. But... if I assisted others who were repressed by cruelty to free themselves and keep peace in the realms, then my people would look favorably upon my actions."

"All right, then." I said, sitting up straighter and clapping my hands together. "It sounds like we have the beginnings of a plan. You mentioned enacting it the night of my wedding."

"To secure his connection to the reaver elves, Azarn wants you to join the family as soon as possible. We will take advantage of that desperation and insist the ceremony takes place tomorrow at the Fire Court's traditional wedding time of nine in the evening."

A wave of dizziness washed over me. "Tomorrow night?"

"Yes, and prior to the actual ceremony, there will be at least half an hour of rituals before the vows are spoken—poetry readings, songs. So at approximately nine o'clock, I'll begin holding Nukala under water. On the dais, you must keep testing your reaver cloak. When it activates, you'll only have about twenty minutes to get out of Taln."

"How do we remove the mergelyn anklets?"

"With Melaya's power blocked, you simply unfasten them. You'd be wise to kill Azarn and Melaya first. And my son if you must." She wiped a silver tear from her cheek. "I fear nothing less will stop their quest for power."

"What will happen to the kingdom without the mages? A book I found in the library said Taln would fall."

"Certain books were written to boost the egos of countless fire kings. If Azarn dies, his power will transfer to a new ruler, and the Sun Realm will stand."

"And you would willingly rule?" I asked.

"I would cede the crown to Arrowyn and yourself and return to my beloved home."

"We have no wish to take your kingdom from you, Estella."

"Which is precisely why you will be its best caretakers."

"And if you can't submerge Nukala?"

"I will use my power to subdue him if there's no other choice." She shifted to face me. "I apologize for not seeking you out earlier. Marcella told me you wished to speak about the wedding, but I've been distracted, wondering how I could get you out of Taln while keeping Bakhur safe. Now it is clear I cannot achieve all my goals, and instead, must help those who will strive toward peace for all."

"Thank you. How can I ever repay your kindness?"

"By maintaining balance in the realms. Rule with your heart. That is all I require of you."

"If we do make it out of Taln, I promise we will work tirelessly to weave the threads of peace throughout the Star Realms until its fabric is stronger than Auryinnian silver." I braced my weight on my palms, preparing to stand up. "Before I go, what did you mean when you said you were spying on your court?"

Soft laughter tinkled, then she cleared her throat and spat in the pond, its surface darkening. "Watch closely."

Thousands of stars appeared floating on the water's surface. The queen waved her palm, and an image came into focus. A birds-eye view of a line of shadowy mountains, the sparkling lights of a city in the distance. The view in the pond changed fast, as if we were flying across the sky, then through an arched window into a dazzling throne room.

"Is that your home? It's stunning!" I squinted at a crimson ball glowing through the glass on one side of the hall. "Strange, that almost looks like—"

"Yes, that is our sun. It's always nighttime in the Crystal Realm of Night and Stars. Once a month, our moon is so bright that it looks similar to the Earth Realm's daylight. For a few days, we feast and celebrate Mother Moon, while paying our respects to our dark Father and his children, the stars."

"You must miss the Star Court terribly."

"Yes," she said, another tear slipping down her pale cheek. "But I must stop distracting you, Zali. Arrowyn will be waiting to speak to you. Here, you must wear this."

Estella removed the smaller of her two pendants, and then held its black stone between her palms, reciting a spell under her breath. "Wear it against your skin, and you will be invisible to everyone, even Ruhh. Put it in your pocket, separated from your body by cloth, any type of cloth, and you'll become visible once again."

"Thank you, Estella."

"The cells you seek are beneath the fire moat. Show the khareek my pendant, and they will grant you immediate access."

I threw myself at the queen, squeezing her in a tight hug. "Please be careful with Nukala, and thank—"

"No need to thank me again." She pushed her palm out, emitting a high-pitched note from deep within her throat.

Then everything changed.

The realms seemed to stop spinning, light and sound sucked from existence as a cold, dark void enveloped me.

I fell backward through space and time, my arms wheeling and my mind screaming. It felt like eons, though in reality, it was probably only a few minutes. I spun through darkness until the churning vortex spat me out, and I landed in the bushes outside the conservatory, away from the guards' line of sight.

I pressed Estella's onyx pendant against my chest, and then ran as fast as I could toward the kitchen.

Chapter 29

LEAF

The moment I arrived, the khareek lurched up from the depths of the moat as if they'd been waiting for me to wander by.

"A lovely liar comes," one said, its flaming body shivering with anticipation.

The three creatures sniffed the air, swinging their heads around and searching for me.

"Oh, sorry. I forgot I was still invisible." I flipped Estella's pendant to the outside of my tunic and stepped closer to the moat.

Sparks showered me as the khareek leaned down and inspected the jewel. One of their arms broke off, landing on the path beside me in a mound of flames.

"That necklace belongs to the Night Queen," said the creature, its limb already reforming as it nudged one of its companions.

"No, the necklace is mine," I lied, smiling in what I hoped was a charming manner. "It always has been."

Laughter crackled. "Two lies," they shrieked. "So sweet. So tasty."

"Why did you call Estella the Night Queen? Surely she's the Queen of Fire."

"To us, she will always be the Queen of Night and Stars. Cosmic Witch. Mother of All Time and Warden of All That is Good, tethered to this realm by her love for an unworthy child."

"That's quite a title," I said.

"You are eager to enter the moat," said the fire creature, extending its hand toward the churning lava. "Balance must be restored. Release the Storm King, and then let no being in the realms live under tyranny. Go quickly."

A staircase materialized before my eyes, the steps disappearing beneath the fiery water. "You mean I have to actually walk under the moat?"

"It's the only entrance to the dungeon. Do you trust us?"

"Oh, of course I do," I said, stepping onto the edge of the moat.

"Another lie," they cackled, licking their bubbling lips. "This human feeds us well."

"When I go down there, I hope I don't get burned alive and turned into a khareek. No offense."

Making no reassuring comments, the khareek moved aside as I took a deep breath, held it in my lungs, and began my descent.

Wet warmth rushed over my body, but I felt no pain, and could breathe and see clearly under the fire water. The khareek swam in circles above the staircase balustrade, their bodies entirely transformed.

They reminded me of the Ice Realm's water sprites from books that I'd read as a child, two females and one male, their sleek, angular forms shining with a cold, beautiful light.

The stairs spiraled past two empty landings, the third one leading to a door that opened smoothly into an air-filled chamber as I approached. I took a long breath of stale air, relieved to be out of the moat.

Another door revealed a long, torch-lit corridor, where two dark-marble statues stood guard. Dressed in Fire Court armor and holding long spears of gold, only their black eyes showed signs of life, moving from side to side and scanning their surroundings.

Making sure Estella's pendant touched my skin, I strolled straight past the creepy, spellbound guards and into a rectangular room, the right side of it lined with bars. Both relief and terror surged through me as I spotted Raiden, Zaret, and Esen inside the first cell. But no Arrow.

Was he even alive?

A quick inspection of the cell revealed a water pipe on the back wall, a single canvas bed, a pile of blankets, and a bucket in the corner. Even if the fire fae improved the lighting and added two more beds, the living conditions would still be dire.

Esen slept on the stretcher, with Zaret curled on the stone floor nearby. Only Raiden was awake, sitting with his arms wrapped around his knees, glaring at his boots.

"Raiden," I hissed, tucking the pendant over my tunic, becoming visible again. "It's me."

"Leaf!" He lurched up and clutched the bars. "I've never been so happy to see anyone."

"Except maybe the Sayeeda," I corrected.

Even in the dim light, I saw his cheeks darken.

"Are you all right?" I whispered. "Where's Arrow?"

"Three cells along. They've done something... I don't know... unpleasant to him. Those fucking statue guards came down, and since then, he's stopped talking to us."

"*Shit.* Do you think the guards can hear us?"

"Doubt it. We've tried yelling to find out, but they only came down twice. Once to deliver food and another time to... do something to Arrow that didn't sound good."

I closed my eyes for a moment and steadied my breathing. "Estella has a plan to get you out of this shithole. And hopefully, out of the Sun Realm."

"Thank fuck. Please, tell her to hurry."

"Tomorrow night. Not long past nine o'clock, your powers should return."

His dark eyes widened. "How?"

"I haven't got time to explain it twice. I'll tell Arrow. Just be ready, Raiden."

"We will be. Good luck."

I shoved my hands through the bars, squeezed his face, and kissed his cheek, my gaze falling on Esen and Zaret, still sleeping. "Are they all right?"

"Yes. They fought like trolls earlier today, so Azarn's guards put a sleeping spell on them. Said it would wear off soon."

I gave Raiden what I hoped was a comforting smile over my shoulder, then hurried to Arrow's cell, gasping when I peered through the bars.

Slumped against the back wall, the Storm King was fast asleep. Or dead. If they'd killed him, I vowed I would murder Azarn with my bare hands, regardless of the consequences.

The cell contained no bucket, blankets, or even a stretcher bed, and the only sounds were the drip, drip, drip of a water pipe and Arrow's soft moans.

Wait... he was alive!

Dark wings spread out, dirty and limp on the floor. He lay on his side with his head resting on his chained hands, fingers from one hand shielding his eyes, like a sleeping child.

My heart pummeled against my ribs. "Arrow, wake up," I shouted.

Slowly, his head rose, and unfocused steel-gray eyes scanned my body, their usual silver glow extinguished. "Leaf?" he slurred.

"Yes! Yes, it's me. I need you to concentrate. Can you move?"

"Think so." With his wingtips dragging along the wet floor, he slowly pushed onto his feet, then stumbled toward me.

Dark-gold hair clung to his damp cheeks as he leaned into the bars and pressed his face to mine like a caged lion begging for a pat. I squeezed his shoulders, ran my hands down his biceps before reaching down and tugging the cuffs around his wrists. Naked from the waist up, bruises bloomed over his skin, his feather glyphs faintly pulsing, activated by my touch.

I gripped his face and pressed soft kisses on his cheeks. "What have they done to you?"

"Just dished out an unhealthy serving of Fire Court hospitality. I'll be fine. Azarn needs me alive. How did you get in here?"

With a grin, I flipped the pendant in and out of my tunic, disappearing then reappearing.

"Estella gave that to you?" he whispered.

"Yes. Now listen closely. We don't have much time. She's arranging my wedding for... for tomorrow night."

"What the *fuck*? No!"

"It's the only way. We have a plan. Just be quiet and listen. The ceremony will begin at nine o'clock. Sun Realm marriages include approximately half an hour of preamble. Poems and songs. As close to nine o'clock as possible, Estella will hold Nukala under water for about twenty minutes. During this time, Melaya's power will be disrupted, the block on your magic released. Blow the cells up, do whatever you must to get the hells out of here fast."

I pulled orchid petals from my pocket. "Rub one of these on your skin, over your heart is best, then hurry to the hall so I don't end up married to Bakhur."

As I tucked the petals deep into the pocket of his leathers, a filthy laugh rumbled from his chest, causing bumps to erupt over my skin. "Be careful, Leaf," he said. "There's still life in me yet."

"Not much you can do through these bars, big fella."

"Try me." He nodded at the bulges in my tunic. "What have you got there?"

"A present for you. Persimmons."

His eyebrows twisted into a hard scowl.

"Only two of them. They were all I could find in the kitchen. But they'll help strengthen your magic, right?"

The Storm King made a gagging sound. "Yeah, but I hate the damn things."

"I know. Sorry."

I held a persimmon up to the bars, and he bit into it. "The things I do for love."

"And also for your kingdom. For all *five* kingdoms, in fact," I said, stifling a laugh as he chewed the fruit like it was full of bitter poison.

Bending, I reached inside his cell and placed the second persimmon on the floor near the side wall, where I hoped the guards wouldn't notice it.

"Eat some more," I said, raising the first fruit to the bars again.

A single brow arched. "Kiss me, and then I will."

I peppered his face with kisses, the last one lingering on his lips before I stepped backward.

"*Leaf.* Come on," he rumbled. "That's not what I meant."

"Promise me you'll eat the other one as soon as your hands are free."

"Say you love me, and I will. Tell me at least once. I need to hear you say it before I die."

"Oh, Arrow, I promise I won't let anything happen to you."

He groaned, a bead of sweat tracing the sharp curve of his cheekbone. "And *I'm* begging you to have mercy. After all, you may never have the pleasure of seeing me again."

I clicked my tongue. "Arrogant right up to the end."

"The end?" His pupils flared. "You just promised to get us out of here."

I scanned his wonderful, maddening face, holding it between my palms, then kissing him through the bars whisper soft. "Although I've tried countless times to rip you from my heart, I admit defeat. Arrowyn Ramiel, I will love you, adore you, and long for you with each beat of my heart through this life and the next."

A dopey smile spread over his face.

"Does that satisfy you?" I asked.

"If you say it again, it will do for now."

"Leaf, you should leave while you still can." Raiden's voice hissed along the dim corridor as I pressed another kiss to the Storm King's lips. "The magic in the dungeons is fucked up. Anything could happen."

"All right. I'm going," I shouted over my shoulder, then grabbed the points of Arrow's ears and tugged him closer, breathing a promise over his lips. "I love you. Always and forever. Please forgive me for ever doubting your loyalty."

"I'll forgive you for any mistake or deed as long as you're mine and I am yours."

"I'd better go, but I'll see you tomorrow night. Please don't be late, and make sure you eat that last persimmon the moment you break free of the chains."

"Fine. I'll think of you with every bite."

Dragging my eyes from the heart-wrenching sight of the Storm King in chains, I forced myself to turn away and leave the dungeon, not stopping as I passed the inanimate guards.

The khareek led me through the fire water and out of the moat, then I hurried toward the palace and sneaked into the chamber next to Azarn's, where I hoped he was keeping the Sayeeda.

Entering the room, I found Ari in a meditation pose, cross-legged in front of the large windows that overlooked the palace's tallest spires set aglow by a burnt-orange sunset.

"Ari," I whispered, not wanting to startle her. "I'm sorry to interrupt, but I need to speak with you about—"

"Estella has already shared the plan with me."

"Do you think it will work?"

"It must. It's our only option."

I sat beside her on the red alnarah rug, the wool soft between my fingers. She squinted at my hair, a mass of unraveling braids, ran her fingers over the shorter side, then brushed dirt off my tunic. Other than a bit of filth, the lava water had left no mark on me.

"I've been in the cells below the moat. Arrow is weak, but he and Raiden are ready for tomorrow. I gave him persimmons."

Ari laughed. "Oh, he must've been *thrilled* by such a gift. The effect of the fruit on his powers will be minimal, but it *will* help him heal faster from the beating Azarn said his guards had inflicted. As soon as Melaya's power is disabled, Arrow's strength will return. Do not worry about him. We must beg the gods to help Estella subdue Nukala."

"So, let's say she succeeds... picture me standing beside Bakhur, Sun Realm rituals droning on as our friends burst into the hall. We'll draw our reaver cloaks around us, remove the mergelyn anklets, and then what happens? Will Arrow turn the hall to dust, like he did with Gorbinvar's smithy?"

"And kill hundreds of innocents, perhaps including us, destroying Taln in the process? No, the Fire Court must stand. Unfortunately, we cannot know in advance who will attend the ceremony or their positions during it. Our best chance is to target Azarn, Bakhur, and Melaya, then fight like the existence of the realms depends upon us winning."

Because in truth, it likely did.

If Azarn controlled Arrow and then the gold trade through me, life for the fae of the realms would become extremely unpleasant. We had to win. There was no other option.

Ari embraced me tightly, insisting I get a good night's sleep—an impossible task—before sending me back to my chamber to meet the court's royal cloth workers.

They dressed me in a black gown featuring a neckline that plunged to my stomach and a long, flared skirt with slits reaching my thighs. Sheer fabric adorned with white gemstones, shimmering in rainbow hues with each step, covered my chest and arms.

The red flames and golden birds embroidered on the main part of the gown no doubt symbolized that the Sun Realm claimed ownership of me—the Earth Realm Princess with reaver blood flowing through my veins—and all of the Light Realm's gold.

But tomorrow, we would not fail. We *couldn't* fail.

Azarn and Melaya were finished, doomed. We *would* defeat them.

I whispered those words like a mantra, a spell, praying that if I chanted them hard enough, my fervent wishes would come true.

The image of Arrow, weak and in chains, kept plaguing me, and I thumped my forehead against the wall three times before resolving to channel my fear more productively.

Instead of resting, I spent most of the night practicing sword strikes with a broken broom handle. A poor excuse for a weapon, but wielding it soothed my anxiety.

The last thing I wanted was to toss and turn for hours in bed, mulling over my fate. Because if we failed tomorrow night, I'd be married to Bakhur, and the only man I had ever loved would be dead.

Or worse, I thought. A horrific image flashed through my mind—the Storm King hanging helpless over the Sentura Pyre.

Chapter 30

ARROW

Trapped inside the dungeon below the fire moat, I had no way to tell the exact time of day. But the moment night fell over the city, my blood quickened in my veins, and I began my vigil, pacing across the cell, cursing Azarn's soldiers for chaining my wrists in front of my body.

In a nearby cell, boots scuffed against flagstones as my friends muttered to each other, the low hum of their voices tethering the chaos of my mind to a bare semblance of sanity.

Questions ricocheted through my brain, torturing me until my palms were slick with sweat. What if we failed and left Leaf alone to face a life of servitude to Bakhur and the corrupt Fire Court? What would happen to Coridon without me? To my people, the Zareen, and the elves of Auryinnia?

Tonight, I couldn't lose. That much was certain. I had to destroy Melaya, Azarn, and Bakhur, too.

If I could break out of the dungeon with my power restored, I would summon a catastrophic storm. Melt the flesh off Azarn and Melaya. Then wrap my hands around Bakhur's throat and squeeze the life from his veins with unbridled joy.

Jerking to a halt, I pressed my forehead against the bars of my cell, each shuddered breath echoing through my lungs, pure agony.

For daring to hurt my Aldara, I would kill Bakhur slowly, savoring his death. I'd play with the fucker. Taste each sour tear as he begged for mercy, for relief that I would never grant.

Hands chained in front of me, I cracked my knuckles, Leaf's face flashing through my mind again. I imagined her expression as she watched me dispense justice—first fear, then disgust—the vision a reminder of how much she despised cruelty.

So be it.

For *her*, I would show leniency. To a *point*. A small, sharp one. And I'd behave like a male who deserved Leaf's love.

Perhaps I wasn't her equal yet, but I would never *ever* give up trying to be.

"Raiden," I called out. "Don't forget as soon as I hand you the petals, you must waste no time and rub one over your skin."

"Does it matter where we apply it?" asked Zaret, the over-thinker of our group.

"Over your heart is best, but anywhere you can in the space of three seconds will do," I replied.

"Will you do the same?" Esen asked, suspicion resonating in her tone.

"No. Fuck that. When Azarn's organs start boiling, I need him to see my face. I'll target Melaya first, then the king. And, Raiden, remember that away from Coridon, your storm magic might be weaker. Gold knows what will happen to Esen's mutated power, but we can only hope both elements will continue to work well together. Grab swords from the nearest fae and kill the king's guards or anyone wearing armor. If any soldiers flee the hall, let them leave. I guarantee they despise Azarn and will help us build a better Taln after we've defeated him."

"You want the entire royal family dead?" asked Zaret.

"No," I replied. "Just the males. And Esen, Raiden, be sure to always have Zaret's back. He may be as fierce a fighter as the strongest Light Realm fae, but he has no magic. I can feel you scowling, Zaret. Don't take stupid risks in the hall. I need you alive."

"Why? So you can keep your promise to Zali? And hers to my mother?"

"I will never break my word to my Aldara. She is more precious than every kanara feather in Coridon. But this is not why I need you by my side. You and Leaf have taught me that I was a fool to reject an entire species because of the crimes of a few. You are as valued a friend as Raiden and Esen, and my trust in Esen is stronger than ever now that I know her true story. Believe me, Azarn will pay for exploiting an innocent fae child."

"I would gladly give my life to save your future queen," said Zaret, his voice determined, bearing no trace of sorrow.

"If it comes to that, so be it," I replied, knowing the young human was as headstrong as my Leaf, and nothing could deter him from following his conscience, seated in the center of his heart.

Not even me.

Time passed as I paced in darkness, and before long, terror took hold, sliding through my veins like a curse, my limbs shaking with suppressed adrenaline, nausea churning my gut. I clutched the bars, certain too much time had passed.

"Estella's plan must've failed," I ground out. "Melaya probably found her before she could subdue Nukala. Leaf might already be dead."

That idea sent shock waves of pain radiating through my body. If my Aldara was dead, I had no wish to go on living.

"No way," said Raiden. "I'm sure all is well. Have patience. Check your glyphs. How do they feel?"

Good question.

Closing my eyes, I tuned out the sound of dripping water, the scuttle of a nearby rat, and ignored the stench of misery that emanated from the walls, barely breathing as I focused internally.

A subtle warmth vibrated over my skin. I concentrated harder, feeling a slight buzz from my glyphs, evidence the magical tether that pulsed from my heart to Leaf's remained unbroken, even in this gold-forsaken shithole.

For the hundredth time, I tried connecting to the elements above the dungeon. To move the clouds. Entice the wind. But once again... nothing.

I paced. Stopped moving, focused, and tried again.

Still nothing.

I repeated the actions until I was ready to smash my skull against the wall in desperation.

"For gold's sake, what the fuck is going on out there?" I yelled, slamming a shoulder into the bars.

Power crashed into my chest and threw me across the floor. "Fuck, *yes*. Estella did it. It fucking worked."

A moan parted my lips, my body shaking and shuddering as my magic returned. Thunder rumbled in the distance, and then roared closer as I called the storm clouds toward me. Blinding light filled the room before snaking down my throat.

I retched, then planted my boots firmly on the stone floor, forcing my arms out in front of me, breaking the chain between my wrists. I pushed a small beam of lightning magic through my palm and blasted the lock off the cell door.

On my way out, I swiped the persimmon from the ground, taking a single bite, because I'd promised Leaf that I would. Then I burst into the passage and blew the door off the cell containing my friends.

Raiden dashed forward and slapped my back. "Finally."

"We have about twenty minutes." I handed Esen an orchid petal. "Here. Start rubbing."

She grinned slyly, wiping the petal over her face, neck, and arms, unable to reach beneath the armor covering her chest. "You have no idea how badly I once wished you'd give me such an order, Arrow."

I snorted, handing Raiden and Zaret petals. They applied them fast, their bodies dissolving into blank space before my eyes.

"Let's go," I said.

Wings folded behind me, I bolted around a corner onto a long, torch-lit corridor where the stone guards waited, the sound of boot scuffs and ragged breathing the only indication my friends followed at my heels.

The guards' spear arms creaked and moved as the magic that animated them sprang to life. I conjured two balls of lightning and threw them at their chests, ducking away from the spray of rocks and fine powder, their remains forming a pile of debris in the corner.

"Too easy," Raiden said as I opened the only door in sight and began climbing a walled-in staircase.

Two levels up, the khareek appeared, stripped of the fiery bodies and their true fae forms revealed.

"King Arrowyn. Come quickly," the female said. "We will guide you through the moat safely."

"Escorts. Excellent," I said, extremely glad to see them. "I was wondering how we'd get out of here without blowing up your moat. Let's go. We haven't got much time."

The khareek nodded, and then led us through the fire water. In no time at all, we stood on the grass beneath a star-filled sky, the violence of my storm clouds rumbling above Taln Palace.

"Those fire fuckers took your chest plate," Raiden said, his voice sounding next to my right shoulder.

I glanced at my bare chest and the feather glyphs flowing like veins of molten gold over my skin.

"Get to the hall," I told my friends, wishing I could see their faces in case everything went to shit and I never got to look upon them again. "Run, and don't stop until you find a soldier or six to kill. I'll meet you there."

As my wings snapped out, I leaped into the air, hovering above the ground with my arms crossed and my heart thundering against my ribs.

Esen yelled, "Arrow, wait. Where the fuck are you going?"

"To make a grand entrance."

With a single, hard beat of my wings, I shot higher, hurtling toward the domed roof above Taln's hall. Toward my Aldara. Zali Omala. Leaf. My forever love and the queen of my heart.

And gold help anyone who tried to keep me from her.

Chapter 31

LEAF

Two enormous dragons soared through the night sky, their fiery breath setting the forest aglow with orange light. Their growls and shrieks sent chills down my spine and fear surging through my blood.

Perhaps as soon as Melaya's powers failed and chaos broke out, the dragons would simply turn us all to ash before we dispatched a single Sun Realm soldier, let alone their king.

Nausea churned in my belly as I stood on a dais in the center of the Arena of Ashen Souls, praying that I kept my dinner down.

Nearly half an hour had passed since Estella's maid appeared in the arena and informed Azarn the queen was ill and would be late to the wedding. Despite Bakhur begging the king to wait, he'd bullied his son into proceeding with the ceremony without his mother. Much to my disgust and horror.

Surrounded by the cold stares of the fire fae, who hadn't warmed to me in the slightest over the past fortnight, I attempted to calm my shaking limbs, telling myself there was still time for Estella's plan to work. Any moment, Melaya's power block might release. And then Arrow would arrive.

I had finally accepted that as long as the Storm King was alive, he would come for me, no matter the danger. But as I listened to the Master of Matrimony drone on, a terrified part of me feared that Melaya had discovered Estella, and my love was already dead.

The court's best singers distracted me with enchanted songs meant to kindle love between a soon-to-be-married couple. And they worked to a point, because desire and longing simmered inside me. But not for the prince who stood beside me, dressed in gold and currently scowling at the sword that hung from his lean hips.

After I'd torn off the mergelyn anklet, that sword would be my first quarry. I'd snatch Bakhur's weapon and cut his pretty head from his shoulders. But wait... had Estella said she wanted him alive?

No.

Her exact words were: *Kill my son if you must.* Which, to me, sounded like permission to send him to the hell realms.

With subtle glances, I studied the ghastly scene around me. The king was perched stiff-backed on his black throne, Estella's chair beside him empty, and Ari stood slightly behind him, like his very own personal slave. On the king's other side, Melaya loomed like a pissed-off crow, seething at the sight of me.

Well, when his twin's head got dunked shortly, I guessed that he'd be significantly more irritated.

Dressed in a black gown with a hood covering her golden hair, Ari melted into the background of dark stone, and Ruhh hovered above her left shoulder. I wondered how much the Sayeeda had told the ghost girl about tonight. Hopefully

JUNO HEART

nothing. Ruhh was an unreliable ally, and when mayhem erupted, she could turn on us, or at the very least, get in our way.

With a sigh, I turned my focus toward the fae that I prayed would never ever be my husband. I gazed at him with fake affection, as if the song kindled attraction, playing a role. But he stared at his boots, or the swooping dragon shadows on the trees, the growling, snickering courtiers. Anywhere, but at me.

When he finally gazed my way, I blasted him with the sweetest smile I could muster, creating the illusion that all was well. Pretending I didn't mind the too-heavy dress emblazoned with aggressive, shit-stirring symbols that scratched my skin. Or my hair coiled in braids so tight that the skin beneath my cheekbones looked gaunt, and the side I preferred shaved slick with perfumed oil.

I hated this fucking dress. Despised pretending to be a willing participant in the ceremony. Loathed waiting while I counted each ragged breath, measuring my fear by the irregular thuds of the aching pump in my chest.

Any moment, my dust-damned heart might explode.

Our plan was terrible, dangerous, and certain to fail. I couldn't stand one more minute of not knowing what was happening underneath the moat. If Estella succeeded with Nukala, how would Arrow find me?

We weren't even supposed to be in the fucking Fen Forest.

And time was running out.

Melaya remained in position on the king's left side, his flaming eyes pinned on the Sayeeda. Marcella wafted through the crowd, surrounded by the fawning admirers she referred to as friends, but I called beautiful parasites with sharp teeth and talons.

Without any warning, sheet lightning flashed in the distance, near the sea cliffs. Three heartbeats later, thunder rumbled, and clouds raced past the moon, gathering in an angry cluster above the palace spires.

If Arrow's returning magic had caused the brewing storm, then Estella had succeeded. A wave of euphoria rippled through me as I dropped my gaze, hiding my excitement from the prince.

"So this is it," murmured Bakhur. "We will soon be forever bound through the trials of pain and fury, commonly referred to as the state of matrimony."

"Doesn't sound pleasant," I admitted, hands flexing at my sides. "For both our sakes, we should at least work on becoming friends."

He made a scoffing sound, and I dug my fingernails into the outside of my thigh to stop myself from attempting to activate my reaver cloak. I had to be patient. The bride couldn't give away the game too early and disappear into thin air. Although, Bakhur would likely be pleased if I did. Initially, at least.

While I waited for the others to arrive, I needed to keep my almost-husband distracted.

"Don't you think we could create a good marriage if we tried?" I asked with a teasing smile.

"Perhaps a tolerable one... if you're obedient."

The blue-skinned fae conducting the ceremony continued with the spoken rituals. His long white hair coiled around his wrinkled bare feet, and he looked as old as the moon, with twice as many craters on his face. His words were a meaningless drone.

I focused my energy on standing still, thinking only about Arrow and my friends, wondering if they were safe. I prayed to the all-seeing Zareen that they would find me fast after they realized Taln's hall was dark and deserted.

I examined Melaya.

Right now, the crimson hair that normally undulated around his shoulders, as if affected by his magic, lay motionless down his back. Distracted by the Sayeeda, he hadn't even noticed. Neither had he glanced at the clouds that were currently hurtling toward us, or reacted to the crackling charge in the air.

It had worked. Estella had fucking done it. She was a goddess. A supreme shining star.

The energy was intoxicating, and I swayed slightly on my boots that were hidden under the excessive fabric of my gown.

Ari stood next to Melaya, her face close to his as she whispered through a rare smile, deliberately charming the fire mage. Exploiting his fascination with the famous Sayeeda of Coridon—the beautiful, wise sister of the great Zareen.

I'd bet the Light Realm's last kanara feather that Melaya was currently imagining the glorious power he and Ari could wield if only they joined forces.

But that would never happen.

Ari wanted peace, Melaya chaos.

Another blast of lightning turned the sky silver, the forest floor shuddering as thunder shook the arena.

Finally, Melaya looked up.

The Master of Matrimony closed his mouth and ceased reciting bad poetry.

Azarn shot to his feet as Arrow crashed through the treetops, his dark wings flared wide and veined with streaks of lightning.

Without delay, I whispered, *"auron khaban ana,"* focusing on each syllable.

The moment the reaver magic slid over my skin, I tore Bakhur's sword from its belt, stepping back and swinging at his neck. He ducked, popped up again, and then ran, his legs wheeling fast. I gave chase, and with a second sweep of the blade, I hacked his head from his shoulders. It tumbled off the dais, chestnut curls framing the gaping grimace on his face as it bounced along the ground.

I ripped the mergelyn anklet from my leg as a wave of terror engulfed the crowd below. Shouts and screams tore through the air, and I squinted, seeking my next target.

I was thankful for two things: one, that no one could see me, and two, for the queen's necklace and orchid petals that I'd tied to my leg in a cloth pouch when the chamber servants who'd dressed me tonight weren't looking.

Melaya had disappeared from the dais, and if he was as clever as he fancied himself, he'd be searching for Nukala right now. Saving his brother and protecting his own power instead of Azarn's life.

Ari was invisible, too, but the path she cut on the dais toward the Fire King was more than clear. As guards raced forward to surround and protect him, bloodied bodies with missing limbs fell one by one, as if struck by an invisible demon.

Zaret, Esen, and Raiden fought soldiers in the crowd below, only the human boy visible as screams of agony split soldiers' pale lips and blood splattered courtiers' fine clothes.

The Fire Court fought back, jagged balls of fire whizzing through the air and setting each other ablaze. A burst of confidence shuddered through me as I realized that fighting an invisible enemy was near impossible. Victory would surely be ours.

It had to be.

But where was Arrow? He'd crashed through the trees, and I hadn't seen him since.

At this moment, I couldn't worry about him. Ari needed my assistance. Because Azarn had to die.

Now.

Lunging forward, I slashed a guard in front of me, and his steaming entrails spilled over the delicate patterns on the dais's painted wooden floor. My sword raised again, I moved to step around his body, but a band of steel crossed my middle, pulling me against a wall of warm flesh.

Arrow stood behind me.

"Sh, little Leaf. Stay still. I must act quickly. Renew the bond," he whispered against my neck before his fangs sank into my flesh.

I muffled a moan with my palm.

Three long pulls of my blood, while I swayed to the sounds of death throes and madness, a terrible bliss swelling in my chest. The air stank of fear and gore, yet I only felt peace in the Storm King's arms, my back pressed against the warmth of his chest and stomach.

"*Go now, and please be safe,*" his voice echoed in my mind. "*Despite how much I wanted to hurt him, I let you take Bakhur. Excellent work by the way, my ferocious love. But Azarn... Azarn is mine. Help Raiden keep the way clear for me.*" Arrow searched blindly for my face, stroking my cheek. "*It breaks my heart not to see you. Kills me not to know if you are well.*"

"I'm doing great. Make sure not being able to see me is the only thing that slays you tonight," I said, pulling out of his arms. "Hurry. Time's passing swiftly."

Praying Ari had left the dais, I dropped a kiss on Arrow's lips. Then I leaped into the crowd, shoving my way through the fae, and stopping where bolts of storm magic and the most soldiers were being flung through the air.

"Azarn," boomed Arrow's voice behind me. "You forgot to invite me to the ceremony." He shot a silver beam of lightning from his palm and lifted the Fire King out from the dwindling circle of guards, raising him high above the dais. "I find myself quite offended by your oversight."

Azarn kicked his legs like a child held aloft by an adult, and he screamed like one, too, throwing weak fire orbs carelessly and setting his own soldiers and random fae alight.

"*Melaya*," he cried out. But the fire mage didn't come.

He shouted for the greivon dragons and the guardians, but the grymarians didn't show, and the dragons continued to fly in haphazard patterns above the forest and arena, as though Melaya's obstructed magic affected their ability to navigate.

Out of nowhere, a guard landed a lucky strike, his blade slicing the back of my arm. The orc was tall and fast, spinning and slashing in a brutal onslaught that backed me toward a stone wall. I tried to duck left or right, to slip away, but fae were packed tight on both sides, and my reaver cloak flickered on and off, allowing the soldier to continue his attack.

I was out of practice and had forgotten how to split my focus between fighting and concentrating on holding the cloak in place. Tired, with my energy waning, visions of my gruesome death floated through my mind.

"*Move hard left*." Arrow's voice cut into my thoughts, sharper than the blade I wielded. "*Now, Leaf*."

I obeyed, throwing myself into a gap between the fighting fae.

A fork of lightning struck the soldier, and he melted into a pile of sizzling flesh and bones. "*Thank you*," I told Arrow through the bond.

Even at a distance, the stench of burning flesh hit me hard, and I retched before hurtling toward the last group of soldiers still fighting, loyal to Azarn until their last breaths.

Many courtiers fled the arena, and I did my best to avoid them, to keep them safe as horrific screeches rattled the air.

The dragons.

Near the cliffs, flames exploded, then a ball of whirling dragon limbs tumbled fast toward the sea, a loud hiss sounding as they landed in the water. The poor fucking things must have collided midair.

But better Azarn's pets were dead than any of my friends. Or Arrow.

The Fire King dangled in a lattice of crisscrossing storm magic, cursing and sobbing, his crown of black flames inert, like charcoal husks twisted through his long brown hair. His short beard was on fire, and dark smudges streaked his face. Any moment, he'd probably beg for his life.

Arrow used to love that—having another being, fae or human, at his mercy. I thought he'd changed. But perhaps not entirely.

"*Kill him already,*" I said, deep laughter through the bond his only reply. "*Gloat too long,*" I warned, "*and you'll regret it.*"

"*That's true,*" he said, amusement in his tone. "*You are wise, Aldara, and it pains me to admit, nearly always right.*"

The sky flashed blinding white as an ear-splitting thunderclap shook the kingdom. When I opened my eyes, blinking away pain...

The Fire King was dead.

Chapter 32

LEAF

A rrow launched himself into the air, his body spinning inside a vortex of blue storm magic, silver lightning forking out from the center of his chest as he flew over the arena in a jubilant victory circuit.

For a moment, I stood frozen deep in the crowd, my fists clenched, breathing raggedly as screams from the remaining courtiers and howls from forest creatures pierced the air. Shock at the Fire King's death rippled throughout the kingdom.

"*I thought a knife to the heart was the only way to kill a king,*" I told Arrow silently as he swooped low over the crowd.

"*A bolt of lightning is quite an effective stand-in for a blade. Have you seen Melaya?*"

"*No,*" I replied. "*He's probably with Nukala. And hopefully not killing Estella as we speak.*"

Arrow made a grunting sound through the bond, then shot high into the starry sky, disappearing from view. "Be safe," I whispered.

Ruhh, absent for most of the mayhem, now floated above the pile of ash that was once the king and his last few loyal soldiers.

"It was you, brother, who bound me to your corrupt kingdom, to my rotting flesh and this tattered gown. You deserve this wretched fate. I hope you spend eternity in the hell realms."

Fae still trailed out of the arena's scrolled gates and into the Fen Forest, either flying, running, or trampling over others, likely terrified that the Storm King was about to raze the entire city to the ground.

"There you are, filthy human," a low voice snarled behind me. "I've been looking for you."

I whipped around, my boots scraping over stones, and found Neeron, the Sun Realm envoy, grinning before me. He scanned my body, now flickering in and out of visibility, and fixed me with a predatory stare, hungry for revenge.

"Come get me," I said as I gripped my sword hilt with two hands, holding it vertically along the center of my body. "I'm more than happy to finish what we started back in Coridon."

Wishing I could tear my horrible, movement-restricting gown off, I chanted the Mydorian war song in my mind. *By branch and root, soil and stone, lend strength to muscle, heart, and bone.*

"Why should I bother fighting with a sword when I can simply destroy you with these?" Neeron asked, spinning several balls of fire magic on his palms.

I ducked and whirled as he threw them at me in rapid succession, missing me and setting many fae ablaze as they fled the arena.

"Why? Because I'm too good at dodging them," I replied, running up a wall and landing directly behind Neeron. "If I were you, Envoy, I'd try using your sword." I swiped my blade diagonally and a line of blood wept from his right shoulder to his left waist.

I hissed my people's chant through my teeth. *Crush all to live. Conquer and prevail. Mydor blood will never fail.*

But Mydor blood *had* failed Quin after he'd polluted his veins with enough gold serum to dishonor the blood of our ancestors. And if I could kill my own brother—an addict jacked-up with fire magic—surely I could take out a whining envoy without breaking a sweat.

Neeron whipped around, snarling like a newborn troll as he drew his sword, lunging and slashing at me three times. I blocked each strike, the third catching his collarbone, another dark stain blooming over the royal blue material of his jacket.

Dropping my right shoulder, I pretended to hack with a downward strike, but went in for the kill instead, raising the blade fast and aiming for his head. Neeron spun out of the blow just in time, then we pushed back and forth, the clash of swords dull thuds over the din in the arena.

Concentrating on precise movements and rhythmic breathing, I lifted my sword above my head, feigning another downward strike, and as the fae moved in to counter it, I kicked him in the balls.

Neeron fell backward, groaning before immediately springing back onto his feet.

Before I could launch another attack, Arrow landed between us.

"I thought you were hunting Melaya," I grumbled.

"Changed my mind. I've been watching the Sun Envoy closely instead. *Neeron*," Arrow said calmly, as if he'd just bumped into him at a garden party. "Good to see you again. You've been well?" he continued, his wings folded along his spine and the arches raised above his shoulders, reminding me of a bristled cat preparing to tear its prey to shreds.

Neeron mumbled an incoherent response. Sweat beading his brow, he collected himself and bowed. "King Arrowyn, I apologize. I wasn't aware you were still interested in the human's welfare."

"Consider me *deeply* invested in my Aldara's wellbeing."

The envoy's knees shook, a dark stain spreading on the crotch of his pants.

Arrow looked at me over his shoulder. "Do you trust me, Leaf?"

"More than I trust myself."

"Good answer." He grinned, tipping his chin toward Neeron. "So then, may I have the pleasure?"

Pointing my blade toward the ground, I considered Arrow's question.

First, it was nice of him to ask permission before killing Neeron on my behalf. And second, I *was* exhausted. In addition, I hadn't spied Melaya since the fighting had commenced. Perhaps he'd already fled the kingdom and was halfway across the realm. Or perhaps he hadn't and would appear any moment and burn us all to crispy cinders. Therefore, I had to conserve my energy and be ready for anything.

I nodded at Arrow. "By all means, go ahead."

Thunder cracked, and with a smirk, he spun a vortex of storm power on his palm. Threads of lightning whirled so fast they blurred into mini-twisters of blinding light. Neeron turned and ran, and Arrow raised his hand, but his magic just... fizzled out and disappeared.

Frowning, he tried to connect to the storm again. Once. Twice.

But nothing happened.

With a snap, my failing reaver cloak completely slid from my skin.

Shit. Our magic was dead. Had twenty minutes passed since we began our attack? It only felt like ten at the most. Something must have happened to the queen or Nukala. I glanced around the arena. Still no Melaya in sight.

Fuck.

What was going on?

Arrow frowned at my solid body. "Time's up," he said, grabbing my sword and running forward, splitting the envoy in half from head to groin before throwing the blade back to me.

I caught it and spun the hilt in my hand. "Nicely done."

A dark-gold eyebrow cocked. "High praise indeed coming from you."

"True," I agreed with a dark laugh, then sobered and asked, "Are we fucked now? As good as dead?"

He shrugged, and we both scanned the arena.

The chaos showed signs of easing. Most soldiers had fled, and Raiden, Zaret, and Esen, their blood-splattered bodies flickering in and out of visibility, were busy helping injured courtiers who'd gotten swept up in the battle.

Where was Ari? The last time I saw the results of her invisible sword wielding, she'd been in the crowd. Icy fear slithering through me, I wiped ash from my face with my sleeve, the smoke from scores of fires stinging my eyes.

I patted my leg. But the pouch containing Estella's pendant and my remaining orchid petals was gone. Fuck.

The last of Arrow's storm clouds dissolved. Then, with a loud crack, Melaya appeared in the sky, his body surrounded by flames and crimson wings that I never knew he possessed, spreading wide.

Arrow moved in front of me, then sighed, wrapping a wing around my shoulders as I sidestepped to stand beside him.

"Your king is dead, Mage," he said. "And the fight is over."

Melaya landed on the dais just above us. "Debatable. By old Talnian law, if I don't kill you now, then you'll become the Sun Realm's new ruler. Or perhaps you would allow our queen to hold power."

Arrow crossed his arms. "Whatever Estella wishes, she shall have. Where is she?"

Melaya's lips formed a savage smile. "I'm more interested in your Sayeeda's whereabouts."

Arrow frowned as Ari called his name from the other side of the arena and stepped through a group of fae that she appeared to have been healing. Raiden shouted, but she kept her face averted, shoulders stiff as she climbed the dais steps, not stopping until she stood four feet in front of the mage.

"Stay there, Leaf. Don't move." In a blur of wings, Arrow left my side and flew onto the dais, landing next to Ari.

"Give me your Sayeeda, Arrowyn," ordered Melaya, "and I'll bind your power to the land, making you king of two powerful realms. Let her depart Taln with me now, and I vow to leave you in peace for now."

A laugh rumbled from Arrow's chest. "You think I'm a fool? You can't have the Sayeeda. She is bound to my kingdom, to our friendship, and her heart is forever linked with another's."

"Her heart is worth nothing to me. I need the gold in her veins, not her *friendship*, and I care not who she's bound to, lover or king."

Arrow thrust his hand toward me, the word *sword* sounding in my head.

Without hesitating, I threw Bakhur's sword to him.

He caught it one-handed without taking his eyes off Melaya. "Stop talking, Mage, and fight me instead."

This time, Melaya laughed. "You cannot defeat me. Not without storm magic."

"Guess I'm fucked, then," said Arrow. "Let's find out for sure." He lurched forward, stood on the tips of Melaya's boots, and then shoved him off the dais, leaping after him with his sword raised.

Power surged around the mage, and a whooshing sound tore through the air at the same time blinding orange light exploded. I squeezed my eyes shut, opening them two heartbeats later.

Arrow was gone.

Heart pounding, I scanned the arena.

No sign of him.

Where in the hells was he?

Spying the sword on the ground where Arrow must have dropped it, I ran forward, snatching it up and turning toward Melaya as he walked back up the dais stairs toward Ari with slow, deliberate steps. She unsheathed a knife from the belt on her hip and bent her knees, ready to pounce on him.

"Sayeeda, wait!" Estella's voice rang through the air. She strode across the arena with Nukala slumped in her arms, a knife sticking out of his heart and blood pouring from the wound.

The flames in Melaya's eyes flared brighter. "Star Witch," he shouted, his voice reverberating with fury and banked power. I closed my eyes for a moment, praying the death of his twin had diminished his strength, just as we'd hoped it would.

"I saved my brother from drowning. Blocked your magic. And yet, you undid it. *How?*"

"That's my business, Mage. And I believe we are now even," said the queen. "Your greed has caused the death of my *only* child. But unfortunately for you, I am not so easy to kill. You shouldn't have left Nukala's bathroom so soon. But you were too eager to hurry off and attempt to claim more power, and now you've paid the price. Your twin is dead, and all you have left without him is limited magic. So how will you choose to use it?"

Melaya's black robes swirled as he shot forward, swooped Ari up, then blasted into the sky, tucking her under his arm. Then they disappeared.

"No," I yelled at the same time Raiden howled like a wounded wolf.

Estella dropped Nukala, and his body crumpled on the dirt. She released a high-pitched scream, the sound as terrifying as a thousand banshees wailing at a funeral.

With her head back, mouth open wide, she raised her palms to the sky and crouched low, her entire body shaking. An answering drone reverberated from the planets above, growing louder and shriller, until the ground shook, and I thought my eardrums might explode.

The air in the arena pulsed as the stars embroidered on Estella's black gown peeled away from the material and swirled in a spiraling mass into the celestial dome above. It changed color from sparkling silver to flat black, creating a strange void directly above us.

Bats, birds, and glowing insects spun through the sky, sucked into the black hole's gravitational pull. I ground my teeth and did my best to keep my boots planted on the ground, my flesh crawling as though the force of the dark chasm pulled me toward its depths.

Wind whipped, tearing at my clothes and hair, and with horror, I watched my fingernails grow, as if every part of me yearned to merge with the cosmic void.

New screams of terror pierced the night as everyone in the arena experienced the same symptoms, nearly drowning out Estella's chanting. She had the voice of a goddess, resonating with ancient, destructive power. The queen was a realm destroyer.

Just when my organs felt like they would burst through my skin, Melaya suddenly appeared in the sky again, his wings beating wildly against the void's force.

Estella's power had reeled him back like a fish caught on a hook.

The mage's mouth tore open in a grimace of terror as he screamed and screamed, the Sayeeda hanging limp in his arms.

"Ari," I yelled.

Estella stopped chanting, her eyes closed and hands moving in an elaborate pattern. Melaya cried out again, clawing desperately against the hungry void as a ball of light, the queen's star magic, exploded on his left shoulder.

He released Ari, and as she tumbled down, the queen whipped her hand toward the ground, and a blanket of light appeared a few feet above it, glittering as if it was made of stars.

Ari landed on the protective barrier, rolled off and onto her feet, and then ran toward the exit. I'd never seen her move so fast, but she was wise to put as much distance between herself and Melaya as possible.

I looked up and watched the void swallow the tail of Melaya's cloak—the rest of him had already disappeared inside it. *Good fucking riddance*, I thought, as Estella crumpled to the ground.

Stars flowed from the void, reversing their spiral and spreading across the sky. And the moment the night reabsorbed the cosmic hole, the droning sound stopped, silver pinpricks glittering serenely in the sky, and the unruly wind settling at last.

"Help the queen," I said to anyone nearby who might respond. I couldn't stay. I needed to find Arrow and Ari, make sure they were all right.

Ruhh appeared at my side and pointed at the group of fae gathering around Estella. "Don't worry, Zali. I will oversee the queen's treatment."

"I don't know why you're helping us," I said, "but I'm very grateful."

Ruhh circled me like a wasp about to get tangled in my hair. "My brother bound my body to this realm, but the Zareen has promised to restore it." She bared decaying teeth in a deranged smile. "Just think, one day soon, I may be able to hug you."

I laughed. "Are you sure you wouldn't rather throw me off a cliff?"

"Since my death, I have realized many men are stupid, making decisions with their egos and cocks instead of their hearts and brains. We females must stick together and clean up their messes. But, please, tell Arrow not to get too comfortable in Coridon. If I know Melaya, he will find a way back from the fringes of the cosmos and cause him more trouble."

With a heavy heart, I nodded, and then spun on my heel, wiping sweat and blood from my face as I moved quickly through the arena, searching for my friends. For my love.

"Leaf!" Ari shouted.

I ran toward the sound of her voice, finding her back in the arena and huddled over a dark shape slumped beside the ancient gates. A body. A large male with his wings flung limply over his bare torso.

Arrow.

No, no, no, no, no.

Please gods, no.

I'd do anything if only he was alive.

Anything.

I let out a scream and bolted forward. Skidding across the dirt on my knees, I knocked Ari sideways as I crashed into her, then stopped by Arrow's body.

Golden tears painted her face, and she wrapped an arm around me, an offer of comfort that I shrugged off as I leaned over Arrow, sobs wracking through me.

I smoothed hair off his face, tucking strands behind the points of his ears. Blood trickled from his mouth, his feather glyphs a dark flesh color. No pulse thudded through his veins.

"No, Arrow. *Please*. Please, no. Come back to me. I can't do this without you." I kissed the blood from his lips and soaked his blanched skin with my tears.

"Help him, Ari," I said. "Please. I'll do anything. If you need blood, I have plenty to spare. A life in exchange for his? I'll gladly give mine. Just don't let him die. I couldn't bear it."

Fires raged around the arena, small ones merging and growing, smoke obscuring the stars. The flames roared around us, cleansing, purifying, clearing space for new beginnings.

New blades of grass.

New saplings.

New kings and queens.

My Aldara mark suddenly flashed, searing the flesh of my neck as white sparks from its magic singed my hair. That was a good sign. It meant Arrow was reviving.

Didn't it?

But then the magic faltered, falling dormant with a final, soft hiss.

And I knew without a doubt...

The Storm King was dead.

Chapter 33

LEAF

I flung myself into Ari's arms, my mind and heart shattering into a thousand painful shards that tore through my trembling flesh as sobs wracked over me.

"No. I refuse to live without him. I don't even *want* to. How can I keep going?"

Ari stroked my back. "You survived when you thought he had betrayed you, but at least now, Leaf, you'll have the comfort of knowing that you were everything to him. That he sacrificed his life to protect you."

My sobs turned into howls. "That's so much worse. I can't do this... *please*..." I let my words trail off as the wind picked up and lashed my hair, strands sticking to my wet face as I turned back to Arrow.

"Please, my love. Please come back. I'm so fucking mad at you. Don't leave me alone. I'm sorry. I'm so sorry for every horrible thing I ever said or did. Please... just don't die." I thumped his bare chest twice, tried to lift him by the shoulders, needing to shake the life back into him.

"Leaf, let him go. *Look*," Ari whispered urgently, grabbing my arm.

I stared at the limp shape of my lover. Skin pale. The iridescent color leeched from his wings, the feather tips fluttering at the mercy of the hot breeze that swept through the arena.

Then his eyelids flickered.

Barely. Hardly perceptible. But still...

Arrow wasn't dead!

He.

Wasn't.

Fucking dead.

Not yet.

But he *was* dying.

My heart flipped and stuttered, then resumed its grim thudding.

Since my arrest in the desert, I'd wished countless times that my hate-filled gaze would be the last thing Arrow saw. And now, if I could take back every tear shed in service of my mistaken loathing, I would happily choke and drown in them.

I pounced on Arrow, holding his cheeks between my palms, chanting his name as if it would save him from a fatal enchantment.

"Please, Leaf. Move aside," said Ari, digging an elbow into my ribs. "I need room if I'm to help him." I gave her space, and she tipped three drops of glittering liquid from a dark vial between his lips.

"Gold serum?" I asked.

"Yes. It's a risk, but unfortunately our only hope. The right dose might just save him. Too much, and it will finish him off."

I swallowed a lump of fear, praying Ari had administered the correct amount.

Please let him be okay. Let him live. Let him wake up and say something outrageous, make me laugh and cry again.

"Leaf, is he going to be all right?" asked a gruff voice.

I turned to Raiden, who stood behind me, and smiled through my tears at Esen and Zaret. "Not sure yet. I thought he was dead, but then he moved. Ari's just given him gold serum."

They crouched next to me, and we huddled around Arrow's lifeless form, holding each other tightly, barely breathing as we waited for the Storm King to come back to us.

"Ari, it's taking too long. It hasn't worked. Should I massage his heart? Try to get it going?"

"No. Don't touch him yet." She drew another breath to continue, but Arrow coughed, interrupting her, and splattering another layer of blood over the battle filth on my neck and collarbone.

I'd never been so happy to be spat on.

"My love. My love," I chanted, pressing gentle kisses on his brow, his cheeks. "You're alive. I can't believe you're alive."

"Not getting rid of me so easily," he croaked through a lopsided grin.

Another bout of sobbing seized me—this time triggered by overwhelming joy.

"How do you feel?" Ari asked, her fingers pressing against the pulse at his neck, her golden eyes scanning his glyphs as they sparked back to life.

"Melaya? Where is he?" Arrow asked, pushing onto his elbows.

"Gone," replied Esen. "Estella pulled him through a cosmic void, a massive black hole in the sky that I pray he can never return from. And Azarn and his horrible son are dead. So that's something."

"A lot more than *something*." Slowly, Arrow looked at each of us, his eyes shining bright. "My Aldara, Ari, Raiden, Esen, and Zaret, you're all safe. Every one of you. Which means, in answer to your question, Sayeeda, I feel fucking fantastic. Good as new."

"What about me?" asked a breathy voice near my ear. "Are you pleased I'm still here?"

My hair fluttered over my face as the ghost girl appeared, bringing with her a gust of cooler air.

Squinting, Arrow frowned. "Oh, shit. Is that Ruhh?"

"It's all right," I soothed. "The little turncoat is on our side now."

"Gold help us, then," Arrow rumbled, lurching onto his feet in one ungraceful movement. He swayed, and I held my breath as Raiden moved to his side, ready to catch him if needed.

"Come," Arrow said, offering me his hand. "Let's survey the damage."

Slowly, we weaved through piles of ash, countless spot fires, and the misshapen bodies of fallen soldiers. He led me up the dais stairs, and then onto Azarn's throne, drawing me onto his lap.

Sweeping his palm across the scene before us, he said, "Not long ago the king of this land used you for his entertainment, and now, you're the Queen of Fire and Flames."

My gaze skimmed his strong jaw, the firelight glinting over the beginnings of stubble. Dark smudges rimmed his eyes like kohl. He looked exhausted. Relieved. Relaxed. Like a desert lion after a difficult but satisfying hunt.

A laugh burst out of me. "Taln already has a queen."

"Estella? She is now free to return to her lover in the Crystal Realm. I'd bet my life she'll renounce the crown."

"Please don't make stupid wagers. You were so close to death, Arrow. And if not for Ari's quick thinking and the gold serum she was smart enough to carry with her, you would have *no* life to bet with. Why would Estella hand her crown to me?"

He scratched his chin, stroking my hip with his other hand. "Think of Sun Realm succession like a pack of brutal werehogs fighting over a bone. As Azarn's killer, I take his place at the head of the pack and can claim ownership of everything around me."

"And that means?"

He waved his hand between us. "Behold, the new King of Fire and Flames and his lady wife, the queen."

"*Wife*? Unless I slept through a ceremony, we're not married."

"Not yet. But we will fix that shortly. If you'll have me, of course." His smile turned into a smirk. "But then again, why would you not?" He sobered as he trailed a finger through the gore on my neck. "Is any of this blood yours?"

"Barely any. I feel wonderful, in fact. Tired, but so happy, Arrow. We did it. Azarn is dead and Melaya's gone."

Appearing fully recovered, Estella walked through the arena, mounted the stairs, and sat cross-legged on the dais beside Azarn's throne. "Discussing your plans for this miserable realm?" she asked.

"Our only plan is to fulfill your wishes," replied Arrow. "Whatever they may be."

"I wish to return to the Crystal Realm. To my home."

"I suspected you would. Will you stay for a while to help ease the court through the transition?" he said.

The queen hugged her knees to her chest and sighed. "Yes, of course."

I leaned forward. "How will the kingdom survive without the twin mages?"

"Quite well. Melaya and Nukala wrote their own legends into our history books centuries ago and have played the rulers of Taln like puppets ever since. Veins of fire bubble beneath the kingdom's soil, heating the water, fertilizing the plants and trees, and blessing the fire fae with magic. With Melaya gone, the people must build their natural power, the power that the mage's magic curtailed. We must train their magical skills as we would strengthen soldiers' muscles for battle."

Estella stood up, rubbing her bruised arms. "I must return to the palace and see to the courtiers. And you two have somewhere else you wish to be, I think."

"Yes," said Arrow. "Coridon. As soon as possible. But we'll return in a couple of days at the latest."

I shot him a surprised look, then addressed Estella. "One day, I hope you'll tell us the story of what happened in the bathroom with Nukala and Melaya."

"Visit me in the city of my birth." She rose and started down the stairs, but stopped three steps down, and said over her shoulder, "Only then, will I speak of it."

Arrow's hands wrapped around my waist, lifting me onto my feet, then he stood up and tugged me into his arms.

His breath warmed the top of my head. "Think back to who we were that day at the gilt market... A lost, fury-filled princess. A king burdened by prejudice and bitterness. And soon, together, we will rule three realms—the kingdoms of Earth, Light, and Sun."

"Well..." I lifted my cheek from his chest and grinned up at him. "Only if I decide to name you my King of Dust and Stones."

Arrow shrugged. "As long as you named no other, I would be satisfied. But know this, if you *do* name another male your king, this unfortunate being would not keep his title for long."

"Hah! A threat. Ruthless even now."

He laughed, entwining our fingers. "You're as vicious as a storm, and I am your ruthless thunder."

My grin widened. "I'm not sure what you mean by that."

"Only that we were made for each other." He squeezed my hand. "Let's go. The others can take care of Taln while we fly back to Coridon. Estella will inform our friends."

"You nearly died, Arrow. Shouldn't you rest for an hour or two? Recharge your power?"

"My Sayeeda is not called the Mistress of Potions and Spices for nothing. The serum has renewed me."

"If I'm not mistaken, her title is the Mistress of *Slaves* and Spices?"

"Not anymore. You'll see when we return home."

"*Your* home. Mine is—"

His thumb pressed my lips together, then dipped between them and rubbed the gap in my teeth. "If you like, you may have a home in every city in the realms. But they will all be *our* homes. I'm never leaving you again. Look what happened the last time I left you to your own devices for a few weeks."

"I'd love to come to Coridon with you." I hesitated, shuffling my boots. "But I couldn't possibly leave Luna behind."

"Your horse? Yes, you can. She'll be fine. I won't keep you apart for long. I promise."

"All right," I said before giving him a sly smile. "But perhaps you should eat another persimmon before we leave. I can probably find one in the garden."

"What a terrible suggestion." He smacked my butt, wrapped his arms around me, then bent his knees as if ready to launch straight into the air.

"Wait! We could use the portal. It should be working again now that Melaya's gone."

"Good try, Leaf. But flying's a lot more fun than stepping through a fucking portal." He laughed, then exploded off the ground, shooting into the night sky.

My scream echoed across the Sun Realm and possibly all the way to Coridon.

Sighing, I wrapped my arms around Arrow's neck, snuggling into his warmth. "Please don't drop me."

His deep voice rumbled against my ear. "I will never let you fall, my love. Ever."

Chapter 34

ARROW

"I thought you liked flying," I said against her ear, hoping she could hear me over the wind, since the Aldara bond was too weak to speak through. "Remember at Auryinnia Mountain, how you begged me to take you on a flight instead of returning to our tent?"

"I do, but you hadn't nearly died that night, Arrow."

"Yes, but *you* almost did. Later. After you left me and escaped on Enyd the *blind* eponar."

She laughed as if I'd said something funny, and I squeezed her tighter, so fucking thankful that after everything we'd been through, she was finally safe. And mine.

"Have faith," I told her, chuckling. "If we fall to the ground, I promise I'll shield your body with mine."

Her fingers clawed my neck.

"I'm only teasing," I said. "I'm fine. *You're* fine, Leaf, and we'll be home before you know it."

There was zero chance that I'd drop her. Ever.

I would destroy anything, including myself, if it would keep her safe. Keep her with me. Every auron kanara in my city. Palaces. Kingdoms. Galaxies.

"The view is so beautiful up here," she whispered, not staring at the glimmering stars or the lanterns of Farron Gilt Market far below, but at me. Her master, her slave, her dearest friend and forever ally.

On the day I'd bought her, when we arrived at the river, instead of showing fear, she taunted and defied me. But had I known what she would come to mean to me, I would've begged then and there for mercy.

But back then, I was foolish, my heart rotting in a cage of bitterness. My fucked-up mind focused only on revenge. Nothing else.

Since then, Leaf had taught me many priceless lessons. And I couldn't wait to show her everything I'd learned.

With my gaze fixed on her precious face, navigating the skies by body memory alone, I could only agree with her statement. "Yes, the view is unmatched in all the realms."

Moonlight painted the Aureen mountains ashen gray, then a little farther along, it turned the palms beside Auron K's river a shiny, iridescent silver. I fucking loved the sight of Light Realm towns tranquil in the deepest of night, knowing their inhabitants slept peacefully in their beds. Happy and content.

A short distance away, before I even saw them, I felt the corroding spikes of Bonerust's gates spearing to the left. To distract Leaf, I quickly pointed to the desert in the opposite direction. I didn't want her to be reminded of the short, but distressing time she'd spent in that shithole of a town.

She snuggled closer, her cheek warm against my chest, and I was glad I wasn't wearing my breastplate. I only hoped that when the fae of Taln found my plate of gold feathers, they would take good care of it. And if they didn't, heads would roll. Just kidding—the new King of Storms and Feathers was a pussycat, not a villain.

Below, the desert's dark hills undulated like rippling velvet cloth thrown across a gigantic table, then before long, Coridon's golden domes and spires impaled the indigo sky, amber and bronze glinting amongst the shadows.

"Nearly home," I said, flying higher before swooping down fast.

Wind tore our hair, and Leaf screamed at the shock of the sudden descent. I laughed, decelerating and gliding around the golden pillars of the pavilion that was once her gilded prison. Her heart pounded against me when the breeze parted the sheer curtains and we glimpsed inside my apartment, gently lit by floating balls of lighting.

Thunder growled in the distance, rumbling closer, seeking me out, and I had to focus hard to push the power away as it shuddered along my spine.

"Are you causing that?" she asked.

"Not on purpose."

As far as I could tell, in my absence, no harm had befallen Coridon, my people, or my quarters. I could hardly wait to hold my Aldara inside my bedchamber. Wrap her in my wings. Feed her grapes. Kiss every inch of her creamy skin. Marking her. Blanketing her in everlasting love.

Each glide past my apartment showed soaring columns supporting three levels of black-and-white marble. Palm leaves glittered in the river room, and the double staircases still swept up to the sitting room connected to the pavilion, where the auron kanara stirred, sensing my arrival. And finally, my crescent-shaped bedchamber, where I planned to give Leaf a very pleasurable welcome back to Coridon.

We were home at last.

All was well. Exactly as I'd left it.

I just hoped Leaf felt that it was *her* home, too.

Adjusting her body in my arms, I squeezed her a little tighter. "When you lived in the pavilion," I said. "I loved watching you sleep. It was an addiction. I couldn't stop. Every night flying around, fooling myself my obsession grew because of the hate I bore humans and the gold chasers that killed my family. Yet looking back now, I know I loved you from the moment I saw that first flash of fire in your eyes through the bars of that fucking market cage."

"I bet you loved seeing me chained to the pavilion, too," she teased. "Helpless. At your mercy."

"No. All I thought about was setting you free. But you wouldn't stop defying me. Keeping you there was the only way I could ensure your safety until you realized what was at stake."

"Our hearts?" she asked.

"Yes. But also your life, which is worth more to me than the moon, the stars, the mountains, every speck of Mydorian dust, and the desert sky. *That's* what I was protecting. You are everything to me. Always will be."

"You're such a charmer," she said, her voice soft and trembling.

I grinned. "Let's see if you still think so after this."

"After what?"

Without explaining, I plunged forward, hurtling downward, but instead of landing inside my chambers as she probably expected, I set her down near a narrow doorway. An entrance to the palace she likely remembered all-too well.

The scent of night jasmine and cinnamon floated on the warm breeze as we retraced the steps we had walked a few months ago—a pissed-off king and an angry, frightened slave. I hadn't stopped thinking about her since the moment she stabbed Esen, and I chased her through Farron Gilt Market.

But now I walked beside her, my arm slung over her shoulders, hers around my waist, and my wing warming her back. Together. Our steps in sync.

The moment we entered the palace, the auron kanaras fluttered and chirped in greeting, and I felt a shiver roll over Leaf's shoulders. I recalled how deeply she had sympathized with their plight and had longed to set every bird in the city free.

She knew what it was like to live imprisoned behind bars of gold, at the mercy of the Light Realm fae, at *my* mercy, and as much as I wanted to gift her with the release of the birds, I couldn't. They needed us and would die without our lightning magic.

But soon, I hoped she would understand just how much her compassion had taught me.

"Why are we here, Arrow?" she asked as we passed the golden cages lining the corridor and stopped in front of the elevator's barred doors. "Shouldn't we be attacking each other in your bedchamber right now?" She grimaced. "After a hot bath, of course."

Illuminated by flames from the wall sconces, the sweet, dusty red of desert roses flushed her cheeks.

I smiled and nodded at a passing servant whose eyes widened at the sight of me. "I thought the most romantic thing I could do, Leaf, before any bathing or attacking, would be to demonstrate the extent of your influence."

"Oh. Sounds intriguing. Please lead the way."

The same two soldiers who had guarded the elevator the night she first arrived in the city, bowed, then opened the scrolled-metal doors. They clanged shut behind us, and we plunged down two levels.

Underfloor.

Memories of the putrid stench of suffering battered my senses, and beside me, Leaf shuddered and swayed, taking a step backward as I exited the elevator.

"It's all right," I said. "Trust me."

Taking my hand, she stepped out, not into the dark tunnel from her nightmares, but into a space now painted gold and lined with light, honey-colored wood. No slaves dwelt here anymore. The cells had been ripped out, and in their place, learning spaces, partitioned rooms with desks, comfortable furniture, and shelves stuffed with books and scrolls invited her to investigate.

Her fingers relaxed around mine as she inspected every gleaming nook and cranny, finding new wonders with each step. Running her palm over metalworking tools, she turned to me and said, "You're teaching your people the skills needed to improve their lives."

"Yes. Well, not me personally, but our tradespeople are. Remember the mineral pool through there?" I pointed toward the door nestled in the far wall, indicating the entrance to the torch-lit cavern where I'd been told guards had thrown Leaf and her human friend Grendal into the water before they began work as kitchen servants.

She nodded.

"That's a place of healing now. The minerals in the spring water are very powerful, did you know that?"

Shaking her head, she laughed gently. "Your face... Arrow, you look so proud."

"I *am* proud. Extremely so. After thousands of years, the slaves of Coridon are no more. Our servants, even those who were once gold chasers, live in a newly built area of town. All workers are paid a fair wage. We don't *create* addicts with our serum bracelets anymore, we help them recover. But I need to know... are *you* proud of me, my Leaf?"

Illuminated by lightning globes, she spun on her heel, taking in Underfloor's new warmth and beauty, then gripped my forearms and held my expectant gaze. "Are you saying that you reformed Coridon, even reformed yourself for *me?*" she asked.

"No. I changed *because* of you. Because you showed me by word and deed that rulers must reflect upon their actions and even more so on their *inaction.* Your blunt criticisms made me realize I wasn't exempt from bearing the responsibility of the systems my father and his father before him had put in place. Not correcting them was as bad as if I had created them myself."

"Oh," she said, a hand pressing over her heart. Seemingly lost for words, she smiled, her warm expression of unfiltered love one I'd only dreamed of seeing on her face again.

If I could only make her happy every single day of her life, then I'd have a legacy to be proud of.

"While you were alone in Mydorian, I took a hard look at myself and my kingdom and realized what my reign was built on. Terror. And I felt only deepest disdain for myself. I hope one day to deserve you, Leaf, and I want nothing to stand in your way of loving me. If you cannot see me as a partner of value, then I am done for. Kill me now. I have no wish to live if you cannot even *like* me."

"Rather drastic," she said, pulling me close and kissing me. "You've been extremely busy. How was this achieved in no more than a month?"

I grinned and wriggled my fingers, lightning flickering between them. "Light Realm fae are very strong and clever."

"*And* have storm magic. Well, you've certainly put it to good use. Impressive Underfloor transformation and commendable personal growth aside, I'd really like to hear your plans for me when we reach your apartment."

With my finger, I caressed the diagonal line of tiny buttons along her collarbone. "First, I'll undo these, and perhaps a few other things, too. Not long after, I plan to make you scream my name about a hundred times. Possibly more."

"Sounds wonderful. Shall we get on with it, then?" She held out her arm, and I linked mine through it, tilting my head toward a new exit near the springs.

Walking quickly, I guided her down a corridor lined with tropical plants to a glass door that led into an outdoor courtyard. "Hold on tight." I grabbed her and shot into the air. "Don't scream," I said at the same time she screeched in my ear and almost permanently destroyed my hearing.

"Too late," she said. "Sorry."

Her breathy laugh aroused my desire, hot flames licking over me.

We spiraled through the air, our bodies pressed together, arms wrapped tightly around each other, and our lips tender as we kissed. Time slowed to a standstill, the night sounds of hunting hawks, the rushing wind, fading into a dream. Nothing else existed but my Aldara and the erratic beat of her heart. The silk-soft caress of her lips.

Twirling slowly downward, we landed in the pavilion, and I tried to imagine how it felt for her to be here again. The warm tiles. The violent mosaic above. The caress of the auron rose-scented breeze. The shackle anchors in the floor. Coridon's glittering lights.

Memories seemed to rush over her, her skin flushing hot, cold, then hot again as she pulled out of my arms and paced around the pavilion's edge. No doubt a track she had walked many times over while fear, rage, humiliation, possibly even desire had shuddered through her.

Back when she was my captive. My lost girl. My fiercest adversary.

"Leaf, stop," I said, agony twisting my features. I couldn't bear to see her suffering. I curled my fingers and beckoned her closer. "Please. Come here."

She unclenched her fists and did as I asked, stopping an arm's length away. I closed the distance between us with one step and found myself looming over her.

"You know, Arrow, your tallness is rather annoying," she said with a smile.

"That's funny." A smirk tugged the corner of my mouth. "I was just thinking the same thing. It can be challenging to reach you all the way down there. And it's strange, but I don't find anything about you annoying, my Aldara."

"Liar." She laughed.

As I gathered her in my arms, lightning flashed over the mountains, and the room's loose kanara feathers rose in the air, rushing toward us and swirling around our bodies, like iridescent black snow.

The heady drug of anticipation thrummed though my veins as I stroked her cheek, my fingernail gently scraping a trail of dried blood before I lifted her chin to my kiss with a finger.

Our eyes locked as we inched closer. My palms framed her face, and I took a long breath. "I love you," I said. "More than I ever thought I could love anything or anyone. You've surprised me at every turn."

My lips brushed hers. "Fascinated me."

A stroke of my tongue against the wet silk of hers. "Challenged me."

A nip of my teeth. "I am a better fae, king, lover, and friend because you taught me how to break free from my past."

I pressed my fingers into the base of her skull. "Thank you, my Aldara." Another whisper-soft kiss. "Thank you."

Shifting her head to the perfect angle, I kissed her as if it were our last time together. As if I would never again be allowed to look at her, touch her. I wound my fingers through her hair, tipping her head back to deepen the kiss.

I could have stayed like that forever, content, in bliss, but my hand, apparently, had other ideas and slowly traced the curve of her body, settling on her hip, desperate to delve lower.

I sighed, dropping soft kisses on her eyelids before forcing myself to step backward. "You must be so tired," I said. "Also, you're—"

"Soaked in the blood of our enemies?" She grinned. "So, yeah. I'd really love a bath."

"You can have anything you desire. Simply name it."

Raising one dark eyebrow, she bit the edge of her smile and gave my body a slow perusal, her emerald eyes lingering on the hard outline pressing against my leathers.

KING OF FIRE AND FLAMES

I laughed. "And you can have that, too. As many times as you wish tonight. Only speak the words and I'll be your slave. Do with me what you will. Forever, if you like."

"Mm, I do like the sound of that."

I pressed my forehead to hers and sighed. "Quickly, then. Let's go. I can't wait much longer."

Chapter 35

LEAF

Before I could beg to take the elevator, we were flying again, swooping into Arrow's domed apartment, then gliding up to the bathroom perched on a platform of raised marble inside the river room.

Arrow ran the bath, not taking his eyes off me as I peeled off my blood-soaked wedding gown and boots. He took a bucket from the corner of the room, guided me to stand over the drain and poured warm water over my head, sluicing most of the blood and dirt from my skin.

My mouth dried as he removed his leather pants, then ambled to the sink and splashed water over his face, the flames from the wall sconces highlighting the mesmerizing shift and glide of muscles.

Arrow's body was a work of art.

Picking up the bucket, he sloshed water over himself, staring at me with a hungry glint in his eyes.

"Mind if I join you?" he asked.

"Please do," I said climbing carefully into the copper tub and swallowing groans of pain. "Before you get any big ideas, touching and kissing in here are fine, but nothing else. We're saving the best stuff for dry land." Grimacing, I swished the red-tinged water. "And clean sheets."

He bowed his head, strands of hair framing the brutal lines of his cheekbones. "I'm yours to command, of course, but let me check if I have this right. Hands and lips are fine, but a cock is out of the question?"

I laughed. "Hurry up and get in before I turn into a wrinkled prune."

"If you do, I promise I'll love every single crease on your skin."

"Arrow, I don't fancy the idea of looking like your grandmother one day."

His glyphs glowed bright gold, his erection bobbing as he slid into the tub and entwined his legs with mine. "Having my storm magic around and inside you will slow the human-aging process. When you bear our children, some of their power will transfer to you. We will live a long and blissful life together, my Aldara, all we must do is enjoy it."

"*And* work on bettering our kingdoms for our people."

"Of course. Instead of hoarding peace and happiness for ourselves, we'll ensure everyone in the realms experiences it, too."

"There's nothing sexier than a reformed villain. When are you planning on kissing me?" I asked.

Smirking, he scratched the stubble on his chin. "Hm... perhaps next Friday I could find time to do it properly."

I splashed water on his chest, then took his face between my palms, kissing him ruthlessly.

"Slow down," he whispered, his palm covering my pulsing Aldara mark. "I'm about to lose control. I want to love you properly. Take care of you."

"Okay," I said, struggling to catch my breath. Then between soft kisses we washed each other gently, fingers stroking, hushed voices soothing.

"I thought I'd lost you in that horrible arena," I said, the tears I'd been suppressing flowing freely.

"No, never. Come here, Leaf." He dragged me closer, wrapping me in his arms and the dark canopy of his wings. "Even death can't keep us apart. I would fight my way back to you from the deepest hell realms. I promise."

"Ugh, now I'm thinking of Ruhh, bound to her corpse forever."

Arrow grimaced. "Don't think about *her*." His fingers trailed over my stomach, then ventured lower. "Does this help redirect your focus?"

I moaned in pleasure. "Yes. It absolutely does." Heat flushed through my veins, my muscles trembling with need. "I can't wait to have you inside me. Please, let's get out of here."

In a blur of limbs, feathers, and splashing water, he leaped from the bath, his glyphs moving over his skin as he pulled me onto the wet floor.

We dried each other quickly and threw our clothes into the blood-tinged bath water. Then he wrapped a towel around my shoulders.

"Please, no flying this time," I begged. "Can we walk through the river room? I want to see the waterfall window again."

"The one you jumped out of? Certainly. But forgive me if I hold on to you too tightly."

I laughed. "I wouldn't dream of fleeing. I couldn't possibly be a more willing guest."

"Not a guest, a permanent resident," he corrected. "I hope."

As we entered the river room, deep peace enveloped me, the large leaves of tropical plants brushing my arms and legs and soothing my fractured nerves. The sounds of the river teased my senses. A bubbling lullaby where it entered the room, growing into a raging chorus as it tumbled over a sloping marble ledge, through the window, and into the pool in the city street below.

It could have triggered traumatic flashbacks of my time held captive here. But it didn't. Instead, the past and the present collided, and memories of the green-eyed boy I'd once loved—the brother I had killed—raced through my mind.

Our loud yelps as we ran through the lush forest of our childhood, then leaped over a waterfall into a rumbling river below. The Mydorian palace. Running with our hands linked through white-washed hallways into our parents' loving arms.

Then the images changed, and I saw myself jumping from the very window I now leaned upon. Smelled the stench of Bonerust. Gorbinvar's forge. Watched the Storm King blow it all to ash.

I shook the past off, turned and smiled at the fae who I loved and trusted with every part of my fragile human heart. He smiled back, folding a wing around my shoulders.

Together, we leaned over the sill, our palms braced on the window frame. He whistled long and low. "Quite a distance from here to that pool. You're brave, love. And stubborn. Reckless. Perfect. And forever mine."

"I do adore arguing with you, but I can't disagree with anything you just said."

"Never thought I'd hear you say that, Leaf."

We laughed, and then raced each other up the staircase to the sitting room. "You let me win," I said at the top, adjusting the towel under my armpits.

"Can you blame me?" he teased, his hungry gaze roaming over my body. "In this case, the loser's view was spectacular."

Through fluttering gauze curtains, I caught glimpses of the shimmering city lights and the silhouette of distant mountains. I looked with longing toward his crescent-shaped bedchamber on the next level up, but ignored the stairs leading to it and walked instead along the stone pathway that connected my pavilion to the sitting room.

"Follow me," I said over my shoulder, entering the gilded prison.

Crouching, I snatched two large feathers from the tiles and waved them under his amused nose. "Remember when I thought these belonged to a rare breed of night hawk?"

"Yes, and instead, they belonged to *me*—your stalker."

Laughing, I walked to the edge of the pavilion and tossed them into the breeze, the warm tiles a comfort under my bare feet as I watched Arrow's feathers float toward the desert.

I remembered lying naked on my back in the center of this very floor, my restless feet scraping against the tiles as forbidden desire heated my blood, and Arrow above me, taunting and teasing until I thought I'd break apart.

But my feelings for him were no longer forbidden. I could do what I liked with the King of Storms and Feathers, and he would happily allow it. I could break him if I desired. Cleave his heart from his chest. *Kill* him.

But at this moment, violence was the furthest thing from my mind.

Letting my towel drop, I eyed his still-damp body, drinking in the sight of smooth, hard planes flowing into dips and valleys between muscles. His cock twitched under my scrutiny, a bead of moisture already forming at its tip.

I licked my lips. "Lie on the floor."

His eyebrows rose as he pointed at his chest, mouthing a silent question, "*me?*"

"Yes, you. And hurry, please."

With his eyes on mine and his fists clenched at his sides, he did as requested.

I nudged his hand with my toe. "Arms over your head and keep your wrists together. If you move them even slightly, this ends. Do you understand?"

Throat bobbing, he nodded.

As I climbed over him, his head rose like he wanted to kiss me.

"Nope." I pushed against his bulky shoulder, and he flopped back without resistance. "Don't touch me. It's my turn to be *your* master."

"Fuck. If you keep talking like that, I won't last three minutes," he ground out, his fangs already lengthening.

My lips and tongue glided along his neck, and I bit the muscle that ran from behind his ear to his collarbone. I sucked his hard nipples, then moved lower, pressing hot kisses over his twitching stomach. When my mouth brushed his weeping tip, his hips lurched off the tiles.

"*Please*. I'll erupt if you do that..." he broke off, panting hard. "And fucking die if you don't."

"Don't worry. I'll go easy on you." With one hand, I balanced my weight on his chest, gripping his pulsating length with the other.

He released a volley of curses, but his wrists stayed crossed above his head, not moving an inch, as if I'd chained them together.

I guided the broad head through my slickness, teasing up and down, until we both quivered and shook, panting with desire. Cuffing his throat with my fingers, I placed him at my center, and with a sigh, slid slowly down his length until our hips met.

"Bliss," I whispered, motionless and losing myself in the wild storm of his eyes. In the sensation of perfect fullness.

"What are you waiting for?" he asked, staring up at me through heavy lids. "Fuck me hard before I die from wanting you."

I leaned forward, my face close to his, the change of angle inside me divine. "Do you remember that time you left me staked out in this exact spot?"

He groaned. "I wish I could forget. It plagues me still, and by the glint in your eyes, it might be the death of me now. I pray to any and all gods, past and future, that you won't be as foolish as I was and torture us for one heartbeat longer. I've begged you before, and I'll beg you again. Every day, if I must, Leaf. *Please*, make us one again."

"As you wish, my king, my obedient *slave*."

His laugh cut off abruptly as I squeezed his throat tighter, and then did as he asked, fucked the Storm King ruthlessly, with neither shame nor mercy. A delicious symphony of moans, growls, and rasped incantations of my name urged me to punish him harder. And I did.

Our bodies rocked in flawless rhythm, our breathing rough as waves of pleasure quaked over us. My movements grew erratic, every muscle coiling tighter and my attention narrowing to the pleasure building at my core.

"Such a good girl," he growled. "Use me. Take what you need."

"Oh, gods." I moved faster, shaking and moaning as I slid up and down his length, our hips slamming together.

It was sublime. It had to end because I couldn't bear anymore. Yet, at the same time, I never wanted it to stop.

"Leaf," he moaned. "I can't... Oh, fuck. Don't think I can hold on."

I cried out, rubbing the points of his ears as I broke apart, coming in hot waves, my physical body dissolving and flowing like lava down a mountainside.

Arrow froze, his mouth forming an agonized grimace as he battled against the end.

Just as I'd instructed, and even while my body pulsed around him, his arms didn't move an inch. But his wings were another matter.

The dark feathers shifted and trembled hard, his wings quivering and arching, and when he came with a growl that made me clench and spasm, they shuddered along with the rest of his body.

Dazed and panting, his arms banded my waist, and I collapsed on his damp chest, my cheek pressing against the thudding heart that I'd sworn to cut out.

But I could *never* harm this male.

Never forsake him.

From the moment our eyes met through the bars of the Farron Gilt Market cage, we had belonged to each other. I knew that now for a fact.

"Do I finally have permission to kiss you?" he asked.

I grinned, brushing my mouth against his. "Yes, please."

Soft lips took mine, and then he flipped our bodies, his fangs flashing as he smiled. "Now it's time for the feeding *and* the fucking."

"My favorite part," I replied.

Tears streamed down my face as he brought me to ecstasy again and again, drinking reverently from the veins in my thighs, my breasts, and my throat, while I whispered, "More. Don't stop. Not yet. Please, not yet."

Finally worn out, he wrapped me in his wings, and we perched on the edge of the pavilion, overlooking our sleeping kingdom.

With a gentle finger under my chin, he tilted my face to meet his gaze. "After tonight, you must promise to stay with me always. We have three kingdoms to oversee, but I'm sure we can—"

"You're still issuing orders," I said, interrupting.

"Not an order, an ardent request. I hope you want the same—to never be parted from me again."

"I do want that, Arrow. I want you to stay with me forever. Marry me. Be the father of my children. Be my dawn, my gloaming, my endless night sky. Always and forever."

"Finally, you're speaking sense! Nothing would make me happier. Before we leave for your Mydorian coronation, we'll marry in a simple Light Realm ritual."

"Sounds perfect."

He looked away, his heels thumping against the pavilion's stone wall.

"What's wrong?" I asked. "Tell me."

"Well... in old Coridonian marriage ceremonies, the king bequeaths his queen with a new name. A formal one, if you like. Will you let me do this?"

"Why would I need a new name?"

"Because it's the greatest honor a Light Realm king can bestow upon his Aldara." He leaned closer and whispered, "If you don't like the name I choose, we can negotiate for change."

I cupped his cheek. "Negotiations are always... appealing. Tell me what you'd choose."

"Leaf Zali Omala Ramiel."

"Why put Leaf before my birth name?" I asked.

"Because it suits you. And it will serve to remind me of everything I have taken away from you and all that I plan to give back."

"Well, then, I like it very much. Can we go to bed now, please? I'm exhausted."

Without warning, he gathered me close and flew us up to his chamber, while I giggled into the crook of his neck. Flying without clothes was certainly an interesting experience.

"Do you still have nightmares?" I asked, sighing as his silk sheets enveloped me, and I curled into the sanctuary of his arms. I breathed him in deeply, the hint of rosemary and mint in his hair making me smile.

"Yes, but only when you're not with me."

"Then you'll never have another one again."

"Never," he agreed. "Sleep soundly, my Aldara. I'll see you soon in our dreams."

"See you there," I whispered, pressing my lips against the strong column of his neck, my Aldara mark pulsing in a soothing rhythm. "Please don't crush me during the night. You're extremely heavy," I teased.

He chuckled. "I'd rather die."

The night sounds of Coridon lulled my eyes closed—the contented chirping of the auron kanara from the floor below, a bell chiming in the distance—and I released a deep sigh of happiness.

I was home at last.

I had finally found what I'd been seeking since the moment I woke up in that horrible market cage. Arrow's love. Wherever and whenever he held me, that was my home and where I belonged.

A rumble came from his chest, then a nonsensical jumble of words from his lips.

"What was that?" I asked.

"Remind me to feed the birds when we wake."

"Somehow, I don't think they'll let you forget."

"Sleep well, my Aldara. Love you."

Then we drifted into heavy slumber, safe in each other's arms, beneath the golden domes of our apartment.

Chapter 36

ARROW

Several weeks later...

I opened the door to Leaf's Mydorian bedchamber, and stopped in my tracks, my heart thundering against my ribs.

"Hi," she said, her cheeks flushing as I studied her, decked out in coronation finery.

She looked exquisite. I took a few steps forward, wondering how I'd stop myself from grabbing hold of her and never letting go.

"Nearly ready?" I asked, my gaze trailing over the creamy skin of her back draped in a gown of finely woven gold thread.

Satisfaction and a dash of fury surged through my blood at the sight of what remained of Bakhur's rune marks, barely visible since I'd been sloughing them off daily at Leaf's request with lightning magic.

It destroyed me to know that when he'd hurt her, I hadn't been there to stop him that night.

"Almost," she said, her reflection smiling at me in a long mirror as she tucked loose strands of hair into her crown of golden peacock feathers. "If only my dust-damned hair would co-operate."

"Where's Ari?" I asked. "Wasn't she supposed to help you get ready?"

My Aldara laughed. "Oh, she did. My hair is just rebelling against all her hard work."

The disobedient hair was currently tumbled high on her head, revealing the graceful line of her neck. Her rose-red lips, curved in amusement, matched the rubies sewn sparingly over the dress. Sheer material hung from her bare shoulders, covering her arms, and an embroidered neckline dipped low, highlighting her glorious curves. Splits swept up to her thighs and revealed more creamy skin, making my mouth water.

As she walked toward me, a frown grew between her eyes, marring the picture of a radiant, happy princess about to be crowned queen.

"Are you wearing that?" she asked, stopping in front of me.

My heart galloped as I glanced at my attire, checking my human-style outfit hadn't dissolved in a fit of malfunctioning storm magic. Nothing had changed. I still wore expertly tailored pants, a fine linen shirt, and a well-cut jacket, the whole ensemble black and embroidered with subtle silver-and-gold feathers.

"I'd planned to. What's wrong with it?"

"Is your feather plate hiding beneath the shirt?" she asked, running her palms over my chest, and finding out the answer herself.

I nodded.

"Arrow, please don't take offense, because you look wonderful. It's a beautiful suit and absolutely does you justice. But tell me, do you feel comfortable wearing it?"

Silence hummed between us as I considered my answer. Should I give the reply that I knew would please her? Or tell the truth?

Closing my eyes, I sighed.

Had I learned nothing?

If Leaf had taught me anything, it was this: only the truth would satisfy her. Even if it hurt.

"No. To be honest, I'd prefer my chest plate was in easy reach, so I can better protect you if needed."

"Says the man with lightning magic that can melt flesh off bones." She unbuttoned my jacket and swept it off my shoulders, tossing it onto the white-washed wooden floor.

She reached for my shirt buttons, and I grabbed her wrist. "What are you doing?"

"Helping you get ready for my coronation."

Releasing her hand, I gripped her waist, my fingers flexing over her warm skin beneath the gown's cool material.

She slid the shirt off my back and ran her palms over my shoulders, lightly over the gold feathers, and then down to my twitching stomach muscles.

"There you are, my golden Storm King. Muscles flexing, glyphs swirling bright," her hand moved lower. "And rock hard at my touch. Just how I like you."

"For gold's sake, keep doing that, and I won't be able to walk out there with you." I tugged her close, kissing her sweet mouth.

For several moments, everything but her dissolved.

She cupped my hardness and squeezed. "As soon as the formalities are over, let's meet back here and have some fun."

"I'll be counting down the minutes."

"Shall we go, then?" she asked.

"Not yet," I replied. "You're not quite ready."

A dark brow arched, an uncertain smile dancing on her lips.

I wiped my damp hands on my pants. "I have something... something I'd like to give you." I dug a silk-wrapped parcel from my pocket and offered it to her on my palm. "Would you wear this, my Aldara? Only if it pleases you, of course."

Her green eyes sparkled. "What is it?"

"Open it and find out."

She peeled the dark silk away, revealing a faceted, red prulite stone, the largest known specimen of the rarest jewel in the realms, flanked by two smaller stones glistening like blood on a chain of finely wrought gold.

She stroked the stones, gazing at me with tears in her eyes. "It's so beautiful, Arrow. Thank you. I would love to wear it."

Grinning, I dropped a kiss on her cheek, then stepped behind her and fastened the chain around her throat, letting the center stone rest in the notch between her collarbones.

I turned her toward the mirror, hugging her from behind. "It used to be my mother's. As a child, it was my favorite thing in her chambers, and I begged to hold it and stare through the gemstone at the sun outside her window. Both light and dark can be found in the jewel's heart. For some reason, that always appealed to me, and my fascination greatly amused my mother."

Leaf smiled as she stroked the pendant. "Now I adore it all the more."

"My mother gave it to me when I came of age, instructing me to keep it safe for my beloved."

"What was your mother's name?"

"Samara," I said, wiping a tear from Leaf's cheek. "She had silver hair with matching eyes and was almost as skilled with a blade as you are."

"I'm sure I would've loved her." Leaf spun away from the mirror, turning to face me. "We really should go."

She took my arm, hugging it close to her side as we left her chamber and made our way to the Mydorian hall. Today, the weather was perfect, the sun shining in a clear, blue sky. Leaf was perfect, too—mine, and about to become the Queen of Dust and Stones. Everything was fucking perfect, and my heart was full. I should have been ecstatic, but as my boots echoed through the corridors, something niggled at the back of my mind.

"Leaf, before you're crowned, will you do one thing for me?"

"Anything," she said softly.

I dragged in a long breath. "For weeks, when you first came to Coridon, I made you suffer. I made you beg and cry out my name many times over, both in fury and in bliss. That is behind us now, and our future shines brightly before us. But I must know if you understand the truth."

"What truth, Arrow?"

"That you're mine, and I am yours forever. A truth as eternal as the stars circling the Crystal Realm. As powerful as Light Realm storms, as constant as the Sun Realm's flames, deep as the seas in the Ice Realm, and as enduring as the Earth Realm's stones—the most wonderful of all the five realms, because you were created from the dust of its forests."

"Of course I know it. And I'll love you always, Arrow. I promise."

"As I will love you."

We began walking again, and peace settled over me.

Standing behind the Mydorian dais, Leaf peeked through the curtain at the crowd gathered under the bone-white branches that held up the high ceiling, waiting patiently for the ceremony to begin.

"Arrow, there's Zaret standing with Stormur, Ildri, and Van. They all look very fine in their coronation outfits. See Raiden and Ari nearby? And Esen is making them laugh. Who would ever have imagined it?"

"I did. For a very long time now, I've hoped to see Esen happy."

Gasping, Leaf elbowed my ribs. "And who's that large fae on the left? The one with long dark hair wearing a crown of ice?"

"Where?" I asked, peering over her shoulder. "Oh, that's King Ren from the Ice Realm, practically your neighbor since the Kingdom of Sea and Snow lies just east of the Earth Realm. I've heard rumors that he'll soon be taking a bride as tribute for maintaining peace with the other fae courts." I hesitated, scanning the side of her face, wondering if this was the best time to reveal the whole of it. "A human wife. Willing or not. No doubt you'll have lots to say to him later this evening."

"There are humans in the Ice Realm? And to think I thought him incredibly handsome, with those ice-blue eyes and that lovely pouting mouth. Now I despise him."

Good, I thought to myself, lest they got too friendly, and Ren decided to steal my human. Which would be a stupid fucking mistake. "Mm, probably best to wait until you meet him, Leaf. Then decide how you feel."

Raising her stubborn nose, she gave me a familiar smile. The one that told me to take my advice and shove it deep in the fiery hell realms.

She pointed at the back wall of the hall, then clapped a hand over her mouth. "Estella came! But, oh, my gods, look at Ruhh next to her. It's still a shock to see the little fiend walking on the ground with her extremely solid legs and feet. I keep bumping into her, thinking I can walk through her. I suppose I'll get used to it one day."

"You will eventually," I said, offering my arm, ready to lead her onto the dais. "Happy?"

"Ecstatic." The fire in her green eyes flashed as her fingers wrapped around my forearm. "Shall we join our friends and family?"

I grinned. "To be honest, I'd rather keep you to myself. But that would be selfish, and since I'm no longer a villain, guess we'd better get out there."

"Fear not. In the bedroom no one is as wicked as you are."

"Praise the gods," I joked.

"Do we really deserve such happiness, Arrow?"

"Every day. And forever," I replied, tugging her through the curtain as the crowd released an ear-splitting cheer.

She let go of my arm and raised hers high in a sign of triumphant joy.

The crowd roared, and musicians took up their instruments.

Leaf shimmied to the front of the dais, waving and greeting her people. Then she turned to face me, ran, and leaped into my arms.

As she wrapped her legs around my waist, laughing and kissing my cheek, not for the first time, I thought to myself: *humans sure know how to have fun.*

And the party hadn't even started.

Acknowledgements

Thank you for reading King of Fire and Flames!

I absolutely love hearing from readers, and I'm so grateful for every lovely review I've received, no matter how brief.

Thank you so much for taking the time to recommend my books to other readers. Your support and enthusiasm is what me keeps writing stories.

And massive thanks to my amazing beta readers Rosemary, Ken, Amelie, and Saskia, and my wonderful ARC readers!

Until next time,

Juno
X

Also By Juno Heart

If you enjoyed King of Storms and Feathers and King of Fire and Flames, check out the audiobooks and special edition print books featuring character art. And there are even character covers that star our very own Leaf and Arrow!

The Black Blood Fae series, swoony fated mates, enemies-to-lovers stories that are a little lighter in tone, not as steamy as the Courts of the Star Fae Realms books, but packed with angst and bantery humor is complete and ready to binge in Kindle Unlimited!

Book 1: Prince of Never
Book 2: King of Always
Book 3: King of Merits
Book 4: Prince of Then, the full-length prequel

Stay tuned for Wyn's story, book 1 in a new series, and the tale of King Ren from the Ice Realm and his stolen human bride. He made a cameo at the end of King of Fire and Flames.

About the Author

Juno Heart writes both swoony and spicy enemies-to-lovers fantasy romances about arrogant fae heroes and the feisty mortal girls that bring them to their knees.

When she's not writing, she's probably busy herding her cat and dog around the house, spilling coffee on her keyboard, or searching local forests and alleyways for portals into another realm.

Join Juno's newsletter on her website for new release and special deal alerts!

Email: juno@junoheartfaeromance.com

Printed in Dunstable, United Kingdom

67539178R00211